Roberta Kray was born in Southport. In early 1996 she met Reggie Kray and they married the following year; they were together until his death in 2000. Through her marriage to Reggie, Roberta has a unique insight into the world of London's gangland.

# ROBERTA KRAY

# BAD GIRL

sphere

SPHERE

First published in Great Britain in 2013 by Sphere
This paperback edition published in 2013 by Sphere

7 9 10 8

A CIP catalogue record for this book
is available from the British Library.

ISBN 978-0-7515-4983-6

Typeset in Garamond by M Rules
Printed and bound in Great Britain by
Clays Ltd, St Ives plc

Papers used by Sphere are from well-managed forests
and other responsible sources.

MIX
Paper from
responsible sources
FSC® C104740

Sphere
An imprint of
Little, Brown Book Group
Carmelite House
50 Victoria Embankment
London EC4Y 0DZ

An Hachette UK Company
www.hachette.co.uk

www.littlebrown.co.uk

# BAD GIRL

# PART ONE

# 1959

# 1

Lynsey Quinn unlocked the back door to the Fox and closed it softly behind her. She leaned against it for a while, taking a moment to prepare herself for the onslaught that was coming. It was two hours since Fat Pete had clocked her up West, and she knew that he'd have gone straight to the nearest phone box to call her dad. And Jesus, wouldn't the bastard have been smug about what he'd seen: Joe Quinn's daughter snogging a copper in a café in Soho! She could imagine the excitement in his voice, his big wet lips pressed against the receiver, his gut rumbling with the thrill of passing on bad news.

She took a deep breath, feeling the mad churning in her own stomach. She loathed her father, but was scared of him too. He'd never thought twice about raising his fists to her mum, and that poor woman had never done anything worse than pander to his every need. What he'd do on finding out that his daughter had been sleeping with the enemy was anybody's guess.

Lynsey plunged her hands anxiously into the pockets of her coat while she listened to the noise coming from the bar. She could sniff all sorts in the air: tobacco smoke, beer, sweat and the cloying scent of stale perfume. The smells rolled along the corridor along with the chinking sound of the glasses and the raucous laughter of the drunks. She strained her ears, trying to separate her father's voice from the wild babble coming from the saloon. Was he dealing with last orders, or was he waiting for her in the flat?

She didn't dare go into the bar to find out. Instead she peered up the stairs, wondering if she could make it to her bedroom before he realised she was home. Not that being in her room would make the slightest bit of difference; Joe Quinn had no respect for anyone else's privacy. And with a few pints inside him, he was more than capable of walking straight in and dragging her from her bed by her hair. It wouldn't be the first time.

Lynsey's right hand automatically rose to her scalp. She gave a shudder. She wished that she hadn't come back. She had wanted to get the inevitable row over and done with, but now she was having second thoughts. There was no reasoning with him when he was in one of his black tempers. She should have stayed over at a mate's house and given the dust time to settle.

Still, it was too late to change her mind. And anyway, why should she hide away? Indignation replaced a little of her fear. She wasn't ashamed of loving Alan Beck. He was smart and good-looking and he made her laugh. No, he was much more than that: he was the best thing that had ever happened to her.

Her thoughts were interrupted by the heavy tread of footsteps on lino. Someone was heading out from the bar. Quietly but quickly she fled up the stairs. At the top, she leaned over the banister to see who it was. The breath slipped from her lungs in a low gasp of relief. It was okay. It was only her older brother Tommy. He glanced up at her and she grinned back.

Tommy wasn't smiling, though. 'Jesus, have you got any idea what—' But he never made it to the end of the sentence.

'Lynsey!' bellowed her father from the living room. 'Get yer bleedin' arse in here!'

She turned sharply, feeling her stomach hit the floor. Oh God, now she was for it. For a few seconds she thought about legging it, but she couldn't move. Her thighs felt heavy as lead, incapable of transporting her body down the single flight. And even if she did manage to make it, he would still come after her. She had no doubt about that. Better, she thought, that they had it out up here rather than in the more public arena of the bar.

Taking a deep breath, she forced herself forward. The thin pointy heels of her stilettos clicked against the bare wooden boards. Behind her she could hear Tommy climbing the stairs. It wasn't a good sign. If he was worried enough to follow her up, then . . .

'Lynsey!' her father roared again.

There was a single lamp on in the living room, throwing shadows across the frayed green carpet. She stood in the doorway and stared at him. 'What are you shouting about?' she snapped, trying to keep the fear from her voice. Her plan, if it could be called that, was to act innocent and deny everything.

Joe Quinn was sitting in an armchair in the corner. He was an ugly man in his mid-fifties, stocky and with a clearly defined beer gut. His eyes, a dark shade of grey, glared at her from beneath a pair of bushy brows. 'Decided to honour us with your presence, then?'

'It's not late,' she said. There were three empty beer bottles on the table beside him, but that would be the tip of the iceberg. She could smell the booze from where she was standing. He'd have been knocking it back all night.

'So what have you got to say for yourself?'

She shook her head, pretending not to understand. 'What about?'

Her father got slowly to his feet. 'Don't give me that,' he growled. 'You think I was born yesterday? You think I'm a bloody moron? You think I don't know who my slut of a daughter's been shagging?'

Lynsey took a step back. There was anger in his eyes and if she wasn't careful she would infuriate him even more. But for some reason she still didn't have the sense to keep her mouth shut. 'And who would that be, then?'

'A fuckin' copper,' he hissed. 'That's who.'

Lynsey knew how she should respond, knew that she should vehemently deny it, but something inside – something that had perhaps been growing for years – rebelled against his bullying. She had a right to her own life, didn't she? A right to make her own choices? She was seventeen years old and she knew exactly what – or rather who – she wanted.

Tommy came up behind her, laid his hands lightly on her upper arms and then slid sideways through the door. He stood in front of their father, creating a physical shield. 'Why don't we leave this until tomorrow, eh? Fat Pete's been on a bender. You know what he's like, Dad. He's seen a blonde, thought it was Lynsey and . . . well, he made a mistake.'

Joe Quinn gave a snarl. His hands curled into two tight fists. 'Yeah, there's been a mistake all right, a mistake that involves your whore of a sister dropping her knickers for the filth.'

'That ain't true,' Tommy said. 'You know it ain't.' He gave a sigh and quickly turned to Lynsey. 'Tell him. Tell him it's a pile of bollocks.'

She looked at him, wishing for his sake that she could. But instead all she could manage was a tiny shrug.

'Ah, Jesus,' murmured Tommy. 'Are you crazy? What the hell were you thinking?'

'It's serious,' she said. 'It's not just—'

'And he's a copper, a bloody copper?'

Even Tommy, the one member of the family she could usually rely on, was disgusted by the revelation. He ran his fingers through his short fair hair as his forehead crunched into a frown. The Quinns and the police didn't mix. It was an unwritten law. They were chalk and cheese, oil and water. They stood on opposite sides of that thin blue line.

'You see?' spat Joe Quinn. 'The little cow isn't even denying it!' He lurched forward, trying to force a way past.

Lynsey jumped, her brown eyes widening. Fortunately, her brother was more than a match for the older man. Grabbing hold of his father's arms, Tommy pushed him back down into the chair. He was about the same height and build as Joe Quinn, but had the advantage of being thirty years younger and stone-cold sober.

'For God's sake,' Tommy said. 'This ain't solving nothin'.' He glanced over his shoulder at Lynsey. 'Just tell him, yeah. Tell him that you ain't gonna see this guy again. It's over, right? It's done with.'

She shook her head. 'I can't.'

'What d'ya mean, you can't? Tell him, for Christ's sake.'

But Lynsey knew that if she gave in now, her fate would be the same as her mother's – a lifetime of being under the thumb, of being controlled, of being manipulated, until all the hope was eventually sucked out of her. 'It's my choice,' she said stubbornly. 'I've a right to see whoever I want.'

'You hear that?' Joe Quinn said. A thin, mirthless laugh escaped from his lips. 'Your treacherous bitch of a sister reckons she's got rights.'

'She don't mean it,' Tommy said. 'Leave it to me. I'll sort it out.'

'There's nothing to sort,' Lynsey said.

Her father leaned forward menacingly, his big hands splayed across his thighs. 'While you're living under my roof, girl, you'll do as you're damn well told.'

'Well, that's easily solved,' she said. 'You think I like living in this dump?'

'Reckon you can do better for yourself, then?'

Her eyes made a quick sweep of the room. Since her mother's death two years ago, the place had gone steadily downhill. Even in the dim light of the lamp she could see the neglect, the beer stains on the carpet and the thick layer of dust. Every available surface was littered with used cups and plates. 'I couldn't do much worse.'

Suddenly, with a primitive roar, her father launched

himself out of the chair. He hurtled past Tommy and shoved Lynsey back against the door, slamming her so hard that a jolt ran the length of her spine. But that was the least of her worries. The next thing she knew he had his hands around her throat, his grip growing tighter and tighter until he was squeezing the very breath from her. She clawed frantically at his thick wrists, but he was too strong.

'No one talks to me like that!' He shook her like a rag doll and spat into her face. 'You hear me? You hear me, bitch?'

But even if Lynsey had wanted to reply, she couldn't. His thumbs were pressing so hard on her windpipe that stars were starting to dance in front of her eyes. As Joe Quinn's curses rained down on her, she had one of those life-flashing-by moments, only it wasn't the past that reeled through her head but the future – all the things she wouldn't do, the people she wouldn't meet, the babies she would never have.

'Bitch! Whore!'

The words drilled into her head. At the same time she was faintly aware of Tommy shouting and pulling and trying to drag her father off, but nothing would make him release his grip. Fuelled by booze and rage, he was lusting for blood. Her blood. So this was it, she thought. The end. The bastard was finally going to kill her. She could feel herself weakening, the life draining out of her body. A few seconds more and . . .

But then the crash came, not a heavy or solid sound, but rather a thin, splintery kind of noise. Abruptly the grasp on her throat was released. Her legs gave way and she slumped to the floor, wheezing and choking. Doubled up, she fought to catch her breath again. As her vision gradually cleared, she saw her father laid out beside her, his eyes closed, a soft moaning sound leaking from his mouth. Beside her, scattered on the carpet, were the broken remains of a dining chair.

'Are you okay?' asked Tommy, crouching down beside her.

She couldn't speak, but managed eventually to nod her head.

'Come on then,' he said, quickly standing up, grabbing her wrists and hauling her to her feet. 'You need to get out of here before the bugger comes round.'

Lynsey stood, swaying, her legs still unsteady. She held on to the door handle and gazed down at the man lying at her feet. Anger swelled in her breast. She wanted to kick him in the guts, to drive the heel of her stiletto through his chest – payback for all the beatings he'd inflicted – but she knew that to do so would mean that he had won. If she resorted to his methods, her soul would be as black as his.

'Come on,' Tommy urged again. 'Don't hang about.' He dragged her out of the room and down the stairs. 'You need to stay away, keep your head down for a few days. Go to Moira's, yeah? I'll let you know when it's safe to come back.'

'That's the . . .' Lynsey began, but the words came out as a croak. She rubbed at her throat and tried again. 'That's the first place he'll look.'

Tommy opened the back door and pushed her out into the chill night air. 'Don't worry about it,' he said. 'Moira's old man knows the score. You'll be safe there. You don't need to—'

'I'm not going to Moira's.'

'So where are you going?'

She turned her face away, not wanting to meet his eyes. 'You know where.'

Tommy gave a grunt. 'Huh?' And then he realised what she was saying. 'You can't,' he said. 'You go to him and Dad will never let you come back.'

Lynsey lowered her chin into the collar of her coat. She glanced up the stairs, gave a shiver and looked at Tommy again. 'I'm not coming back. Why should I? Next time he'll bloody kill me.'

'He'll bloody kill you if you shack up with some copper.'

'He'll have to find me first.'

Tommy closed the door and they walked rapidly round to the front of the pub and then along the road. 'Are you sure you know what you're doing? How long have you even known this bloke?'

'Long enough.' She didn't want to admit that it had only been a couple of months. For her, the amount of time they'd been together was irrelevant; the only thing that mattered was their feelings for each other. 'Look, you should get back. You're going to freeze to death out here.'

'You're only seventeen,' he said, continuing to stride along beside her. 'You're too young to be leaving home. What are you going to do for readies, for a job?'

'I'll manage. There's plenty of pub work out there. Anyway, you weren't that much older when you got together with Yvonne.'

'Yeah, but you're not up the duff. There's no need for you to—' He stopped dead and turned to face her. 'Jesus, Lynsey, tell me you're not.'

Lynsey gave another of her shrugs. 'Don't have a go. It happens. *You* know that. It's not the end of the world.'

'And he's happy about it, this bloke of yours?'

In truth, Lynsey hadn't got around to telling Alan yet. She'd been planning on doing it tonight, but then Fat Pete Turnbull had walked into the café and she'd had enough to worry about without breaking *that* news as well. 'Course he is. It's what we both want.'

Tommy pulled a face. 'I take it he knows who you are?'

She started walking again, not wanting to see the expression on his face. She didn't care about what most people thought, but Tommy's opinion mattered. She knew that he was disappointed in her. 'What's that supposed to mean?'

'You're Joe Quinn's daughter,' he said. 'It makes a difference. At least, it does if you're the filth.'

'Alan loves me,' she said simply. 'Nothing else matters.'

'Not even family?'

She frowned at him. 'Don't say that. You saw what that bastard did to me back there. What kind of family is that?'

'Connor's gonna do his nut.'

But Lynsey didn't give a stuff about Connor. Her other brother, currently banged up in the Scrubs, had the same filthy temper as their father. 'Let him. It's none of his business.'

'He'll make it his business.'

'Not if he wants to stay out of nick, he won't.' They had reached the corner and Lynsey stopped by the phone box. 'You'd better go now. You don't need to worry. I'll be okay.'

Tommy screwed up his eyes and peered at her. 'Will you?'

'Promise,' she said, forcing a smile. The immensity of what she was doing was just beginning to dawn. She felt afraid and excited, anxious and relieved, along with a crazy jumble of other emotions that set her heart racing. 'I'll get in touch when I've got things sorted.'

'I could get the motor, give you a lift.'

But Lynsey didn't want him to know where Alan lived. Although she trusted Tommy not to tell anyone, she needed time to get her head sorted. It wouldn't help to have her brother knocking on the door every five minutes. 'He's got a car,' she said. 'I'll give him a bell. He'll come and pick me up.'

Tommy put his hand in his pocket and pulled out a roll of pound notes. He peeled off twelve – more than she earned in a week – and held them out. 'Here, take this.'

She shook her head. 'I can't.'

'Please,' he said, pressing the notes into her hand. 'Just do it for me. This way I know you'll be okay.'

'Thanks,' she said, putting the money into her bag. 'I'll pay you back.'

'No worries.' Tommy leaned forward and gave her a quick hug. 'Take care, yeah?'

'You too,' she said, pulling away. 'And watch your back. Dad's gonna be well pissed off about what you did tonight.'

'He wouldn't dare try it on with me.'

Lynsey reckoned he was right. Her father was a bully, but he was also a coward. He didn't ever pick on anyone who might give as good as they got. 'Bye then,' she said, opening the door to the phone box. 'I'll see you soon.'

'You sure you don't want me to hang about until he gets here?'

'He won't be long. I'll wait in the station. It'll be warm there.'

Tommy still seemed reluctant to leave. He stood with his white shirt sleeves flapping in the wind, staring glumly back at her.

'Go on,' she said. 'If you don't get back soon, he'll come looking for you.'

'Go to Moira's,' he said.

Lynsey shook her head. 'Don't start that again. I can't, and I don't want to.'

The corners of his mouth turned down. 'Don't burn all your bridges, sis.'

'I'm only doing what I have to do. Take care of yourself, Tommy. And thanks for tonight. I owe you one.'

She went inside the phone box, letting the door close behind her, and picked up the phone, pretending to be looking for change in her purse. Finally Tommy got the message. She glanced over her shoulder and saw him heading towards the pub. At that moment she felt a sudden rip of panic in her chest. What would she do without him? They had always been a team, the two of them, watching out for each other. Now everything was changing.

She had chosen Alan Beck, a copper, the enemy, and nothing would ever be the same again.

# 2

Lynsey waited until Tommy had gone inside the pub before putting down the receiver and stepping out of the phone box. Quickly she crossed the road and turned right into Kellston High Street. She couldn't have called Alan even if she'd wanted to. There was no phone in his flat. Still, it wasn't as if he lived far away. At a brisk pace – if that was possible in the heels she was wearing – she could be there in fifteen minutes.

She turned up the collar of her coat. It was a cold night, and a thin, drizzly rain was starting to fall. Rummaging in her bag, she found a blue silk scarf, which she took out and tied around her head. It wasn't much, but it was better than nothing. The carefully contrived waves in her fair hair wouldn't last long without some protection.

She glanced at her watch and saw that it was almost eleven. Not that late. There were still plenty of people around, walking in twos and threes, on their way home or going on to a club. It was less than half an hour since Alan had dropped her off outside the Fox. Maybe he'd already gone to bed – she knew he had an early shift in the morning – but he'd understand why she'd come, why she had to be with him. Soulmates, that was what they were. Made for each other. Like two perfect pieces of a jigsaw.

Her hand rose to her throat, still sore from the tightness of her father's grip. God, she hated that man. He'd made her life a misery from the day she'd been born. From now on she was having nothing more to do with him. He could rant and rave as much as he liked; there was no way she was ever going home again. She and Alan would start their own family. Of course they wouldn't be able to stay around here, but London was a big place. They'd find somewhere else to raise their child.

'Lynsey Beck,' she murmured to herself, liking the sound of it.

All the shop windows were wreathed in darkness, but as she continued heading north, a light across the street caught her eye. Tobias Grand & Sons, the undertakers, were still at work. And that could only mean one thing. As if someone had walked over her grave, a shiver ran through her. Tonight somebody had died, somebody's mother, somebody's husband or wife. She thought of her own mum and bit down on her lip. Irene Quinn's life had been one of unrelenting misery, her death slow and painful.

Lynsey hurried on, trying to shake off the image of her mum laid out in the chapel of rest. A woman who didn't quite look like her mother. A woman with waxy skin and too much rouge on her cheeks. She blinked hard. No, she couldn't bear to think about it. Her hands clenched in her pockets, her long nails digging into the soft flesh of her palms.

She turned right at Mansfield Road and skirted around the perimeter of a wide stretch of wasteland. What remained of the old back-to-back terraces – bombed in the Blitz – lay strangled in weeds. She had played there as a kid with Tommy and Connor, clambering over the rubble, searching for treasure in the dust and the dirt. There were rumours that the land was going to be developed, that three high-rise towers were going up, but nothing had happened yet.

Here, away from the main street, it was quieter. The click of her heels against the pavement sounded unnaturally loud. She peered warily into the black shadows, at the humps and bumps, at the shapes that appeared almost sinister in the darkness. When she was six, Connor had whispered in her ear that the place was haunted, that the souls of the dead roamed forever through the wreckage of their old homes. Connor, like their dad, had always taken pleasure in tormenting her.

Suddenly there was a small clattering sound. Lynsey jumped, her heart missing a beat. A drunk, perhaps? Or a cat? Or maybe something more ghostly. Before her imagination could begin to riot, she took to her heels and ran as fast as her shoes would allow her.

Alan's flat was in Lime Road, above a butcher's shop. When she got there, she paused for a moment to catch her breath, gazing up at the window on the first floor. The curtains were closed, but a sliver of light crept between the join. She took off the headscarf, put it in her pocket and gently patted her hair. Her mouth widened into a smile. A thrill of anticipation ran through her. Now, she thought, now her *real* life was about to begin.

She pressed the bell and waited. It was over a minute before she heard the soft thud of footsteps on the stairs. As the door opened, she prepared to throw herself into his arms, but was brought up short by the appearance of a man she had never seen before. He was older than Alan, in his late thirties, with a plump face, glasses and thinning light brown hair.

'Yes?' he said.

'Oh.' Lynsey peered over his shoulder. 'Is Alan in?'

'Sorry, he's not.'

Lynsey looked at him and frowned. Alan had told her he was driving straight home, so why wasn't he here? She'd been gearing herself up to tell him everything that had happened, and now she wasn't sure what to do. Her shoulders slumped in disappointment. 'Would you mind if I came in and waited?'

'There's no point,' he said.

She shook her head, wondering who the man was. A friend? A relative? 'What do you mean?'

'I mean you'd be wasting your time.'

'Oh,' she said again. 'Why's that? Has he gone in to work?'

The man hesitated, as if he wasn't sure what to say. His gaze slid sideways and he shifted uncomfortably from one foot to the other. 'Not exactly.'

'I don't understand.' Lynsey's frown grew deeper. From upstairs she could hear music from a record player: Connie Francis singing 'Who's Sorry Now?'. A bad feeling was starting to stir in her guts. 'I mean, he does live here, right?' Of course he did. Hadn't she been round dozens of times? She

18

could describe the living room and the bedroom in intimate detail. Although now she came to think about it, she had never actually been here at night. Their secret assignations had always taken place in the afternoon.

The man's face took on a pained expression. 'Well ...'

'Well?' she echoed, a slight tremor entering her voice. 'He either does or he doesn't.'

'Perhaps you ought to talk to Alan about this.'

Lynsey could feel the colour rising in her cheeks, a red flush of anger and humiliation. She couldn't believe it. After everything she'd been through, now a whole new nightmare was beginning. 'Alan isn't here,' she snapped sharply. 'So it looks like it's down to you.'

The man gave an awkward shrug. 'He's a mate. He stays here sometimes, that's all. It's handy for the station.'

'So what you're telling me ...' She swallowed hard and tried again. 'What you're saying is ... this isn't his flat?'

The man retreated a step, his hand reaching for the door. 'Like I said, you'd better talk to Alan.'

But Lynsey wasn't going to let it go. How could she? She was pregnant and homeless and in one unholy mess. 'You'd better give me his real address, then.'

'Sorry, but I really can't—'

She moved forward quickly so that he couldn't slam the door on her. 'Do you know who I am?' she asked in desperation. She didn't wait for an answer before continuing. 'I'm Lynsey Quinn, Joe Quinn's daughter. I take it you've heard of him?' She couldn't be sure in the dim light from the hallway, but she thought his face paled a little. 'So it's like this. You give me Alan's address, right here, right now, or you'll have my old man to deal with.' She glanced up the stairs again, pretty sure from the choice of music that there was a woman in the flat. 'And believe me, you wouldn't want him coming round here to ruin your evening.'

He thought about it, but not for long. Any loyalty towards Alan was clearly outweighed by Joe Quinn's vicious reputation. 'It's Camberley Road, out in Farleigh Wood.'

Lynsey had a lump as large as a boulder in her throat, but she wasn't going to cry in front of this stranger. 'What number?' she demanded.

He hesitated, glanced down at the ground and looked up at her again. 'Twenty-four,' he said eventually.

'You'd better be telling me the truth, or—'

'That's where he lives,' the man said firmly. 'Now do you mind getting out of the way so I can close my door?'

Lynsey glared at him before taking a step back. Then, without another word, she turned and walked off down the road. It was raining much harder now, but she didn't bother to put her scarf back on. What did a drenching matter when she was already drowning in despair? Alan had lied to her. *Lied* to her. The bastard had told her he loved her, taken her to bed, taken her virginity, taken bloody everything. Oh Jesus, what was she going to do now?

At the corner, where Lime Road met the high street, there was a long, low wall. With her legs trembling, she sat down and put her head in her hands. Her palms were sweating, her teeth chattering with the cold and the shock. She suddenly thought of all the questions she wished she'd asked the man: had Alan taken other girls to the flat? How many of them? Was he married? Oh God, what if he was already married?

And maybe there were kids, too. Slipping a hand between the buttons of her coat, she pressed her fingers against the flat panel of her cotton dress and groaned. Perhaps she was mistaken about being pregnant. She was only a few weeks late, after all. 'Please God,' she murmured. 'Let me be wrong.'

While she sat on the wall, she thought about the first time they'd met, at Connolly's. A Saturday afternoon, just before Christmas. The café warm and steamy, busy with shoppers, with frazzled mums and tetchy kids, and teenage girls like her and Moira with time to spare and nothing much to do with it. He'd come in with another bloke and sat down at the next table. She hadn't been able to stop looking at him.

It was his eyes she had noticed first, a dreamy shade halfway between green and blue with long, dark lashes. Incredible eyes. Then his mouth, wide and sensual, with even white teeth. Dark brown hair flopping over his brow. It had only been a few minutes before they'd got talking, although it was another hour before she'd discovered that he was a cop. Usually she could sniff out the filth without even trying. Enough of them came into the Fox, trying to mingle with the crowd, to eavesdrop on the local villains. But she'd never have clocked Alan Beck, not in a thousand years. He was too stylish, too cool, too breathtakingly gorgeous. Anyway, by the time she found out the truth, it was way too late. Her heart was never going to listen to her head.

Feeling the rain seeping under her collar, Lynsey shivered and lifted her face. What now? She had to make some decisions, and fast. She wanted to confront him, but Farleigh Wood was miles away. Perhaps it would be better to go round to Moira's, stay there for the night and . . . and then what? She couldn't go crawling back to her dad's. She'd rather die than do that. He'd almost killed her just for sleeping with a copper. What would he do when he found out she was pregnant?

Wearily, she got to her feet. At least Moira would provide a shoulder to cry on, although Lynsey would also have to endure the lifted eyebrows and the inevitable *I told you so.* Moira had never liked Alan, never trusted him. Lynsey had put it down to jealousy, but perhaps her best friend had been right all along. *Perhaps?* She shook her head. What was she thinking? There was no perhaps about it. But even now, she acknowledged wryly, there was a part of her that still refused to believe in the betrayal.

She trailed back along the high street with her shoulders hunched and her hands deep in her pockets. She was almost at the turning for Silverstone Street when a car drove quickly past, its wheels sending up a spray of water from the puddles in the gutter. Lynsey tried to jump out of the way, but she was too late. As the motor disappeared from view, she gazed dolefully down at her wet legs and stockings.

'For God's sake,' she muttered, wondering if the night could get any worse.

It was at that very moment that she saw the black cab approaching. On impulse she put out her arm and flagged it down. After clambering into the back, she leaned forward and said, 'Farleigh Wood. Twenty-four Camberley Road.'

The cabbie didn't move. She could see him staring at her in his mirror. 'That's quite a way.'

'I've got money,' she said, glaring back at him. She grabbed her purse from her bag, took out the handful of notes that Tommy had given her and waved them at him. 'See?'

Satisfied, the cabbie gave a shrug and pulled away from the kerb.

Lynsey sat back and huddled into the corner, gazing blindly out at the street. Whatever the truth was, she had to know it. Good or bad, she couldn't wait until tomorrow.

# 3

It was three quarters of an hour before the cab got to Chingford and another ten minutes before it finally reached the leafy suburb of Farleigh Wood and began to wind through the back streets. Lynsey had spent the journey in a state of agitation, desperate to get there but terrified of what she might discover when she did. Now, as the moment drew closer, her fear increased, her pulse starting to race, her heart thrashing against her ribs.

How would Alan react when she turned up out of the blue? Not well, she imagined. He'd be less than pleased to be exposed as the lying love rat he was. She remembered the first time they'd gone to bed, his mouth pressed close against her ear, his voice barely a whisper. She remembered all those afternoons spent in the flat, the evenings up West, the pubs and clubs, the bright lights of Soho and Mayfair. She remembered the parties where they'd danced together, their bodies so close they could feel each other's heartbeat. And then there was that time when—

'What number was it, love?' the cabbie asked, interrupting her reverie.

'Drop me here,' she said, assailed by a fresh burst of panic. She wasn't ready yet. She needed more time to get her head together. 'This is fine.'

The taxi drew up and Lynsey stared out at the row of large semi-detached houses. It was close to midnight and most of them were in darkness. The people who lived here clearly didn't keep late hours. Reluctantly, she passed the fare over, not bothering with a tip. It had cost more than she'd expected, and anyway, he didn't deserve the extra after the way he'd looked at her in Kellston. She got out of the cab and slammed the door behind her.

Once the taxi had gone, she began to walk along the road, searching through the soft glow of the street lamps for a number on one of the houses. When she located number fifteen, she crossed over and shortly found herself outside Alan's place. She stood at the gate and peered along the drive. From what she could see, the house looked much the same as all the others, a Victorian semi with a porch, a large bay window and a garden filled with shrubs. There was no light on in the front, but she could see a glimmer coming from a back room. Good, someone was still up.

Lynsey took a deep breath, pushed open the gate and walked up the path towards the front door. There was a knot in her stomach like a big fat snake coiled around her guts. Preparing for the worst, she let her finger hover by the bell for a few seconds before she made contact and heard it ring inside. Almost immediately a light went on in the hall. Through the opaque glass panes she could see a figure approaching.

'Who is it?' asked a female voice.

'My name's Lynsey. I'm a friend of Alan's.'

'He's in bed.'

'Yes, I'm sorry it's so late, but it's important. I really need to talk to him.'

There was a short pause before a bolt was pulled back and the door was opened. A young woman in her early twenties appeared. She had a long, horsy-looking face with a wide mouth and slightly prominent teeth. Her auburn hair was tied back in a ponytail. Lynsey's gaze slipped down to the girl's left hand, searching for a wedding ring, but the finger was bare. His sister, perhaps? She had a vague idea that he had mentioned a sister.

'I'm so sorry to disturb you. I know it's late, but I have to see him.'

The girl's eyebrows shifted up a notch.

Another female voice, this one older, came from the rear of the house. 'Who is it, Janet?'

'A friend of Alan's.'

'He's in bed.'

'I've already told her that.'

'Tell her to come back in the morning.'

Lynsey's eyes widened. She hadn't come all this way to be turned away at the door. And where would she go? The chances of finding another cab were slight, and anyway, she didn't have money to burn. Tommy's cash wouldn't last for ever. 'No,' she insisted firmly. 'I have to see him now.'

The girl gave her a cool look and then glanced over her shoulder. 'Mum, she says she has to see him now.'

Lynsey was soaking wet and starting to shiver. 'Please, just tell him it's Lynsey Quinn. He'll want to see me, I know he will.'

An older woman emerged, perhaps from the kitchen, and walked along the hallway towards the door. She was wearing a plaid dressing gown and slippers. Her face, with features similar to her daughter's, had been stripped bare of any make-up and carried the greasy sheen of night cream. She looked Lynsey up and down, and frowned.

'My son's in bed. Is this some kind of police business?'

Lynsey could imagine how she must look, like a drowned rat in all probability. She could feel her wet hair clinging to her scalp. But still she managed a smile, relieved that this was Alan's family home and not anything else. 'No, I'm a friend of his. Something's happened. I . . . I really have to talk to him.'

Alan's mother appeared dubious, as though it was unlikely that her son could have any personal business with the working-class girl who was standing in front of her. Her eyes made a quick sweep from head to toe, her gaze lingering for a moment on the rain-splashed stockings. Lynsey could feel herself being judged and found wanting. *Common as muck* was what the older woman was thinking. Not the type of girl her son should be mixing with.

Although it was with a clear show of reluctance, Mrs Beck eventually stood back and said, 'Well, I suppose you'd better come in, then.'

'Ta,' said Lynsey. 'I mean, thank you.'

'Janet, go upstairs and wake your brother.'

Lynsey stepped inside the house. It was only marginally warmer than outside, but at least it was dry. She followed Mrs Beck into a large living room that had patterned wallpaper, a busy carpet with blue and green swirls, a sofa and a couple of easy chairs. The fire in the grate had long since gone out and all that remained was grey ash and cinders.

'He won't be long,' Mrs Beck said icily before retreating into the hall and closing the door behind her.

Lynsey perched tentatively on the edge of the sofa while she waited. She could have done with a brew, but no offer had been forthcoming. It was too chilly to take off her wet coat, and so she sat shivering as she made a more thorough examination of the room. There were a couple of rugs, a lamp with a tasselled shade and a large television in a mahogany cabinet. Another glass-paned cabinet was set against the wall, containing rows of figurines, bits of silver and a collection of china thimbles. Family photographs were lined up on the mantelpiece, including one of Alan in his police uniform.

Noticing a gilt-framed mirror hung above the fireplace, Lynsey jumped up, hoping to make herself presentable before he came downstairs. If they were going to have a row, she wanted to be sure that she looked good in the process. But her reflection soon put paid to that idea. Her mascara had run, and her fair hair lay in wet straggles around her face. As she rubbed at the dark shadows, tears of anger and frustration sprang into her eyes. Everything had gone wrong, horribly wrong. She wasn't sure how much more she could cope with.

At the very second the thought came into her head, the door opened and Alan walked in. He'd got quickly dressed in a pair of trousers and a dark red sweater she hadn't seen before. His hair was uncombed, his eyes still dull with sleep. She'd intended to play it cool, but the sight of him shattered her resolve and sent her running into his arms. She felt his body instantly tighten as she leaned against him.

'Lynsey, how did you . . . I mean, what are you doing here?'

She pulled back and gazed up at him. 'The bastard went for me, didn't he? He went crazy and . . . I thought he was going to . . . He found out about us. I didn't know what else to do.' And then, remembering that she was supposed to be mad at him, her mouth took on a sulky pout. 'I went to the flat, but you weren't there.'

'Jesus, your dad knows about me?'

Lynsey could hear the fear in his voice. He was clearly more concerned about his own safety than any traumas she might have been through. 'Don't worry,' she said peevishly. 'You're a cop. He won't touch *you*.'

'Sorry, I didn't . . . Did he hurt you? Are you all right?'

Lynsey rubbed at her arms where her father had grabbed her. 'Just about. But I can't go back there. He'll kill me next time, I know he will.'

'No, of course you can't.'

'So I can stay here?'

Alan pulled a face. 'I don't think my mum would . . . Well, it would be a bit awkward.'

'I can't go back,' she said again.

'We'll think of something. Look, you're soaked. You need to get out of those wet things. Why don't I drive you over to Chingford? There's a couple of guest houses there. We can find you somewhere to stay and then have a chat tomorrow.'

'Tomorrow?' she echoed softly.

'Yeah, it won't seem so bad after a good night's sleep.' He took hold of her elbow and gently but firmly started to propel her out of the room. Lynsey, angered by his obvious attempt to get rid of her, snatched her arm away.

'Why didn't you tell me that you lived here?'

'What does it matter?' he said dismissively. 'I spend some time here, some time at the flat.'

'But the flat isn't yours. It belongs to that other guy.'

Alan raised his eyes to the ceiling, as if she was being completely unreasonable. 'Sure, it belongs to him, but I help out with the bills and stuff.'

'So why didn't you tell me?'

'God, Lynsey, can't we do this tomorrow? I've got work in the morning and I'm going to be knackered.'

'Do you take other girls there?' She put her hands on her hips and glared at him. 'Do you?'

Alan shook his head. 'I'm not having this conversation now.'

'I want to have it now. I want to know the truth.' She sat back down on the sofa, making it plain that she wasn't going to leave before she got the answers she wanted.

'Don't be like this.'

'Like what?'

He raked his fingers through his hair and sighed. 'You know what I mean.'

She leaned forward, dropping her gaze. If he thought things were bad now, they were about to get a whole lot worse. 'Yeah, you're making it pretty clear.' She splayed her fingers across her thighs, studying the carpet while she searched for the right words. A short silence filled the room before she lifted her eyes again and said, 'There's something else you need to know.'

'What's that?'

She tried to speak again, but couldn't. Her throat was as tight, as painful, as when her dad had pressed his fingers against her windpipe.

'Lynsey?' he said impatiently.

She swallowed hard and eventually managed to gulp the words out. 'I'm pregnant.'

Alan's intake of breath was clearly audible. 'What?' He gave a short, barking laugh, as if he thought she might be joking. But when he saw her expression, his face grew ashen. 'No way,' he said. 'You can't be. Are you sure? Have you seen a doctor?'

'Of course not.' Dr Harris, the family quack, would have been straight on the blower to her dad. Nothing was private when it came to Joe Quinn's family.

His eyes contained a flash of hope. 'So you could be wrong?'

'I'm three weeks late. I'm never late.'

He paced up and down the room while the news sank in. Then suddenly his legs seemed to give way and he slumped down on the sofa beside her. 'Does he know? Have you told your father?'

Lynsey gave a snort. 'You think I'd be sitting here now if I had? I'd be laid out in the bloody morgue.'

'Christ,' he murmured. She heard him take a few deep breaths before he turned to her, put his hand on hers and said, 'It'll be okay, love. You're not on your own. You don't need to worry.'

Lynsey felt a wave of relief roll over her. 'Are you serious? Do you really mean that?'

He squeezed her fingers. 'Of course I do.'

'So we can—'

But before she had the opportunity to tell him about her plans for the future, he'd jumped to his feet again. 'I've got some money. It'll be okay. We can sort this.'

Lynsey felt her stomach turn over. 'Sort it?' she said softly.

'Sure. There are people . . . you know . . . I'll take care of it.'

Lynsey stood up too, her face pale and angry. 'You want to . . . you want to kill our baby? Is that what you're saying?'

'It's not like that. We're both too young. We're not ready to be parents.'

'You mean *you're* not bleedin' ready!' she yelled. Her blood was boiling now, her rage and frustration bubbling over. She launched herself at him, battering her fists against his chest. 'You bastard! You rotten filthy bastard!'

He grabbed hold of her wrists, forced her away from him and glanced towards the door 'Keep your voice down, for God's sake.'

'Why? Scared your precious family might find out what you're planning to do?'

'Just calm down. There's no need to shout.'

'There's every bloody need!'

Alan pushed her back on to the sofa and leaned over her, his eyes cold and angry. 'This isn't just to do with you. There are two of us in this.'

Lynsey bared her teeth. 'Three, actually. And I don't give a damn about what you want. I'm keeping this baby and there's nothing you can do about it.'

'You're crazy!' he hissed. 'You're out of your tiny little mind.'

And it was in that moment, as Alan Beck stared down at her with pure loathing on his face, that she knew there would be no fairy-tale ending. He didn't love her. He'd never loved her. But there was no going back now. She had made her bed, as her mother used to say, and now she would have to lie in it.

# PART TWO

# 1970

# 4

The first thing Helen saw as they turned the corner into Camberley Road was the long line of cherry trees, their branches laden with soft pink blossom. The blooms must have been there in the morning, but somehow she had failed to notice them. She felt an overwhelming urge to leap up and try to grab a handful of the flowers, but even if she had been tall enough – which she wasn't – she knew that the attempt would be met with disapproval.

She glanced at the long, thin face of her grandmother. Joan Beck disapproved of a wide and varied list of things: drinking, smoking, swearing, short skirts, pop music, make-up, sleepovers, glossy magazines, queers and Roman Catholics. And that was just the stuff that came to mind. If she really thought about it, the list would probably be as long as a book.

At eleven years old, Helen considered herself too grown-up to be met from school, but she didn't bother to protest. To voice an objection would be to invite a lecture on ingratitude or the dangers to children of walking the streets alone. If her grandmother was to be believed, Farleigh Wood was awash with evil. Lewd men lurked behind bushes or loitered in parks, waiting patiently for their victims. *Never talk to strangers. Never take sweets from strange men.* These frequently voiced pieces of advice were as familiar to Helen as the dull Sunday sermons at the red-brick church of St James's.

No matter how hard she looked, Helen had yet to spot one of these elusive perverts. In daylight she was sceptical of her grandmother's claims, but at night, even in the safety of her own bed, she was less certain. The men came to her in dreams, their gnarled hands reaching out to her, their sly eyes turning her bones to jelly. As fragments of these nightmares floated back into her head, a small shiver rattled the length of her spine. Momentarily distracted, she lost track of what her legs were doing and stumbled on a bit of uneven pavement.

'Pick your feet up,' her grandmother said sternly. 'Those are new sandals you're wearing. Look where you're going.'

It was at that very second, as Helen lowered her gaze, that she saw the police car parked outside the house.

'What now?' Joan Beck muttered under her breath.

Helen glanced at her again, knowing exactly what and who she was referring too. This wasn't the first time the police had appeared at number twenty-four – in fact, it was the third time in eight months – and it could only mean one thing: Mum was in trouble again. Helen's own feelings about this were mixed. On the one hand, it would mean rows and a whole lot of bad feeling; on the other, it meant that before long, she would see her mother again.

It was this mixture of emotions that caused her stomach to

flip as they approached the gate. She watched as the uniformed policeman got out of the car. She'd expected to see PC Wainwright – he was the one who usually delivered the news – but this man was older and greyer, with three white stripes on the sleeve of his jacket.

'Mrs Beck?' the officer asked.

Joan Beck gave a curt nod.

'Sergeant Mills,' he said. 'Are you Lynsey Beck's mother?'

'Mother-in-law,' she replied sharply, eager to dispel any notion that she might actually be a blood relation. 'What's the stupid girl gone and done now?'

The sergeant glanced briefly down at Helen before looking at her grandmother again. 'Perhaps we could talk inside.'

'If we must.'

The three of them walked in silence down the drive. Once the front door was unlocked, Helen was ushered inside. There were stripes of sunlight on the floor and the hallway smelled of beeswax. Her grandmother took her coat and gave her a little push towards the stairs.

'Go up to your room for a while. We won't be long.'

Helen was used to the procedure. As she climbed the stairs, she was aware of the adults going through to the living room. She wondered what her mother had been arrested for this time. Shoplifting? Drunk and disorderly? Soliciting? She rolled this last word around on her tongue, not entirely sure what it meant.

On reaching the landing, she leaned over the banisters and tried to eavesdrop on the conversation, but the door had been firmly closed. Oh well, she would find out soon enough. And before long, her mum would be here again, for a few days, or maybe even a week. Or perhaps, just perhaps, she might decide to stay for ever.

Helen went into her bedroom and bounced down on the bed. She knew that her mum did bad things sometimes, that she got in trouble and got herself arrested. And then, when she was finally bailed, she was usually released to this address. The truth was that Lynsey Beck wasn't like other mothers. She didn't bake cakes or wash clothes or do the ironing. She didn't even live in the same house as her daughter. But none of that mattered. To Helen, she was still the most beautiful and the most important person in the world.

She jumped up and went to stand by the window so she could see when the sergeant left.

Impatiently she hopped from one foot to the other. It would probably be tomorrow, Friday, before her mum got here. Then on Saturday there would be a trip to the cinema or to the shops up West. She didn't much care what they did, so long as they did it together.

Before that, of course, there would be what she had come to think of as 'the battle'. Helen's forehead creased into a frown. Her mum would arrive and make a rambling apology for whatever she had done. Gran would say, 'Sorry isn't good enough. When are you going to grow up? You've got a child. You've got responsibilities.' And Mum would say, 'I don't remember Alan taking much notice of his responsibilities.' And then the two of them would go at it hammer and tongs.

It was an old, well-worn record that Helen had heard countless times before. She didn't fully understand the bad feeling between the two of them, but she knew that it was to do with her father. She glanced over her shoulder at the photo on the dressing table. It was a picture of her parents on their wedding day. Her mum, standing on the steps of the registry office, looked happy and radiant. Her dad wore a more solemn expression. When Gran asked if Helen remembered him, she always said yes, but the truth was that she wasn't really sure. She'd only been five when he'd died, and her memories of that time were dim.

While she waited, Helen thought some more about him. Once a month she was taken to Chingford cemetery to lay flowers on his grave. Her father was a hero. That was what Gran said. He'd died in the line of duty, a serving police officer murdered by a pair of violent thugs. Helen had the same dark brown hair as him, and the same grey-green eyes. Although it made her feel guilty, she couldn't help wishing she looked more like her mum. She wanted her eyes to be brown, her hair to be long and straight and blonde.

She heard the front door close and quickly turned her attention back to the window. She watched as the policeman walked smartly down the drive, hesitated for a moment, glanced back at the house and then got into his car. She waited for her gran to call her downstairs. A couple of minutes passed, but nothing happened. She heard the light ting as the telephone was lifted and knew that a call was being made. Carefully she opened the bedroom door and crept out on to the landing.

Helen heard the murmur of her grandmother's voice, but couldn't make out what she was saying. She leaned over the banister, straining her ears. She thought she caught her mother's name being mentioned, but couldn't be sure. Was it Auntie Janet on the other end of the line? Another ting signalled the end of the call and she quickly retreated to the bedroom.

Five minutes passed, and then ten. What was going on? Excited at the thought of seeing her mum again, Helen couldn't keep still. She danced from one side of the room to the other, stopping at the window to gaze out at the street before retracing her steps. Her stomach made a tiny grumbling sound, reminding her that she hadn't eaten since lunch.

She went to the door again, opened it, peered and listened. Nothing. She frowned, disturbed by the silence. Usually she would have been summoned by now. Too impatient to wait any longer, she made her way downstairs. She looked into the living room, but it was empty. She went on to the kitchen and gently pushed open the door. Her grandmother was sitting at the table with a cup of tea by her elbow.

'Gran?'

Joan Beck's eyes narrowed in confusion. 'What are you doing here?' she said. 'You should be in school.'

'School's finished, Gran.'

'Finished?'

Helen glanced at the clock on the wall. 'Over an hour ago. We walked back together, remember?'

'Oh yes, of course.' She gave a faltering smile. 'You'd better get yourself a drink.'

Helen went to the fridge and poured a glass of milk. This wasn't the first occasion her grandmother had acted strangely. The episodes had started after Grandad had died, over a year ago now. Usually they didn't last long, a few minutes of vagueness, of absent-minded confusion, but sometimes – like last month, when Gran had got up in the middle of the night, turned the oven on and started cooking – they were more prolonged.

'Gran?' she asked tentatively. 'What did the policeman want?'

Her grandmother seemed baffled by the question. Her hands rose, hovering briefly in the air before fluttering back down to the table again. She glanced at Helen and then out of the window. Her brown eyes were vague and unfocused. 'The policeman,' she murmured, as if struggling to understand.

'You know,' Helen prompted. 'The man who was here earlier. He came about Mum. Is she coming tomorrow? Is she coming to stay?'

'Oh, I don't think so, dear.'

Helen felt a sharp stab of disappointment. 'But I thought—'

But she never got a chance to articulate her thought. Her grandmother pushed back her chair, slowly got to her feet and wandered off towards the hall. 'Now where did I put that shopping list?'

Helen finished her milk, washed out the glass in the sink and placed it neatly on the drainer. Then she went out into the garden, where she leaned against her grandfather's shed and wrapped her arms tightly around her chest. She didn't like it when Gran acted oddly. It made her feel unsteady, unsafe, as if the ground was shifting beneath her. Like at the fairground, when you got off the ride but your knees continued to feel wobbly.

She thought about the policeman again. Why wasn't her mum coming? It was weeks now since she'd last seen her. And only one phone call since then. *I'll see you soon, baby,* that was what she'd said on the telephone. Helen worried at her lower lip. The sergeant had asked Gran if she was Lynsey Beck's mother. She'd heard it with her very own ears. So something must be going on.

The old wooden shed was warm from the afternoon sun. She turned, pushed open the door and stepped inside. It smelled musty and abandoned. There was a row of tools hung up on the wall, a lawnmower in the corner, flowerpots and seed trays stacked on the shelves. Nothing had been touched since her grandad had died. She ran a hand along the edge of the table, picking up dark smears on her fingertips. There was dust in the air, and cobwebs had gathered in every nook and cranny.

Helen could feel the shadow of her grandfather's presence. He had been a quiet man, but a kind one too. He'd also been the peacemaker in the house, bringing calm to the stormy relationship between his wife and daughter-in-law. Yes, even her mother had liked him; he was the only one of the Becks she'd ever had any time for. Everything had changed now that he'd gone. Nothing would ever be the same again.

She backed out of the shed and closed the door behind her. As she glanced towards the house, she saw Janet through the kitchen window. Their eyes met and her aunt beckoned her inside. Helen walked up the path, wondering what she was doing here. Janet had two small children of her own and usually only came around at the weekend. She remembered the phone call Gran had made earlier, and a sense of uneasiness stirred inside her.

By the time Helen stepped into the kitchen, the two older women were already seated.

'Come and sit down,' Janet said solemnly. 'I've ... we've got some news for you.'

Helen glanced from her aunt to her grandmother before obediently pulling out a chair.

'Now you're going to have to be a brave girl,' Janet said. 'You can do that, can't you?'

That was when Helen's stomach really sank. You only ever had to be brave for bad news, not for good. She managed a small nod, despite her inner trepidation.

'You see ...' Janet began, but then abruptly stopped. Her hands wrestled with each other on the table, and her eyes darted away from Helen's face, as if she couldn't bear to look at her.

It was her grandmother who took over, her voice a little shaky. 'I'm afraid there's been an accident, dear. It's your mother.'

Helen felt a flutter of panic in her chest. 'Is she ... is she in the hospital?' That was where they took people when they were ill or hurt. The doctors made them better. Or at least sometimes they did. She had a sudden vivid memory of her grandad propped up in the hospital bed, the sheets stiff and white around him. His wasted body had seemed far too thin for the pair of blue and white pyjamas he was wearing.

Her grandmother shook her head. 'No, dear.' She gave a long sigh. 'I'm sorry. She's not in the hospital.'

'She's in heaven,' Janet said softly. 'She's with Jesus now. He's taking care of her.'

Helen felt a pain like a knife slicing through her. No! She wanted to stick her fingers in her ears, to block out the words. If she couldn't hear them, then it couldn't be happening.

45

What right did Jesus have to interfere? Why couldn't he find someone else to take care of? She didn't want her mum in heaven. She wanted her here, smiling and laughing, making plans to go up West.

'It's a shock, I know,' her grandmother continued. 'Terrible news. And of course we're all extremely upset, but ... Well, we can only do our best and try to carry on. You'll have to be a brave girl for your mum, Helen. I know it's not easy, but it's what she would have wanted.'

Helen had a lump the size of a boulder in her throat, a hard stone of grief that had lodged in her windpipe. She was faintly aware of Janet's hand reaching out to touch her own but then slowly retreating. The Becks weren't comfortable with displays of emotion. 'Can I go upstairs?' she eventually managed to croak. She wanted to get away from their scrutiny, to grieve in the privacy of her own bedroom.

'I don't think—' Janet began, but her grandmother interrupted her.

'Of course you can, dear.'

Helen rushed out of the kitchen and took the stairs two at a time, hurtling into her room and launching herself on to the bed. She curled into a ball and waited for the tears to come, but nothing happened. It was as though something had frozen inside her. After a while, she sat up again, wrapping her arms around her knees. Her mother was gone, gone for ever. *Dead*. How could that be? She didn't even know how it had happened. An accident. That could mean anything.

As she sat gazing bleakly down at her feet, she noticed a tiny flattened clump of blossom protruding from the sole of one of her sandals. Carefully she peeled it off and held it in the palm of her hand. If only she could turn the clock back, return to that moment when she had turned into Camberley Road and marvelled at the row of cherry trees. Then, in her head at least, her mother had still been alive. For the first time in her life, she understood the meaning of the saying that ignorance is bliss.

It was then, suddenly, that the tears began to flow, slowly at first but getting faster and faster until her body was racked with heaving sobs. She buried her face in her arms, not wanting anyone to hear.

# 5

Tommy Quinn pushed his breakfast around the plate, the untouched bacon and eggs already starting to congeal. He had a sick feeling in the pit of his stomach, and the smell of the food was making it worse.

'What's wrong with it, then?' Yvonne asked from across the table.

He shoved the plate aside. 'There ain't nothing wrong with it. I'm just not hungry.'

She took a puff on her cigarette and exhaled the smoke in a quick, resentful stream. 'You could've thought about telling me that before I started cooking. You think I haven't got better things to do than slave over a hot stove all morning?'

Tommy took a slurp of his tea and glared at her over the rim of the mug. 'Don't start. In case you've forgotten, it's my sister's bloody funeral today.'

'Well, don't think I'm coming with you.'

'Nobody's asking you to.'

She tapped her fag in the vague direction of the ashtray.

'It's not as though you've even seen her for years. I can't see why you're bothering.'

Tommy stared at the tiny cylinder of ash that had landed on the table. He thought of the crematorium, of a body laid out in a coffin, of the flames that would engulf a young woman's flesh and bones. The thought of it made his stomach turn over again. He should have made more of an effort, tried harder to heal the breach between them. But Lynsey was stubborn like him. She'd never admit that she'd made a mistake. Once she'd married that copper, there was no going back.

'What time are you leaving?' Yvonne asked.

Tommy glanced at his watch, pushed back his chair and stood up. 'Now.'

'Now?' she repeated, scowling up at him. 'I thought you said the funeral wasn't until one.'

'I've got a bit of business to sort first.' He wasn't actually due to meet Frank Meyer for another hour, but he wanted to get away before he said something he'd regret. Tommy neither loved nor even liked his wife, but preferred to keep things on an even keel. After fifteen years of marriage, he knew all there was to know about her, and most of it did his head in.

'Don't be late,' she said. 'You'll need to open up. If you think I'm doing it again, then—'

'I'll be back in plenty of time.' Since Connor had been arrested a few months ago, Tommy had been running the Fox on his own. It was hard work, but that didn't bother him. He'd grown up in the pub and was more than happy to be living there again. Yvonne, on the other hand, couldn't stand the place. Given a gallon of petrol and a match, she'd have gladly razed it to the ground.

He took his black jacket off the back of the chair and slipped it on. As he walked out on to the landing, he gave a small nod of satisfaction. Yes, it was good to be back. This was where he belonged and where he intended to stay. For the past seven years they'd been renting a semi on the south side of Kellston, but Tommy had never felt comfortable there. It had always seemed more like Yvonne's house than his, a place where he had eaten and slept but never really felt at home.

Connor's arrest – for demanding money with menaces – had turned out to be a blessing in disguise. It had given Tommy the excuse he needed to move back to the Fox. Someone had to keep an eye on Dad and his cronies, or they'd drink all the profits away. At least that was what he'd told Yvonne. And money was tight these days, so what was the point in shelling out for rent when they could live above the pub for free? The flat was big enough for all of them, and with the business to run it made sense, financially and practically, to live on the premises.

Tommy jogged down the stairs, eager to be away from his wife. If it hadn't been for the girls, he'd have kicked the marriage into touch years ago, but he didn't want to be one of those part-time fathers who only saw their kids at weekends. Thinking of his girls reminded him that Lynsey had a daughter too, a child who no longer had a mum or a dad. Helen, that was her name. She must be eleven by now. Jesus, his own niece and he'd never even seen her.

He headed outside to the car park and climbed into the white Cortina. For a change, it started first time, and he drove down the road on to the high street and parked outside

Connolly's. He was early, but it didn't matter. He just wanted to drink a mug of tea in peace without Yvonne giving him earache.

The caff was pleasantly warm, smelling of damp coats and cigarettes. On his way to the counter he nodded to a few of the fellas but didn't stop to chat. He didn't want to have to listen to their expressions of sympathy: *Sorry to hear about your Lynsey, mate.* How many times had he heard that over the last week? And as soon as his back was turned, they'd be gossiping like women, raking over old history about how Lynsey Quinn had got knocked up by a copper, and noting that even her own father wasn't going to the funeral.

Tommy got a brew and went to sit in the corner by the window. The glass was steamed up and he cleared part of the pane with the palm of his hand. He stared up at the sky, dark and heavy, the grey clouds swollen with rain. Hard to believe that only a few days ago the sun had been shining.

It had been raining, he remembered, on the Friday night Lynsey had come home all those years ago, bringing with her the kind of news that no self-respecting family of villains wanted to hear. If only the poor cow hadn't got herself pregnant. She'd have got over Alan Beck in time, seen him for the scumbag he really was. Tommy hated bent coppers even more than straight ones. You chose one side or the other – that was his philosophy – and didn't dabble in the shades of grey.

He lifted his mug to his lips and sighed into the tea. Why hadn't she packed her bags when it had all started to go wrong? But he already knew the answer to that. Lynsey was too proud to come crawling back. She'd rather have thrown herself in the Thames than admit to Joe Quinn that she'd made a mistake. Every now and again he'd heard snippets of news from Moira Sullivan, the only person Lynsey kept in touch with – that the baby was a girl, that they were living out Ilford way, that the marriage wasn't a happy one.

Later, after Beck had got his just rewards, there had been all sorts of rumours about what Lynsey was doing. Tommy's mouth turned down at the corners. They were the type of rumours he didn't want to dwell on. Maybe if he'd made the first move, if he'd gone to talk to her, things could have been different; but he hadn't, and that was the end of it. It was too late to start stressing over might-have-beens.

He sensed a movement and looked up. The tall, broad-shouldered figure of Frank Meyer was striding towards him.

'You're early,' Tommy said.

Frank looked at his watch and smiled. 'Says the man who's been sitting here for how long?' He pulled out a chair and took a seat on the other side of the table. 'I dropped by the Fox. Yvonne told me you'd already left.'

'Yeah, well, there's only so much grief you can take of a morning.' Tommy fingered his tie, feeling overdressed in the casual surroundings of the caff. 'You'd think she'd give it a rest today of all days.'

'What time do you have to be there?'

'One o'clock.'

Frank looked towards the counter, caught the eye of Paul Connolly and ordered another two brews with a quick gesture of his hand. Then he turned his attention back to Tommy. 'Joe's not changed his mind, then? He's not coming with you?'

'What do you think? He never gave a damn about her

when she was alive, so why should he bother now? The bastard can't even be arsed to go to her funeral.'

'You want me to come along?'

Tommy was touched by the offer. Even his own wife wasn't prepared to set foot in the crematorium. It was at times like this that you found out who your real friends were. He thought about it for a moment, but then shook his head. This was something he needed to do on his own. 'Nah, it'll be fine.'

'Well, the offer's open. Just give me the nod if you change your mind.'

Tommy had only known Frank Meyer for a year or so, but in that time he'd come to trust him. They'd first met in the Red Lion in Bethnal Green. It had been a Tuesday, a cold night, and Tommy had been doing a bit of business in the area. He and Yvonne were at each other's throats over something and nothing, and not relishing the prospect of round three, he'd nipped into the pub for a few loin-girding Scotches before heading home.

Frank had been sitting at the bar nursing a pint. He was in his early thirties, a man with a square-jawed face and a bored expression. The place had been quiet, and they'd fallen into the kind of aimless conversation that was probably taking place in a thousand pubs around the country between a couple of blokes who had nothing better to do and who would in all likelihood never meet again.

Tommy had downed his third short and was preparing to leave when the door had opened and two of the Gissing brothers, Lennie and Roy, had walked in. Not good. Not good at all. The brothers were tanked up and looking for trouble. It was only a year since the Krays had gone down, and other East End firms were jostling for dominance. There was a gap in the market, and the Gissings had ambitions to fill it.

Tommy was handy enough with his fists, but he didn't relish the prospect of two against one. He was off his home turf, with no one to watch his back. If the place had been busier he would have tried to slip away, but as things were, he was standing straight in their line of vision.

It only took a moment for them to spot their prey. Like a pair of hungry hyenas they padded softly across the bar and stood directly in front of him. None of the Gissing brothers – there were three of them in all – was blessed with good looks, but Lennie took the prize for sheer unadulterated ugliness. He was in his forties, a former bare-knuckle fighter with the facial scars to prove it. Leaning in, he expelled a rush of booze-laden breath. 'Well, if it ain't Tommy Quinn.'

Tommy smiled as if he didn't have a care in the world. Never show any fear. That was the number one rule. 'Lennie. How are you doing? Long time no see.'

Lennie gave a snarl, revealing a row of chipped yellow teeth. 'Ain't you got a pub of yer own to drink in?'

Tommy held his gaze, trying to keep his voice casual. 'Fancied a change, didn't I?'

Roy Gissing narrowed his eyes. He wasn't as tall as his older brother, but what he lacked in height he made up for in sheer viciousness. 'Quinns ain't welcome in the Lion. In fact, now I come to think of it, Quinns ain't much welcome anywhere.'

Lennie sniggered. 'Now ain't that a fact.'

Tommy glanced towards the door, but the two men were

effectively blocking his path. He could see what was coming and there was no escape from it. Unless a bloody miracle happened, he was about to get a kicking.

It was then that Frank Meyer stood up. 'Is there a problem, gentlemen?'

Three heads turned to look at him. Until that moment, Tommy hadn't realised how big Frank was – six foot three or four at least – and solid with it. Glancing back at the brothers, he could see surprise blossom on their faces. Having come into the pub just as he was about to leave, they'd thought he was drinking alone.

'What's it to you?' said Lennie, but his voice had a less aggressive edge. He might have been pissed, but he wasn't completely stupid.

Frank loomed over him, his cool grey eyes looking faintly amused. 'And here was me about to ask the very same question. Mr Quinn and myself were about to go. If you've got a problem with that, please feel free to join us outside.' He left a short pause before adding, 'Be a shame to smash up this nice tidy bar.'

Lennie exchanged glances with his brother. They were both in the mood for a scrap, but something about Frank – and it wasn't just his size – made them think twice. They shifted slightly to the side, leaving room for the two men to pass them. 'You'd better fuck off, then.'

Once they were safely on the pavement, Tommy took Frank's hand and shook it. 'Thanks, mate. I owe you one.'

'No worries.'

'No, I mean it. My old man's got a pub in Kellston, next to the station. It's called the Fox. Drop by any time.'

'Kellston,' Frank repeated, as if the place meant something to him.

'Yeah, you know it?'

'Used to. I imagine it's changed a bit since then.'

Tommy hadn't really expected to see Frank again, but a couple of nights later he had turned up at the pub. They'd been mates and business partners ever since.

Now Frank leaned across the table. 'Tommy? Have you been listening to a single word I've said?'

'Sorry, I was just—'

Frank waved a hand. 'It's okay. You've got things on your mind, yeah? We can do this some other time.'

'Nah, go ahead. I'm listening.'

The two fresh brews arrived and Frank waited until Connolly was out of earshot before resuming the conversation. 'I may have found a fella,' he said softly. 'Over Romford way. His name's Blunt, Alfie Blunt. I reckon he could be our front man.'

'And he's sound?'

'Yeah, I've checked him out. He's clean and he's well up for it.'

'Good. Let's set up a meet and get things moving.' Tommy hadn't even considered long-firm fraud until Frank had suggested the idea, but once he'd got his head around it he could see the advantages. The MO was simple. First, you got a front man, preferably one without criminal convictions, to open a shop or a warehouse. Goods would then be ordered on credit and the suppliers would be paid promptly. This would continue over a longish period of time, with more and more business being done, until the moment came for the final big

56

bang: there would be a series of massive orders and the credit-bought goods would be sold at knockdown prices in a 'liquidation sale'. After that, the premises would be closed and the profits pocketed.

Tommy took a slurp of tea. 'So how long do you reckon we're talking, start to finish?'

'About a year, maybe longer. You need patience in this game, Tommy. You can't rush things. It's all about building up trust.'

'I can do patience. I'm married to the lovely Yvonne, remember?'

Frank grinned back at him. 'You've got a point.'

'So we'll go ahead?'

'Sure. I'll set up a meet and we'll take it from there.'

Tommy gave a nod, pleased that the plan was going ahead. Joe Quinn preferred the quicker, more basic approach to business – protection, intimidation, poncing off the local villains – but Tommy was looking for less risky ways of making a living. If Frank was right, the long-firm fraud could bring in a hundred, even a hundred and fifty grand – and with little chance of getting caught. By the time the creditors had realised they'd been done, it would all be too late. The front man would have disappeared and the trail would be cold.

'What's the news on Connor?' Frank asked. 'Got a trial date?'

'Not yet.' That was something else to think about. When the date was set, there'd be witnesses to be sorted, money to be paid out. Connor was a liability, but family was family. Tommy would do whatever was necessary to make sure his older brother wasn't sent down. 'He's still doing his nut about not getting bail.'

'You found out why yet?'

Tommy shook his head. 'I just don't get it. I mean, it's not as though it's a bleeding murder charge or anything.' After Connor had been arrested, Tommy had paid a visit to the Albion at Ludgate Circus and given a grand to Bernie Humber to sort it, half down, the other half to be paid on completion of a successful bail application. Humber was a professional straightener, with connections in high places. Usually the arrangement would go like clockwork – the coppers being paid off and agreeing in court (with a feigned show of reluctance) that the defendant was unlikely to abscond – but not this time. A day after the money had been handed over, Humber had returned it, claiming that on this occasion his contacts weren't prepared to play ball.

'Someone doesn't like your brother,' Frank said. 'Mind, when I say *someone*, what I really mean is everyone. He might be family, but he's not worth the bother.'

'So I just leave him to rot?'

'Why not?'

'Like I left Lynsey?'

Frank gave him a long, steady look. 'That won't change anything.'

'Huh?'

'Blaming yourself, beating yourself up about it. She made her own choices. None of it was your fault.'

Except it didn't feel that way to Tommy. He averted his gaze, looking out at the street. The clouds had finally burst and the rain was pouring down. It pummelled against the window, making the pane vibrate. It beat down on the pavement. It ran in fast streams along the gutters, washing away the dirt and the dust and the litter – cleansing everything apart from his own troubled conscience.

Tommy's guts were beginning to churn again. His hand tightened around the mug he was holding. How the hell was he going to get through today? His sister's funeral. God, it made him sick just to think about it. It should be about coming to terms, laying the past to rest, but that didn't seem possible. Lynsey might be gone, but what had happened could never be buried.

# 6

It was ten to one when Tommy pulled up outside Farleigh Wood crematorium and turned off the engine. By now the rain had eased, and he wound down the window, lit a fag and tried to prepare himself for what was to come. He tugged hard on the cigarette, aware that the service was due to start soon. There was no one near the building, no one going in or coming out. In fact the whole place was eerily quiet.

Tommy looked at his watch, saw that it was almost time and quickly checked his reflection in the rear-view mirror. He smoothed down his fair hair and straightened his tie. 'Okay,' he said softly. 'You can do this, Tommy Quinn. You can do this.' He got out of the car, ground the fag end into the gravel with his heel and strode purposefully towards the door.

Inside, the chapel was almost empty. There were only six

other people there, all of them female. Three were sitting together up front; the other three were scattered around. He thought for a moment that he'd come to the wrong place, but then, as he glanced up the central aisle, he recognised Moira Sullivan. She turned her head and gave him a nod. He could have gone to join her, but instead he slid into a chair on the back row.

Tommy leaned forward and frowned. What kind of bloody turnout was this? The Lynsey he'd known had always been popular, always surrounded by friends. He wished now that he'd taken Frank up on his offer. At least there would have been one more person to swell the numbers and mourn her passing. He gazed dolefully at the pale wood coffin. On top were a large spray of white lilies, and the wreath of yellow and white chrysanthemums that he'd ordered from the florist in Kellston. She'd always liked yellow.

The service began, and while the priest jabbered on, Tommy's gaze slid from the coffin to the three figures seated at the front. It was the kid he was most interested in. Helen. The niece he had never set eyes on until today. Unfortunately, he could only see the back of her bowed head. The nape of her neck was ivory pale and her hair, a muddy shade of brown, was cropped short like a boy's. She was wearing a plain black woollen dress that looked a size too big for her.

To Helen's right was a woman in her sixties, her back as straight as a ramrod. That must be the grandmother. From what Moira had told him, there'd been no love lost between her and Lynsey. The remaining woman, on Helen's left, would be Joan Beck's daughter, Janet. She was the one who had called the Fox to pass on the news and discuss the arrangements for the funeral.

Tommy gritted his teeth as he recalled that short telephone conversation. He could still hear her clipped tones in his head; her manner had been brusque, her voice devoid of any emotion. The death of Lynsey, he suspected, was nothing for the Becks to grieve over. Except for Helen, of course, but then he didn't consider her to be a Beck. She might bear her father's name, but to Tommy she would always be a Quinn.

It was a short service, lasting only fifteen minutes. No one got up to speak about Lynsey, to say what she'd been like, to share their memories of her. Moira was the only one who wept, a tissue pressed hard against her eyes, her shoulders gently heaving. The priest talked of the resurrection and the life. Prayers were spoken before the coffin slid back and the curtain swished silently across in front of it. Tommy closed his eyes at that moment, feeling a thickness in his throat. So this was it. The end. Lynsey Quinn was gone for ever.

Tommy slipped out of the door and went to stand on the drive. He lit another fag, greedily drinking in the nicotine, and stared longingly at the white Cortina, wanting to jump in and roar away as fast as he could, preferably to the nearest boozer. Christ, he needed a drink, something to take the edge off it all. But it would have to wait. He had one last duty, and that was to check that Helen was all right. It was the least he could do for Lynsey.

After a minute or so, Moira Sullivan appeared and joined him on the drive. Her eyes were red and puffy. She stuffed the mangled tissue into her pocket before laying her hand gently on his arm. 'Are you all right, love?'

He gave a shrug. 'Not much to show for a life, is it? I mean, seven lousy people, for Christ's sake. And two of them didn't give a damn about her.'

As if on cue, the Beck women appeared in the doorway. Joan Beck was talking to the priest, making spare nodding gestures. She was a tallish woman with a wrinkled neck and a thin, sour face.

'Don't be too hard on them,' Moira said. 'It can't have been easy losing Alan like that. Things were difficult with Lynsey, but they've always been good to Helen. She's been living with her grandmother for most of her life.'

Tommy took another drag on the cigarette. That was Moira all over, kind and big-hearted, always ready to forgive. He looked at her, remembering the gawky teenager with the wild red hair and the generous smile. The hair had been tamed now, but the smile was the same. She'd been forever in Lynsey's shadow but was never resentful about it.

'Poor little thing. She's got no mum or dad to take care of her. It's not right, Tommy.'

Tommy glanced towards the door again and saw his niece clearly for the first time. He felt a rush of disappointment. He'd expected to see something of Lynsey in her, but there was nothing. She was a small, skinny, colourless creature, not exactly plain but hardly pretty either. He quickly pushed the thought to the back of his mind. It wasn't important what the kid looked like. All that mattered was that she was Lynsey's flesh and blood.

'I'm going to get off,' Moira said. 'Take care of yourself, yeah?'

'You want a lift?'

Moira shook her head. 'Thanks, but I'm fine. I've got the car.'

Tommy was relieved that he wouldn't have to take her back to Kellston. He liked Moira well enough, but he was gasping for that drink. The pub was the only place he wanted to be at the moment. He watched as she climbed into the Morris, catching a glimpse of thigh as her coat rose up. Hastily he blinked the image away. This wasn't the time to be eyeing up his sister's best friend. He raised his hand as she drove off, watching until she disappeared from view. He should have married someone like Moira, he thought, someone kind and loyal and decent.

Tommy turned his attention back to the chapel. The priest had gone inside and the trio had been joined by the two other women who'd been at the service, both plump and middle-aged. One of them left a minute later, giving Tommy a sidelong look as she walked past. It wasn't a friendly look. He dropped his fag on the ground and winked at her. She scuttled on, her lips pursed and disapproving.

He waited for the other woman to go, but after a while the group started to head towards a blue Ford Escort. They must all be leaving together. He moved to intercept them, wondering what to say. The usual standby, *I'm sorry for your loss*, didn't seem appropriate in the circumstances. In the event he settled for, 'Hello, I'm Tommy Quinn.'

He was met by a wall of silence.

Janet was the only one to respond, and that was with a curt nod.

He looked down at the kid. 'Hi,' he said. 'I'm your uncle Tommy.'

The girl gazed blankly up at him, as if she'd never heard the name before. Maybe she hadn't. Was it possible that Lynsey hadn't told her about her family in Kellston? As he gave her his most winning smile, he noticed that she wasn't quite as nondescript as he'd originally thought. Her eyes were a deep blue-green, almost startling against the paleness of her skin.

'It's nice to meet you,' he said.

As if Tommy was the type of man who lured small girls into his car, Janet placed a hand protectively on the kid's shoulder. Her thin, tight mouth finally managed to squeeze a few words out. 'Well, thank you for coming.'

Tommy bristled. It was meant, he knew, as a form of dismissal. 'I just wanted to make sure she was okay.'

Joan Beck peered hard at him for a moment, and then turned her head to address her daughter. 'Who is this man?'

'He's Lynsey's brother, Mum.'

'Lynsey? Who's Lynsey?'

Tommy stared at her. 'Is that supposed to be funny?' But then he saw the confusion in her eyes, the genuine bewilderment. The old bat didn't know what day of the week it was, never mind whose funeral she was attending. He looked at Janet. 'What's going on here?'

'Nothing's going on. She's fine. She's just a bit . . . stressed. It's been a long day.'

'Stressed?' Tommy echoed. He could see that it was more than that. 'No, I'm not having it. This isn't right. How can she take care of a child when—'

Janet raised a hand, stopping him in mid-flow. 'Brenda, could you take Mum and Helen to the car? I'll be with you in a minute.'

The middle-aged woman, who was clearly relishing the exchange, reluctantly ushered the two of them away.

Once they were out of earshot, Tommy said, 'I need to know she's being taken care of properly.'

'Oh yes? And how much care have you been providing, proper or otherwise, for the past eleven years?'

Tommy glared at her. He opened his mouth and then closed it again. He didn't like her attitude, but she had a point.

'Exactly,' she said. 'So unless you've got a better idea, we'll just have to struggle on as best we can. Helen isn't in any danger. I pop in every day and make sure that she's all right. Mum's more than capable most of the time.'

'Most of the time isn't good enough.'

Janet's eyebrows shifted up an inch. 'So what would you suggest?'

'Couldn't she live with you?'

'No, Mr Quinn, she couldn't. I've got two small boys of my own, and that's enough to deal with. She's your family too. Perhaps *you'd* like to take her for a while?'

Tommy shuffled from one foot to the other and heaved out a breath. He could imagine Yvonne's reaction if he turned up with Lynsey's kid in tow – not to mention what his old man would say. 'Well, it's kind of—'

Janet gave a snort. 'No, I didn't think so. Well, if there's nothing else, I'll be getting on. Some of us have responsibilities to attend to. Goodbye, Mr Quinn.' And with that, she turned on her heel and walked away.

'Snotty cow,' murmured Tommy under his breath. He could understand now why Lynsey had clashed so badly with the Becks. He watched as Janet got into the Escort and slammed the door with rather more force than was strictly necessary. As the car pulled away, he saw Helen's face pressed up against the window. He forced a smile and gave her a wave. She didn't smile back. She didn't wave either. My, he was popular today.

Crossing the car park, Tommy kicked up the gravel with the toe of his shoe. Some women were just bloody impossible! However, it wasn't only Janet's attitude that was bugging him. He'd come here to tie up the loose ends, to close the final chapter, but things hadn't quite panned out that way. Maybe the old woman wasn't a danger to Helen, but she was still sixpence short of a shilling. She wasn't a fit guardian and he knew it.

Tommy got into the Cortina, turned on the ignition and took off down the drive. At the gate he veered left and headed towards Chingford. He had to find a pub and fast. He'd come here to say goodbye to his sister and to reassure himself that everything was fine with Helen. But it wasn't fine. And what was he doing about it? Absolutely sod all. He needed a stiff drink, maybe even two or three, to silence his conscience.

He'd travelled a couple of miles when that little voice inside his head started nagging him again. What if it was one of his own girls? How would he feel if they were orphaned and living with someone like Joan Beck? The thought made him shudder. None of this was right. Damn it! She was Lynsey's kid. She had Quinn blood. He couldn't just abandon her.

Tommy checked the road behind him. When he saw that

it was clear, he slowed down and pulled up on the grass verge. For a while he sat there, the engine idling while he drummed his fingertips against the steering wheel. He ran through the options, always coming to the same conclusion – there was only one decent choice to be made. Before he could change his mind, he did a screeching U-turn and headed quickly back towards Farleigh Wood.

# 7

For Helen, the day had acquired an odd, almost bleary quality. Everything felt unreal, like in one of those dreams where you thought you might be awake but weren't entirely sure if you were or not. She was still hoping to blink her eyes and find that her mum hadn't been in that coffin at all, that she was alive, that she was coming back to see her soon. And now, perched on the edge of the bed, she found herself watching in a daze as her aunt neatly packed up underwear and skirts and jumpers into an old brown suitcase.

'It'll only be for a while,' Janet said as she moved around the room, opening and closing drawers. 'Your gran's been a bit under the weather recently. She needs a break, a rest, so she's coming to stay with me. You'll be all right with your uncle Tommy.'

Helen thought about the stocky blond man who was waiting downstairs, the man who had smiled at her outside the church. She didn't understand grown-ups. On the one hand they told you never to talk to strangers, then the next minute they were sending you away with one. 'How long for?'

'Just a week or two, until your gran's feeling better.' Janet looked down at the suitcase. 'Now, is there anything else you'll need?'

Helen got up from the bed and went over to the dressing table. She picked up the framed photo of her parents and the shell-covered box that her mum had given her for Christmas. Inside was her mother's wedding ring, a silver christening bracelet – too small for her now – some loose beads, a couple of plastic bangles and the flattened piece of cherry blossom. She would be back soon, but she didn't want to leave these things behind. They felt like the only connection to her mother she had left.

Janet looked as though she was about to say something, but then changed her mind. She took the items from Helen's hand and placed them carefully between the folds of a jumper. Then she closed the case and snapped shut the metal fasteners. 'Now, you be a good girl for your uncle Tommy, won't you?'

Helen gave a nod. She didn't want to go. She didn't want to leave her bedroom or the warm familiarity of the house. Although Gran might behave strangely at times, it was a strangeness she was used to. Suddenly everything was shifting in a way she had no control over.

'Come on then,' Janet said briskly. 'We don't want to keep everyone waiting.'

Helen followed her obediently downstairs and into the

living room. They entered a space heavy with silence. Her grandmother was gazing blankly at the wall, her hands doing a restless dance on the lace-covered arms of the chair. Tommy Quinn was leaning forward with his palms on his thighs. He jumped up as soon as he saw them, clearly eager to get away. 'Here, let me take that,' he said, reaching out for the suitcase.

Janet gave Helen's shoulder a nudge. 'Say goodbye to your gran, then.'

'Bye, Gran.' Helen bent and kissed the dry, powdery cheek. 'I'll see you soon.'

There was no response from the old woman.

Now that it was real, now that she was actually leaving, Helen felt a flurry of panic in her chest. She bit down on her lip, feeling that lump growing in her throat again.

Janet, perhaps fearing tears, turned quickly and headed for the front door. 'Now, you know my phone number, don't you, Helen?'

'Yes.'

'Good. Well, if you need to get in touch about anything, you can always give me a call.'

A thin, drizzly rain was falling. They walked in single file to the end of the drive, where a white Cortina was parked beside the gate. Uncle Tommy put the case in the boot and then opened the door to the front passenger seat. 'Hop in, then,' he said.

Helen hesitated. She wasn't scared of him, but she still didn't want to go. She wanted to run back inside the house and lock the door.

'Go on,' urged Janet. 'Before you get wet.' She bent and

gave Helen a brief, awkward hug. 'Everything's going to be fine. You'll be home again before you know it.'

And because Helen had been raised to always do as she was told, she reluctantly got into the car. Inside, it smelled of tobacco. There were empty cigarette packets on the floor, along with crinkly strips of cellophane, crumbs and sweet wrappers. With the edge of her shoe, she gingerly nudged the rubbish aside, clearing a patch for her feet.

Uncle Tommy closed the door but remained standing by the car. She heard him say to Janet, 'Er, about the ashes ... '

'I'll let you know when they're ready to be picked up. You can decide what to do with them.'

Helen caught her breath. Ashes. All that was left of her mother. Although no one had discussed the matter with her, she'd presumed that they would go in her father's grave. Her uncle said something else that she couldn't quite catch, before walking around the Cortina and getting in beside her.

'Okay, love? You ready for the off?'

Hoping for a last-minute reprieve, Helen gazed pleadingly out of the window at her aunt.

Janet gave a breezy wave before starting to walk back into the house. Just as she turned away, Helen caught a glimpse of the expression on her face. She wasn't sure, but she thought it might have been relief.

Uncle Tommy loosened his tie and undid the top button on his shirt. Then he wound down the window and lit a cigarette, before switching on the ignition and sliding the car away from the kerb. 'You okay, love? Been a bit of a day, huh? Let me know if you're feeling cold.'

Helen huddled down in the seat, getting as close to the

door as she could. She was feeling a lot of things, but cold wasn't one of them. She gave one last glance over her shoulder as they left Camberley Road, her gaze drinking in the houses, the gardens and the row of cherry trees.

Her uncle drove in a casual, almost careless manner, his right elbow leaning on the ledge of the window. She watched him surreptitiously out of the corner of her eye. He had the same colour hair as her mother, the same easy smile.

'You ever been to Kellston before, Helen?'

She shook her head.

'That's where your mum and me grew up. It's in the East End, not that far from here. We'll be there before you know it. And you'll have plenty of company, too. Did anyone tell you about your cousins?' He paused, looked at her and carried on. 'Me and Yvonne – that's the missus, by the way – we've got two girls, Debra and Karen. Debs is a bit older than you, but Karen's only just gone twelve.'

And now suddenly Helen had even more to worry about. She'd heard about the East End from her gran – a wild, godless place full of thieves and drunkards and murderers. Did Janet know that she was being taken there? And as if that wasn't bad enough, she also had to deal with the prospect of sharing a house with other children. Some of her school friends had brothers and sisters, older ones who teased and bullied them, or younger ones who followed them around and messed with their stuff.

'It must get lonely on your own,' her uncle said.

Helen gave a small shrug of her shoulders. 'It's okay.'

'Now your mum, she couldn't spend two minutes by herself. She was always gabbing with her mates. Jeez, she could talk for Britain. Once she got started, you could never shut her up. She—' He stopped abruptly, as if it had just occurred to him that Lynsey Quinn would never speak again. He chucked his cigarette end out of the window and rubbed his forehead with the heel of his hand.

Helen, avoiding his eyes, studied the silky blond hairs on his wrist and the gold signet ring on his little finger. Uncle Tommy, she realised, probably knew more about her mother than anybody else. There was a question on her lips, but she didn't yet have the courage to ask it. Instead she turned her face away and stared out of the window.

They went through Chingford Mount, passing the entrance to the cemetery. She thought of her father lying buried with his father beneath the white marble headstone. When had she last been here? Three weeks ago, or four? She tried to trace back time, counting off the Sundays. She could visualise the day. A slight breeze, a pale sun sliding between the drooping branches of the willow trees. She had put blue hyacinths on the grave. She remembered the smell of them, heady and sweet.

The rain was coming down harder now, lashing against the windscreen. Uncle Tommy wound up the window. The wipers swished back and forth, a rhythmic, almost hypnotic sound. Soon they were passing through unfamiliar places, the streets flashing by, leaving a trail of hazy imprints in her head: a cinema, a red dress in a shop window, a woman struggling with an umbrella. And all the time they were getting closer and closer to their destination.

Eventually, afraid that she might not get another opportunity, she took a deep breath and spoke. 'Uncle Tommy?'

'Why don't you just call me Tommy, hon. Less of a mouthful, yeah?'

'Oh, okay.'

'So what's the question?'

She almost had second thoughts, but then blurted it out. 'Do you know what happened?'

He glanced at her. 'Happened?'

'To Mum. I know there was a fire at the flat, Janet told me that, but ... but do you know why?' She swallowed hard, the words thick on her tongue. 'I mean, do you know how it started?'

He hesitated before replying. 'It was an accident, love. Could have been faulty electrics, something like that. Or maybe a fag that was left burning. They haven't finished the investigation yet.' He cleared his throat, staring straight ahead. 'But she wouldn't have felt anything. She wouldn't have known about it. She was asleep, you see. It was the middle of the night. The smoke would have ... Well, the smoke would have overcome her before she had the chance to wake up.'

But Helen didn't see how he could know this for sure. What if she *had* woken up? What if she'd been scared? What if she'd struggled to get out of bed and ... Her hands clenched instinctively. She could feel the dampness of her own palms. Quickly she tried to block the thought, to think about something else. Her mother's flat had been in Kilburn. Last week, when no one was looking, she had taken her grandfather's well-worn *A to Z* from the bookcase and checked the index to find out where it was. North-west London, that was where she'd been living. Her mum had

place for long: a few months, sometimes
two. Helen had found the road, Samuel Street,
ed her thumb down on it.

ou okay?' Tommy asked.

She gave a nod. 'Janet says that Mum's in heaven now.'

He grinned back at her. 'Sure. Why not? Probably causing mayhem already. Those angels won't know what's hit
them.'

For a long while after, there was silence, but it wasn't an
uncomfortable one. It was getting on for five thirty when
Helen saw the signpost for Kellston. By now, the roads they
were driving along were busier, greyer and dirtier than the
ones in Farleigh Wood. Three tall concrete towers dominated
the horizon. As they got closer, she gazed up at the top storeys
of the high-rise flats, wondering what it was like to live so
close to the sky. There were flashes of colour fluttering on the
balconies: shirts and towels hung out to dry by optimistic residents.

'This is the high street,' Tommy said. 'And there's a
market three times a week. The girls usually go there on
Saturdays.'

Helen, not wanting to appear rude, pretended to be interested. They passed a cinema, Woolworths and a café with a
group of lads loitering outside. The youths looked rough and
hard-faced, their hands stuck deep in their pockets as they
lounged against the wall. Recalling her grandmother's warnings about the dangers of the East End, she felt a spurt of
anxiety. But she didn't have to worry, she told herself. She was
in the car. She was safe. Nothing could happen to her. But her
heart continued to beat a little faster.

Tommy flicked on the indicator and turned left at a set of traffic lights. The first thing Helen noticed was the railway station. Men and women were streaming from the exit, an almost liquid crowd that flowed out on to the pavement. She was still watching this when her uncle swung right across the line of traffic and entered the car park of a pub called the Fox.

'Here we are,' he said, pulling the Cortina into a space by a stack of empty beer barrels. 'Home sweet home.'

Helen's eyes widened. She had never even been inside a public house before, never mind lived in one. As she got out of the car, she stared anxiously up at the Fox. It was a large but slightly shabby building, three storeys high, with the paint peeling from the windows. Tommy took her suitcase out of the boot and they sloshed through the puddles to the back door. Inside, there was a dimly lit corridor leading into the pub rooms – she could hear the murmur of voices, the chink of glasses – and a staircase going up to the first floor.

Her knees started to shake as she followed him up the stairs. Her eyes, downcast, took in the threadbare carpet, the scuff marks on the skirting boards and the battered lower part of the banisters. On reaching the first floor, Tommy swung around to the right, walked a short way along the landing and went through an open door that lay directly ahead. It led into a living room that overlooked the street. Two big green sofas, their arms worn thin with use, dominated the space. There was a patterned easy chair, a television, an electric fire – currently turned off – and a modern-looking record player. A pale blue Trimphone sat on a low table by one of the sofas.

The room was clean but untidy, with newspapers and magazines strewn around.

A female voice came from the room beyond. 'Tommy? Is that you?'

'Yeah.'

A second later, a woman flounced in from the kitchen beyond. She was slim and blonde and attractive. Or at least she would have been attractive if her face hadn't been contorted in an angry scowl. 'Where the hell have you been? Do you have any idea what the bloody time is?' She stopped dead in her tracks as she saw Helen. 'Who's this?'

'This is Helen,' he said. 'Lynsey's kid. She's come to stay with for us for a bit.' He put the case down and gave Helen's shoulder a reassuring squeeze. 'This is the missus, love. And don't worry, it's me she wants to kill, not you. I should have been back hours ago.'

Yvonne put her hands on her hips and stared at Helen. 'Stay?' she repeated stiffly. Her gaze flicked back up to her husband. 'What are you talking about?'

Helen shuffled awkwardly from one foot to the other. Her cheeks were beginning to burn and she wanted the floor to open up and swallow her. She hadn't asked to come here, hadn't wanted to come. If it had been up to her, she'd have turned straight around and gone back to Farleigh Wood.

'Don't start,' Tommy said. 'It's an emergency. Her grandma's sick.'

'And you didn't think to call, to let me know?'

'There wasn't time. Jesus, it's only one more. What's all the fuss about? You'll hardly notice she's here.'

Yvonne, however, didn't seem convinced. 'Oh, and you'll

78

be looking after her, will you? Cooking her meals, washing her clothes?' It was clearly only the presence of Helen that prevented her from really letting rip. Instead, she said through gritted teeth, 'We'll talk about this later, Tommy Quinn.'

Tommy grinned, backtracked to the door and shouted up the stairs. 'Girls? Come on down and meet your cousin.'

There was the soft thud of footsteps on the stairs, followed shortly by the appearance of two extremely pretty blonde girls. Apart from their height, they were almost identical, with long fair hair flowing down their backs, heart-shaped faces and wide brown eyes. They looked, Helen realised with a start, more like her mother than she did.

Uncle Tommy made the introductions. 'Debs, Karen, this is Helen. She's going to be staying with us for a while.'

The two girls, dressed in flared jeans and tie-dye T-shirts, looked her up and down blatantly. Helen squirmed under their scrutiny, aware of being judged. Her clothes, she knew, were drab in comparison to theirs – a pair of dark grey trousers and a striped jumper that was a size too big for her. Gran had always insisted on buying clothes that were 'practical' and that she could 'grow into'.

'Where you from, then?' Debs asked.

'Farleigh Wood,' Helen said. 'I live in Camberley Road.'

'What kind of music are you into?'

Sensing that this was some kind of test – and one that she could easily fail – Helen gave a small shrug. 'I like lots of things.'

'I like the Jackson Five and David Cassidy best,' Karen said. 'Debs reckons she's going to marry Mick Jagger.'

Helen, who had been grudgingly allowed to watch *The Partridge Family* on Saturday nights, said, 'I like David Cassidy too.'

Karen gave a giggle. 'How come you speak funny?'

Tommy gave his daughter a nudge with his elbow. 'She doesn't speak funny, love. She just speaks different. She's not common like you.'

Helen, who was not used to any kind of banter, was shocked by the remark, but Karen found it outrageously funny. She threw back her head and laughed out loud. Grabbing her father's arm, she tugged on his sleeve and gazed up at him.

'Am I, Dad? Am I really common?'

'Common as muck,' he said. 'Perhaps your cousin can teach you some manners. Although I doubt it. I reckon you're a lost cause, darlin'.'

'A lost cause,' Karen repeated, clearly pleased by the verdict.

'There's nothing wrong with her manners,' Yvonne snapped. 'But if she has got any bad habits, we all know who she's picked them up from.'

Tommy raised his eyebrows, but didn't seem overly stung by the criticism. 'Yer old dad's in the doghouse again,' he said, grinning from ear to ear. 'She'll be sending me up to me room next.'

Suddenly a loud, barking voice came from behind them. 'Oh, so you're back, are you? Good of you to honour us with your presence. I thought you were supposed to be running this bleedin' pub.'

Helen whirled around to see a fat, ageing man standing in

the doorway. He had a large drooping face with folds of flesh under his chin, red-veined cheeks and sparse grey hair combed over a pinkish scalp. His eyes, dark and menacing, glowered at her uncle.

'Five minutes,' Tommy said. 'I'll be right down.'

'Five minutes, my arse. It's packed down there.'

'Okay, okay. Don't lose yer rag. I'm coming.'

The man gave a grunt, apparently satisfied. It seemed as if he was about to go, but then Yvonne piped up.

'Aren't you going to introduce Joe to his granddaughter, Tommy?'

Helen heard a thin hiss of breath escape from Tommy's lips. She saw him look daggers at his wife before shifting his gaze back to his father. 'This is Helen,' he said finally.

Joe, who until that moment had completely ignored the third child in his living room – perhaps presuming she was one of Karen's school friends – now focused all his attention on her. His dark eyes seemed to bore into her soul and there wasn't an ounce of friendliness in them. 'Tell me this is a fuckin' joke.'

'No joke,' Tommy replied.

'No way. No fuckin' way! I'm not having Lynsey's brat in this house.'

Helen shrank back, moving closer to her uncle. Yvonne's welcome hadn't been exactly enthusiastic, but this was something else entirely. She could feel her legs beginning to shake again. The man was vile, horrible. How could he possibly be her grandfather?

'It's only for a week or so. She's got nowhere else to go.'

'Over my dead body.'

'If you like,' Tommy said. And there was something in his voice that Helen hadn't heard before, something hard and cold and determined. The two men locked eyes in a battle of wills. There was a scary silence in the room that seemed to go on for ever. Joe Quinn was the first to look away.

'Ah, do what you want. Just keep her out of my way.' He waved a hand dismissively, then turned and stormed out of the room.

Tommy put a hand on Helen's arm. 'Sorry about that, love. Don't worry about the old bastard. He's all mouth. He'll get used to the idea soon enough.'

Yvonne gave a snort. 'You reckon?'

Tommy ignored her. Instead he said to the girls, 'Look, why don't you take Helen upstairs and help her unpack. Grab her case, will you, Debs. It isn't heavy. She can bunk in with you, Karen.'

Helen glanced warily at her cousin, wondering if she would protest at this invasion of her space. But Karen didn't seem to mind. Perhaps she was used to sharing her bedroom with waifs and strays.

As she followed Debra and Karen up the stairs, she heard Tommy say to Yvonne, 'Well, thanks a bunch for that.'

'You had to tell him sometime.'

'Yeah, but not in front of the kid. What the hell were you thinking?'

'What the hell were you thinking bringing her here in the first place?'

'Christ, don't start, okay? You think today hasn't been bad enough without you giving me an earful too?'

The door suddenly slammed shut, cutting off the argument.

Helen could feel her heart beating hard in her chest. This was awful, a nightmare. She wanted to burst into tears. Perhaps she could run away. But where would she go to? Janet would be mad if she just turned up on her doorstep, and there was no room at her house anyway. No, she had no choice but to tough it out. It was only for a week or two. She'd be quiet. She'd be no trouble. She'd keep out of everybody's way. And then, after the time had passed, she'd be allowed to go home again – wouldn't she?

# 8

Yvonne poured two double vodkas, added some ice and a splash of lemonade and took the drinks round the bar to a table in the corner of the Fox. Her friend Carol Gatesby shuffled up to make room on the bench.

'I mean, can you believe it?' Yvonne said tetchily, continuing the conversation where she'd left off. 'He just turns up with her out of the blue. As if I've not got enough on my hands without another kid to take care of.'

'Yeah, it's a liberty, love. Ain't she got no one else to stay with?'

'Not according to Tommy. Mind, I wouldn't be surprised if those two saw him coming. Now that Lynsey's kicked the bucket, I reckon they've decided to get shot, to offload the kid on to some other poor sucker. But if he thinks that's going to be me, he's got another think coming.'

Carol took a sip of vodka and ran her tongue along her upper lip. 'So what's she like, then, this Helen?'

Yvonne gave a shrug. 'I dunno. She's a plain little thing, to be honest. Looks more like a boy than a girl. Not that that's her fault or nothin', but you'd have thought being Lynsey's daughter, she'd be . . . well, you get what I'm saying.'

'Yeah, Lynsey was a right stunner. That Alan Beck was a looker too, even if he was the filth.'

'I can hardly get a word out of her,' Yvonne continued. 'She just sits there staring at me like I'm an alien from outer space. I'm starting to wonder if there's summat wrong with her.' She gave a light tap to her forehead. 'You know, if she's not quite right up here.'

'She's probably upset and all. She'll settle down in a while.'

'It's the while I'm worried about,' Yvonne sighed. 'Oh, it's not just the kid.' She gazed around the Fox, her mouth turning sulky. 'I hate this dump. And now I'm stuck with living here again. And with Joe bloody Quinn. The old goat tries to feel me up every chance he gets; I can't make a cup of tea without him creeping up behind me. I could kill Tommy, I really could.'

Carol patted her on the hand. 'It's not for ever, love. You'll be out of here as soon as Connor gets back. And believe me, there's worse in the world than your Tommy.'

Yvonne wrinkled her nose. She'd thought Tommy Quinn was a catch when she'd married him all those years ago – part of a successful criminal family, good prospects, a man going places. Except Tommy wasn't going any further than this lousy pub. He had no ambition, no drive. 'Well, that may be true, but there's better, too. He's still sneaking around with that tart, Shelley Anne. It's pathetic. He thinks I don't know about it, but that man is the worst liar I've ever come across.'

85

'He'll get bored of her soon enough.'

'That's not the point.' Yvonne, by choice, rarely slept with Tommy these days, and she didn't really care who else he was shagging. But she didn't like being made a fool of. 'Why should I spend my time taking care of Lynsey's unwanted sprog while he's getting his leg over his latest squeeze? It's not on.'

'So what are you going to do?'

Yvonne thought about it, and then gave a small shrug. 'Nothing – for now. But I'll make him pay. You see if I don't.'

'Just watch your step,' Carol said softly. 'You've got the girls to think about, remember? If you cross Tommy, you'll be crossing Joe and Connor too. And let's face it, they're not what you'd call the forgiving sort.'

'Oh, I can handle them.' Yvonne glanced across the pub to where Tommy was leaning forward with his elbows on the counter. He was deep in conversation with Frank Meyer. 'And those two are up to something. They've been whispering in corners for weeks.'

'Perhaps your Tommy's got a big job planned.'

Yvonne gave a mirthless laugh. 'That'll be the day. The biggest job he ever does is dragging them crates up from the cellar. I tell you, getting any readies out of him at the moment is like getting blood from a stone. You'd think with Connor being away he could make himself more useful to Joe. The old git must be raking it in, but there's not much comes in Tommy's direction.'

'You still after that holiday in Spain?'

'Fat chance,' Yvonne said. 'The way things are going, we'll

be lucky to get a week in Clacton.' She flicked her eyes towards the bar again. 'I really don't like that guy.'

'Who, Frank?'

'I mean, just who the hell is he? He turns up out of the blue – no one has a clue where he's come from or knows sod all about him – and suddenly he's Tommy's best mate.'

'That was ages ago, love.'

'So what? I still don't trust him. He could be the filth, for all we know.' In fact, Yvonne had other, more personal reasons for disliking Frank Meyer. Most of the guys who hung around the Quinns you could have a laugh with, a joke, a bit of a flirt, but not Frank. The first time she'd tried it, he'd completely blanked her. The guy was like a piece of stone. And he had a way of looking at you. Superior, that was what he thought he was. She took a gulp of her vodka and returned the glass to the table with a small bang. As if he was anything special. Lifting a hand, she quickly patted down her fair hair. She might be in her thirties now, but she was still worth a second glance.

'You okay?' asked Carol.

'I'm fine.' She looked at her friend and smiled. Compared to Carol – a blowsy bottle blonde with a thickening waistline – she reckoned she was wearing pretty well. At least she still had her figure. This thought cheered her up somewhat. Nudging her friend's shoulder, she said in a low voice, 'Tell me something. Have you ever seen Frank with a girl?'

'I'm not sure. I don't think so.'

'Exactly!' Yvonne said triumphantly.

It took a moment for the penny to drop. Carol's eyebrows shot up. 'You don't think he's . . . ?'

Yvonne sniggered. 'That's be a turn-up for the books, wouldn't it? Tommy snuggling up to a queer. Jesus, he'd never live it down.'

The women's gaze automatically swivelled towards the bar. Aware of being under scrutiny, the two men looked back at them. Yvonne gave them a wave. Carol put a hand over her mouth and dissolved into a fit of giggles.

'Best not say anything, though,' Yvonne said. 'It'll be our little secret.' She sat back, feeling smug. If there was a good way to start a rumour, it was to whisper a 'secret' in Carol Gatesby's ear. The girl couldn't keep her mouth shut if her life depended on it.

Suddenly the door from the street swung open, bringing with it a burst of chilly night air, and a young, dark-haired man strode into the pub. He shook the rain from his head and made his way towards the bar. He had a lean, handsome face with cheekbones like razor blades.

'Evening, ladies,' he said, winking as he passed them. 'Looking gorgeous, as always.'

Yvonne smiled back at him. 'Evening, Terry.' She studied his tight little arse as he sauntered over to join her husband. Then she leaned in towards Carol and whispered, 'Now I wouldn't kick that out of bed.'

'You'd be so lucky. You're old enough to be his mother.'

'He's only ten years younger than me.'

'And some,' Carol said. 'He can't be a day over twenty.'

Yvonne gave a shrug and knocked back the rest of her drink. Terry Street was her kind of man – good-looking, sexy, smart and charming. He might be young, but she could tell that he was going places. There were lots of lads who hung

88

around the Quinns, but only a few who made it to the inner circle. Joe Quinn might be a dirty old bugger, but he still recognised a prospect when he saw one. Terry was an asset to the firm, and everybody knew it.

'Fancy another?' Yvonne said, waving her empty glass.

'Ta. I wouldn't say no.'

As she sashayed over to the bar, Yvonne started thinking about Tommy and his tart again. She could confront him, but it wasn't worth the effort. No, if she wanted to be free of the Quinns, she was going to have to bide her time and wait for the right opportunity. It might not be tomorrow or the day after, but when it came along, she was going to grab it with both hands.

# 9

DI Tony Lazenby put his glass down. He slid the envelope on to his lap, opened it and started counting out the notes.

'It's all there.'

Tony glanced up. 'Sure it is. I know you wouldn't deliberately screw me over, Lennie. But best to make sure, huh? Just in case you made a little mistake.' When he was satisfied that all the cash was there, he slipped the envelope into the inside breast pocket of his jacket. 'So, have you thought any more about what we talked about?'

Lennie Gissing leaned forward, putting his heavy elbows on the table. They were sitting in an otherwise empty corner of the Cat and Fiddle, with no one near enough to overhear what was being said, but still he kept his voice low. 'Yeah, we've been giving it some consideration.'

'Some *consideration*?' Tony frowned. 'And what exactly is there to consider? Either you're in or you're out. I don't like being messed about and I don't like wasting my time.' He made as if to get to his feet. 'You're not the only firm in the East End.'

Lennie hurriedly waved him back down. 'Hold on. I didn't say we wasn't interested, did I?'

Tony sank back into his chair. 'So what's your problem? Connor's inside for the next few months – I've made sure of that – which only leaves old man Quinn and his henchmen. They're hardly the bleeding Krays, are they? It's there for the taking, Lennie. You could double, triple your profits if you made a move now.'

Lennie gave a nod. 'Yeah, I get it.'

'Do you?' Tony asked. 'Because this opportunity isn't going to be around for ever. Miss this bus and you'll have a damn long wait for the next one.' He knew what was holding them back. Reggie and Ronnie had gone down for thirty years, and nobody fancied a piece of that. There might be a gap in the market, but all the local players were biding their time, waiting to see how things panned out, making edgy little forays but nothing on a grand scale. No one wanted to be the first to put their head above the parapet in case they got it shot off.

'Joe's no pushover,' Lennie said darkly. 'He's been around since the bloody Ark.'

Tony shook his head. 'Believe me, he's past it. Take him out and you've got a clear run. You can have it all: the protection, the toms, the whole shebang. You can get their dealers off the streets and get your own in. By this time next year, you could be running the East End.'

Lennie took a long pull on his pint. Tony could see him thinking it over, the wheels slowly turning in his primitive brain. The Gissings weren't the sharpest knives in the drawer, but that was one of the reasons he wanted them as his partners. They were brutal enough to exert their authority but not bright enough to double-cross him. 'So, have we got a deal?'

Lennie Gissing narrowed his eyes, his mouth opening a little to reveal his chipped yellow teeth. He put down his pint. Then he spat on his palm and extended his hand. 'You've got a deal.'

Tony shook the proffered hand and immediately stood up. 'Good decision. I'll be in touch.' He walked across the bar to the gents', and as soon as the door had closed behind him, wiped his hands on his trouser legs. 'Jesus,' he murmured, wondering how much more Gissing saliva he'd have to put up with before the month was out. Still, it would be worth it in the end.

He went over to the urinal, unzipped his pants and took a slash, then washed his hands and examined his reflection in the mirror. Most of what he observed – a decent-looking face, blue eyes, a strong jaw with a cleft in the chin – was entirely to his satisfaction. There was only one fly in the ointment. Although he was just knocking on forty, his brown hair was starting to recede. He took out a comb and made a few adjustments. He was, he knew, only papering over the cracks. What really pissed him off was how a bunch of scientists was able to put a geezer on the moon but was still damn well incapable of finding a cure for premature male baldness.

Tony put the comb away and tapped the cash in his pocket. It was enough for now, but it wasn't a fortune. Not to worry. The more powerful the Gissings became, and the more they controlled, the bigger his kickback would be. He would keep them informed about any police raids that were being planned and make sure the girls and the dealers could work freely. Basically, he would watch their backs, and in return they'd give him a cut of everything they earned.

He took one last look in the mirror and then went back into the bar. There was no sign of Lennie Gissing. Walking out of the door, he took a right and strolled down the street. It was barely five o'clock, but already Soho was heaving, the porn shops doing brisk business, the toms touting for trade, the strip joints opening their doors for the first evening shows.

Tony thought about the deal he'd just made. It was important to him, and not just because of the money he'd be making. No, this was much more personal. He hated the Quinns with a vengeance. It was time to finish them once and for all. It was the very least he could do for Alan.

Mates, especially ones you could trust, didn't grow on trees, and he still missed Alan Beck. Together they'd made one hell of a team. How long was it now since he'd been gone? It must be getting on for six years. Jesus, they'd had some good times together until *she* had come along, getting herself up the duff and forcing Alan to marry her. The bitch had probably done it deliberately. And even then she hadn't been happy. Nothing was ever good enough for Princess Lynsey Quinn.

Tony scowled as he pushed his way through the crowd. He wondered, not for the first time, how the fates could conspire to ruin the life of a good man. He could still remember walking into Connolly's that day. What if they'd decided to go to the pub instead? What if they'd sat at a different table? Maybe

Alan would never have caught the eye of the stunning slim blonde sitting drinking coffee with her friend. Maybe the two of them would never have got talking.

In some ways it only felt like yesterday. It was all still so clear to him. He'd ended up chatting to the blonde's pal, a gawky-looking redhead whose name he had long since forgotten. Something Irish, he thought. He hadn't fancied her, but those were the rules. If your mate had his sights set on someone, you had to keep the friend occupied.

Tony breathed out a sigh. Alan should have run a mile when he'd found out who Lynsey Quinn really was. Screwing a villain's daughter was never a smart move. But then Alan had always liked to live dangerously. It was part of her appeal, perhaps, that she was forbidden fruit, that there was a big red danger sign flashing above her head.

He turned into Brewer Street, a deep frown settling between his eyes. If only the clocks could be turned back, the bad decisions made good. If only the bitch hadn't been so adamant about keeping the kid. It could have been sorted quietly, discreetly, if she hadn't decided to turn up on Mrs Beck's doorstep shouting her mouth off. Once the family was involved, there was no chance of making the problem go away.

The last thing Alan had wanted was a nagging wife and a kid, but that was what he'd landed himself with. It wasn't any wonder that he'd ended up at Jeannie Macklin's place that night. Everyone needed a break from time to time. Jeannie had run a tidy little brothel above a takeaway in Whitechapel, with clean girls and no bother. Or at least there had never usually been any bother. Unfortunately Jeannie hadn't realised that two of her other clients were a pair of East End mugs wanted for the murder of a jeweller in Hatton Garden.

The bastards, about to head down the stairs, had recognised Alan as he was coming in and thought he was part of an undercover operation to arrest them. Retreating back along the landing, they'd watched as he'd gone into a room with one of the toms, waited for five minutes and then charged in all guns blazing. The poor sod hadn't stood a chance.

Tony's hands clenched into two tight fists. Alan wouldn't have had to go there if he'd been getting it at home. The frigid bitch wouldn't even put out for him. The official party line, of course, was that DS Beck had been at the brothel on police business. He was hailed a hero, his face splashed all over the front of the papers. It was never mentioned that he was stark bollock naked when they found him with three bullets through his chest.

Yes, the Quinns had a lot to answer for. He'd heard all sorts about Lynsey after Alan's murder – that she'd dumped the kid with the grandmother, that she was screwing around, that she was on the game. Ironic, he thought, that she refused to sleep with her husband but she'd shag anything else in pants. Well, the bitch might be dead, but he wouldn't rest until he'd scourged the earth of the rest of the family too. He'd already paid off Humber to make sure that Connor Quinn wouldn't get bail. With the older son out of the picture, it shouldn't take long to finish off the others.

# 10

Helen was woken by the thin morning light sliding through a gap in the curtains. She turned her head to look at the alarm clock. A quarter to seven. She frowned. Although wide awake, she didn't want to get out of bed yet. What was there to get up for? It was the beginning of the summer holidays – a time for most kids to be excited – but she was dreading it. The weeks stretched ahead of her, long, empty days, hours and hours that would need to be filled.

It was over two months now since she'd first arrived at the Fox. She could remember it vividly: the fear, the confusion, the sense that her place in the world had changed irretrievably. That first night, unable to sleep, she'd gone over and over it all – the funeral, the journey to Kellston, the vicious look in Joe Quinn's eyes – as if by constant repetition she might finally arrive at a different outcome. Eventually, at about three o'clock, she had drifted off to the low tinny sounds of Radio Luxembourg coming from Karen's transistor radio.

For the first few weeks she had clung on to a thread of hope. Her grandmother would get better. Tommy would take her home. Everything would be as it had been before. But gradually the hope had faded. Janet's Sunday telephone calls had become increasingly grim, until finally there was news of a stroke. With her gran in hospital, it was clear that there was no chance of an early return to Farleigh Wood.

Helen linked her hands behind her head. Her hair, without the constant attention of her grandmother's scissors, had grown an inch or so, covering her ears and the back of her neck. Thankfully, she was starting to look less like a boy. The second the thought popped into her head, she felt guilty for it. Gran had always tried her best. She knew that. And for all her strictness, for all her peculiarities, Helen still missed her like mad.

There had been no visits to the hospital. Helen hadn't been allowed. 'It'll only upset her, you seeing her like that,' Janet had said. 'Best to wait until she's feeling brighter.' But brighter never happened, and Janet's phone calls, once so predictable, had become increasingly irregular. How long now since she'd last heard from her? Almost two weeks, she reckoned.

Helen gazed at the wall. The bedroom was painted purple and covered with posters. From where she was lying she could see Michael Jackson smiling down at her. She'd been allocated the lower bunk and could hear the creak of the springs whenever her cousin turned over. Karen seemed indifferent to her presence, neither pleased nor angry about it. They had not become friends, but at least they weren't enemies.

Helen hadn't seen any of her real friends since leaving

Farleigh Wood. She'd exchanged the odd letter with Ruth and Susan, but now – like with Janet's calls – their communication was starting to tail off. She was only a few miles away, but she might as well be living on the other side of the world. *Out of sight, out of mind* was one of her gran's favourite sayings, and Helen was beginning to grasp what that meant.

Starting a new school could have been the chance to make new friends, but that hadn't worked out too well. When it had become clear that she wouldn't be going home in a hurry, she'd been enrolled at Kellston Comprehensive. The building, a sprawling, low-slung concrete construction, was a daunting maze of corridors, and the other kids – of whom there seemed to be thousands – scared her half to death.

On her first day, the teacher had sat her at a desk beside another new girl called Andrea Moss. Andrea, who had moved from Bournemouth, wore her hair in a long brown plait hanging down her back. As the two new kids, they were glad of each other's company, safety in numbers and all that. They spent break times and lunch together and everything was fine for a week. But then, on the following Monday, Helen had gone cheerfully into class only to find herself shunned. Andrea had moved desks and was apparently no longer her friend.

Helen briefly squeezed her eyes shut, remembering the shame and humiliation. It was another girl who, either through pity or relishing the prospect of passing on bad news, had finally told her the reason why.

'It's 'cause you're a Quinn, ain't it? Her mum and dad don't want her hanging out with you.'

'But I'm a Beck,' Helen had protested.

The girl had shrugged her shoulders as if this was a mere technicality. 'Don't make no odds. You're living with 'em, ain't you?'

This was a fact Helen couldn't dispute. She could have tried to make other friends, but she didn't really have the heart for it. And anyway, it had soon become clear that she didn't fit in. There were the 'nice' girls like Andrea, who didn't want to be associated with someone from a family like the Quinns, and then there were the rougher ones, who, perhaps because of the way she spoke or the way she acted, wouldn't accept her either.

Helen had taken to hiding out in the library whenever she had free time at school. This excused her from the horror of standing alone in the playground but did little to enhance her reputation. She had become known as a swot. Such a label could have made her the target of bullies, but ironically, she'd been saved from this fate because she was a Quinn. No one messed with the Quinns. That was common knowledge.

Knowing that she wouldn't get back to sleep now, she pushed back the covers and swung her legs over the side of the bed. She sat there for a moment staring at the photograph of her parents. It had pride of place on the small chest of drawers that had been emptied for her. The sight of her mum's face still sent a pain through her chest, the thought of never seeing her again almost too much to bear.

'Mouse?'

Helen glanced up towards the upper bunk. 'Yes?' She couldn't remember exactly when her name had morphed into Mouse. It was Debs, she thought, who had first started it, teasing her about how quiet she was. Now everyone had taken it up.

'What are you doing?'

'Nothing. Just going to the loo.' Helen pulled on her underwear, her jeans and a T-shirt. She pushed her bare feet into her sandals and stood up.

'Mouse?'

'Yes?'

'Who do you like better, David Cassidy or Terry Street?'

'David Cassidy,' Helen said. Then, concerned that this might not be the right answer, she quickly added, 'But it's close.'

Before Karen could interrogate her any further, Helen slipped out of the room and padded along the landing to the bathroom. Terry was nice enough, good-looking and funny, but she didn't share the crazy crush that both her cousins had on him. Whenever he was in the flat they'd stare at him all wide-eyed like he was some kind of film star. Even Yvonne became fluttery in his presence.

Helen locked the door and went to the loo. Then she washed her hands, brushed her teeth, splashed water on her face and rubbed it dry. She stared into the mirror for a moment, not liking what she saw. Her gran had always said that it was what was on the inside that was important, but she already knew that what you were judged on first was your appearance. It might not be right, but that was the way of the world.

She left the bathroom and went downstairs. Just before she reached the landing, she peered cautiously over the banisters and listened for any signs of movement. The last thing she wanted to do was to run into Joe Quinn. His bedroom, unlike the other three, was on the first floor. He didn't usually get up until late morning, but there was a first time for everything.

When she was sure that the coast was clear, she walked smartly through the living room and into the kitchen, where she made a peanut-butter sandwich and shoved it into a carrier bag. Her plan was to make herself scarce for a while. At around nine o'clock she'd come back and help Tommy bottle up before the pub opened. She liked the satisfaction she got from filling the shelves, arranging the beers and the mixers in neat straight lines. But most of all she just liked hanging out with Tommy. He was the one sure ally she had in the household.

Helen ran down the next flight of stairs and let herself out of the back door. Although the sun was shining, its warmth had barely registered. She enjoyed the feel of the cool breeze against her skin. Later, the air would be filled with exhaust fumes, with the smell of frying, with all the various human scents and stinks, but for now it still seemed fresh and new.

She jogged to the corner and then slowed to a walk as she turned on to the high street. It still amazed her how she had the freedom to come and go exactly as she wished. She was hardly ever questioned, and on the rare occasions that she was, she would always claim that she was visiting the Mansfield Estate to see her friend Ella. She had plucked the name from the air, some lingering memory perhaps of her mother's love of Ella Fitzgerald. No one was interested enough to wonder why the mysterious Ella never came to the Fox.

Helen crossed the road and strolled on to the green. This patch of land, about twice the size of a football pitch, was the nearest Kellston had to offer in the way of a park. It ran between the high street and Barley Road, a stretch of grass with a few scattered shrubs and trees. She had the place to herself – even the local dog-walkers hadn't risen from their beds – and went straight over to her favourite seat. This wooden bench, set off to the left, was positioned beneath a lilac tree. She looked up. The violet blossoms, once so pretty, had now faded to brown and were hanging limply from the branches.

The reason why she always chose this spot was that her mum had often sat here when she was young. Or so Moira Sullivan had told her. Moira had told her lots of things, about where the two of them used to go and what they liked to do. Tommy didn't talk much about his sister – he went all gloomy and quiet whenever her name was mentioned – but Moira's face would light up whenever she shared her memories.

Sometimes, after school, Helen would go round to Moira's. She lived above the undertakers', Tobias Grand & Sons, at the far end of the high street. The funeral parlour spooked Helen, but the flat was neat and cosy. She liked to hang out there, to eat chocolate biscuits and listen to Moira's tales about the past.

Thinking about the biscuits made her stomach growl. She took out her sandwich and chewed it slowly while she decided what to do next. Since arriving in Kellston, she'd spent hours wandering the streets. She was familiar with the bright colours and sounds of the market, the neat rows of identical terraces, the maze of alleyways and the dim, threatening corridors of the Mansfield Estate. The latter, with its three high towers, both drew and repelled her. Although the place was unnerving, she couldn't resist going there.

Helen chucked her bread crusts on the grass, watching the scruffy pigeons strut over to share her breakfast. When all the food was gone, she stood up and headed back to the high street. Recently she had started to explore further afield, travelling west into Shoreditch or east into Bethnal Green, but today she didn't have the time. She would stroll up to Connolly's, she decided, and see if Moira was working this morning. Sometimes she did a weekend shift.

Now that it was past seven, the street was getting busier. The shops were still closed, but the market would be opening in an hour. Already the vans were starting to arrive, packed with fruit and vegetables, with flowers and clothes and kitchen goods. As Helen idly watched them turning into Market Road, she found herself thinking about what she'd learned since joining the Quinn family: to keep her head down, never to speak unless she was spoken to, to keep out from under Yvonne's feet, to always avoid Joe Quinn. Since that first time they'd met, he hadn't said two words to her, but whenever their paths crossed she would see the loathing on his face.

Helen shook her head, trying to dislodge the image from her mind. She crossed the road, drew adjacent to the café and peered in through the window. Paul Connolly was behind the counter frying up eggs and bacon, but there was no sign of Moira. Helen delved into her pocket to find the shilling that was lying there. No, she mustn't call it a shilling. It was a bob.

And sixpence was a tanner. Every day she was learning new words, some of the language of Kellston being as foreign to her as French.

Anyway, she had more than enough money to buy a Coke. She was thirsty, but still she hesitated. Through the glass she could see the other customers, and they were all male. She felt too intimidated to go in. The men leaned forward, their sturdy elbows on the tables, their big hands grasping the white mugs. A fug of cigarette smoke hung in the air.

One of the men got up to leave, and as the door opened Helen caught a snatch of Mungo Jerry's 'In the Summertime' coming from the radio. She wanted to be brave enough to go in, but she wasn't. Everyone would look at her and someone might even speak or make a joke. Her chronic shyness was an almost intolerable burden. She wished she was more like her cousins, outgoing and talkative and unafraid of life.

Reluctantly she turned away and ambled back towards the market. She spent almost an hour wandering between the stalls, watching the sellers as they laid out their wares, listening to the bangs and the clatters and the easy banter. Recently she had bought a couple of cheap T-shirts here, including the red and white one she was wearing now. Tommy gave her ten shillings a week pocket money, most of which she tried to save and which she kept hidden in an old sock in her chest of drawers. She had no idea what she was saving for, but the money made her feel more secure.

Helen's wardrobe had increased dramatically since she'd come to Kellston. She was now in possession of two pairs of blue jeans, as well as numerous shirts and blouses that Karen or Debs had grown out of. She didn't mind wearing their cast-offs. Anything was preferable to the dull, old-fashioned clothes that her grandmother had bought for her.

When she heard the town hall clock strike eight, Helen headed slowly back towards the Fox. She let herself in through the back door, walked along the corridor and looked into the bar. She wrinkled her nose. The place smelled of stale beer and tobacco. Someone had already begun the tidying up – there were dirty glasses stacked on the counter, and a couple of the tables had been wiped clean.

Helen was about to go in when she heard the heavy tread of footsteps on the stairs. Tommy? She looked over her shoulder, intending to call out, but then her heart missed a beat. She heard a familiar wheezing breath, followed by a cough. It wasn't Tommy at all. It was Joe Quinn, on his way down.

She felt a flutter of panic in her chest and instinctively looked for somewhere to hide. It was bad enough crossing paths in the flat, but at least upstairs there were other people around. Down here she would be alone with him. Her first thought was to slip into the bar, to hide in the ladies' perhaps, but if Joe was going to finish cleaning up, then she could be trapped in there until the pub opened. She glanced towards the back door, but she already knew that she wouldn't make it before Joe reached the bottom of the stairs.

That only left one option. As quietly as she could, she ran along the passageway, pushed open the door to the cellar and closed it softly behind her. She flicked on the light – a bare bulb hanging from a fraying piece of string – and went quickly down the old stone steps. Her left shoulder brushed against the wall, the mortar flaking off and covering her arm in a thin white dust. At the foot of the steps, she stopped and listened, but she couldn't hear anything.

Across the far side of the basement was another, more solid door. It led out into the car park, but she knew it was locked. The key was hanging in the bar on a hook by the optics. Helen resigned herself to a wait. If she hung on for five or ten minutes, she could hopefully sneak past Joe and get back up to the flat without being spotted.

# 11

Helen perched on the edge of a barrel and looked around. The cellar, crammed full of old crates, had a musty, beery odour. Cobwebs hung in the corners of the ceiling and there were fag ends scattered on the tiled floor. Boxes of spirits were stacked up to her right, beside the bottled beer and the sherry and the mixers. She scanned the floor for spiders, hoping something large and black wasn't about to make an appearance.

Joe Quinn reminded her of a spider. She gave a quick, involuntary shudder. It was impossible to think of him as a grandfather; her *real* grandad had been kind and gentle, but Joe was something else entirely. Fortunately, he didn't spend much time in the flat, and any occasion he was there, she was careful to steer clear. She understood that he'd fallen out with her mother, but why did he hate her – Helen Beck – so much? What had she ever done to him? Her very existence, it seemed, was enough to send him into a rage.

Two minutes passed, and then another two. Helen kept glancing at her watch, aware of how slowly the hands were moving. Was it safe to go yet? She decided to venture back up and take her chances. She had just jumped off the barrel when she heard a noise from above. She stood very still, straining her ears. Voices. Yes, there were definitely voices. And then, horror of horrors, she heard the door at the top of the steps open.

'Down here,' Joe Quinn said.

'What's wrong with the bar, then?'

'You want to do business or not?' This was followed by a hissing sound. 'For fuck's sake, can't he ever turn this bleedin' light off?'

For a second Helen was paralysed. Unless she moved quickly she was going to be caught. How was she going to explain why she was lurking in the cellar? And what would Joe do when he found her? Panic finally propelled her into action. She scurried over to the rear of the room, where the empty barrels were stacked up awaiting collection. Crouching down, she wedged herself between the barrels and the wall.

She was only just in time. Seconds later, peering out, she saw two pairs of feet descending the steps. Joe's black boots came first, followed by a pair of smart brown brogues.

'Nice place you got here, mate.'

Helen didn't recognise the other voice. She was holding her breath, her arms wrapped around her knees, her heart thumping wildly in her chest.

Joe gave a grunt. 'You got a problem, son? 'Cause if you have . . .'

There was a low laugh. 'No, mate. Don't sweat. I get it. Just saying, that's all.'

Helen kept her head down as the two men walked to the centre of the cellar. It was dim in the corner and she prayed they wouldn't see her. *Please God. Please God.* She couldn't have made herself any smaller if she'd tried, but in her mind she was the size of an elephant.

'How much we talkin', then?' Joe said.

'Five, and that's a bloody good deal.'

'You reckon?'

'You'll make ten times that out on the street and you know it. It's good stuff, Joe. It's none of your shit.'

There was a brief silence, followed by the sound of a match being struck. Helen could smell the burnt match and then the drifting cigarette smoke. She felt sick to her stomach. She shifted slightly, careful not to make any noise. Her trembling shoulders were beginning to ache from the hunched position she'd assumed. When would they go? She didn't want to hear any of this, didn't want to listen. If only she'd never come down here. If only she'd stayed outside, safe and free.

Joe's voice again. 'When are we talking about?'

'Thursday. Cash on delivery. I can bring it here or you can choose a place.'

'Not here.'

'Like I said, it's up to you.'

Joe began to pace around the cellar, striding from one side to the other. His boots creaked as he walked. 'Where's it coming from, then?'

'Straight from sunny Morocco. Top quality, no messing. You'll shift it in no time.'

'Morocco,' Joe grunted. 'I don't trust those bloody bastards. They could be palming off any old crap on you.' He changed direction again. Helen could hear his footsteps getting closer. She shut her eyes tight. If she couldn't see him, then he couldn't see her.

'I'm telling you, it's damn good stuff.'

Now Joe was only a foot away. If he looked down, if he lowered his gaze just a fraction . . . She could sense him looming over her and instinctively she shrank back. It was then that disaster struck. Although the movement was a small one, her body make contact with the edge of one of the empty barrels. There was a thin scraping noise as the metal shifted against the tiles. Her heart instantly jumped into her mouth.

'Who's there?' Joe called out roughly. 'Who the fuck's there?'

Helen tried to scrabble backwards, but the wall was blocking her escape.

Joe lunged forward, leaned over, grabbed the top of her arm and hauled her out. 'You!' he said, almost spitting in her face. She struggled to get free, but his hold was too tight. Terror streamed through her blood as he grabbed her other arm too and began to shake her.

'What's your game, girl?' he roared. 'What you playin' at? What you fuckin' playin' at?'

Helen couldn't have answered even if she'd wanted to. Her jaw had gone rigid with fear, her teeth clamped together so hard she thought they might break. The rest of her body was as limp as a rag doll. There was no fight left in her at all; she was helpless and he knew it.

Joe's grasp tightened as he shook her ever harder. He was

shouting now, yelling at the top of his voice. 'Tell me, you scheming little cow! Who sent you to spy on me? Who was it?'

'Hey, take it easy, Joe,' the other man said. 'She's just a kid.'

Joe's lips were twisted in a snarl, his breath coming in short, fast pants. 'Keep out of it! This is none of your damn business.'

Helen looked pleadingly at the man, hoping he might intervene, but instead he took a step back. Whatever his feelings on the matter, he clearly wasn't going to cross Joe Quinn. She had time for only the most fleeting of impressions – longish brown hair, small mouth, pointy chin – before Joe started in on her again. Helen was convinced she was going to die, right now, right here in the cellar, when suddenly another voice rang out.

'What the hell's going on down there!'

As Tommy jogged down the steps, Joe abruptly let go of Helen's arms. Her legs instantly gave way and she crumpled to the floor. Without the will or the strength to try and stand, she stayed on the ground, her face on her knees, her eyes brimming with tears. She gulped in air, her chest still heaving. She wasn't going to cry. She wasn't going to let the bastard make her cry.

Tommy knelt down, putting an arm around her. 'Mouse? Mouse, are you okay?' He looked up at his father. 'What the fuck have you done to her?'

'What have I done to *her*? You're asking the wrong bloody question, son. She's the one who's been sneaking around. Spying on me. Hiding right here in the cellar, listening to every bleedin' word.'

'I'm out of here,' the stranger said, heading for the steps.

'We've still got business,' Joe growled.

'Later.'

As soon as the man had gone, Tommy glared at Joe. 'What's wrong with you? Jesus, don't bother answering that. You never did pick on anyone your own size.' He ran a hand gently over the top of Helen's head. 'You okay, love? You hurt?'

Joe growled. 'There ain't nothin' wrong with her. I barely touched the kid.'

Tommy carefully helped Helen to her feet, placing one arm protectively around her shoulders.

'But she's a wrong 'un,' Joe continued, 'and you know it. This is what happens when you bring a brat like her into your house. She's got bad blood. What do you expect? Her mother was a whore and her father was a bleedin' copper.'

Tommy stiffened. 'Don't talk about Lynsey like that.'

'Why not? It's the fuckin' truth.'

Helen stared at Joe Quinn, her eyes blazing with hate. She knew what whores were. They were the girls who worked Albert Street, selling their bodies. Sometimes they'd come into the pub of an evening in their short skirts and low-cut tops, their faces empty, their mouths an angry slash of scarlet.

'Don't listen to him,' Tommy said. 'He's a goddamn liar. He ain't got a clue what he's talking about.'

Joe barked out a laugh. 'And her old man weren't even straight filth. That piece of shit were as bent as they come.'

'That's enough!' Tommy said. 'Shut your bloody mouth!'

But Joe Quinn wouldn't be told. He took a few steps towards Helen, baring his teeth. His voice was a menacing hiss. 'That's where you come from, love – a bent copper and a dirty whore!'

Helen's stomach was turning over again. It wasn't true, none of it was. How could he say these things? Her mother had been beautiful; her father had been a hero. She felt the tears pricking her eyes again. Quickly, before anyone had the chance to grab her, she ducked free of Tommy's arm and made a dash for it.

'Mouse!' Tommy called out.

But she didn't stop, not even for a second. She sprinted up the stone steps and along the passage, and launched herself at the back door. Yanking it open, she stumbled outside. And then, as fast as her legs would carry her, she ran and ran and ran . . .

# 12

Helen kept on running for another five minutes until she passed between the black wrought-iron gates of Kellston cemetery. Even then she only slowed to a jog after she was certain that no one was behind her. Her chest was starting to ache as she cut away from the main avenue, skirted around the chapel and stumbled into the older, wilder part of the cemetery. Here, where the tall, wide-branched trees formed a canopy, she advanced into shadow and finally slowed to a walk.

The long grass brushed against her legs as she forged a path between the tilting gravestones. Some of the smaller ones were stacked up against each other, in fours and fives, neglected remembrances of people long gone, long forgotten. Further in, the grass grew shorter, with weeds and wild flowers forming a carpet beneath her feet. She lifted a hand to her face and found that it was wet. Quickly she brushed away the tears. Even in this place, where only the dead could see her, she refused to cry.

'I hate you, Joe Quinn,' she muttered. 'Hate you, hate you, hate you.'

She knew that it was wrong to feel this way, but how could she help it? Every part of the man was bad, every bone in his body, every greasy hair on his head. She scowled. What kind of father called his own daughter a whore? It went against everything that was natural. She had sat through enough church sermons on the subject of turning the other cheek, of being the better person, but she still couldn't find it in her heart to forgive him.

Eventually she emerged into a clearing flooded by sunlight. In the centre was a large white stone lion set up on a plinth. It was not the first time she had come across him, but the sight still made her eyes widen. He was the very image of Aslan from *The Lion, the Witch and the Wardrobe*. She reached up to run her palm across his paw, the stone worn smooth by years of touching.

'Hi there,' she said.

Aslan had come back from the dead to fight against evil. She wished that he could rise again and sort out Joe Quinn. If there had been a magic wardrobe she could go through in her bedroom at the Fox, she'd have run straight into Narnia without a second thought. She leaned against the memorial, letting the sun warm her body. If only she was still living in Farleigh Wood. If only Gran wasn't sick. She wanted to go home, to feel safe again, to wake up in the mornings without that heavy ball of dread in her stomach. She gave the lion one last look before turning away and retracing her steps.

Once she'd reached the main avenue again, she glanced warily towards the gates. There were three cars parked there, but none of them was Tommy's. She thought that he might have come to look for her. A jogger, a middle-aged man in a blue tracksuit, thudded past, breathing heavily. An elderly woman hobbled across the grass clutching a bunch of flowers. Helen kept on walking until she came to a curving path that led off to the left. She followed the path until she came to its end. Here, not far from the wall, was the pink granite head-stone with fine gold lettering. *Irene Elizabeth Quinn. Beloved wife and mother. Born 29th May 1912. Died 10th January 1957. Rest in peace.*

Helen sat down by the side of the grave, pulled up her knees and wrapped her arms around her legs. There was no mention of her own mum, but this was where they had scattered her ashes. It had been Moira's idea to bring her remains here, to reunite mother and daughter.

They hadn't told another soul, especially not Joe Quinn. It was a secret only the three of them shared.

Thinking back to the May afternoon, Helen remembered how the sun had been shining that day too. A blue sky, a thin breeze rustling through the yew trees. First of all Tommy had made sure that no one else was around. You were supposed to ask permission before placing ashes in a grave. When he was sure they were alone, he'd crouched down, swept away the white marble chips and dug into the earth with a small metal trowel. Moira had said a prayer and then they had taken it in turns to empty the urn into the hole. The ashes had been a pasty kind of white, the feeling of them grainy as they slipped through her fingers.

Helen still found it hard to connect her mum to those ashes, to fully accept that she was gone for ever. Or perhaps not for ever if there truly was life after death. But what did that mean? She screwed up her eyes as she peered into the sky. Was that where heaven was? Up high above the clouds and the sun? And if it was, then why hadn't those astronauts noticed it when they'd gone to the moon? She felt a sudden spurt of resentment at her mother's abandonment. It wasn't fair that she'd been left here alone to cope with the likes of Joe Quinn.

Helen slowly rubbed at her arms, still sore from where she'd been grabbed. Already the skin was turning brown and yellow as the bruises started to emerge. She was studying the damage when a voice behind her made her start.

'Mouse?'

She whirled around to see the tall figure of Frank Meyer looming over her. 'What are you doing here?'

'Looking for you.'

'What for?'

'Because I was worried. We all are. Moira said you might be here. She'd have come herself but she reckoned you might go to her flat, so she's hanging on there instead.'

'I'm not coming back,' Helen said defiantly, wrapping her arms tightly around her knees again. 'You can't make me. I'm not ever coming back.'

Frank lifted both his hands, showing her his palms. 'Hey, I'm not here to make you do anything you don't want to.' He lowered himself on to the grass a few feet away from her and stretched out his long legs. 'Look, what Joe did was bang out of order. It'll never happen again. Tommy will make sure of that.'

'Where is he, then?'

'Driving around, seeing if he can spot you on the streets.'

Helen stared at him for a moment and then lowered her gaze. She didn't know Frank Meyer that well, but there was something trustworthy about him. Unlike most of the men who came to the Fox, he was the sort who didn't need to talk loudly or show off to make his presence felt. And he didn't work for Joe Quinn, which was another plus. The only business Frank did was with Tommy.

'So, you got plans, then?'

Helen looked up again. 'What?'

'For where you're going to go next.'

She gave a small shrug. 'Might have.'

'Well, it's a big old world out there. I guess you can go just about anywhere you want.'

In truth, Helen hadn't thought much beyond the never-going-back bit. She could always get on a bus to Farleigh Wood. Would Janet really turn her away when she found out what had happened, when she showed her the bruises on her arms? Maybe not, but that didn't mean that she'd be welcome, either. Her aunt had always been distant with her, tolerant but never loving.

'China, for example,' Frank continued. 'Now I've heard that's a very interesting country. Or how about Peru?'

Helen pursed her lips and frowned. 'Stop making fun of me.'

Frank Meyer's mouth crept into a smile. 'As if. You know, Kellston might not be perfect, but there are worse places to live. And you've got people who care about you here.'

'No one cares about me.'

'Sure they do. Tommy cares. Moira cares. I care.'

But not Joe Quinn, she thought. Or Yvonne. Or her two cousins. The girls, although never cruel, were not especially friendly either. After the initial burst of curiosity had worn off, they had ceased to take much notice of her. Helen picked at the grass, carelessly pulling out clumps with her fingers. She stopped abruptly as it suddenly occurred to her that maybe it was her fault. Perhaps when push came to shove, she simply wasn't a likeable kind of person.

Frank lifted one knee and leaned his elbow on it. 'What's on your mind?'

'Nothing.'

'You're looking mighty thoughtful for someone with an empty head.'

Helen gave another shrug. She glanced towards the headstone and then back at Frank. He was wearing light grey trousers and a white shirt with the sleeves rolled up. His face, lightly tanned, wasn't exactly handsome, but it wasn't ugly either. It was a pleasant face, the eyes grey and clear, the full mouth curled up slightly at the corners. He looked completely at ease, as if tracking down runaways was all part of his daily routine.

'Did you know my mum?' she asked.

Frank shook his head. 'Sorry, love.'

'What about my dad?'

'No, I didn't know him either.'

'He was a policeman,' Helen said. 'Joe says he was bent.'

'Joe says a lot of things. Doesn't mean they're true.'

'What does Tommy say?' she asked. 'He must have talked about it.'

Frank hesitated, and then glanced away. 'You'd have to ask him.'

But that glance was enough to give her the answer she wanted. Or rather didn't want. 'I'm asking you,' she persisted. 'I want to know the truth.'

'What for? Will it make a difference to the way you feel about him?'

Helen gnawed on one of her knuckles, watching him over the edge of her hand. She thought about the photograph of her dad in uniform, the one that had pride of place in her grandmother's living room. 'Policemen aren't supposed to be bad.'

'No,' he said. 'I guess not. But some of them are. And for all sorts of reasons. They do it because they're greedy, because they see the villains with the big houses and the flash cars and they think, *I want a piece of that*. Or they do it because they're disillusioned and don't care any more. Others bend the rules because they see it as a battle, the good guys against the bad, and in their eyes the end always justifies the means.'

'And what kind was my dad?'

'I don't know, and that's the honest truth. Perhaps he's the only one who could really answer that question.'

Frank reached into the pocket of his shirt for a pack of cigarettes. He lit one and inhaled deeply. Helen watched him blow out the smoke in a long, fine stream. Everyone at the Fox smoked. Well, all the adults, at least. There were ashtrays scattered all over the flat. She had hated the smell at first, but now she was growing used to it.

'The thing is, Mouse, you can't choose your parents. You get what you're given and you have to make the best of it.

Take mine, for example. When I was a baby, they put me in an overnight bag and dumped me at the railway station.'

'The station,' she repeated, astounded. 'What station?'

'Waterloo,' he said.

Helen's mouth had fallen open. She had an image in her head of a tiny baby abandoned in the centre of a bustling forecourt, hungry perhaps, lonely and cold. She could imagine the sound of the trains, of the travellers hurrying past. 'But that's terrible. That's—' She stopped suddenly, and frowned again. The corners of his mouth were twitching. 'You're making it up.'

'Maybe,' he said, leaning back and laughing.

She glared at him. 'Why would you do that?'

'Well, it made you think about something else for thirty seconds.'

This was true, although she wasn't about to admit it. 'I'm still not going back to the Fox,' she said stubbornly.

'Okay, how about if we make a deal?'

Helen stared at him suspiciously. 'What kind of a deal?'

'You agree to give it another try for a while, see how things work out, and then if you're still determined to leave, I'll drive you to wherever you want to go.'

'How long is a while?'

Frank scratched his head. 'Say ... a month? That's not so long.'

'Two weeks,' she said.

'Okay, we'll split the difference. Let's make it three.'

'And you'll take me anywhere?'

'Anywhere.'

'But Joe doesn't want me at the Fox. He hates me.'

'He hates everyone, love. And I've told you, Tommy's sorting it. There won't be any more trouble.' Frank rose to his feet and stretched out a hand towards her. 'Come on, let's go.'

Helen glanced at the ground in front of the headstone. What would her mother tell her to do? Not go cap in hand to Janet, that was for sure. But she wouldn't want her in the same flat as Joe, either. Three weeks, she thought, rolling the deal around in her head. Maybe she could manage that. Finally she took Frank's hand and allowed him to pull her up. His fingers were strong and warm and slightly callused. Was she making the right decision? There was no way of knowing.

# 13

Tommy put the phone down, then heaved a sigh of relief and walked through to the kitchen, where Yvonne was sitting at the table flicking through a magazine. 'It's okay, Frank's found her. She's fine. She ain't hurt or nothing. He's taking her over to Moira's for a while.'

'Mm.'

He frowned at his wife. 'You could at least try and look interested. Anything could have happened to the poor kid.'

Yvonne glanced up at him, her expression one of exasperation. 'God, she's only been gone an hour. What was all the panic for? It's not as though she's been missing for days. She'd have come back in her own good time.'

But Tommy wasn't so sure. Mouse had fled from the cellar like her heels were on fire. 'Come on, the old man had a real go. He must have scared the living daylights out of her.'

'I don't get what she was doing down there in the first place.'

'Does it matter?' he said. 'She was probably just messing about.'

'Well, I told you it was a bad idea to bring her here. You know how Joe feels about Lynsey. He was hardly going to welcome her sprog with open arms, was he?'

'The old bastard's a bully, always was and always will be.'

Yvonne closed the magazine, pushed it away and folded her arms. 'Right,' she said. 'But you still think it was a good idea bringing our kids to live here with a man like that.'

Tommy might have guessed that she'd bring it round to this again. She hated living in the pub and couldn't stop herself from reminding him of the fact twenty times a day. She'd use any excuse to try to get him to move out again. 'He'd never touch them. You know that.'

Yvonne gave a light shrug, as if to say that you could never be certain of anything. Tommy briefly raised his eyes to the ceiling. 'He dotes on those girls. He spoils them rotten.' And it was true that Joe seemed to possess an affection for his two granddaughters that he'd never been able to feel for his actual daughter. Going over to stand by the window, Tommy gazed down on the street and watched the women passing by. He absent-mindedly bemoaned the decline of the miniskirt, which was rapidly being overtaken by longer and less revealing styles. Then his thoughts shifted back to Lynsey, to the times they'd spent together here in this room and how in the end everything had gone so horribly wrong.

'Where did Frank find her, then?'

Tommy glanced over his shoulder. 'Huh?'

'Mouse,' she said. 'Where did he find her?'

'Oh, in the cemetery.'

Yvonne gave an exaggerated shudder, her mouth twisting into a moue of distaste. 'What the hell was she doing there?'

'I dunno,' he said, although that wasn't strictly true. He was, however, unwilling to share the vital piece of information about where they'd scattered Lynsey's ashes. Yvonne wouldn't be able to keep it to herself. She might not tell Joe, but she would tell that Carol Gatesby, which was pretty much the equivalent of splashing it over the front page of a newspaper. 'It was somewhere to hide, I suppose.'

'That kid's got a screw loose, I'm telling you.'

'Ah, don't say that. She's just upset. She's been through a lot lately.'

Yvonne's eyes narrowed slightly. 'And I don't suppose you've heard from that Janet Beck, have you?'

'It's Janet Simms. She's married. And no, I ain't heard from her, not for a couple of weeks.'

'What did I tell you? They've got no intention of taking that kid back. She's been dumped on us good and proper.'

Tommy gave a sigh. 'For God's sake, woman, the grandma had a stroke. What do you expect them to do?'

'That's what *they* say. I reckon they just wanted to get rid.'

'Yeah? And what do you base that theory on, then?'

'Doesn't take a genius,' Yvonne said. 'You're the only one who can't see it.'

Tommy gave a snort. 'Well, I don't give a damn whether she's been dumped on us or not. I like having her here.' And it was true that he'd grown fond of Mouse over the past couple of months. She was a quiet little thing, but there was no harm in her. Given time, she'd probably become as noisy as his own two girls. 'Anyway, I'd better get on or I'll never

125

open up on time. Don't suppose you want to give me a hand?'

'Isn't Fiona coming in?'

'Yeah, in half an hour or so.'

Yvonne pulled the magazine back towards her and started flicking through the pages again. 'You'll be all right, then.'

Tommy didn't bother pressing her. He'd rather get stuck in on his own than have to listen to her moan about chipping her nails or working as a drudge in an East End pub. The lazy cow didn't know when she was well off. She might not be rolling in diamonds, but she didn't go short. She had a roof over her head, more clothes than any woman could wear in a lifetime, and cash in her pocket. There were plenty who'd be grateful for half of what she had.

He trotted downstairs and into the bar. Most of the clearing up had been done last night, but there were still the tables to be wiped down and the bar to be restocked. Usually Mouse helped if she wasn't at school, but of course his dad had put the kibosh on that this morning. Unsurprisingly, there was no sign of him either. Not that Joe Quinn ever contributed much even when he was on the premises. The old man hadn't done a hard day's work in his life.

As Tommy picked up a cloth and got started on the tables, he went over the stand-up row they'd had earlier. He'd come seriously close to thumping the bastard. What kind of scumbag picked on a kid like that? It was beyond the bloody pale.

'Shithead,' he murmured.

Tommy had threatened to leave if his father ever lifted a finger against Mouse again. If Connor hadn't been banged up, the threat would have been an empty one, but he knew that he was needed at the moment. Joe Quinn had no interest in actually running the pub. The profits, yeah, he liked those well enough, but he couldn't be arsed with dealing with deliveries, pulling pints or any of the other day-to-day necessities. And he wouldn't fancy getting a manager in either; managers had eyes and ears, and there were things that went on at the Fox that Joe wouldn't want a stranger to know about.

Tommy went behind the bar, wondering where his dad was now. At Connolly's, probably, having a brew while he slagged off his younger son to his cronies. He leaned forward with his elbows on the counter and took a good look around. He loved this pub, but it needed smartening up a bit, a fresh coat of paint and some new upholstery. Joe never spent a penny on the place.

In his mind, Tommy could see what the Fox *could* be like with a cash injection and a bit of TLC. He had a plan that he hadn't shared with anyone yet – he wanted to buy the pub off Joe. Just the thought of it brought a smile to his face. Eventually, when his father kicked the bucket, the place would come to him and Connor anyway, but he didn't want to wait that long. The old man could hang on for another twenty years. If Tommy could get his hands on it now, he could improve it before it got too shabby. Connor wouldn't mind – he'd be only too happy to take his share of the cash and run – but Yvonne would take some persuading.

The thought of his wife brought a frown to Tommy's brow, so he instantly stopped thinking about her. Instead he turned his attention to the long-firm fraud he had going with Frank Meyer. Everything was running smoothly at the moment. They'd set up an electrical goods outlet in Romford and were doing a brisk trade. In another ten months or so they'd have built up enough credit to stock the place to the ceiling and have one mighty final closing-down sale. And if it all went according to plan, that was when Tommy would have the cash to buy the Fox.

He glanced across the pub again. Owning the Fox would give him and his loved ones some security for the future. Although he'd been raised in a criminal family, Tommy wanted to be free of his father's dealings. He was sick of always having to look over his shoulder. If it wasn't the filth giving them hassle, it was one of the other East End firms trying to muscle in. There would always be money in protection and tarts, but the business was beginning to revolve more and more around drugs. It was a profitable trade but a risky one too. One bad deal and they'd all end up in the slammer.

Apart from a few brief spells on remand, Tommy had never served a proper prison sentence, and that was how he wanted to keep it. Some villains viewed it as an occupational hazard, but he wasn't one of them. He hated being locked up, being confined to a cell the size of a toilet. He hated having to breathe the same air as psychos and nonces. He hated being apart from his daughters. If he could buy the Fox, he could make his own money and put some distance between himself and his father.

Tommy caught sight of the clock and gave a quick shake of his head. If he didn't get a move on, he wouldn't be ready for opening time. For the next twenty minutes he flew up and down the steps of the cellar, replenishing the supplies of bottled beers and mixers, restocking the shelves of the bar. He put out clean ashtrays and beer mats and sorted the float. When he finally stopped again, it was ten to eleven.

There was a knock on the main door, and Tommy crossed the bar to open it. He pulled back the bolts to find Fiona Soames waiting there.

'Hi,' she said, breezing in. She brought with her a gust of summer air and a soft, musky scent of perfume. 'You okay?'

'I've had better mornings.'

Fiona went behind the counter and peeled off a cream mackintosh to reveal a calf-length red skirt and a thin cotton blouse. She went through to the hallway to hang her coat on a peg. 'Problems?'

Tommy followed behind, his gaze fixed on her butt. Although he didn't fancy her – he preferred his birds with more meat on them – he couldn't resist checking her out. Fiona was a skinny mare with long legs and a neat backside but nothing much up top. 'Oh, family stuff. The usual. It's sorted now.'

'Good,' she said, flicking back a strand of long dark hair. 'Is it just us today?'

Tommy gave a nod, quickly lifting his gaze as she turned around. 'Yeah, just the two of us. Dad's done his usual disappearing trick.'

'Well, I'm sure we'll survive.'

'Doubt we'll notice the difference.'

They exchanged a quick conspiratorial glance. He knew that Fiona had about as much time for his father as he did. She was, however, too polite to say it out loud. Joe Quinn had wandering hands and a lewd mouth, and no self-respecting woman was safe within ten feet of him.

'Term's finished now,' she said, 'so if you've got any more shifts going . . . '

'Sure. We'll sort something out.'

She gave him a winning smile as she headed back into the bar. 'Thanks. You're an angel.'

Tommy still hadn't figured out exactly why Fiona was working at the Fox, but reckoned it was something to do with paying her own way and proving a point to her rich Surrey family. She was a nineteen-year-old student, well-spoken and with nice manners – what the lads commonly referred to as 'posh totty'. Personally, he preferred his women a little rougher around the edges, but the customers liked her and that was all that mattered.

A few minutes later the pub opened for business and the first punters of the day began drifting in. As Tommy served up drinks, chat and a sympathetic ear to anyone who needed it, his thoughts drifted off to his plans for the afternoon. At two o'clock, as soon as the shift was over, he was heading over to Hoxton to see Shelley Anne. The prospect of it caused a faint stirring in his groin.

It was six months now since Shelley Anne had first started working at the Fox, and the attraction between them had been instant. She was a real firecracker, a small, curvy blonde with wide blue eyes and a sulky mouth. Everything about her had set his blood racing, and sadly Yvonne hadn't been slow to realise it. Three months ago she'd insisted that Tommy give Shelley Anne the sack.

'What for?' he'd asked, assuming his most innocent expression.

'You know what for.'

'She's a good barmaid.'

'Well, she can go and be a good barmaid somewhere else.'

And that had been that. Once Yvonne set her mind to something, there was no point in arguing. She'd nag and nag until she made his life a misery. It had, however, probably been for the best. Although Tommy still missed working with Shelley Anne, she had been a constant distraction; he'd spent more time thinking about shagging her than he had pulling pints. A few quick calls to his mates had secured her a job at a pub in Finsbury Park, and now he was free to see her whenever he could slip away.

Tommy didn't feel any guilt over his lack of faithfulness. The magic between him and Yvonne – if there had ever been any to begin with – had long since disappeared. They rubbed along for the sake of the kids, but that was about the sum of it. And a man had needs, needs that at the moment could only be satisfied by a cockney girl with a generous mouth. He glanced at his watch again, willing the hands to move faster.

At a quarter to two, just before Tommy was about to call last orders, Frank Meyer strolled into the pub. After finding Mouse and delivering her to Moira's flat, he had driven up to Romford to go through the books with Alfie Blunt.

'All okay?' asked Tommy, eager for some good news. 'You want a pint?'

Frank gave a shake of his head. 'Jesus, who did you upset?'

'What?'

'Your car.'

Tommy frowned at him, confused. 'What about my car?'

'You're telling me you haven't seen it?'

Tommy looked over at Fiona. 'I'll be two minutes,' he said.

In the car park, he walked around the white Cortina, cursing loudly as he surveyed the damage. 'Fuck, fuck, fuck!' Some bastard had slashed every one of his tyres. His first thought was that his dad must have done it, revenge for their earlier altercation. It was the type of petty, spiteful act that was typical of him.

'I bet this was the old man.'

'I don't think so,' said Frank, gesturing with his head towards Joe's silver Jaguar parked near the cellar door. 'Well, not unless he's completely lost the plot.'

Tommy looked over to see that the Jag had received exactly the same treatment. Quickly he scanned the other dozen or so other motors that were parked outside the Fox. They all appeared to be fine. Whoever had done this had clearly been targeting the Quinns and the Quinns alone. 'Jesus, I can't believe this!'

'Hey, it's not the end of the world,' Frank said. 'Give Billy Kent a call. He'll come over and sort it for you.'

Billy ran a garage over in Dalston, a hotbed of stolen motors and getaway vehicles. 'But I need the car this afternoon. I've got stuff to do.'

Frank raised his eyebrows. 'Stuff?'

Tommy raised and dropped his arms in frustration. 'I'm supposed to be seeing someone, that's all. A bit of business.' If he had to stay and sort this out, he'd never get to see Shelley Anne. Sensing the much-anticipated assignation slipping away from him, he kicked out at the rear left wheel hub, stubbing his toe in the process. 'Ah, Christ!' As he hopped about on his one good foot, he was beginning to wish that he'd never got up that morning.

Frank Meyer reached into his pocket, took out his own car keys and threw them over. 'Here, you can take the MG, but try and get it back in one piece. If you call Billy, I'll hang around and wait for him.'

The black cloud hovering over Tommy's head instantly lifted. 'Really? You serious? Ah, thanks, Frank. You're a mate.'

'You owe me one.'

'Come inside. I'll get you a pint.' As they made their way back into the pub, Tommy's improved mood briefly darkened again as he pondered on who might have been responsible for the attack. Had Joe been stepping on another firm's toes? If he had, Tommy didn't know about it. Someone, however, was clearly out to get them. His money was on those Gissing bastards, and if he was right, then the trouble was only just beginning.

# 14

Terry Street paid for the two brews and took them back to the table. It had been pure chance that he had walked into Connolly's today to find Joe Quinn sitting on his own, and he was determined to make the most of the opportunity. Usually Joe was surrounded by his henchmen, his cronies or the group of young wannabes who followed him around like hungry dogs waiting to be thrown a few scraps.

Terry was nineteen and he had ambition. He'd chosen the firm he wanted to work for with care and attention, watching, listening and weighing up all the pros and cons. The Quinns weren't the most powerful or the most vicious firm in the area, but he believed – so far as his own future was concerned – that they had the most potential. At the moment he was still working his way up the ranks, fetching and carrying and doing the jobs no one else wanted to do, but he didn't intend to stay there for long.

Joe gave a grunt of acknowledgement as the mug went

down in front of him. He finished rolling a cigarette, rotating the cylinder deftly between his fingers and thumb before raising it to his fleshy lips, lighting it and drawing in the smoke. Only then did he resume his monologue where he had left off.

'Fuck knows why I bother. A bleedin' waste of space, that's what he is. Useless. Calls himself a Quinn? Jesus, he's not fit to have the name.'

Joe was stuck in a groove, like a needle on a scratched LP. Terry had been subject to the diatribe on Tommy for the last ten minutes. While he continued to listen, making the appropriate responses of sympathy and disgust whenever the older man paused to take a slurp of his tea or a drag on his fag, he waited patiently for the chance to pursue his own agenda.

Eventually, when Joe finally appeared to run out of steam, Terry turned the conversation to his other son.

'So how's your Connor doing? The trial must be coming up soon.'

'Not soon enough,' Joe growled.

'You'll sort it, Mr Quinn. No problem. You always do.'

Joe narrowed his eyes for a second. Although not immune to flattery, he was nobody's fool. Terry held his breath, wondering if he'd been too obvious. No one wanted to be known as an arse-licker. But then Joe gave a curt nod and almost smiled.

'You're not wrong there.'

'And if there's anything you need me to do, you just say the word.'

Joe sat back and stared at him. It was a long, penetrating

stare that seemed to bore straight through Terry's eyes and into every crevice of his brain. For a moment he felt completely transparent. Did Joe realise what his plans were? Perhaps he could see straight through him.

'Shall I give you a piece of advice, son?'

Terry put his elbows on the table and leaned forward. It was a rhetorical question – the advice was going to come whether he wanted it or not – but it was wise to act respectfully. 'Sure. I'd appreciate that.'

'You ever heard that saying about not trying to run before you can walk?'

Terry gave a shrug. 'I just want to get on, Mr Quinn. Nothin' wrong with that, is there?'

'You're still a kid.'

'A smart kid, though,' Terry said, gently tapping the side of his forehead. 'Why do you think I came to work for you?'

Joe barked out a laugh, revealing a row of large tombstone teeth. 'You've got a bleedin' cheek, I'll give you that.'

Terry grinned back at him. Since joining the firm, he had quickly sussed out that humour and charm could be as effective as brute force, particularly when it came to dealing with the 'clients'. Every Friday night he did the milk round with Vinnie Keane, a six-foot-six giant of a man, collecting money from the clubs and bars, the bookies and the scrap-metal dealers who paid for the pleasure of Joe's protection. He had soon discovered that a bit of friendly banter helped to ease the pain of the transactions.

'I've got ideas,' Terry said. 'Lots of 'em.'

'You and the rest of the world.'

Terry took the dismissive retort on the chin. He wasn't

going to push things. He had wanted to make an impression, to stand out from the others and to let Joe know that he could be more than a money collector. It might take a while, but eventually he hoped to prove how much of an asset he could be to the firm. With Joe getting older, there was likely to be a gap at the top before too many years had passed.

Connor, of course, was the natural successor to the Quinn empire, but he wasn't smart enough to run it. He was nasty and unpredictable – both useful assets when it came to putting the fear of God in people – but he didn't have his father's guile. Connor never knew when to stop, which was why he was banged up yet again. Even if he did manage to get off this time, he'd be back behind bars before too long. As for Tommy – well, he wasn't even a contender.

Joe idly stroked the grey stubble on his jaw as he continued to stare across the table at Terry. 'As it 'appens, son, there is something you could do for me.'

'Anything, Mr Quinn.'

'You could fuck off and leave me to drink this brew in peace.'

Terry didn't take offence. Joe was hardly renowned for his good humour, or his nice manners, come to that. Pushing back his chair, he quickly got to his feet. There was nothing worse than outstaying your welcome.

'Right, I'll be off, then.'

Joe didn't bother to reply. He stubbed his skinny fag end out in the ashtray and instantly began rolling another.

Terry left the café and swaggered down the high street in an excellent mood. He'd done what he'd intended to do and hopefully left a lasting impression. There was still a long way to go – he had no illusions about that – but at least he'd laid the foundations. He would build on those, brick by brick, until he was the one who was running the show.

At the pawnbroker's, he stopped to examine the goods in the window, his eyes greedily alighting on a gold signet ring with three small diamonds. That would look mighty good on the little finger of his left hand. He considered going in and trying it on, but then decided against it. For now, he needed to save his cash, to squirrel it away for when the big deal came along. Speculate to accumulate, that was what they said, and Terry was a staunch believer in the phrase.

Shifting his gaze, he focused instead on his own reflection. Nothing much there to complain about. He knew he had the kind of face and high cheekbones that women found attractive. Carefully, he smoothed down his dark hair and adjusted his tie. He nearly always wore a smart suit, no matter what the occasion. If you wanted to be someone, then you had to dress like someone. It was the only way to be taken seriously.

Moving away from the shop, he headed back towards the Fox, where his second-hand Capri was parked. One day he'd own a fancy motor like Joe's, a penthouse flat in the West End and a house in the country. Other people dreamed about such things, but he was going to have them. Nothing and nobody would stand in his way.

'Hello, darling,' he said as he drew level with a slim, attractive redhead coming from the opposite direction. He saw her eyes flicker towards him, making a rapid assessment of his face, his body and his clothes before her lips deigned to curl into a smile. The next moment he was past her, but he knew that if he stopped and looked back over his shoulder, there was every chance that she would too. He considered it for a second, but kept on walking. There were plenty more fish in the sea.

Terry was never short of female attention; he could walk into any club or bar and pick up a bird in ten minutes flat. The trick was not to get too serious about them. A bit of fun, that was all it was. He knew too many blokes who'd been forced into marriage by an unwanted pregnancy – including Tommy Quinn, if the rumours were true – and he didn't intend to get trapped like that. Young, free and single was the only way to be.

Without waiting for the lights to change, Terry jaywalked across Station Road, nimbly dodging the cars and the buses and the honking black cabs. As it happened, he had a lot of time for Tommy. The guy was sound, a good laugh, but he lacked the edge to make a truly good villain; when push came to shove, he would always put the interests of his family above those of the firm. And when Terry said family, he meant Yvonne and the kids rather than Joe. There was clearly bad blood between Tommy and his father, which was all to Terry's advantage.

As Terry strolled into the almost empty car park of the Fox, he saw Frank Meyer standing by Joe's silver Jag. One of Billy Kent's vans was parked by the side entrance to the pub, and a man in greasy overalls was kneeling by the rear left wheel.

'Hey, Frank. What's going on?'

Frank gave him a nod. 'Some scumbag slashed all the tyres on Joe's motor. Tommy's too.'

Terry quickly looked towards his own Capri, relieved to

discover that it hadn't been touched. 'Does Joe know about this?'

'Not yet,' Frank said, with just a glimmer of a smile. 'You want to be the one to break the good news?'

'You're kidding me, right? The mood he's in, he'll shoot the bleedin' messenger.' Terry walked all around the Jag, surveying the damage. 'And no one saw nothin'?'

'Nothing out of the ordinary. But it's a pub. People are coming and going all the time.'

'It ain't just spite, though. Not if Tommy's was done too.' There would always be people who envied the possessions of others, but this obviously wasn't a random attack. 'This is personal.'

'Looks that way,' Frank agreed.

'Is Tommy around?'

'Not for a couple of hours.'

Terry decided to be smart and make himself scarce too. Joe wasn't going to be happy when he found out about the Jag, and was more than likely to take out his frustration on whoever was closest to hand. After all the hard work he'd put in at the caff, Terry didn't intend to be that person. Glancing at his watch, he made out as if he had a pressing appointment. 'Okay, I'd best be getting on.'

Frank gave his almost-smile again. 'You're not going to hang around, then?'

'Things to do,' Terry said. He suspected that Frank wasn't fooled, but he didn't really care. 'Catch you later.'

'See you.'

Terry got into the red Capri and made a hasty exit from the car park. The attack on the motors had only confirmed the rumours he'd been hearing about other firms trying to muscle in on Joe's business. The Gissings especially were looking to expand. As old enemies of the Quinns, they were clearly in the frame for this latest act of provocation. He tapped his fingers against the wheel, smiling widely. He wasn't worried by the turn of events. On the contrary, he was well pleased by it. Trouble was good, very good. Trouble would give him a chance to prove himself.

# 15

Tony Lazenby flicked through the newspaper again while he waited. The headline news was still the same doom and gloom as it had been the first time he'd read it: troubles in Belfast, an imminent state of emergency over the forthcoming docks strike and some less than reassuring pronouncements from the PM, Ted Heath. The damn country was going to the dogs. He lit another cigarette and checked out the time on the dashboard. It was almost three o'clock, only half an hour since he'd followed Tommy Quinn to this small block of flats in Hoxton. Time passed slowly when you were sitting doing nothing.

He wound down the window to let in the fresh summer air. Earlier, Lennie Gissing had sent one of his boys to the Fox to set things in motion. Slashing the tyres on the Quinn cars was only the beginning, a warning shot across the bows, a preliminary to what was to come. If you wanted to wind up Joe Quinn, there was no better way of doing it than having a go at his precious Jag. The guy thought more of that motor than he did of his own kids.

Tony had been parked way down Station Road, but still with a decent view of the pub. He grinned as he thought about the expression on Tommy's face when he'd seen the state of his Cortina. It was a shame Joe hadn't been around too – seeing his reaction would have been priceless.

When they'd discussed the plan last night, Lennie hadn't been too keen on the whole car idea. 'I don't get it. If we do that, then they're gonna be waiting for something else to happen. It's like tipping them off in advance.'

'You reckon? That arrogant bastard doesn't believe anyone has the nerve to take him on. He'll be pissed off about the motor, but he won't be worried enough to take any precautions. That's the joy of it. He'll be kicking himself when you go in for a second time. You'll have made him look a bloody fool.'

Lennie had eventually come round to his way of thinking. For Tony, this wasn't just about moving in on the business; it was about taking steps to destroy the Quinns once and for all. If you wanted to ruin a man, you had to ruin his reputation too. Joe wasn't going to know what had hit him.

Having followed Tommy Quinn to the flats, Tony had gained an unexpected bonus. After parking up, Tommy had walked across the road and rung one of the bells to the side of the main front door. A minute later the door had been opened by a small blonde wearing a red dress so short and so low-cut that it left nothing to the imagination. She was a slim, slutty-looking girl in her early twenties with a wide mouth and an ample cleavage. Her affectionate greeting had left little doubt as to the nature of their relationship.

Tony pulled on his cigarette and grinned again. So, the dirty bugger was playing away. It was a piece of information that could be useful in the fight that lay ahead. He wondered how much Tommy told her about Quinn business; some men could be less than discreet when it came to pillow talk.

'Careless talk costs lives,' he murmured with a sly smile.

With nothing else to do, Tony gazed along the road, rating the girls out of ten as they walked by. Most of them were only a six or a seven. Either there were no hot babes in Hoxton or they'd all gone shopping up West. Although he tried not to, he couldn't help comparing them to his ex-wife, Dana. Physically, she had been his ideal woman – tall and slender, with long dark hair. Classy, unlike the tart Tommy Quinn was shagging. All she had needed was a personality transplant and she would have been perfect.

Tony chucked his fag end out of the window and snarled. It had been two years now since Dana had left him for some toff architect with a silver spoon up his arse. She'd claimed it was nothing to do with the money, but he didn't believe her. It was his moods, she'd said, that had driven her away. Jesus, what kind of a reason was that? Everybody had their off days. She should have tried doing his job for twenty-four hours, mixing with the lowlifes and the scumbags and the psychos, and seen how bloody cheerful she felt at the end of it.

It disgusted him to think of how much time he had wasted in trying to get her back. Some women weren't worth fighting for. In fact, come to think of it, none of them were.

Underneath the slick, glossy exteriors, they were all bloody bitches. He should have made her pay for what she'd done to him, and still regretted that he hadn't. A simple hit-and-run or an overenthusiastic mugging and Mr Silver Spoon could have been lying flat on his back in the morgue. The thought of this sent a pleasurable shiver down his spine.

Alan Beck had understood how women could wreck your life. That Lynsey had trapped him good and proper; the poor bloke had been done up like a kipper and no mistake. A wedding ring on his finger before he'd had time to get his head straight, and then a screaming sprog to support. Tony heaved out a breath. He should have learnt from his mate's mistakes and stayed single.

It was twenty past four before Tommy Quinn finally emerged from the building, crossed the road and climbed into Meyer's MG. He was checking the buttons on his shirt and wearing a smug expression like a kid who had got away with doing something he shouldn't.

'Make the most of it, shitbag,' Tony muttered under his breath. 'This could be the last happy day you have for quite some time.'

He thought about following him, but then decided against it. Tommy was probably going back to the Fox to open up. No, he'd stay here and see what he could find out about the tart. It meant more hanging around, but it could be worth it in the end. Once the MG had driven off, Tony got out and strolled casually towards the flats. There were eight bells in all, four flats on each floor, but no names on any of them. He went back to the car, turned on the radio and settled down for another wait.

In the event, it was only twenty minutes before the small blonde appeared again. She had changed into a flowery minidress, only marginally longer than the one she'd been wearing for Tommy, and was tottering along the pavement in a pair of white stilettos. She was so top-heavy that she looked in imminent danger of tipping forward. Still, she didn't have far to fall. She stopped at the bus stop and gazed hopefully down the street.

Tony lowered his head, pretending to read the paper as he watched her from behind the dark lenses of his sunglasses. He didn't find her any more appealing close up than he had from a distance. Her skin was very pale, a shade that made her look almost anaemic, and her bare shoulders were faintly pink from where the sun had caught them. He wondered, apart from the obvious, what Tommy Quinn saw in her. But then again, maybe it was the obvious that was the big attraction.

Within a couple of minutes a bus turned up, and Tony pulled the car out from the kerb, swinging behind the red double-decker. He had a fleeting glimpse of her climbing the stairs before she disappeared from view. Following a bus was a tricky business. There was always some moronic bastard behind you, getting the hump because you weren't overtaking when it stopped to let passengers on and off.

Tony kept his eyes peeled as he trailed the bus through the traffic down to Old Street and around the roundabout. With no idea of her destination, he had to be ready for whenever she might make a move. From what she was wearing, he had no idea of whether she was going to work or planning a night on the tiles. Maybe Tommy Quinn wasn't the only man in her life.

It was another forty minutes, just as they were skirting the green expanse of Finsbury Park, before he noticed her coming down the stairs again. As soon as the bus stop came into view, he pulled into the first available parking space and watched as she got off and continued to walk along Seven Sisters Road.

Tony got out of the car and pursued her, keeping a discreet distance. Over the years he had noticed that some people had a sixth sense when it came to being followed. It was as though a tiny alarm went off in their head, a primitive warning that someone had their eyes on them. This girl, however, didn't turn around or even glance over her shoulder.

After a hundred yards, she stopped outside a pub called the Dog and Duck and made a few minor alterations to her hair before walking through the door. Tony didn't immediately follow her inside. Instead he lit a fag and leaned against the wall, deciding to wait a while before putting in an appearance.

Five minutes later, he pushed open the door and went in. It was still early, and the place wasn't busy yet. He scanned the tables, most of them empty, but couldn't see her. Had she gone to the ladies'? Had she clocked him and done a runner through a back exit? But then he suddenly caught sight of her behind the bar. Ah, so Tommy's bit of fluff was a barmaid. That made sense. Tommy Quinn didn't strike him as the adventurous type; he probably liked to stick with what he knew.

Tony went up to the counter and gave her his widest smile. 'Hello, love. A pint of lager, please. And have one yourself.'

'Oh, ta, darlin'. That's nice of you. I won't say no.'

She had a broad cockney accent and a mouthful of teeth.

Decent teeth, as it happened, straight and white, although there seemed to be too many of them. Her bright red lipstick was made more garish by the paleness of her skin.

'So, what's a beautiful girl like you doing in a place like this?'

'What you after, then?' she giggled.

Tony gave her a look of mock incredulity. 'Can't a guy give a compliment these days without being suspected of ulterior motives?'

'Not to me, love. I've heard every line going and then some.' She put his pint on the counter and took the pound note from his hand. 'But don't let me stop you. I like a good laugh.'

Tony watched her as she wiggled over to the till and rang up the drinks. Her fingernails were long and red, the same shade as her lipstick. When she came back with his change, he gave her another of his smiles. 'I'm Tony, by the way.'

'Shelley Anne,' she said as she placed the change in his palm.

'So, Shelley Anne, how are things with you?'

'Could be better,' she said. 'But I ain't complaining.'

'Ah, I like an uncomplaining woman.'

'I bet you do.'

Tony grinned. 'Why do I get the feeling that some ungrateful man's been breaking your heart?'

'It's a long story, darlin'.'

Tony leaned forward, his eyes full of sympathy and understanding. 'Well, I'm not going anywhere; why don't you tell me all about it?'

# 16

Helen was in bed, lying on her back with her hands behind her head. She knew without glancing at the luminous green dial of the alarm clock that it was just after eleven. The bedroom was at the front of the flat, overlooking Station Road, and the customers were starting to leave. People always talked too loudly when they had the drink in them. Sometimes there was shouting, rows and fights, but tonight it wasn't so bad.

She was tired, but she couldn't sleep. She was thinking over the day and the deal she had made with Frank Meyer. Three more weeks and then she could leave if she wanted to. He had promised to drive her anywhere, but where would she go? Perhaps by then Gran would be better and she could return to her life at Camberley Road.

After the two of them had left the cemetery, Frank had walked her up to Moira's and stayed for a cup of tea. Helen had watched him surreptitiously from over the rim of her

149

mug. He was the kind of man, she thought, who made you feel safe: big and solid, with an easy manner. Maybe, when she was older, she would marry a man like Frank, someone who was kind and funny and never mean to her. That was if she ever got married at all. Would anybody want a girl with bad blood?

After Frank had gone, Moira had leaned across the table and laid a hand over hers. 'Are you sure you're okay, love? That Joe Quinn's a nasty piece of work. If you want me to have a word with him ...'

But Helen shook her head. 'It's fine. Really it is.' She couldn't bear the idea of anyone else getting involved. All she wanted to do now was to try and forget about it. Her grandmother, who adhered to the stiff-upper-lip school of thought, had always disapproved of people who 'made a fuss'. She had been raised to put a brave face on things and not to whine about what you couldn't change.

Moira, sensing her awkwardness, changed the subject smartly. 'So how about something to eat, then? You must be starving.' Before Helen could reply, she had jumped up and started bustling round the kitchen. 'What about an omelette? You go and put some music on while I get them ready.'

Helen had flipped through Moira's extensive collection of LPs, examining the covers while she tried to decide what to play. It was mainly soul music – Otis Redding, Marvin Gaye, James Brown – with a bit of pop thrown in. She had chosen Aretha Franklin's *Soul '69* and they had listened to it while they ate their lunch.

Afterwards, she and Moira had taken their chairs outside to

the rickety fire escape that led down to the alley. They had sat in the sun and chatted about nothing in particular. For the first time that day, Helen had actually started to relax. Joe might be her enemy, but she wasn't completely alone. She had Tommy and Moira on her side, and Frank Meyer too.

At four o'clock, they had walked back to the Fox together. Moira had stopped by the back door and laid a maternal hand on her arm. 'You can always come to mine, Helen. If you're worried about anything, or if you just want to get away from here for a while. You're always welcome.'

'Thanks.'

'Would you like me to come in with you?'

Helen had shaken her head. She was anxious about entering the pub again, scared that she might walk straight into Joe, but she had to do it some time. And she had to do it on her own. 'Thanks for lunch. I'll see you soon.'

After Moira had left, Helen had unlocked the back door and stepped gingerly inside. She had held her breath while she listened for any noises coming from the bar or from upstairs. All she could hear was the faint sound of the television. After a few minutes, she had climbed quietly up the stairs.

As it happened, she'd had no need to be worried. There was no sign of Joe in the living room, and everything was calm. Her two cousins had shifted up to make room for her on the sofa and even Yvonne had made an effort to be nice.

'You okay, love? Sit yourself down. I'm just making tea. It won't be long.'

Food, it seemed, was the common answer to any upset. No one had come straight out and asked her about what had happened, but she could tell that they all knew. Karen and Debs had given her curious sidelong glances, clearly eager to ask for all the gory details but probably under strict instructions not to do so.

They had eaten tea on their knees, eggs, chips and beans, and everything had been fine until Tommy had come back. As soon as he'd stepped through the door, Yvonne had started sniping.

'Where the hell have you been?'

'A bit of business,' he said.

'Yeah, and we all know what kind of business that is.'

Tommy had raised his eyes to the ceiling. 'The kind of business that keeps this family fed and clothed, woman. What's your problem?'

'My problem is you disappearing and not telling me where you're going.'

Helen had bowed her head, not wanting to listen. She hated it when they bickered; it reminded her of her mum rowing with Gran, and that in turn reminded her of everything she'd lost. For her uncle, however, it was like water off a duck's back. He gave an indifferent shrug and headed for the kitchen.

Helen had gone to bed early so that she could pretend to be asleep when Karen joined her in the room. Out of earshot of Yvonne, her cousin might be tempted to start asking questions. Now, an hour later and still awake, she turned over and lay on her side, gazing at the thin stripe of light that ran along the bottom of the door. The landing light would stay on until Tommy locked up and came upstairs.

From the bunk above, she heard Karen's light snuffling

snores. There was the sound of laughter from outside, and then the clatter of an empty tin can as it rolled along the road. She closed her eyes, willing oblivion to come. Her body felt heavy and exhausted, but the events of the day continued to haunt her. Her eyes blinked open again. Had Joe come in yet? What if he was still angry and he . . . No, if she started thinking like that, she'd lie awake all night.

It was only when she heard Tommy's heavy tread on the carpet outside the door that Helen finally relaxed. She was safe so long as her uncle was close by. Joe wouldn't come for her when his son was around. There was a murmur of voices from the master bedroom, and then it went quiet. She closed her eyes again and began to drift into sleep.

Helen had just dozed off when she was woken abruptly by a huge crash. There was the distinctive sound of breaking glass, followed by a soft whooshing noise. She sat bolt upright, her heart hammering in her chest. It had come from downstairs, either the first floor or the bar.

Seconds later, she heard Tommy thumping along the landing. 'For fuck's sake!'

Helen leapt out of bed, opened the door and leaned over the banisters. She saw the top of Tommy's head as he turned the corner on the first-floor landing and lunged down towards the pub. There was a thin, crackling noise and smoke started to drift up the stairwell. Oh God, the Fox was on fire! For one crazy, panic-stricken moment, she thought that Joe was trying to kill her, before reason kicked in. He was hardly likely to burn down his own pub, especially when his two granddaughters were fast asleep in the flat above.

Yvonne came out of the bedroom, her fingers fumbling

with the sash on her pink silky dressing gown. 'Get Karen,' she yelped as she rushed into Debs's room.

Helen dashed back, jumped on the bottom bunk and reached up to shake Karen awake. 'Get up, get up! Quick! There's a fire!'

Karen half climbed, half fell out of bed, and the two of them ran out on to the landing. Yvonne grabbed her daughters' hands and started pulling them down the stairs. Helen followed behind, her legs feeling weak and shaky. They stumbled down the two flights into the smoky atmosphere of the ground-floor hallway.

As Yvonne yanked the key off the hook in the hallway and began to fumble with the lock on the back door, Helen looked across at the entrance to the bar. The central pillar was alight, blazing fiercely, and there were other, smaller scattered fires. Tommy, dressed only in his jeans and trainers, was spraying the floor with the fire extinguisher, trying to stop the flames from spreading. His back was gleaming with sweat, his shoulders grey and ashy.

Helen felt another wave of panic rising in her chest. What if he got caught in the fire? What if he couldn't escape? From where she was standing, she could see the gaping hole in the window, its edges sharp and ragged. She heard an ugly splintering sound and saw one of the tables collapse to the ground. The acrid smell of smoke filled the hallway.

'Come on,' Yvonne urged, finally getting the door open. She quickly pushed her daughters out into the cool night air and then grabbed Helen's arm and propelled her out too. She called over her shoulder. 'For God's sake, Tommy, get out of there! Leave it!'

But Helen suspected that he'd take no notice. Tommy loved the pub and he'd do anything to try and save the place. As Yvonne dragged them all towards the far side of the car park, Helen kept looking back, willing him to run out through the door, to do exactly as his wife told him for once in his life. Please, Tommy, she silently begged.

'Stay here,' Yvonne ordered, before flopping clumsily down the street in her slippers towards the red phone box on the corner. There were two phones in the pub, one upstairs and one down, but there hadn't been time to use them.

While she was gone, the three girls huddled together and gazed helplessly at the burning building. The orange glow of the fire could be clearly seen through the back windows of the bar, the flames licking at the glass. From where they were standing, they couldn't see any sign of Tommy. Karen started to cry, a thin, mewling sound like a frightened kitten.

'He'll be all right,' Debs said, trying to comfort her.

'Your mum's gone to call the fire brigade; they'll be here soon,' Helen offered, although in truth she had no idea how long they would take. She wished Frank Meyer was on his way too. He'd know what to do. He wouldn't let Tommy get hurt. Hopping from one foot to the other, she hugged her chest with her arms. Perhaps she was being punished for not going to church. She stared up at the starlit sky, making a private deal with the God she had ignored for the last couple of months. *Please don't let him die. Please keep him safe and I'll always be good.* When she thought of fire, she thought of hell and damnation. She thought of her mother going to sleep and never waking up.

Yvonne returned and went as close to the back door of the

pub as she dared. By now the smoke was billowing out in thick black clouds. 'Tommy!' she yelled again. 'I've called the fire brigade. Get out of there!'

Helen strained her ears but couldn't hear any reply. She lifted a hand and chewed on her fingernails. They should never have left him alone. He was going to die. He was going to burn to death. She watched, terrified, as Yvonne retreated, beaten back by the smoke. And then, just when she thought there was no hope remaining, Tommy suddenly came barrelling out of the pub with a jacket over his head. He got as far as the centre of the car park before his legs gave way beneath him and he crumpled to the ground.

The girls were on him in a second. 'Dad? Dad? Are you okay?'

Tommy sat on the concrete, his head between his knees, his body racked with great heaving coughs. His fair hair was singed at the ends and blackened by the smoke. There were cuts and burns across his shoulders, back and arms. After a while, the coughing began to subside and he gulped in the fresh night air.

While the girls fussed around Tommy, Helen stood back. Her instinct had been to run straight to him, but she had fought against the impulse. She might be family, but she wasn't his daughter. Relieved as she was, she didn't want to push in where she might not be wanted. Instead she briefly squeezed shut her eyes and whispered, *Thank you, God. Thank you, God.*

'What about Grandad?' Debs asked, whirling round to stare at the pub.

'He's not home, hon,' Yvonne said. 'You don't have to

worry.' She looked down at Tommy and scowled. 'What the hell were you thinking, you moron? You could have been killed in there!'

It was another ten minutes before two fire engines, their sirens shrieking, arrived at the Fox, along with an ambulance. By now a small crowd had gathered, a group of neighbours and people who were just passing by. They stood around in clumps, pointing and whispering as they viewed the spectacle.

A middle-aged woman with her hair in curlers laid a blanket around Helen's shoulders as she sat perched on the low wall of the car park. Up until that point she hadn't even realised she was shivering. Becoming suddenly self-conscious about the fact that she was dressed only in her pyjamas, she wrapped the blanket tightly around her.

As the firemen fought to extinguish the blaze, she sent up another prayer that the Fox wouldn't be destroyed. It was probably asking too much – whatever limited credit she might have had must have been used up by now – but she had to try at least. It occurred to her that everything could be her fault. Perhaps she had more than bad blood – perhaps she brought bad luck as well. Misfortune seemed to follow her around. First her mother, then her gran, and now . . .

Helen gave a tiny shake of her head. The fates might not have been kind to her recently, but the blaze at the pub wasn't down to any accident. She had heard the crash of the window breaking just before the fire started. Someone was out to hurt the Quinns. They had only partly succeeded this time, but what about the next? Her stomach turned over. This might be bad, but she had a feeling that things were going to get worse.

# 17

Tommy sat quietly in the corner of the living room, drinking a beer while he listened to his father rant and rave. It was three days now since the Molotov cocktail had been hurled through the front window of the Fox, setting the place ablaze. The word on the street was that the Gissings were responsible, and not one member of that family had come forward to refute the accusation.

Joe, egged on by his entourage, was busy plotting revenge. If the Gissings wanted a war, he was more than happy to oblige. An eye for an eye was his mantra, and his retribution would be suitably violent. The Gissings owned a nightclub in Shoreditch, and his intention, for starters, was to burn it to the ground. Such was his rage that he was unable to sit still, and continuously paced the floor from one side of the room to the other. 'Fuckin' bastards! Fuckin' bastards!' he repeated endlessly. His face, flushed with booze, was a bright florid red and his eyes were dark with hatred.

From downstairs came the sound of hammering and sawing as a team of builders worked to repair the damage to the pub. Tommy was torn between the desire for revenge – his own kids had been put in danger by the attack – and the anxiety of embarking on a full-scale battle with the Gissings. Once Joe retaliated, the violence would escalate rapidly, and when that happened, it wouldn't just be buildings that were targeted. There could be no backing down without losing face; the battle would continue until one family or the other was finished.

Tommy glanced over towards the kitchen, where Mouse was busy making mugs of tea for the workmen. Yvonne had taken the girls and gone to stay at Carol Gatesby's house until the pub repairs were finished. She could have stayed put – the flat was still perfectly habitable, apart from the lingering smell of smoke – but he hadn't tried to dissuade her. With all the shit going down, he preferred them out of the way. It was one less thing to worry about.

Mouse, however, had refused to leave, although he wasn't sure why. He thought she would have jumped at the opportunity to get away from his father, especially in his current mood. He wondered how much she understood about what was really going on. She hadn't asked a single question about the fire, and he couldn't figure out whether she thought it was accidental or simply didn't want to talk about it. On balance, he favoured the latter. She might be the quiet sort, but she had eyes and ears.

Fat Pete leaned forward in his chair and slapped his palms against his thighs. 'I'll take a couple of the boys over there tonight, suss the place out.'

'Yeah,' said Joe. 'The sooner the better.'

Terry Street, who had been sitting as quietly as Tommy until this point, leaned forward too. 'They'll be expecting you.'

'So what?' Joe snapped impatiently. 'Who gives a fuck?'

By which he meant that when they did retaliate, they'd be tooled up. Tommy felt his guts tighten. He wasn't afraid of a scrap – in his younger days he'd have been more than up for it – but this one would end in major casualties. If the truth be told, he could do without the grief.

Terry gave a thin smile. 'I heard a rumour that Lennie Gissing's been cosying up to the filth.'

'And?' retorted Joe impatiently. There wasn't a firm in London that didn't pay off the law. It was all par for the course.

'Thing is, I did a bit of asking around, and it turns out the geezer's not local. He's a DI called Tony Lazenby, and he works out of West End Central. I mean, the Gissings ain't got any interests up West, so what the fuck's the connection?'

Tommy's ears had pricked up. 'Hang on. What does he look like?'

Joe gave a snort. 'What the hell does that matter?'

''Bout forty,' said Terry, ignoring Joe's comment. 'Six foot, solid-looking, brown hair, thinning a bit at the front. You know him?'

'Not me,' Tommy said, 'but I reckon it may have been the same fella who was sniffing round Shelley Anne on Saturday night. She's working at the Dog and Duck now, over at Finsbury Park. He came into the pub just after she'd started her shift and she clocked him for the filth straight off but didn't let on. She played along, you know, just to see what he was after. He said his name was Tony. He was doing a lot of digging, asking her stuff.'

'What sort of stuff?' Terry asked.

Tommy gave a shrug. 'Oh, who she was seeing, how it was going, that kind of thing.'

Joe stopped pacing for a moment and stared at his son. 'So he was chatting her up, so what? Won't be the first or the last time some copper tried to get into a slapper's knickers.'

Tommy glared at him. 'She ain't no slapper,' he snapped back, although he wasn't sure if he was defending Lynsey or Shelley Anne.

'What else did he say?' Terry asked, before the exchange between father and son could escalate into a full-blown row.

Tommy continued glaring at Joe for a few more seconds, and then glanced over at Terry. 'Said he thought he knew her from somewhere else, Hackney maybe, or Kellston. She told him that she used to work here at the Fox, and that seemed to interest him a lot. Anyway, she called me on Sunday after she heard about the fire, reckoned there might be a connection.'

'Bit of a coincidence,' Terry said. 'Don't you reckon, Joe?'

Joe gave a shrug and went over to stand by the window.

Tommy hadn't thought too much about Shelley Anne's call before. Like his father, he had pretty much dismissed what she'd told him as some guy trying his luck. He was having second thoughts now. And shit, if this inspector had teamed up with the Gissings, it would mean even bigger trouble. What if the guy started poking his nose into Tommy's business and found out about the long-firm fraud in Romford? It could result in all his plans going right down the Swanee.

'It don't smell good, Joe,' Terry continued. 'Fact, it stinks. It might not only be the Gissings who'll be waiting if you go for the club. Could be the filth, too.'

Joe Quinn looked over his shoulder. 'What did you say that geezer's name was again?'

'Lazenby, Tony Lazenby.'

Joe's forehead crunched into a frown, and his face took on a strained expression, as if he was struggling, through the haze of booze, to retrieve the name from some lost corner of his addled brain. 'Lazenby,' he murmured.

'You heard of him?' Terry asked.

Joe gave an abrupt flap of his hand. 'Shut it, I'm trying to think.'

A silence descended on the room. When Joe Quinn gave an order, everyone obeyed. For a while, the only sound came from two floors down, a monotonous hammering that never seemed to end. The minutes ticked slowly by, and then suddenly Joe's face cleared and he slapped a fist triumphantly against his thigh. 'Jesus,' he snarled. 'Lazenby, bloody Lazenby.'

'What is it?' Tommy asked quickly.

Joe gave a growl. 'That precious sister of yours might be dead and buried, but she's still causing grief.'

'What the hell are you talking about?'

'Yeah, I remember him now.' Joe gave two abrupt nods of his head. 'Lazenby used to work with that no-good bastard Alan Beck. The two of them were in Vice. They hung out together, too. Yeah, that's who he is.'

Tommy stared at him in surprise. How could Joe have known who Alan Beck hung out with all those years ago unless he'd done some pretty intensive digging? It had always been his belief that his father had cut all ties to Lynsey after she walked out that fateful night, but that clearly wasn't the case. He wondered what his motives had been – to simply check out his daughter's husband, or something more sinister? Well, whatever his plans, he hadn't gone through with them.

'I still don't get it. I mean, I know about—' Terry stopped, not wanting to invite Joe's wrath by even referring to the fact that his daughter had got herself knocked up by a copper. 'But why should he be out to target you?'

'He's the filth, ain't he,' Joe retorted sharply. 'He don't need a fuckin' reason.'

Tommy wondered if the news of Lynsey's death had stirred up old resentments in Tony Lazenby. Beck must have whined to him about his lousy marriage to a villain's daughter, and about how he'd been forced into it. Perhaps, with Lynsey gone, Lazenby had decided to focus his anger on her family instead.

'So the bastard's looking for a fight,' Joe said. 'Well, we'll fuckin' give him one!'

And all end up in clink in the process, Tommy thought. His old dread of prison rose like bile into his throat. The moment they turned up at the Gissings' club, the law would be all over them like a rash. 'It's a stitch-up, for Christ's sake. We lift a finger and they'll have us bang to rights.'

'What's the matter, son?' his father sneered. 'Haven't got the bottle for it?'

Tommy glared back at him, trying not to rise to the bait. His father had all the subtlety of a bull in a china shop. Act first and think later. Which was all very well when you were dealing with lowlife thieving scumbags or the collection of protection money, but not so smart when it came to dealing with the law.

'Sure it's a stitch-up,' Terry said, grinning from ear to ear. 'So why don't we give 'em a taste of their own medicine?'

'What are you thinking?' Tommy asked, eager to encourage a less self-destructive approach.

'I'm thinking why bother to fight your own battles when you can get some other sucker to do it for you.'

'Go on.'

Terry took a swig of beer and stood the bottle carefully on the coffee table. He glanced over at Joe. 'Didn't you say that Lennie Gissing had a run-in with Mickey Stott a few weeks back?'

Joe gave a nod. 'What of it? Those two are always at each other's throats.'

'Exactly,' Terry said. 'And as the Gissings are looking to take over Kellston, it won't come as any great surprise if their next target is Mickey Stott's gaff. He's got a pub on Lincoln Road, ain't he? Be a shame if those Gissings gave it the same treatment as this place.'

Joe narrowed his eyes as the likely outcome of such a scheme slowly sank into his head.

Tommy didn't say a word. It was a brilliant idea, inspired. Mickey Stott was a drug dealer, a man verging on the psychopathic, and he wouldn't think twice about wreaking revenge on the Gissings. However, as his father was likely to reject the idea out of hand if he expressed any enthusiasm for it, Tommy wisely kept his mouth shut and waited for the great man to work out the virtue of the plan for himself.

Joe turned his head away and gazed out of the window. He lit a fag and sucked in the smoke. He scratched at his balls. The rest of the room maintained a reverential silence. Finally, just as Tommy was beginning to lose hope, he barked out a laugh and said, 'Those sonofabitches are going to regret the day they ever crossed Joe Quinn.'

# 18

Helen sat on the lower bunk with her knees drawn up to her chin. It was three o'clock in the morning, fifteen minutes since Tommy and the others had left in the white van. How long would it take them to set the Lincoln alight? And what if something went wrong? Her uncle had almost got himself killed once, and still had the burns to prove it.

Too anxious to sit still, she got up and wandered downstairs to the living room. She'd been in the kitchen this afternoon when Terry Street had come up with his plan. No one had paid her any attention. She was just a kid making tea, and they'd continued to talk freely despite her presence.

Later, she had used more furtive methods to get her information. When she was supposed to be in bed, she had crept down the stairs and along the landing to peer through the crack in the half-open door. There were five of them sitting round the table, speaking in hushed tones. The atmosphere was tense, but excited too. Fat Pete was the one who had made the bombs, emptying out two vodka bottles and carefully filling them with petrol and some motor oil. He had soaked two rags in petrol too and stuffed them into the necks of the bottles.

Helen kept the lights off and peered down the street, willing the van to appear. She knew that what Tommy was doing was wrong, but what the Gissings had done was wrong too. Her grandmother would have said, 'Two wrongs don't make a right', but it didn't feel that simple. Turning the other cheek hardly seemed like a viable option when someone had tried to burn down your home.

'Lazenby,' she murmured, rolling the name around on her tongue. Although she searched her mind, she couldn't recall ever having heard it before today. If he'd been a friend of her father's, then her mum must have known him too. But it was too late to ask her now. Impossible to ask her grandmother either, who was still languishing in hospital. She frowned. Why should this man want to hurt the Quinns so much? It was a question she had no answer to.

Helen scoured the empty street again, her nose pressed against the cool window pane. For the plan to work, Mickey Stott would have to believe that the Gissings were trying to take him out of the game. At least that was what Terry had said. But of course Mickey would believe it, because they'd attacked the Fox in the same way a few days earlier. There would be no reason to suspect Joe Quinn.

She didn't, as yet, fully understand the nature of Joe's business. What she did understand was that he didn't operate inside the law. Joe Quinn was a villain, and she supposed that made Tommy a villain too. It confused her to think of

Tommy doing bad things. He had shown her nothing but kindness since bringing her here. She'd been uprooted and thrown into a world that was completely alien to her, but gradually she was learning to cope.

As the minutes passed by, she grew increasingly worried. Where were they? How long did it take to throw a bottle through a window? If something went wrong, if they got caught by the police, then it could be hours before she even found out. Tommy had wanted her to go and stay at Moira's for the night, but she wouldn't leave and he hadn't insisted. She wasn't afraid of being here on her own, but she was afraid of Tommy never coming back.

She tried to distract herself by thinking about the pub. It wouldn't be that long before it was up and running again. The workmen started at dawn and didn't leave again until it got dark. Already the evidence of the fire was beginning to fade as the interior was stripped out and gradually rebuilt. There would be new paper on the walls and new seating with fresh upholstery. Soon the customers would return and everything would be as it had been before.

Helen crossed her fingers, hoping that was true. She strained her ears, listening out for the sound of the van, peering both ways along the road. They would probably come from the direction of the high street, unless they decided to take a less direct route home. She tried not to think too much about what could go wrong – a panda car passing by, a witness who might recognise them, a random puncture as they attempted their getaway.

Her thoughts drifted back to Tony Lazenby. Maybe she could ask Moira about him. If he'd been a good friend of her dad's, Moira might have met him at some point in the past. But then again, perhaps she was better off just keeping her mouth shut. After all, that was what she did best. She was Mouse, the girl who was seen but rarely heard.

Helen moved away from the window. *A watched kettle never boils*. She patrolled the living room for a couple of minutes, skirting around the furniture. A thin light coming from the street lamp outside cast an almost eerie orange glow. Did Yvonne know what was happening tonight? Had Tommy told her, or was he keeping quiet about it? Tommy kept quiet about all sorts of things. Like his friendship with Shelley Anne, for example. He was always chatting to her on the phone when Yvonne wasn't around.

Unable to resist, Helen returned to the window. The sound of an engine made her heart leap, but it was only a taxi going by. She clenched and unclenched her hands, humming the chorus of Marvin Gaye's 'I Heard It Through The Grapevine'. She could relate to the lyrics: she was just about to lose her mind too.

And where was Frank Meyer? she wondered. There had been no sign of him for a couple of days. He'd turned up on Sunday, but she hadn't seen him since. Had he and Tommy fallen out? She knew that Frank blamed Joe for the fire. He had said as much when he'd been viewing the damage downstairs. Tommy wouldn't let her go into the bar – he said it was too dangerous – but she had stood at the door, her heart sinking as she gazed at the wreckage of the Fox.

'Christ, your old man's going to get you all killed one day.'

Tommy, standing with his hands on his hips, had shaken his head. 'This wasn't down to him.'

'You reckon? He might not have thrown the bomb, but he pissed off someone else enough to make *them* do it.'

Tommy had given one of his shrugs. 'Maybe.'

'There's no maybe about it. And now you're going to have the law sniffing round. It's not good, mate. If they think it's about to kick off big time, they'll be paying you way too much attention. What about Romford? If they start poking their noses into that, then—'

'They won't. They don't know anything about it. How could they?'

Frank had put his hands in his pockets, his shoulders stiff and hunched. 'But what happens next? Joe isn't going to take this lying down.'

'We'll deal with it.'

'That's what I'm worried about.'

Helen frowned as she thought about the conversation. The two men hadn't exactly fallen out, but some sharp words had been exchanged. She understood Frank's frustration, but Tommy was in an impossible position. Unless he helped his father fight back, the Quinns would go under.

Suddenly that niggling fear came back to haunt her, the idea that she was responsible for everything that was happening. If she'd never been born, Tony Lazenby wouldn't be looking for ways to get revenge. If her mum had never met Alan Beck, then . . .

But she didn't have time to complete the train of thought. Her heart gave a leap as she saw a white van turn the corner. It slowed as it approached the Fox, and then she knew for sure that it was them. Quickly she scampered back upstairs and knelt down on the landing, peering between the banisters.

It was a couple more minutes before she heard the back door opening, followed by the heavy tread of boots on the stairs. She could tell from their voices and the sound of boisterous laughter that the mission had been accomplished. Everyone was home without any casualties.

As Joe Quinn's firm gathered in the living room to celebrate their success, Helen tiptoed back to bed. She crawled between the sheets and curled into a ball. Despite her relief, she still felt uneasy. The battle might be won, but that didn't mean the war was over.

# 19

Mickey Stott snorted another line of coke before pulling the balaclava over his head and picking up the baseball bat. He ran his hand along the smooth surface, already anticipating the damage he would do. There was, all things considered, nothing more gratifying than the soft thudding sound of wood against bone.

It was getting near to closing time at the Blue Lagoon, and customers were starting to leave. The strip joint owned by the three Gissing brothers lay on the west side of Shoreditch, and catered for all those City boys who liked to cop an eyeful after a long, hard day at the office.

Mickey and his army of nine were squashed into the back of a van that had been nicked that afternoon. They were parked up across the street, counting down the seconds before they swung the vehicle on to the forecourt and launched their attack. The Gissings were creatures of habit, always getting together on a Friday night to have a few drinks and split the weekly takings.

Mickey gave a long, low growl. No doubt the bastards were busy congratulating themselves on their latest achievement. He still couldn't believe what they'd done. Ten fuckin' years it had taken him to get enough cash together to buy the Lincoln, and now it was nothing but a heap of rubble. There would be the insurance money, of course, but the compensation came at a price: already the pigs had been sniffing round, asking questions and digging into his affairs. The fire had put him firmly on their radar, and that was the last thing he needed. With two firebombings within a week, they were getting jumpy, worried that the East End was about to explode into full-blown warfare.

Mickey felt a red mist descending. He could have dropped a word in the ear of the filth – every villain in Kellston knew that the Gissings were responsible – but that wasn't his style. He was old school. He wasn't a grass. When he had a problem, he dealt with it in his own way. What really wound him up, however, wasn't the fact that the Gissings had set fire to his pub, but that the arseholes thought they could get away with it.

With this grievance bearing down on him, he gave the nod and the guy at the back banged his fist three times against the metal dividing them from the driver. The engine, which had been idling, suddenly roared into life, the van veering at speed across the road and coming to a screeching halt outside the Blue Lagoon.

In a few seconds the advance guard had whipped open the door, jumped out and charged towards the entrance. It was their job to take out security. The attack was so fast and furious that the two bouncers, already preparing to knock off for the night, were taken completely by surprise.

The rest of the crew – with Mickey at the forefront – were able to get a clear run into the club itself. They hurtled into the room, bats flying wildly, swinging at everything in sight. Tables were overturned, with bottles and glasses smashing to the ground. The three strippers on stage covered their tits and started screaming. Some of the punters tried to make a run for it, while others dropped to their knees or sat paralysed with fright.

The lights in the club were dim, but Mickey knew his way around. He thundered towards the rear and was almost at the door marked *Staff Only* when he saw it open and a startled Lennie Gissing peer out. Before the oldest Gissing brother had the chance to close the door in his face, Mickey was on him. He pushed him back into the office and then, with all the fury of a man wronged, swung the bat and slammed it across his enemy's legs. Lennie's mouth was open as he slumped to the floor, but no sound came out of it. And Mickey wasn't finished yet. A couple of broken legs were nothing compared to a man's reputation. Cursing loudly, he put the boot in, kicking Lennie hard in the ribs, in the groin and then in the head. There was no point in teaching a bloke a lesson unless it was one he remembered for the rest of his days.

Once Lennie had ceased to care whether he lived or died, Mickey stopped wasting his energy. He'd been only vaguely aware of the activity going on about him, but his companions hadn't been idle. Roy Gissing was lying on the floor, groaning softly. The third brother, Carl, was doubled over in the corner, spitting out his teeth.

Mickey looked at his watch and grinned. Eight minutes flat. A job well done. Better make an exit before someone raised the alarm. There was just time, however, to reach across the desk and grab the cash that was lying there. He stuffed the notes, a couple of grand he reckoned, into his pockets and went to gather up his troops.

The main part of the club was in mayhem, the girls still shrieking, the whole place turned upside down and smashed to pieces. He liked what he saw. Revenge was sweet. 'Out! Out!' he yelled, waving his arms about. With the adrenalin pumping through his veins, he sped into the foyer, swinging his bat at anything or anyone that stood in his way.

It was only as he stepped triumphantly on to the forecourt that Mickey's bubble finally burst. A powerful beam of light stopped him dead in his tracks and he put his free hand up to shield his eyes. 'What the . . . ?' He squinted quickly to the left and right, his fingers tightening instinctively around the handle of the bat, but already he knew that it was over. There was nowhere to run. The filth had arrived and he was well and truly buggered.

# 20

It was almost one o'clock in the morning when Tony Lazenby was jolted awake by the sound of the phone ringing. Far from being displeased by this interruption to his dreams, he rolled eagerly across the bed and snatched up the receiver. If the news was what he hoped it would be, then sleep was of secondary importance. 'Yeah, Lazenby.'

'Hi, it's Jim. I've got good news.'

Tony pulled himself into a sitting position, grinning from ear to ear. 'You got the scumbags?' After the fire at the Fox, he had informed Jim Morris – a DI working out of Shoreditch – that one of his narks had tipped him off about a revenge attack being planned. It was too late to catch the Gissings in the act, but the Quinns would be easy prey. And one less East End firm on the loose was good news for everybody. As the Blue Lagoon was used as the Gissing brothers' main base, this was the most likely target. A surveillance operation had been mounted and Tony had been waiting for news ever since.

'We got them all right.'

Tony punched the air with his fist. 'Result!'

'Only a couple of minor hitches,' Morris said. 'They came a bit earlier than we expected, turned up before the damn place had closed. They'd done a job on the brothers before we even made it to the door.'

'How bad?'

'Bad enough, but they'll live.'

'Caught you napping, did they?' Tony said, laughing. 'Typical. I give you the best tip you've had in years, and you go to sleep on the job.'

'After closing time, you said.'

'Well, that's what I was told. Still, it makes no difference, does it? You nabbed the bastards and that's all that matters.' Tony leaned back against a pillow, savouring the sweetness of success. Finally he'd managed to nail Joe Quinn. Alan would rest easy in his grave tonight.

'I said a couple of hitches, not just one.'

'Go on then, spill,' Tony said. He didn't much care about the detail but felt obliged to hear the guy out. It was unfortunate that the Gissings had taken a beating, but he wasn't going to lose any sleep over it. 'What else did you manage to fuck up?'

'Not us, mate. I reckon your nark got his facts a bit screwed, though.'

'And how's that?'

'Because it wasn't the Quinns we arrested tonight. It was Mickey Stott and his crew.'

The revelation hit Tony like a thump to the stomach. He slumped forward, feeling the breath fly out of his lungs. It couldn't be. It was impossible. Gripping the phone tightly, he searched for words but couldn't find any. The devastating news had left him dumb.

'Tony? You still there?'

Tony flicked on the bedside light, squinting at the sudden brightness. 'Yeah,' he said eventually, his head still reeling from the shock. 'I don't get it, though. Why the hell would Mickey Stott do that?' Before Jim got a chance to respond, he came up with an answer of his own. 'Shit, the Quinns must have changed their plans, decided to pay someone else to do their dirty work. You need to put the screws on Stott, get him to talk. See if you can make a deal with him. See if—'

'There's no chance of that, mate.'

Tony could feel the rage growing inside him. 'Of course there's a chance. You want to nail the Quinns or not?'

'Who doesn't?' Jim said. 'But I don't reckon they're in the frame this time. This was personal.'

'What do you mean, *personal*?'

'Just what I said. Stott had his own reasons for giving the Gissings a good kicking. He thinks they burned down his pub.'

'What?'

'The Lincoln. You know, the one by the Mansfield Estate.'

'Yeah, I know where it is,' Tony said. 'Christ, I didn't hear about that.'

'It only happened last night. Same MO as the attack on the Fox, except this time the fire brigade didn't get there in time. The place was gutted.' Jim gave a thin, sarcastic laugh. 'Bit like Mickey Stott, now I come to think of it.'

But Tony wasn't in the mood for wisecracks. The only

thing he could think of was all that work, all those weeks of planning, swilling straight down the drain. Everything ruined by a two-bit crazy junkie like Mickey Stott. 'So that's that,' he said roughly.

'Hey, it's still a result. Stott and his crew are going down for sure, and the Gissings won't be back in action for a while. I'd call that two for the price of one.'

'Sure it is,' Tony said, although he couldn't share his colleague's sense of satisfaction. 'Thanks for letting me know.'

'No problem. Give me a bell when you fancy a pint. I owe you one.'

'Will do.' Tony put down the receiver carefully, fighting against the impulse to slam it back into the cradle. 'For fuck's sake!' he muttered, glaring at the wall. Rubbing hard at his face, he tried to scrub the frustration away. Already the truth was starting to seep into his consciousness. He knew that the Gissings hadn't set the Lincoln alight, but he could guess who had. He'd been outwitted and outmanoeuvred by his enemy. Joe Quinn had well and truly screwed him over.

Tony's hands curled into two tight fists. This was a lesson he wouldn't forget in a hurry. It might take a year or it might take ten, but one day he'd make the Quinns pay.

# 21

It was the morning after the reopening party at the Fox, and the pub looked like it had been hit by a different type of bomb. Helen stood in the centre of the bar, her eyes growing wide at the prospect of the task that lay ahead. Every available surface was covered with dirty glasses and plates, overflowing ashtrays and the crusty remains of food. The air stank of stale beer and fag smoke.

'Bet you wish you'd never offered now,' Tommy said.

The party had gone on into the early hours. It had felt like half the East End had turned out for the event, with the three large adjoining rooms packed to the rafters. Helen, together with Karen and Debs, had been allowed to stay up until midnight. Yvonne, if somewhat reluctantly, had finally moved back in, and the family was reunited again.

Helen picked up one of the big refuse sacks. 'It won't take long once we get started.'

'You wouldn't say that if you had a head like mine.'

Tommy winced and rubbed at his temples. 'Thanks, love, you're a star.'

Helen smiled and set to work. As she piled the rubbish into the sack, she thought back to the previous night. Frank Meyer had been there, and Moira too. There'd been music and singing, even dancing at one point. She had drifted through the crowd, sipping her Coke as she studied the men in their slick suits and the women in their party dresses. As she passed by one group and then another, she'd caught endless snippets of conversation. That was the thing about being a kid – no one really noticed that you were there. There had been the usual gossip about one person or another, as well as talk of the fire, the ill-judged ambition of the Gissings and their ultimate downfall.

Joe had swaggered around the pub as if it had been him, not Mickey Stott, who had pulled a balaclava over his head and put the three brothers in hospital. Helen knew, however, that her grandfather hadn't been idle in the weeks since the Fox had been attacked. Stott's fast and violent retribution against the Gissings had given Joe the opportunity to move in on new business, and he had grabbed it with both hands. Although she didn't know all the ins and outs, she had been aware of the flurry of activity and the constant comings and goings of his henchmen.

Karen and Debs had spent most of the evening ogling Terry Street, who much to their annoyance had turned up with a pretty blonde on his arm. Since the bombing of the Lincoln, Helen had noticed a change in Joe's attitude towards Terry. It wasn't respect exactly – Joe didn't respect anyone – but a kind of recognition that the younger man had both cunning and brains. Terry had proved the latter not just by coming up with the plan to oust the Gissings, but by having the sense not to brag about it afterwards.

When Helen had first begun to comprehend the violent, shadowy world that the Quinns inhabited, it had filled her with fear and trepidation. Now, even after the short period she had been here, she was becoming accustomed to its different principles and morals. That wasn't to say that she approved of the way the family behaved – she had listened to too many Sunday sermons for that to happen in a hurry – but she was learning to live with it.

Joe still scared the hell out of her. However, there'd been no repeat of the performance in the cellar. This wasn't, she was certain, down to any softening in his attitude, but purely a result of having more important things on his mind. Occasionally he would fix her with one of his steely glares, but on the whole he just ignored her.

Helen ran a cloth over one of the tables, buffing the wood to a fine sheen. Four weeks was all it had taken to get the Fox open again. It would have been much longer if it hadn't been for Tommy's efforts in preventing the fire from spreading. Had the flames reached the stash of bottles behind the bar, the place would have gone up like a tinderbox. Not that he'd got much in the way of thanks for his trouble. Joe was preoccupied with expanding his empire, and Yvonne would have been more than happy to see the pub burnt to the ground.

Helen had spent every waking hour helping Tommy to get the place up and running. She looked around, proud of what they'd achieved. Reaching over, she touched the new red and gold flock wallpaper. She liked the feel of the raised velvety surface against her fingertips. There were long red curtains too. Joe had wanted to put bars on the windows – thus preventing any future firebomb attacks – but Tommy had managed to talk him out of it.

'Are you kidding? Half our customers have been banged up at one time or another. They ain't gonna want to drink in a bleedin' jail.'

Helen stood up straight and did a three-hundred-and-sixty-degree turn. Yes, the Fox looked better than it ever had. It was the floor, though, that she liked best. The old worn carpet had gone, replaced by a zigzag of oblong wooden blocks. There was a name for the style, but she couldn't remember what it was. Anyway, it would make the cleaning a lot easier.

As she swept a pile of paper plates into the bag, she realised with a start that it was almost the end of August and school would be beginning in the first week of September. Her heart sank. She wasn't looking forward to it. She wished she could stay here in the pub and never step inside a classroom again. The three-week deal she'd made with Frank Meyer in the cemetery was long past, and with the fallout from the fire, she'd forgotten all about it until now. Thinking of Frank reminded her of something else she'd heard last night.

Helen concentrated hard as she tried to recall the exact words. Yvonne had been standing near the bar, and leaning in to her friend, Carol, she had said in a hushed voice, 'See what I mean. Frank's on his lonesome again. He hasn't even looked at a girl since he got here.'

'Maybe there's no one he fancies.'

'If you believe that, you'll believe anything.'

Carol had given a snigger. 'Your Tommy had better watch himself, then.'

Helen frowned, wondering what the two women had meant. The comments puzzled her. It was true that Frank was always on his own, but so what? And what had Carol meant about Tommy? She suspected it was something bad, something smutty, but she wasn't sure exactly what. The little she did know about sex had been gleaned from a furtive reading of the problem pages in Debs's *Jackie* magazine, and none of those dilemmas seemed to cover this particular subject.

Helen's line of thought was broken by the sound of the phone ringing. Tommy came hurrying through to the bar to answer it. She wasn't sure if his haste was down to a desire to prevent the noise from intensifying his hangover, or because he thought it might be Shelley Anne. She often called around this time, when she knew he'd be able to talk.

'Hello? The Fox.' There was a short pause, and then he said, 'Yes, this is Tommy Quinn.'

Helen picked up some glasses and took them over to the counter. She was only listening with half an ear, but suddenly she became aware of a change in his tone.

'Oh, I'm sorry to hear that.'

Helen glanced over at him, but his eyes met hers only briefly before he quickly and deliberately looked away. Such was the evasion that she was instantly aware that the call was connected to her. She felt the breath catch in the back of her throat. There was a tightening in her chest, a heavy sense of foreboding.

'Yeah, of course I will. And the ... the ... it's on Thursday, right?'

Helen stacked the glasses on the bar, her hands shaking slightly. Her legs felt unsteady too, as if the weight of her body had become too much for them. She leaned against the counter while she waited for Tommy to finish the call.

'Ten o'clock. Yeah, that's fine. We'll be there.'

As he put the phone down, Tommy's face twisted. He hesitated for a moment before finally meeting Helen's gaze. 'That was your Auntie Janet. I'm really sorry, love. It's bad news.'

Helen gave a shake of her head, not wanting him to say the words. If he didn't say it, it couldn't be true. A part of her had always known that this could happen, but she had pushed the possibility to the back of her mind. There it had stayed for the last few months, a horror held at bay.

Tommy stepped out from behind the bar and wrapped his arms around her, pulling her close. 'I'm so sorry, hon.'

Helen, who was not used to being hugged, stood awkwardly in his arms. With her face pressed against his shirt front, she breathed in his musky smell. As the finality of the news began to sink in, she felt a shifting inside, a kind of splintering, and she remembered the night of the fire, when she had witnessed one of the pub tables devoured by flames. One minute it was there, and the next it was gone. One minute her grandmother was there, and the next she was gone.

'It was peaceful, hon. She wasn't in any pain.'

Helen thought of the woman who had brought her up, tall and stern and nothing if not constant. Joan Beck had been her anchor for so many years that it was impossible to conceive of her as being dead. She hadn't even had the chance to say goodbye. Not one visit to the hospital. Had that been her gran's choice or Janet's? She felt a wave of grief roll over her, but refused to give in to the tears pricking at her eyes. Even in the presence of her uncle, she couldn't bear to cry.

Tommy eventually released her from his embrace. Standing back a little, he placed a hand briefly on her shoulder. 'You okay, Mouse? Why don't you go upstairs for a bit? I can finish off down here.'

Helen gave a tiny shake of her head. What would she do upstairs? With Yvonne and Debs lounging in the living room, and Karen still in bed, there would be little chance of any privacy. Anyway, she didn't want to be alone with her thoughts. After Grandad had died, Gran had cleaned the house in Camberley Road from top to bottom. Keeping busy had been her answer to grief, and Helen would follow suit. 'It'll be quicker with the two of us.'

'Well . . .' he said doubtfully. 'If you're sure.'

Helen forced a thin, trembling smile. Aware of the croak in her voice, she didn't dare to speak again. Instead, she walked across the bar and started collecting the rest of the glasses. All the time she was aware of Tommy's gaze on her. He stood there for a while, his eyes sad and anxious, before finally retreating to the room next door. It was only then, when she was finally alone, that a single tear escaped and ran down her cheek. Quickly she brushed it away with the back of her hand.

## 22

Helen could hear the radio, Elvis Presley singing 'The Wonder of You', as she turned the corner of the staircase and began walking along the landing. The song made her heart ache. It was Thursday, eight o'clock in the morning and the day of her grandmother's funeral. She wasn't sure how she'd get through it. The dread lay heavily in her stomach, a great boulder of grief wrapped in pain and regret.

She glanced down at the black woollen dress, the same dress she had worn to her mother's funeral. It was too warm for it really – already she felt hot and bothered – but she had nothing else suitable to wear. She could have gone to the market, perhaps, and bought something lighter, but it was too late now. Carefully she smoothed out the creases with her fingertips.

As Helen approached the living room, Yvonne's voice, edged with irritation, floated out to her from the kitchen. 'So what happens next?'

'Next?' Tommy replied.

There was an angry clatter of cutlery. 'Why do you always pretend you don't know what I'm talking about? With her. What's going to happen with *her*?'

'She's got a name,' Tommy said. 'And there's no need to shout about it. What's going to happen next is that we're going to bury her grandmother.'

Helen stopped by the door, too embarrassed now to step into the living room. They would guess that she had overheard them, think perhaps that she'd even been deliberately eavesdropping. There'd be silence and awkwardness. Her cheeks flushed scarlet at the thought of it.

'And then?' Yvonne prompted. 'I take it you're going to have a word with that aunt of hers, find out what her plans are. It was only supposed to be for a few weeks, that's what you promised, and the kid's already been here for months.'

'Ah, don't start all that again. I'll have a word, okay? I'll sort it.'

'Well make sure you do. I know what you're like, Tommy Quinn: you say one thing and do the exact opposite. I'm telling you, you need to put that woman straight before this turns into a permanent arrangement.'

Helen raised a hand to her mouth and bit down on her knuckles. She might have guessed that Yvonne wouldn't want her around, but even Tommy didn't seem that bothered. Maybe he'd had enough of her too. Maybe this would be her last day at the Fox. Not so long ago, the idea of getting out of Kellston would have made her jump for joy, but recently her attitude had changed. She didn't feel at home exactly, but she didn't feel a complete stranger either. And when she weighed up the options – staying here or going to live with Janet – she knew which one she'd prefer.

After backtracking along the landing, Helen climbed softly up the stairs. When she got to the middle, she paused for a moment and then retraced her steps, making sure that she made enough noise to let them know she was coming.

'Morning,' Tommy said. 'Sleep all right? Sit yourself down and have some breakfast.'

Helen wasn't hungry – her stomach was churning – but she pulled out a chair and sat across from her uncle. She tried not to look at the bacon and eggs he was eating, although the smell of it still reached her. She breathed through her mouth, feeling nauseous and hoping that she wasn't going to be sick.

Yvonne, still in her dressing gown, put a plate on the table with a heap of toast on it.

'There's tea in the pot. Help yourself.'

Helen reached for the milk bottle and sloshed some into a yellow mug. At Camberley Road there had always been a jug, but things were done differently here. Every morning she had sat down to eat with her gran, but breakfast at the Fox was rarely a communal event, the members of the household drifting in and out of the kitchen at whatever time they liked. She sipped the milk, thinking it might calm her stomach.

Yvonne plonked herself next to Tommy and lit a cigarette. She stared at Helen for a few seconds before saying, 'So, is that what you're wearing?'

'There's nothin' wrong with it,' Tommy said, throwing his wife a warning glance. 'You look very smart, hon.'

189

Yvonne's eyebrows shifted up. 'I didn't say she didn't. Just thought she might be a bit hot, that's all. It's gonna be a scorcher today. It said so on the radio.'

'Yeah, well, it won't be hot in church. Those places are always cold enough to freeze yer bollocks off.'

Helen, who'd been feeling self-conscious even before she stepped into the room, now felt ten times worse. She didn't know what to say and so she said nothing. Instead, she leaned forward a little, hunching her shoulders as though by such an act she could make herself less visible.

The Elvis song had come to an end and now Freda Payne was singing 'Band of Gold'. Yvonne sang along between puffs on her cigarette.

'Jesus,' said Tommy, winking at Helen. 'What's that noise? Is there a bleedin' cat in here or something?'

'Ha, ha,' Yvonne said. 'Just because you're tone-deaf doesn't mean that everyone else is too.'

'What d'ya reckon, Mouse? Voice of an angel or something that needs putting down?'

Helen forced her mouth into the semblance of a smile. She knew that Tommy was only trying to cheer her up, but nothing could make her feel better today. The lyrics of the song reminded her of her mother's wedding ring, the band of gold lying in her shell-covered box of treasures upstairs. Sometimes she would take it out and slip it on to her own finger, hoping to make a connection with the woman who had drifted so casually in and out of her life.

'Have some cornflakes,' Yvonne said, shoving the packet towards her.

'I'm not hungry, thanks.'

'I can do you an egg if you like. How about that – a boiled egg? It won't take long.'

Helen shook her head. 'No thanks. Really, I'm fine.'

'Have some toast at least.'

'She said she wasn't hungry,' Tommy said. 'Leave the poor kid alone.'

Yvonne frowned at him. 'She's got to eat something.'

'She doesn't *have* to do anything.'

Helen, finding herself not just the unwanted centre of attention but also the cause of another petty squabble between Tommy and Yvonne, cringed inwardly. She wished now that she'd stayed upstairs until it was time to leave.

Yvonne stubbed out the cigarette with a series of quick jabbing movements. She glanced at Helen and said sulkily, 'Well don't blame me if your stomach's rumbling in church.'

Helen, who'd had no intention of blaming her for anything other than a general lack of tact, kept her eyes fixed firmly on the table. On the tablecloth to the right of her unused plate was a brown tea stain in the shape of a cloud. She stared at it intently, then lifted a hand, intending to trace the outline with a fingertip, but stopped herself just in time. Yvonne might think that she was drawing attention to the unwashed state of the cloth. It would be yet another reason for the woman to dislike her.

Tommy poured himself a mug of tea, then sat back and sighed. His gaze raked the room for a moment before coming to rest on a pile of magazines stacked on the corner of the table. There was a piece of paper poking out from the one on top. He slid it out, stared at it and scowled. 'What's this doing here?'

'It's just a leaflet,' Yvonne said.

'I've already told her she ain't going. She's too young and that's the end of it.'

Helen looked at the flier, a guide to the Isle of Wight Festival. On it was a long list of the artists who'd be playing, including Jimi Hendrix, The Doors, and Joni Mitchell. Debs, who was desperate to attend, had been nagging her mother about it for weeks.

'She's almost fifteen,' Yvonne said.

'Exactly,' Tommy said. 'She's *fourteen*. I'm not having it and that's final. It ain't safe. Anything could happen to her.'

'She wouldn't be on her own. All her mates will be there.'

'As will every horny teenage male who can haul himself across the Solent. You really want her up the duff at fourteen?'

'For God's sake,' Yvonne snapped back. 'It's a concert, not a bleedin' orgy. And that doesn't say much for your opinion of Debs. She's a decent kid. She can take care of herself.'

'It's not *her* morals I'm worried about. It's the dirty little bastard who'll ply her with cider, gaze into her eyes and swear undying love while he tries to get into her pants. I've been there, remember? I know every trick in the book.'

'Well, perhaps you shouldn't judge everyone else by your own low standards.'

Helen's gaze flitted anxiously from one to the other. She was relieved that she was no longer the focus of their attention, but she was worried that the sniping would turn into a full-blown row. Tommy's face had already darkened, and even through his suntan she could see the flush of red on his cheeks.

'You reckon?' He gave a snort, pushed back his chair and

rose to his feet. Glancing down at Helen, he said, 'You ready, love?'

Helen nodded and quickly got up too.

'You'll be early,' Yvonne said. 'It doesn't take that long to get to Farleigh Wood.'

Tommy pulled on his jacket and went through to the living room. Standing in front of the mirror, he straightened his tie and smoothed down his hair. Then, without another word, he headed for the stairs.

Helen tagged along behind, musing on whether his fears for his daughter were the result of his own past mistakes or those of his sister. If Lynsey hadn't got herself pregnant, he wouldn't have been landed with taking care of her offspring. At the bottom of the stairs she stopped and took a final look into the bar. Recalling what Tommy had said earlier about *sorting it*, she wondered if this would be the last time she ever saw the Fox. Perhaps today, like some unwanted parcel, she would be handed back to Janet.

# 23

As Yvonne had predicted, they arrived in Farleigh Wood an hour before the funeral was due to start. They found a café round the corner from St James's, where Helen had a strawberry milkshake and Tommy drank another mug of tea and smoked two cigarettes. She was aware of him being quieter than usual, although she couldn't tell if this was down to his spat with Yvonne or the solemnity of the occasion. Either way, neither of them said very much. They sat by the window and gazed out at the street, both preoccupied by their own thoughts.

When they finally got to St James's, Janet was already seated in the front row with her husband, Colin. Tommy shook hands with them both, expressing his sympathy at their loss. Helen stood awkwardly beside him, not sure what to say or do. Was she supposed to lean down and kiss her aunt, to repeat Tommy's words about how sorry she was? But Janet might not welcome being kissed. The seconds ticked by, and the longer she delayed doing anything, the more difficult it became to do *something*.

'And how are you, Helen?' Janet asked eventually.

Helen shifted from one foot to the other. It was a question that didn't seem to have a right answer. If she politely replied that she was fine, it would sound like she didn't care about the death of her grandmother, but if she said what she really felt, that wouldn't be acceptable either. The Beck family prided themselves on their forbearance, on not showing any unnecessary emotion. Her throat had gone tight and her mouth felt dry She chewed on her lower lip, racked by indecision.

It was Tommy who came to the rescue after a brief embarrassing silence. 'She's kind of upset, but we're taking care of her.'

Janet gave a thin-lipped smile. 'Well, it's a difficult time for all of us.'

'Of course,' Tommy said.

With the formalities over, they were finally able to sit down. Tommy sat to the left of Colin, and Helen squeezed in beside him. She glanced over her shoulder, surprised by the turnout. All the other pews were full, and she recognised the faces as being part of the regular Sunday congregation. It was all in stark contrast to her mother's funeral and its pitiful handful of mourners.

The service began, and while the Reverend Moorgate led the prayers, Helen's gaze flicked repeatedly towards the darkwood coffin covered with flowers. She felt grief and despair, but her overwhelming emotion was one of anger. What sort of God could take her mother and her grandmother away from her in the space of a few months? It was not the act of a kind or loving God. Yet she had prayed to him to save

Tommy the night of the fire and he'd come through for her. Was this the price she had to pay for it? One person saved but another sacrificed.

As they all stood to sing 'Abide with Me', Helen's head became flooded with memories. She recalled all those times when she'd railed against being caught in the middle of the rows between her mum and Gran, the pawn in a game they had played out so often. Now, with both of them lost, she felt cut adrift, a girl with bad blood who nobody wanted.

She frowned, knowing that she shouldn't be thinking of herself at a time like this. It was selfish and wrong. But she was scared of what the future held, fearful of its uncertainty. She glanced along the pew towards Janet. Her aunt, stiff-backed and stoical, gazed straight ahead towards the cross on the altar. What if she refused to take her back? With Yvonne having made her feelings clear on the subject, would Tommy decide that the best thing to do was to place his niece in one of those children's homes? She shuddered at the thought of it.

The rest of the service passed in a daze. The next thing she knew, Helen was standing in the churchyard, watching as they slowly lowered the coffin into the ground. Her gran was being buried in Grandad's grave. Next to it was the resting place of Helen's father, Alan Beck. She briefly shifted her gaze to look at the marble headstone. Had her father been a hero or a villain? She still wasn't sure.

As the strong morning sun beat down on them, Helen felt a prickling of sweat on her forehead. The black woollen dress was hot and itchy, and she had to fight against the impulse to scratch at her neck. The vicar dropped soil on top of the coffin. *Earth to earth, ashes to ashes, dust to dust.* It made an eerie smattering sound as it scattered on the wood. And then, too suddenly it seemed, the service was over and the mourners moved away from the grave.

From the church, they all went back to Camberley Road, where there were plates of cold meat, sandwiches and cake laid out on the table in the living room. There was tea and orange juice to drink, as well as sherry for the women and whisky for the men. Helen noticed Tommy pouring himself a large one before going over to talk to Janet and Colin.

Helen watched them surreptitiously, trying to work out if it was her future they were discussing. She was unable, however, to gauge much from their expressions and was standing too far away to hear the conversation. From time to time her surveillance was disrupted by someone coming up, gently patting her arm and murmuring words of condolence. She smiled feebly back, lost as always as to how to respond. 'Thank you, thank you,' was the best she could manage.

After a few minutes, she decided to escape upstairs. There at least she wouldn't have to talk to anyone. She went quickly up to her bedroom and closed the door with a sigh of relief. Sitting on the single bed, she pulled her knees up to her chin and looked around. Everything was exactly as she'd left it. Well, almost. There was a thin layer of dust on the bedside table, something that her grandmother would never have tolerated. Reaching out her hand, she ran a finger through it, creating a single clean stripe. She stared at her fingertip for a moment and then wiped the dust on the sleeve of her dress.

Although the room was entirely familiar, Helen had the odd feeling of no longer belonging to it. It was hers and yet at the same time it wasn't. But still it remained a place of sanctuary, if only a temporary one. Would Janet sell the house now, or would she move into it with Colin and the boys? Either way, Helen knew in her heart that this would be the last time she sat on this bed, the last time she looked towards the window that overlooked the garden. She said her good-byes as solemnly as she had said goodbye to her grandmother.

She wasn't sure how long she'd been there – half an hour, perhaps – when the door opened and Janet came in.

'Oh, here you are,' she said, her voice edged with irritation. 'I've been looking all over for you. I think your uncle's ready to leave.'

Helen climbed off the bed, her pulse starting to race. A part of her wanted to ask if a decision had been made about her future, but the other part was too scared of hearing the answer. She searched Janet's face, but found no clues in it. But of course, by the very nature of this dismissal, it was obvious that she wasn't going to be staying with the Simmses. Tommy was taking her away, but where was he taking her?

She followed Janet silently down the stairs and into the living room. The mourners had thinned out, and those that still remained had largely migrated to the kitchen. Tommy, who was sitting in an armchair, stood up as she came into the room.

'Ready to go?' he asked.

Helen gave a nod.

Janet began walking towards the door, then suddenly stopped. Her voice, previously stern and matter-of-fact, soft-ened a little. 'If there's anything you'd like to have, a keepsake or . . . you know, something to remind you of her . . .'

Helen, startled by this unexpected offer, didn't know what

to choose. She looked wildly round the living room before glancing back at her aunt. She noticed Janet's eyes flick warily towards the china cabinet, as if afraid that she might pick something valuable. But Helen wasn't interested in the rows of figurines or the pieces of silver. Instead she pointed at a tiny black glass cat that she had bought for her grandmother's birthday many years ago.

'Could I have that?'

Janet, looking relieved, opened the cabinet and took out the cat. 'Do you want me to wrap it for you, put it in some tissue paper?'

Helen shook her head. 'It's all right.' She took the cat from her aunt's hand and slipped it into her pocket. It was at that very moment that she looked towards the shelf on the far side of the room and noticed something else. 'And could I . . . could I have the *A to Z*, please?'

'What?'

'The road atlas,' Helen said, indicating shyly towards the shelf.

Janet seemed bemused by the request. 'That old thing. Are you sure?'

'If it's okay,' Helen said.

Janet walked over and took it down. She stared briefly at the cover before handing it over. 'It's completely out of date,' she said, as if Helen might be planning on using it for a tour of London.

'Thank you.' Helen hugged the old book tightly to her breast, knowing how often her grandfather had perused its contents. She could see him now, hunched over its pages, tracing out a route with his fingertip.

'We all done?' asked Tommy.

The three of them walked to the front door, where there was the usual awkwardness of what to do next and how to say goodbye. Before it could become too strained, Janet solved the problem by leaning down and giving Helen one of her swift, uncomfortable hugs.

'Well, take care of yourself.'

Helen noticed that there was no *Stay in touch* or *I'll talk to you soon*. This was it. The end of the road. Her aunt was effectively severing whatever fragile ties there might have remained between them. 'I will.'

'Bye then,' said Tommy. He gave a quick wave, then laid a protective hand on Helen's shoulder and ushered her along the drive.

Helen climbed into the Cortina and sat back, still clutching the *A to Z*. Her heart had started to thump again. She couldn't wait any longer. She had to know what was happening. Before Tommy could start the engine, she asked in a quiet, slightly breathless voice, 'Are we going to the Fox?'

'Sure, where else would we go?'

Helen glanced down at the floor and then up at him again. 'Only I thought ... What about Yvonne?'

'What about her?'

Helen wasn't sure how to phrase it. She struggled with the words, turning them over in her head. In the end, she just came straight out and said it. 'I thought she didn't want me staying with you any more. I thought you were going to send me away.'

'Are you kidding?' Tommy said. 'Why the hell would I do that? You're family. You've got a home with us for as long as you want.'

Helen gazed gratefully into his soft brown eyes. 'Really?'

'Really,' he said, his mouth breaking into a grin. 'You're a Quinn now, Mouse, so you'd better get used to the idea.'

Helen smiled back at him, her body awash with relief. 'A Quinn,' she murmured. It sounded strange on her lips, but she'd get used to it. And in that moment, she made a mental promise: no matter what it took, whatever she had to do, she would never let him down. She would make him proud of her. She would be the very best Quinn that she could possibly be.

# PART THREE

# 1974

# 24

As Helen collected the glasses from the table, she felt a familiar groping pressure on the back of her leg. Without even looking, she slapped the hand off her thigh with well-practised ease. Then she turned towards the owner of the offending paw, looked straight into his eyes, smiling sweetly, and said, 'Do that again, honey, and you'll be eating with a hook.'

The man pulled a face, pretending to be shocked. 'Aw, babe, I was only being friendly.'

'Well, keep your hands to yourself or you can go and be friendly someplace else.'

Helen moved away, unfazed by the exchange. He wasn't the first lecherous customer who had tried it on with her, and he wouldn't be the last. Although she didn't welcome the attention, she was learning to deal with it. Over the past six months – during which time she had celebrated her fifteenth birthday, shot up several inches and developed some unexpected curves – men had suddenly started taking an interest in her. On the whole, this turn of events had proved more bemusing than flattering, but she was trying to take it in her stride.

It was Friday lunchtime and the place was packed. Since Tommy had bought the Fox, he'd increased the takings tenfold, turning it into one of the most popular pubs in the East End. It was down to his skill as a landlord that the clientele, a curious mix of locals, toms, students, artists and villains, somehow managed to mix harmoniously with each other. He was able to make everyone feel welcome, never forgetting a face or a name and always willing to lend a sympathetic ear to any customer with a problem. There was rarely trouble, even during the regular lock-ins, when the booze flowed freely and inhibitions tended to be shed.

As she placed the dirty glasses on the counter, Helen glanced in the mirror behind the bar. Whenever she caught her reflection these days, she was surprised by what she saw. Both her face and her body seemed to be changing faster than she could keep up with them. Her tomboy looks had gone, to be replaced by those of a young woman. She didn't view herself as attractive – Debs and Karen were the pretty ones – but she was more or less satisfied with what she'd got. It had taken a long time, but she was finally beginning to feel comfortable in her own skin.

To her left, Frank Meyer was perched on a stool, nursing a pint that Tommy had poured for him over half an hour ago. Helen caught his eye and smiled shyly.

'That geezer giving you trouble?' he asked, frowning.

'I can handle it.'

'You shouldn't have to. Anyway, why aren't you at school?'

Helen swept back her long brown hair and gave a shrug. 'It's only PE this afternoon,' she lied. 'I may as well be here.' In recent months, she had taken to bunking off more and more often. She hated school and would have left for good if the law had allowed her to. It was only here, in the Fox, that she didn't feel the need to hide away and was able to be herself.

'You're a bright girl, Mouse. You could go a long way. You shouldn't waste your opportunities.'

Helen blushed, as she always did when he paid her any kind of compliment. She couldn't say for sure when her crush on Frank Meyer had started. The feelings had crept up on her gradually, until they were as strong and powerful as her eleven-year-old yearnings for David Cassidy. She was realistic enough to know that he was too old for her, but that didn't stop her heart from missing a beat every time she set eyes on him. 'I'm not wasting them,' she said.

'You could do anything, go anywhere. You don't want to be stuck in Kellston for the rest of your life.'

Helen tilted her head, as if he might have a point, but the truth was that she *did* want to stay here. She had no desire to go anywhere else. Debs was working in a salon in the West End and Karen in a trendy boutique on the King's Road. Although Helen envied them their freedom from the prison of school, she didn't covet their jobs. She was happy here, working alongside Tommy. Before Frank could press her further on the subject of her future, she quickly changed the subject. 'So how's it going at the new flat? Have you settled in all right?'

'It's okay,' Frank said, with all the indifference of a man who didn't really care where he lived.

Helen knew that he travelled light, a fact that made her feel faintly anxious. Last month, when he'd moved out of Bethnal Green and into the second-floor apartment on Barley Road, she had gone along with Tommy to give a helping hand. It hadn't taken long. There had been no furniture to shift – the new flat was already furnished – and there hadn't been much else either, only his clothes, a small TV, a record player, a radio, some kitchen stuff and a few boxes of LPs and books. She had a constant nagging worry that one day he would decide to move on again, throw all his possessions in the back of his car and disappear for good.

'I like it,' she said. 'Do you think you'll stay there?'

'It'll do . . . for now.'

The answer did little to allay Helen's fears. 'For now?' she echoed faintly. The flat, which overlooked the Green, was light and spacious, with clean white walls. It was simply but smartly furnished, a very male space without any feminine frills.

Frank took a sip of his beer and put the glass down on the counter. He didn't answer her question, or maybe he simply hadn't heard. It was noisy in the pub and the jukebox was playing. 'If you got some qualifications, you could go to college.'

'You didn't,' she said, disappointed to find the focus back on education again. 'And you haven't done so badly.'

He gave a wry smile. 'Depends on how you look at it.'

Helen gazed briefly into his cool grey eyes. She'd known Frank for over four years, but she still didn't really know anything about him. His private life – if he had one – was as much a mystery to her as it had been when they'd first met.

Although she now understood Yvonne's sly innuendoes about his sexuality, she didn't want to believe them. It might be true that he didn't ogle women, but he didn't ogle men either.

Frank finished his drink and stood up. 'Right, I'd best be off.'

'Are you coming back later?' she asked, in what she hoped was a suitably casual tone.

'Why? You missing me already?'

Helen blushed furiously. 'No, I just ... I didn't ... I meant ...'

'It's okay,' he said, laughing. 'I was only kidding.'

She inwardly cursed her lack of composure. How come she could deal with all the lecherous oafs that came in here, but dissolved into jelly the minute she was standing close to Frank Meyer? Fortunately, she was saved from any further embarrassment by Tommy placing two pints of lager on the counter.

'Do us a favour will you, hon, and take these over to the old man.'

Helen grabbed the glasses and made her escape as quickly as she could. She was halfway across the room, forging a path through the crowd, when she realised that she hadn't even said goodbye to Frank. Looking back, she was just in time to see him open the door and walk out.

'Eh, watch where you're going or you'll have it all over me!'

Quickly, she turned to find herself staring into the sallow face of Pym, one of the older members of Joe Quinn's entourage. He was a skinny, furtive kind of man who, even when he was speaking to you, was forever glancing over your shoulder as if afraid of missing something or someone more interesting. Although she wasn't certain of his exact job description, she knew that his position was a lowly one. He prowled around Joe like a hungry mongrel begging for scraps from the table.

'Sorry,' she said.

'Clean on, this shirt was,' he grumbled.

The shirt, which had once been white, was now faded and worn. It was a greyish colour, like the 'before' example in the Daz washing powder advertisements. Although some of the lager had slopped out over her hand, not a drop so far as she could see had touched his shirt. 'I don't think any of it went on you.'

Pym pursed his lips. 'Not the point, though, is it? It *might* have done, and then where would I be? You ought to be more careful.'

'Sorry,' she muttered again before stepping to one side and manoeuvring around him. But now that one unpleasant encounter was over, she had yet another to face. Joe Quinn was sitting at his usual corner table, puffing on a fag while he talked to his older son. Connor had come out of jail three weeks ago, and Helen was already wishing that they'd bang him up again. He was a chip off the old block in every way, with the same physical characteristics as his father and the same filthy temper. He was a nasty piece of work, with a split personality. Vicious one minute, nice as pie the next, you could never tell what mood you'd find him in.

Helen placed the pints down on the table and tried to make a speedy escape, but Connor wasn't having any of it. Never one to pass over the opportunity for a spot of niece-tormenting, he grabbed this one with enthusiasm.

'Hang on,' he said, staring at the glass. 'What's this?'

'Lager,' she replied. 'Tommy asked me to bring it over.'

'I know what it is,' he said, frowning at her. 'But where's the rest of it? Isn't it supposed to be a pint?'

Helen glanced down. There was no more than a quarter of an inch of the drink missing. She felt like saying that as he wasn't paying for it anyway – he'd done nothing but freeload since he'd been released – he should be grateful for what he got. And it wasn't as if he was even short of money. She didn't know how much Tommy had given him for his share of the Fox, but it had been enough to buy the brand-new red Triumph Spitfire that was parked out back. 'You want me to top it up for you?' she said through gritted teeth.

Connor sat back and folded his arms across his chest. 'Place has gone downhill since you owned it, Dad.' He scowled up at Helen, his dark eyes full of contempt. 'The staff are too busy chatting up their boyfriends to provide a decent service. Don't you think he's a bit old for you, love?'

Helen stared back at him. 'W-what?' she stammered. Mortified that Connor had somehow worked out her feelings for Frank Meyer, she felt the blood burn into her cheeks again. 'What do you mean?'

'Oh, I think I hit a nerve,' Connor said, smirking. 'You two going steady, then?'

Joe slapped his palm on the table and laughed like a drain. 'Going steady,' he repeated. 'That's a good one!' Then, as quickly as he had started laughing, he stopped. Looking Helen up and down, he gave a sneer. 'Jesus, even Pym isn't *that* desperate.'

211

Helen suddenly realised that it hadn't been Frank they were talking about at all. She glared hard at the two men before turning her back and hurrying away. 'Bastards,' she hissed softly to herself as she pushed through the crowd. Her face was still hot, her heart drumming in her chest. For the past couple of years – ever since Joe had moved out of the Fox – she'd been able to relax, but now Connor was stirring things up again. She wished he was dead. She wished both of them were dead.

Once she was safely at the bar, Helen looked back towards the corner. The two of them were hunched over the table, deep in conversation. Plotting. They were always plotting. Things had been good until Connor had come back, but now all that was changing. She knew with a dull, despairing certainty that something bad was going to happen, and there was nothing she could do to stop it.

# 25

Tommy lay on his back, gazing up at the ceiling. With his eyes he traced a series of hairline cracks that radiated from the light fixture like a spider's web, wondering if they were superficial or indicative of a deeper structural problem. What if one day the whole ceiling collapsed while he was lying here? He had a sudden mental image of the cracks joining up, becoming wider and deeper until finally all the hard white plaster shattered and came tumbling down in a heap. Perhaps he should have a word with the landlord.

Tommy frowned and lowered his gaze to the crown of Shelley Anne's head. He studied the dark roots at the parting of her blonde hair and the swaying movement of her breasts as she tried to suck him off. She was doing all the right things, even making those little throaty noises that usually turned him on so much, but today nothing was happening. He shifted up on to his elbows, hoping that a better view might kick-start his libido. The problem was that he had too many other things on his mind.

He tried to relax, to sweep away the niggling worries, but no sooner had he dismissed one problem than another popped up to take its place. Until a few weeks back, everything had been A1, his life nicely sorted, the future looking rosy. Even Yvonne had stopped giving him grief. A fur coat, a Cartier watch and a two-week family holiday in Spain had finally silenced most of her ongoing complaints about the Fox. She'd done her nut, mind, when he'd first told her he was buying the place. That was a couple of years ago now. Jesus, where had all the time gone? If he had that kind of money going spare, she'd said, he could damn well buy a decent house for his wife and kids to live in.

Tommy tried to get her voice out of his head. It wasn't helping any. He closed his eyes for a moment, but then all he could see was Connor looming over him, his face dark and angry and filled with reproach. Ever since his brother had been released, he'd been gunning for him, blaming Tommy for *not sorting the witnesses, not sorting the jury, not even sorting the bleedin' bail.*

Tommy breathed out a sigh. It pissed him off that he was getting all the flak. And it wasn't as if he hadn't tried. It was hardly his fault if the fixer had returned his cash and the witnesses had all been under police protection. Even the jury had been impossible to nobble, the few weak links and their families being carefully guarded by the filth. And anyway, why was the finger being pointed exclusively at him? The old man hadn't been any more successful in *his* attempts to get him off the hook and yet Connor wasn't throwing any blame in his direction. Still, that was likely to change. Connor and Joe had always been tight, but their relationship was a stormy one.

Tommy shifted his position slightly and scratched at his chest. Yeah, the honeymoon period would soon be over. It might be all sunshine and roses now, but it wouldn't last. Before long, his brother and his father would be at each other's throats again. And that, although it might get Connor off his back for a while, wasn't anything to look forward to either.

Aware that the afternoon encounter was beyond saving, Tommy gently patted Shelley Anne on the shoulder. 'Give it a rest, eh, hon?'

She released him with a show of reluctance, her big blue eyes containing a slightly hurt expression, as if her inability to bring him to climax reflected badly on her womanly skills.

'What's wrong, babe? What's up?'

'Well, we know one thing that isn't,' he said, trying to make a joke of it. 'It's getting late, love. I have to get back to the pub.' He swung his legs over the side of the bed, strapped his watch back round his wrist and reached down for his Y-fronts.

Shelley Anne watched him while he got dressed, sitting sideways on the eiderdown with her pale legs bent at the knees. 'It's not late. It's only five past three. What are you rushing off for?'

'I'm not rushing off. I just . . . ' He stood up and pulled on his trousers. 'You know what it's like at the moment. When Connor's around, there's always trouble. I just want to keep an eye on things.' Quickly, he slipped on his shirt and fastened the buttons. 'It'll settle down in a week or two and then we can get back to normal.'

'Why should it?' she asked.

He glanced over at her. 'What?'

'Why should it be any different in a week or two? Your Connor's got a screw loose. That ain't gonna change no matter how long you wait. He'll still be a pain in the arse by the time Christmas comes around.'

Tommy gave a shrug. She had a point. 'Yeah, but in a few weeks he'll have found someone else to be pissed off at.'

'You reckon?'

'Sure,' he said. 'And until then, I'm gonna watch my back.'

Shelley Anne unwound her legs, slipped off the bed and draped her arms around his neck. 'I could do that for you,' she whispered in his ear. Her lips found his mouth, her tongue flicking against his. 'If you really want me to.'

As she pressed herself up against him, Tommy felt a stirring in his groin. Perhaps after all there wasn't that much urgency about getting back to the Fox. He gave in to temptation for a while, moving against her body, his hands rising to fondle the soft roundness of her breasts. It was only as her fingers scrabbled to undo the buttons on his shirt that the image of Connor leapt into his head again. If ever there was a passion killer, it was that. Pulling away, he gave a quick shake of his head. 'I'm sorry, hon. Sorry, but I've really got to go.'

'Okay, but call me, huh?'

Tommy grabbed his jacket and made for the door. 'I will. Bye, love.' He took the stairs two at a time, left by the main front door and half walked, half jogged along the street to where the black Ford Capri was parked. Before he got in, he had a quick look round to make sure that he hadn't been seen by anyone he knew. Part of the attraction of his relationship with Shelley Anne was the fact that it was a secret. Even after all these years, he still enjoyed the idea of eating forbidden fruit.

He turned the key in the ignition and the engine sprang instantly and smoothly into life. Although he loved the new Capri, he still felt a twang of regret when he thought of his old unreliable Cortina. The trouble was that you got used to things, got attached to them and then missed them when they'd gone. Well, *some* things. He wouldn't miss Yvonne if he ever managed to get rid of her.

Tommy indicated and pulled out into the line of traffic. Another couple of years, he reckoned, and he'd have enough to pay her off. By then the girls would be at the age where they were pretty well leading their own lives. Not that he would ever stop worrying about them; every day they went up West to work he was haunted by the fear of IRA bombs. What if they were in the wrong place at the wrong time and ... No, he couldn't bear to think about it.

There was a smattering of rain against the windscreen. He glanced up at the forbidding grey skies and shuddered. He knew that you couldn't live your life always being afraid of what was around the corner, but these were dangerous times. And it wasn't just the dire political situation that was weighing on his mind. With the return of Connor, there was bound to be strife. His brother was unpredictable and uncontrollable. He'd gone on a week-long bender after he'd been released, boozing and whoring, but now he was back full of anger and bitterness and armed with enough recriminations to start a third world war.

Tommy tapped the wheel as he waited for the traffic lights to turn to green. Connor was already asking awkward questions about where the cash had come from to buy the Fox. He'd fobbed him off with the same story as he'd told his father – that he'd got lucky in a game of poker – but he sensed that Connor wasn't entirely convinced. He didn't want him to know about the long-firm frauds he had going with Frank Meyer. Once Connor started poking his nose in, things were bound to go pear-shaped. The frauds needed patience, and his brother had the attention span of a gnat.

Tommy grinned as he thought about the Romford deal. It had taken two years, but it had been worth it in the end. Now they had another on the go in Dagenham. If this one went as smoothly as the last, he'd make enough to pay off Yvonne, a generous divorce settlement that she wouldn't be able to refuse. And why should she? It wasn't as if there was much love lost between them these days. A good chunk of cash would enable her to buy a fancy house and have all the clothes and holidays she wanted, while he got on with doing what he liked best – running the Fox.

Tommy's smile faltered a little as he considered what he'd do after a divorce. Would he marry Shelley Anne? He knew that was what she expected – and probably what she deserved after waiting all this time – but he wasn't sure if he wanted to be tied down again. He was realistic enough to know that an illicit affair, with all its seductive stolen moments, was a damn sight different to living with someone twenty-four hours a day. It wouldn't take long for the magic to disappear.

Fifteen minutes later, Tommy pulled into the car park of the Fox. After getting out of the Capri, he stood for a moment gazing up at the pub. Sometimes he still couldn't believe that he actually owned it. Every brick, every fixture and fitting, every glass and bottle: it was all his. He couldn't say for sure why he had such an attachment to the place, but he thought it was connected to the happy times he'd spent here as a kid. For five glorious years, from when he was seven to when he was twelve, his father had been banged up and his mum had run the pub on her own. It was the only time he'd ever heard her laugh. Tommy sighed. He would never stop missing her, just as he would never forget how badly Joe Quinn had treated her.

Tommy unlocked the back door and walked into the narrow passageway. Out of habit he sauntered through to the bar, even though opening time wasn't for another hour and a half. A quick glance told him that Mouse had been busy. The room was spotless, the bar polished and gleaming. He smiled. She was a grafter, that one, with the same affection for the pub as he had. It made him sad that neither of his daughters seemed to care about the place, but that was life and he'd just have to accept it.

Tommy was about to leave and go upstairs when he heard a thin scraping noise, like the sound of a chair moving against the floor. 'Mouse?' He waited a moment but there was no response. 'Mouse, is that you?' He leaned down behind the bar, picked up the baseball bat and headed quietly towards the adjoining room. If some little scrote was trying to rob him, then he'd be sorry he'd ever got up this morning.

As he slid through the doorway, Tommy was holding his

breath. What if there was more than one of them? Well, it was too late to worry about that now. He took two steps into the room, his eyes darting left and right, his ears tuned to any hint of a movement. He could feel his heart pumping in his chest. And then it came again, that scraping noise, followed by what sounded like the clearing of a throat. It was emanating from the third and smallest room at the back of the pub.

This time Tommy didn't stop to think about the consequences. With the adrenalin coursing through his veins, he lifted the bat to shoulder height and charged forward, ready to do battle. He saw the intruder immediately; the guy had his back to him and was kneeling on the floor, scrabbling around under one of the tables. Tommy was within striking distance when the man suddenly turned his head and gazed up at him, his eyes widening as he saw the baseball bat.

'Shit, man, what are you doing?'

As Tommy realised who it was, he stopped dead, his arm still in mid-air, poised like a freeze frame in a movie. It was his brother. It was Connor. The breath rushed out of his lungs in one almighty stream. 'What the hell are *you* doing?'

'Dropped me lighter, didn't I?' Connor, who had an unlit fag hanging from the corner of his mouth, held up the silver Zippo with a grin of triumph. 'You gonna put that thing down or what?'

Tommy glared back at him but lowered the bat. 'I meant what the fuck are you doing *here*?'

Connor got slowly to his feet, with all the studied care of a drunk who was trying to look sober. 'Well that's a fine welcome if ever I heard one.'

Tommy glanced towards the table, where there was a half-empty bottle of whisky, a couple of glasses and an overflowing ashtray. 'Not that it ain't bleedin' obvious. You do remember that you don't live here any more?' It had been a relief when his father had decided to move into a fancy new flat down the road, and an even bigger one when Connor had decided to join him. 'You can't just waltz in here whenever you feel like it.'

Connor gave a snort and slumped down on the bench. 'Christ, you don't begrudge your own brother a few drinks, do you? I reckon it's the least I deserve after four years in the slammer.'

And Tommy knew that what he really meant was that he owed him. Connor was never going to forget the Quinn family failure to get him off the hook. 'How many times? I tried, okay? It ain't my fault if the filth had it in for you.'

'Hey, did I say a word? I get it, okay. I'm over it. It ain't a problem.' Connor patted the space on the bench beside him. 'Sit down, for Christ's sake. Let's have a drink together. We haven't had a chance for a proper chat since I got out. And put that bloody bat down. You're making me nervous standing over me like that.'

Tommy looked at him with suspicion. Connor wasn't the type to either forgive or forget, so he must be up to something. Carefully, he leaned the bat against the leg of the table and then pulled up a chair. He watched as his brother poured out a couple of whiskies.

'So who's been rattling your cage?' Connor asked.

'What do you mean?'

Connor pushed the glass across the table. 'I mean, what's with the weapon? You expecting visitors?'

221

'Nah, I just didn't expect to find anyone here.' Tommy took a sip of the whisky. The bottle had come from his better, more expensive stash of malt. 'I gave a shout. Why didn't you say something?'

Connor lit up and took a long drag. 'Do I look like I'm called Mouse?' He tapped his cigarette on the ashtray and glanced up again. 'What the fuck kind of name is that anyway?'

Tommy gave a shrug. 'You could have ended up with your skull caved in.'

'Yeah, right.' The mocking tone suggested that even if Tommy had gone for him, it wouldn't have been his head that ended up in pieces. Connor looked around the pub and nodded. 'Still, you've done a good job on the old place. Very nice.'

'I like it.'

'You've got her well trained.'

Tommy frowned. 'What?'

'Lynsey's brat. I saw her cleaning up earlier.' Connor took another long drag on his cigarette and then laughed loudly. 'A born scrubber, that one, just like her mother.'

Tommy slammed the glass down on the table, anger blazing in his eyes. 'Leave it out, Connor! You've got no fuckin' right to—'

'Hey, no need to go off on one. I'm only saying. It's in the blood, man. She'll turn out just the same as Lynsey. You wait and see. She's a liability. She'll be knocked up before you know it and then you'll have another mouth to feed.'

'You're a sick bastard. You know that?'

'Christ, you're touchy, ain't you?' Connor laughed again. 'You shouldn't take stuff so serious. I'm only kidding around.'

'Well it ain't funny,' Tommy said. 'So keep your filthy opinions to yourself.' He stared at his brother with disgust, wondering not for the first time how the two of them had turned out so differently. It was as if his father's genes had been poured undiluted straight into Connor's body, all the hate and spite and venom pooling in his veins. There wasn't an ounce of decency in the man.

Connor knocked back the whisky and poured himself another. 'Come on, bruv, keep up. You've barely touched that drink.'

'Some of us have to work tonight.'

'Don't call it work, do you? Piece of piss running this place.'

Tommy thought that was rich. Even when Connor had been managing the pub, he'd barely lifted a finger. 'You reckon?'

Connor leaned back, laid his left arm along the top of the bench and gave Tommy a long, sly look from over the rim of his glass. 'You know what I'm still trying to figure out? How the fuck you ever got the cash together to buy the Fox.'

'You know how. I've already told you.'

Connor pulled a face. 'You told me some pile-of-shite story about winning at poker, but that just don't add up. No offence Tommy boy, but you've always been crap at cards. And you ain't the luckiest guy in the world, either.' He gave a low, unpleasant snigger. 'I mean, I'm talking to the bloke who got himself landed with the lovely Yvonne.'

Tommy twisted the glass between his fingers. 'I ain't complaining,' he said, maybe a little too quickly. 'And everyone gets lucky once in their life.'

'Nah, it don't add up. It don't add up at all. I've been think-ing about it real hard, and I reckon I've sussed it out.'

'There ain't nothing to suss.'

'Sure there is.' Connor tilted his head and gave him a cool look. 'I've got eyes, bruv. I've got ears. I know what your game is. You think I'm stupid?'

'I think you're pissed,' Tommy said, trying to keep his voice as casual as possible. God, what if Connor had found out about the long-firm frauds? Frank would do his nut; he might even pull out, decide it was too risky to carry on. And then where would he be? Stuck with Yvonne for the rest of his nat-ural. Jeez, it didn't bear thinking about.

Connor suddenly lurched forward, pointing a finger at Tommy. 'You ain't as smart as you reckon, mate. Good old big-hearted Tommy. Always ready to help anyone out. Except it ain't really like that, is it?'

'You've lost me.'

'The brat,' Connor said. 'They paid you, didn't they? Those stinking Becks. They paid you to take the kid off their hands after our Lynsey kicked the bucket.'

Tommy, more out of relief than anything else, burst out laughing. 'Are you nuts? Where the fuck would they get that kind of money?'

Connor's face grew dark. He didn't like being laughed at. 'Nah, don't give me that. It makes sense. I mean, why else would you take the little bitch in? She ain't nothing to this family, *nothing*!'

'She's my niece, for fuck's sake,' Tommy said. 'And yours too, come to that.'

Connor gave a quick shake of his head. 'She ain't a Quinn.

She don't mean jack shit to me. I wouldn't piss on her if she was on fire.'

'Nice. I'm sure she shares the same warm feelings towards you.'

But Connor wasn't listening. 'Yeah, you and the old man were in this together. There's no way he'd have let Lynsey's brat within a mile of here unless there was something in it for him. The two of you split the cash and then gave me a slice to keep me sweet. How much they give you, then? It must have been some wedge.' He scowled into his drink. He was well bladdered now, and becoming paranoid. 'It ain't right. It stinks. What else have you two been up to? What else you been planning? Maybe I ain't welcome round here no more. Maybe I should be watching my back, huh?'

'You're crazy,' Tommy said, rising to his feet. 'I'm not listening to this.'

Connor shook his head again. 'It's not me who's crazy. And if the old man reckons he can do me over, he's got another think coming.'

Tommy raised his eyes to the ceiling. When his brother was in one of his drunken black moods, there was no reasoning with him. 'Whatever. I'm off. I'll see you later.'

'That's right, you just run away, like you always do.'

'Sure,' Tommy said. 'I'm running all the way upstairs.' When he reached the door, he glanced quickly back. Connor was hunched over, steadily banging his fist on the table and muttering to himself. He made a mental note to get the locks changed first thing in the morning.

# 26

It was dark by the time Helen and Moira emerged from the cinema and headed towards Connolly's. A chill March wind whipped through the air, but Helen barely felt it. Her mind was far away from the grey streets of Kellston, still focused on the tragic fate of Jay Gatsby in a very blue swimming pool in a mansion in Long Island.

'So, did you enjoy it?' Moira asked.

'It was kind of sad.'

Moira linked her arm through Helen's. 'Yes, it was that all right.'

Helen thought about Daisy Buchanan, with her golden hair and cool white dresses. 'I don't get why he loved her so much. I mean, she never really cared about him, did she? Not right down in her heart, not where it matters.'

Moira glanced at her and smiled. 'Well, that's men for you. They always want what they can't have.'

'I guess,' Helen said, although she had no idea if this was

true or not. She wondered what it would be like to be so adored by a man, so loved, that he would do anything for you. That kind of thing, of course, didn't happen to girls like her. It only happened to wide-eyed beauties with perfect skin and soft, seductive mouths.

It had started to rain, so they quickly crossed the road and jogged the last few yards to the café. Helen felt the warmth as she pushed open the door, a welcoming blast of hot air, and gave an involuntary shiver. Connolly's was nearly always quiet at this time – the lull that came between the afternoon shoppers and the evening customers – and today was no different. They made their way to their usual table by the window, sat down and picked up the menus.

Over recent years, it had become part of their regular Saturday routine to see a film in the late afternoon and then come for something to eat at Connolly's. It was a chance for them to catch up on the week's events, to exchange news and gossip and have a good moan about the world in general.

'What do you fancy?' Moira asked. 'I think I'll have the shepherd's pie.'

'Er . . .' Helen scanned down the menu before choosing what she always went for. 'I'll have a cheeseburger and chips.'

Although Helen thought of Moira as more of a friend than a mother replacement, she was aware that the older woman had taken on some aspects of that maternal role. It was Moira, after all, who had taken her to buy her first bra, explained about periods and even had the awkward talk with her about boys and sex. Had the job been left to Yvonne, Helen would have remained in ignorance.

Moira gave the order to the waitress and then turned back to Helen. 'So, how's it going at the Fox?'

Helen gave a shrug. 'Not bad. You know what Connor's like. But it's okay, I can deal with it.'

'Yes, well, he's just like Joe. Neither of them has got a decent bone in their body.'

'Worse,' Helen said. 'At least you know where you are with Joe. Connor's kind of . . . I don't know . . . creepy. There's just something about him. He gives me the shudders.'

Moira looked at her anxiously. 'He hasn't . . . I mean, he hasn't been giving you any trouble? Not hurting you in any way?'

'No, nothing like that. It's just the way he looks at me. And the things he says sometimes. It freaks me out.'

Moira gave a sympathetic nod. 'He always was a nasty little bugger, even when he was young. Best thing is to try and keep your distance. Stay away from him as much as you can.'

'I do.'

'And tell Tommy if he gives you any grief.'

'Of course I will.' Although the truth was that Helen didn't like running to Tommy whenever she had a problem with someone. It felt like grassing, and she knew the rules about that. She decided to change the subject. 'Anyway, do you think you'll ever get married again?'

Moira looked startled for a second, and then she laughed. 'Where on earth did that come from?'

'Oh, sorry, I was just thinking about the film. Daisy didn't love her husband, but she still went back to him. I wouldn't have. I'd have stayed with Gatsby.'

'You and the rest of the female population.' Moira picked

up her fork, tapped it a few times against the tablecloth and then laid it down again. 'And in answer to your question, I doubt it. Well, not unless Robert Redford comes knocking on my door, and the likelihood of that is just about zero.'

'You never know.'

'Only in my dreams, sweetheart. Only in my dreams.'

Helen wasn't aware of all the ins and outs of Moira's failed marriage, but she had gathered enough to know that it had been a miserable and painful affair. Her husband, a feckless gambling man, had squandered most of her inheritance and then turned to drink. By the time she threw him out, the house and the bookies – left to her by her father – had both been lost.

'So how's school?' Moira asked.

Helen averted her eyes, pretending to scrutinise the rain-swept street. 'Yeah, it's okay.'

'Tell me you haven't been bunking off again?' A thin sigh escaped from Moira's lips. 'Helen?'

'Not really.' Helen glanced back at her. 'Well, only the odd afternoon. I can't see the point of it. As soon as I'm sixteen, I can leave and work full-time in the pub. I don't need any qualifications for that.'

'But what if you change your mind or want to run your own pub one day? You're a smart girl, love. You could do anything if you put your mind to it.'

But what Helen wanted was to be free of the shackles of school, to earn some proper money and get on with things. She had never properly explained how lonely it was for her at Kellston Comp. It was only in the Fox, working beside Tommy and surrounded by the customers, that she felt there was any purpose to her life. 'It's all right. I've already had the lecture from Frank.'

'Frank?'

'Yeah, this lunchtime. He was in the pub and . . . and he said the same thing. Kind of. We were talking and . . . well, you know . . . '

Moira watched her carefully for a moment, and then said, 'He's a nice guy, isn't he?'

Helen blushed furiously, wishing that she'd never mentioned him now. She chewed on her lower lip for a while and then gave a casual shrug. 'He's all right.'

Moira gave her a knowing smile. 'When I was your age, I had a mad crush on Tommy. I used to worship the ground he walked on, thought he was the best thing since sliced bread. Of course he never looked twice at me. I was just his little sister's gawky friend. I never told anyone, not even your mum, about it . . . well, not until now.'

Helen took a few seconds to absorb this surprising piece of information before launching into a vehement denial. 'I don't have a crush on Frank. Not in the slightest. I mean, I like him, but not like that. There wouldn't be any point, would there? Him being, you know, the way he is.'

Moira's eyebrows shifted up a notch. 'And what way is that?'

Helen glanced briefly out of the window again. She shouldn't have said anything. She should have just dismissed the idea with a joke and quickly changed the subject. Instead, in trying to cover up her feelings, she was only making it all worse. 'That he . . . ' She hesitated, not wanting to use the word *queer*. 'That he'd rather go out with men than women.'

'Who on earth told you that?' Moira asked. A light huffing

came from the back of her throat. 'Oh, I bet it was Yvonne, wasn't it? God, that woman's such a stirrer. You can't believe a word that comes out of her mouth.'

'So it's not true?'

'Of course it's not true.'

Helen's heart gave a tiny leap, even though she knew her love for him was hopeless. 'How can you be sure?'

'Just because a man doesn't chase everything in a skirt doesn't mean he's homosexual.'

The waitress arrived with the food, along with a glass of Coke and a mug of tea. Moira, who was taking over the woman's shift in half an hour, had a chat with her, and when the conversation was over, neither Moira nor Helen returned to the subject of Frank Meyer.

Shortly after six o'clock, Helen said her goodbyes and left the café. The rain was coming down harder now, and she turned up the collar of her coat. As she walked back towards the Fox, she glanced across the Green towards the windows of Frank's flat. They were in darkness. Did this mean he was already at the pub, or was he somewhere else? She hurried her pace a little, hoping that it was the former.

Crossing the road by the station, her thoughts swung back to Moira's revelation about her teenage feelings for Tommy, and she couldn't help wondering how different things would have been if the two of them had fallen in love and got married. There would be no Yvonne, for starters. Despite her best efforts, Helen had not been able to forge any kind of meaningful relationship with her. From the day she'd arrived, Yvonne had resented her presence, and nothing had changed since then.

Helen strode into the car park, went round to the side of the building and unlocked the back door. As she stepped into the corridor, she heard the familiar sounds of clinking glasses, music and laughter. There was always a buzz to the place, but Saturday night had a particular charge all of its own. With another working week over, the lads had money in their pockets and the girls were looking forward to helping them spend it.

After hanging her damp coat on a peg, Helen shook the rain from her hair and went through to the bar. Tommy was busy serving, along with three pretty barmaids, who were all brunettes. Deciding to follow his head rather than his heart, he had long ago given up trying to hire blondes. It wasn't worth the aggro from Yvonne.

'Hey, Mouse,' he said. 'How are you doing?'

'I'm good,' she said, while her eyes quickly scanned the bar for Frank. There was no sign of him. Disappointed, she grabbed a cloth and headed for the tables. Although it was still early, there was already a decent-sized crowd and plenty of familiar faces. Of these, some she was glad to see and others not so.

Joe Quinn was in his regular spot in the corner, along with most of his entourage, including Fat Pete, Vinnie Keane and Terry Street. But no Connor, she was relieved to see. Although she still loathed and despised Joe, she was no longer terrified of him. But one legacy of that frightening encounter in the cellar still remained. Like glue, his words had stuck tight to the inside of her mind – *bad blood, bad blood* – and no matter how hard she tried, she could never peel them off.

For the next few hours, Helen flitted between the tables,

gathering glasses, emptying the ashtrays and keeping everything clean and tidy. As soon as she had finished one round of the pub, it was time to start again. Yvonne came downstairs at eight o'clock, taking a seat near the bar where she could keep one eye on Tommy and the other on any good-looking men who might enter her field of vision. Carol Gatesby was with her, and the two of them, dressed up to the nines, flirted outrageously with any male who cast a glance in their direction.

Every time Helen went past, Yvonne would lean in to Carol and whisper in her ear. Then the two of them would snigger like a pair of schoolgirls. Helen knew they were laughing at her, putting her down, and although she tried to ignore it, a part of her still curled up inside. Through the years, Yvonne's dislike of her had grown rather than diminished, and now she didn't even try to hide it.

Every time Helen returned to the bar, she hoped to see Frank sitting there. But time and time again she was disappointed. Perhaps he wasn't coming. Her heart sank at the thought. What if he was out with a girl, having a meal up West followed by a romantic moonlit walk along the Serpentine? But then she noticed the windows, splattered with rain, and felt a small wave of relief. No one in their right mind would take a walk in the park in this weather.

The time ticked by and Helen kept a constant watch on the door, looking over whenever it opened, carefully hiding her dismay when the customer turned out not to be him. It was twenty past ten before her vigilance was finally rewarded. Frank came in alone and made his way through the crowd towards the bar. Standing head and shoulders above everyone else, he was easy to spot.

Helen gathered up some glasses, and after a suitable delay – she didn't want to appear too obvious – followed him to the counter. By time she got there, he'd already been served his pint and was standing chatting to Tommy. As she came up behind him, she noticed his elegant grey suit and wondered where he'd been for the rest of the evening. Taking a deep breath, she urged herself not to blush before she sidled in beside him and placed the dirty glasses on the bar.

'Hiya,' she said, overbrightly.

Frank looked down at her and smiled. 'Hi, Mouse. They're keeping you busy tonight.'

'Yeah.' She searched for something witty or interesting to add, but her mind had gone blank. *What's the matter with you? Speak, you idiot. Say something.* But the only thing that came out of her mouth was a thin, despondent sigh. Fortunately, before she was completely crushed by embarrassment, Tommy came to her rescue.

'You want to take a break, love? Let me get you a drink.'

'Oh, okay. Thanks. I'll have a Coke.'

There was a queue at the bar, and she found herself squashed between the line of customers and Frank. She was so close to him that she could smell the dampness of his jacket and the slight whiff of his citrus aftershave. Just above the noise of the crowd, Barry Blue's 'Dancing on a Saturday Night' floated out from the jukebox.

Frank leaned down towards her and said, 'So, did you and Moira go and see a film today?'

Glad that he at least had found a topic of conversation, she gave a grateful nod. '*The Great Gatsby*. It was good. Have you seen it yet?'

Frank shook his head. 'I'm not sure it's my kind of thing.'

'What do you like?' she asked, eager to glean any tiny piece of information about him.

But she was never to find out the answer to her question. Right at that moment, Connor Quinn crashed into the pub, wielding a baseball bat. He staggered over to his father's table in the corner, steadied himself on the back of Terry Street's chair, opened his mouth and started spewing out a tirade against Joe. 'Call yourself a fuckin' father? Four bleedin' years I've done. Four bleedin' years and this is what I come back to. You think I don't know what you're up to? You think I'm fuckin' stupid? You think I ain't got a brain? Well, I get it, I fuckin' get it, and nobody fucks me over, nobody! So if you think—'

The rest of what he had to say was lost as the crowd quickly separated and shifted back, moving just far enough away to be out of swinging distance without actually missing any of the action.

'Oh, for God's sake,' Tommy said.

Helen saw him glance down beneath the counter and immediately knew what he was checking out. He didn't need to. Even she was certain that the bat in Connor's hand, the one with the distinctive blue and red twine wrapped around the handle, was the bat that normally lived under the bar. She was suddenly reminded of what had happened to the Gissings, of how Mickey Stott had paid them back for what they'd done, and she looked nervously towards the corner.

Connor's face was tight and angry, his eyes blazing. Joe, across the other side of the table, had stood up and was trying to calm him down, albeit not in a particularly effective manner.

'Are you off yer fuckin' head? What's wrong with you?'

'*You're* the fuckin' matter, old man. Think you can do me out of my share, do you? Think you can fuckin' rob me! Well, I ain't having it. I know your game, and it won't fuckin' wash.'

Fat Pete and Vinnie jumped to their feet too, at which point Connor swung the bat in the general direction of the three of them. He missed his target, but the bat landed with a thwack on the table, shattering several glasses and showering the men with a mix of glass and lager. 'I'll kill you! I'll fuckin' kill you all!'

The next thing Helen knew, Tommy had rushed out from behind the bar. She went to go too, but Frank laid a restraining hand on her shoulder. 'Stay here,' he ordered, before following his mate. But Terry Street acted before either of them had even got within yards of the table. With one swift movement, he turned, grabbed the wide end of the bat and flipped it neatly out of Connor's hand. Connor, in a vain attempt to wrestle it back, stumbled and fell in a heap to the floor. For a while, he gazed up at the ceiling with a glazed expression in his eyes, then he twisted his head, saw his father looking down at him and burst out laughing. 'Your face! Your fuckin' face! You're finished, man, and you know it!'

A ripple of anticipation ran through the crowd. The Saturday night entertainment had never been so good. Joe Quinn, one of the biggest villains in the East End, attacked and then mocked by his own son in public. Open-mouthed, everyone waited to see what would happen next.

But Joe wasn't prepared to give them the satisfaction. As if he'd discovered something unpleasant lying on the floor, he walked around the table and nudged his son's chest with the toe of his boot. Then he glanced up at Tommy. 'Get the stupid bastard out of here.'

With Tommy taking one arm and Frank the other, the two of them finally managed to haul Connor to his feet.

'Upstairs,' Tommy said. 'Let's get him up to the flat.'

Helen watched as the two men dragged him towards the hall. As they passed by the bar, Connor grinned at her.

'Hey there, Mouse, little Mouse. Aren't you gonna give your uncle Connor a good-night kiss?'

'Just shut the fuck up,' Frank said. 'Haven't you done enough damage for one night?'

'Just shut the fuck up, just shut the fuck up,' Connor mimicked. Then he burst out laughing again. 'His face. Did you see his bleedin' face?'

Helen looked towards the corner, where Vinnie and Terry were picking up the broken glass. Joe was standing with his hands on his hips, still glaring after his older son. Then, becoming aware of the attention still on him, he suddenly turned and addressed the audience. 'Show's over,' he said roughly. 'You can all get back to your drinks.'

But Helen only had to look in his eyes to know that nothing was over yet.

## 27

Terry Street made one complete circuit of the Inner Circle before stopping the car and switching off the engine. He sat and waited for another five minutes until he was certain that he hadn't been followed. There was no reason why he should have been, but the stakes were high and it was better to be safe than sorry.

The sky was low and grey and filled with clouds as he made his way along York Bridge to the Regent's Park tennis courts. It was, he thought, the perfect place for a meeting, with the chances of him bumping into anyone he knew virtually zero. As he walked, he turned up the collar of his overcoat. It was a chilly morning, and that was all to the good. The fewer people around, the better.

All of the tennis courts were empty apart from one at the far end, where a middle-aged man and a boy of about twelve were knocking balls across the net. The guy seemed more enthusiastic than the kid, running back and forth and barking out orders. The kid looked like he'd rather be in bed.

Terry checked out the first bench he came to, saw that it was dry and sat down. He checked his watch and then opened his copy of the *News of the World*. He liked to keep abreast of the latest scandals. It was another ten minutes before he heard the sound of footsteps on the path and glanced up to see DI Tony Lazenby approaching.

'All right?' Terry said.

Lazenby gave a nod, sat down beside him and crossed his legs. 'Interesting choice of venue. You thinking of taking up the game?'

'Not right away. I'm kind of busy these days.'

'Other games to play, huh?'

'Something like that.'

There was a brief silence while the DI took out a pack of cigarettes, prised one from the carton and lit it with a fancy gold lighter. He didn't offer the pack to Terry. 'I hear there was trouble at the Fox last night.'

'News travels fast.'

Lazenby's mouth slid into a sly smile. 'Didn't I tell you? Nothing happens that I don't get to hear about. You fart in your sleep, Terry, and I'll know about it before you do.'

Terry grinned. 'Anyone ever tell you that too much knowledge can be a bad thing?' Lazenby was just flexing his muscles, letting him know who was boss, and he was perfectly happy to go along with it – for now. 'I told you I'd deliver, and I will.'

'One row in a pub doesn't add up to much.'

'You had to be there,' Terry said. 'And anyway, this is just the start. Believe me, everything's going exactly to plan.'

'If you say so.'

But Terry *knew* so. He'd been dripping poison into Connor's ear ever since he'd got out of the slammer: how Joe didn't rate him, how he was cutting him out of deals, how he had plans for the business that didn't include his older son. Oh yes, he and Connor had become best buddies over the past few weeks.

'And how do I know I can trust you?'

'You can't,' Terry said. 'Any more than I can trust you. But ask yourself this: who would you prefer to be running Kellston – Joe Quinn or me?'

Lazenby gave him his hardest cop look. 'You try and screw me over and I'll make you pay.'

'Why would I? I need you as much as you need me.' And it was true. As soon as he got rid of certain obstacles, he'd be able to push into the West End, where the real money was. Once there, he'd need a friendly copper to watch his back. 'Joe's past it. He's pissed as a newt most days, and Connor's the same. I'm virtually running the show as it is.'

'If you say so.'

'I do say so.' For the last four years Terry had fetched and carried, planned and schemed until he had made himself indispensable to Joe. Throughout his steady rise to power he had always showed due deference to the ageing villain and been careful to hide the full extent of his own ambitions. But now the time had come to act before Joe Quinn completely lost the plot and threw away everything he'd helped to establish.

'What about Tommy?'

Terry gave a shrug. 'What about him? He won't be any trouble. The only thing he's interested in is that fuckin' pub. And the others – well, they ain't gonna complain when the cash starts rolling in.'

Lazenby stared over at the tennis players for a while. The middle-aged guy had given up yelling, and only the pock-pock of the balls broke the silence. Slowly he turned to face Terry again. 'When are you thinking?'

'A couple of months, three maybe.'

'That long?'

'You can't rush a good thing. One row in a pub isn't enough. I need the two of them at each other's throats – and everybody knowing about it.'

Lazenby rose to his feet, dropped the cigarette butt on the gravel and ground it in with the heel of his shoe. He pushed his hands deep into his pockets. 'Let me know when you're ready.'

'Don't let me down, because if you do . . . '

'Don't threaten me, Terry.'

'I'm just saying. You stick to your side of the bargain and I'll stick to mine. That way we'll both be happy.'

'Happiness?' Lazenby snorted. 'Is that what you think this is about?' Then, without another word, he turned and headed for the gate.

Terry stared contemptuously after the departing figure. He was making a deal with the devil, but that was the way it had to be. He waited a while, until he was sure the inspector had gone, and then got up and strolled along the path. His thoughts slid back to last night, to how he had hidden the baseball bat under the bench while everyone else had their eyes fixed firmly on the action. Now it was in a safe place, complete with a perfect set of Connor's prints, ready and waiting for when the moment came to act.

Terry had never killed a man before, but he wasn't losing any sleep over it. What choice did he have? He hadn't come this far to back down at the final hurdle. Joe Quinn had become a liability – it was time to get rid.

# 28

Helen took the stairs two at a time, before pausing on the first-floor landing to look towards the living room. The only noise came from the bar, where the midday shift was still in full swing. In the past, she had spent an unnatural amount of time trying to avoid Joe, and now she was doing the same with Connor. Since the row with his father, three days ago, he'd been staying at the flat and kipping on the sofa.

'Just until the dust settles,' Tommy had said.

But there wasn't any sign of that yet. In fact, the very opposite was true. Relations between Connor and Joe were getting worse rather than better. Helen hated having him around. It had been bad enough when he'd come into the pub, but now he had extra opportunities to taunt and torment her.

She tiptoed along the landing and peered into the living room. It was empty, thank God. She walked through to the kitchen and put the kettle on. Karen and Debs were both at work, Tommy was downstairs and she had no idea where

Yvonne was. Shopping, perhaps, or maybe she was down in the bar too. As for Connor – well, she didn't care so long as he wasn't anywhere near her.

Helen had skipped the last couple of hours of school, unable to face double maths.

Somehow the fact that the free time had been stolen made it feel more precious. She poured hot water over the tea bag, gave it a stir, added some milk, dumped the bag in the bin and then took the mug and went to stand by the window, where she could gaze down on the car park and watch the customers come and go. Already there was an inch of snow on the ground, and it was coming down again in gentle flurries. She watched as the tiny flakes hit the glass of the window pane, clinging on for a second before melting away.

She drank the tea in quick little sips, feeling its warmth spread through her body. It was freezing outside, and her feet felt like two blocks of ice. She had sloshed triumphantly through the snow on her way back from school, and now her socks were soaking wet. She wriggled her toes, trying to get the circulation back. She'd just finish her drink and then she'd go upstairs and get changed.

She was down to the dregs when she noticed the woman crossing the car park towards the Fox. She was walking unsteadily, weaving between the cars with a look of intense concentration on her face. Dressed in a red miniskirt, red stilettos and a fake fur jacket, she was holding what looked like a half-bottle of vodka in one hand and a cigarette in the other. Helen recognised her as one of the toms that worked the Albert Road, an older woman in her late forties with dyed blonde hair and skinny legs. What was she called? She couldn't remember.

A few seconds later, Connor appeared. He jogged through the snow, grabbed the tom's shoulder and swung her roughly round to face him. Although Helen couldn't hear what was being said, she could read his expression. It was cold and dark and angry. She felt a spasm of alarm for the woman. Connor had no self-control. He was a violent bully, like his father.

For a while, the two of them had a heated discussion on the forecourt. Helen shifted to the side of the window, worried that Connor might look up and spot her. The woman – Shirley, that was her name – suddenly turned and started to walk away. Connor quickly grabbed her again. This time words weren't enough. He gave two quick punches to her face and Shirley dropped to the ground like a stone. Helen jumped back in shock, her hand rising to her chest, her heart pounding. By the time she looked out of the window again, Connor was striding away towards Station Road.

Helen gazed down at the prostrate woman. She wasn't moving. She was either too badly injured or too drunk to get to her feet. Helen hesitated – what if Connor came back? – but then decided that she couldn't leave her lying there. She might need an ambulance. At the very least she had to get her out of the cold. She rushed down the stairs, unlocked the back door and hurried out into the car park.

Shirley was still lying on her back, the snow beginning to gather like white dust on her jacket. Both her eyes were closed, the left lid red and swollen. Her upper lip was split and a thin trickle of blood was running down her cheek.

'Shirley?' Helen crouched down beside her, gently shaking

her shoulder. There was no response. 'Shirley, can you hear me?'

Eventually the woman moved her head, opened her right eye and gazed blearily up at her. 'Huh?'

'Are you okay?' Helen asked. 'Can you get up? Here, let me help you.' She took hold of her arm and slowly managed to raise her to her feet. But as soon as she was upright, Shirley dropped to her knees again and started scrabbling around in the snow.

'Where is it? Where is it?'

It took Helen a moment to realise what she was talking about. Then her eyes alighted on the bottle of vodka lying in the snow by her feet. Quickly she bent down to retrieve it. 'Here,' she said, passing the bottle over.

Shirley promptly sat down on the ground, unscrewed the cap with shaky hands and took a large swig, gasping as the alcohol touched her split upper lip. She took a few deep breaths, and then, as if the vodka had revitalised her, managed to stand up again without the need of any help.

Helen leaned across and brushed the snow off her shoulders. 'You'd better come inside. It's cold out here.'

'Don't worry, love. I don't feel the cold, me.'

'Your lip's bleeding,' Helen said.

Shirley tentatively touched her mouth with her forefinger and winced. She gave a small, weary laugh. 'Oh, I've known worse, hon.'

Helen frowned, not wanting to imagine what was worse than Connor Quinn punching you in the face.

'Ta for helping me up.'

'That's all right.'

Shirley gazed towards the pub and then towards the street, as if trying to decide where to go next. In the end she settled for the street. She took a step in that direction and instantly stumbled.

Helen grabbed hold of her elbow. 'Watch out.'

Shirley swayed a little, trying to get her one good eye to focus. 'It's just these heels, hon. They're slippy on the ice.'

Helen suspected it was more to do with the vodka or the after-effects of Connor's assault. 'Come inside. Please. Just for five minutes. I can make you a brew. You'll feel better when you've had a sit-down.' She doubted if this was entirely true but couldn't bear the thought of the woman wandering off when she clearly wasn't fit to do so. What if she collapsed somewhere out of the way and nobody came across her until it was too late? She could end up dead, and Helen didn't want that on her conscience.

Shirley tottered from one foot to the other while she considered the offer. 'I dunno.'

'Come on. We'll both freeze to death if we stay out here.' Helen took hold of her arm and started to gently propel her towards the back door. 'There's no one upstairs. It'll only be you and me.'

Shirley didn't offer any further resistance, allowing herself to be led through the door and up the stairs to the living room. Helen prayed that no one had come in during the five minutes she'd been outside, and thankfully her prayers were answered. She could imagine Yvonne's reaction if she came back to find one of the local toms sitting in her kitchen. But what she feared far more was the return of Connor. Wherever he had gone, she hoped he would stay there.

'Grab a seat,' Helen said, before switching on the kettle again. She took two clean mugs off the draining board and set them down on the counter. Then she opened a cupboard, looking for something to put on Shirley's cuts and bruises. There was a first-aid box down in the bar, but she couldn't see any way of smuggling it out without Tommy noticing. Of course, she could just tell him what had happened, but then he was bound to come upstairs. She had a feeling, a gut instinct, that Shirley would do a runner if anyone else turned up on the scene.

Eventually Helen found a fresh pack of J Cloths. She pulled one out of the plastic wrapper and ran it under the cold tap. 'Here,' she said, passing it over. 'Put this on your eye.' She was sure she had heard something about the usefulness of frozen peas when it came to black eyes, but she didn't dare raid the freezer compartment of the fridge. There was no way she'd be able to explain *that* to Yvonne.

While Shirley dabbed ineffectively at her face, Helen made two mugs of tea and brought them to the table. 'Does it hurt?'

'Nah, it's nothin' serious. I'll live. Thanks for the brew, love.'

'That's okay.'

Shirley took a large slurp, wincing again as the hot liquid ran over her lip. Then she unscrewed the vodka bottle and poured a generous measure into the mug. She took another noisy slurp and sighed. 'Ah, that hits the spot. You got an ashtray, sweetheart?'

'Sure.' Helen walked through to the living room and found one balanced on the arm of the sofa. Back in the kitchen, she emptied the contents into the bin and put the ashtray on the table. Always alert to the dangers of fire, she suddenly wondered what had happened to the cigarette Shirley had been smoking when Connor had thumped her, but decided that it didn't really matter. Even if it had still been burning when it fell to the ground, the snow would have extinguished it by now.

She sat down on the opposite side of the table and picked up her tea. From over the rim of her mug, she gazed curiously at the woman. The baggy flesh under her closed eye was turning a blue-grey colour and her mouth looked painfully sore. Although Helen had estimated her age to be late forties, she realised now that she was probably older. There was a thick layer of make-up on her face, but it didn't quite disguise the lines and wrinkles.

Aware of her scrutiny, Shirley gave a wry smile. 'Bet I look a freakin' mess, don't I?' She put the J Cloth down and gave another sigh. 'Course I do. That bastard never does anything by half measures. He's a real fucker, if you'll pardon my French.'

Helen gave a nod. 'I know.'

Shirley stared back at her, her expression full of concern. 'I hope you don't.'

'Oh, I don't mean ... no, he's never ... he just ...'

'Yeah,' Shirley said. 'He's a nasty little sod and there's no getting away from it.' She took a long drag on the cigarette and knocked the burnt end into the ashtray. A few seconds passed before she added, 'You're Lynsey's kid, aren't you? Mouse, yeah?'

'Well, Helen really, but everyone calls me Mouse.'

'Helen,' Shirley repeated softly.

'Did you know her?' With only Moira to talk to about her mother, Helen was interested to find someone else who might be prepared to share their memories.

'Yeah, course I did. She was a lovely kid. I've been in Kellston all my life, love. I was around when Irene ran the Fox.' Shirley topped up her tea with the vodka again and gazed wistfully into the middle distance. 'God, they were the days. I could turn a few heads then, I can tell you.'

Helen smiled at her. 'Tommy doesn't talk about her much.'

'Well, it was terrible what happened to your mum, just terrible. The poor girl didn't deserve that.' Shirley stubbed her cigarette out and fumbled for another. It was then, just as she was lifting the fag to her mouth, that she dropped the bombshell. 'Why would someone want to do that to her? Why would someone kill a beautiful girl like that?'

Helen almost jumped out of her chair. Her heart missed a beat and her pulse began to race. She could feel the colour draining from her cheeks. 'W-what?' she stammered.

Shirley glanced sharply across the table.

Helen began shaking her head, as if by the very action she could shake the words right out of her mind. 'She wasn't . . . it wasn't . . . she died in a fire. It was an accident.'

Shirley's mouth had dropped open. As if suddenly shocked into sobriety, she had a look of horror on her face.

'It was an accident,' Helen continued to insist. 'Tommy told me. He said there'd been an investigation. She fell asleep and left a candle burning. The flat caught fire and—'

'Just forget it, hon,' Shirley said. 'I'm getting confused. Sorry, sorry. It's just the booze talking. I never think straight when I'm on the voddie.' Flustered, she rose hurriedly to her feet, grabbed the bottle and headed for the door. 'I'd best be going. Ta for the brew. Don't get up, sweetheart. I'll see myself out.'

Helen wanted to run after her, to stop her from leaving, but her body felt paralysed. She tried to call out, but her throat was so constricted that only a croak emerged. She gazed at the unlit cigarette that Shirley had dropped and left lying on the table. *Murdered.* It wasn't possible. It couldn't be true. It couldn't.

# 29

It was a quarter to three before Helen heard the familiar sound of Tommy's footsteps on the stairs. She glanced at the clock on the wall, surprised to find that so much time had passed. She had been sitting there for well over an hour. But what did time matter anyway? For her, the clocks had stopped ticking from the moment Shirley had opened her battered, broken mouth and uttered those devastating words.

Tommy bounded into the kitchen, patting her shoulder as he passed by her chair. 'Hey, Mouse. Good day at school?'

Helen didn't reply. She studied him carefully, as if seeing a different Tommy to the one she had lived with for the past four years. She couldn't figure out how you could think you knew someone and yet not really know them at all. Her gaze took in his big, solid hands as he turned on the tap and let the cold water swoosh into the kettle. Safe hands, or so she'd always thought. Now she wasn't so sure.

Tommy took the kettle back to the counter, switched it on, and then, as if sensing her eyes on him, twisted around to look at her. 'You okay, love?'

She swallowed hard and then quickly cleared her throat. 'I need to ask you something.'

'Ask away, sweetheart.'

Now was the moment. But still Helen hesitated, aware that once she started down this road, there could be no turning back. There was a wide gap, she realised, between hearing the truth and being able to bear it. 'It's about ... about Mum,' she finally managed to stutter out.

Tommy's expression instantly grew serious. He leaned back against the kitchen counter and folded his arms across his chest. 'What is it?'

Helen took a deep breath. 'Is it true she was murdered?'

Tommy flinched, a physical reaction that he couldn't disguise. 'Who told you that?' he snapped.

Her heart sank at his answer. Not *Of course it's not true* or *That's just ridiculous*, or any other of a hundred mundane denials that would have swept the horror from her soul. 'It doesn't matter who told me. Was she?'

Tommy opened his mouth and then closed it again.

'Please,' she said. 'I need to know.'

'I've no idea what you've been told, but—'

'Don't lie to me,' she pleaded. 'I can find out. There are plenty of ways of finding out.' She wasn't quite sure exactly what these were, but presumed that the police kept records and that a daughter would have the right to know if her mother had been murdered or not.

Tommy pulled out a chair and sat down beside her. 'I was

253

going to say that it wasn't straightforward, hon. There was ... there was a suspicion that she might have been, but with the fire and everything, they couldn't be sure. The coroner reckoned that the evidence wasn't conclusive.'

Helen raised a hand, briefly covering her face. She didn't want it in her head, that dreadful image of the flames licking at her mother's body. 'What evidence?' she forced herself to ask.

Tommy's mouth twisted. He glanced away, staring at the wall for a few seconds before looking back at her. 'There was some ... some damage to the skull, but it could have been caused by a fall. She might have tripped and banged her head, knocked herself unconscious. Maybe the candle tipped over at the same time. And then there was the fire, and ...' Tommy's voice trailed off. His shoulders lifted and dropped in a regretful shrug.

'But maybe not.'

He reached out and placed his hand over hers. 'I'm sorry, love. I really am.'

As if she'd been burnt by the contact, Helen quickly pulled her hand away. 'Why didn't you tell me? All these years, and ...'

Tommy stared at the rejected hand for a moment and then used it to rake his fingers through his hair. 'Because you were only eleven, Mouse, and you had so much else to deal with. And we didn't know for sure. No one did. We thought ... we thought you'd be better off believing that she died in an accident.'

'So who else knew?'

But Helen only had to look at his sheepish expression to

realise that this was hardly the world's best-kept secret. 'Yvonne?'

He nodded. 'And Dad.'

'And Moira?'

Tommy nodded again.

Helen gritted her teeth, this betrayal feeling far worse than the others. All the times she had chatted to Moira about her mum, and not once had the woman even hinted at the truth. They were supposed to be close, but now it all felt like a sham. Her hand curled into a fist, the nails digging into the soft flesh of her palm. She would never forgive her for this. Never!

'There was an inquest,' Tommy said. 'People hear about stuff. You can't always keep it quiet.' He paused, and then added, 'But not the girls, not Karen and Debs. They don't know anything.'

'Just the three of us, then,' Helen said tightly.

'Don't be angry, Mouse.' He gazed at her pleadingly. 'No one wanted you to get hurt. That's the only reason we kept quiet about it.'

Helen mentally brushed his excuses aside. 'So instead I have to find out from—' But she swiftly bit her tongue. If she told on Shirley, Connor might take his fists to her again. And none of this was Shirley's fault. 'How do you think it makes me feel when everyone knew about it but me?'

'I'm sorry,' Tommy said again. 'I was wrong. I thought I was doing the right thing, but . . . '

Helen fought back her tears. She was as upset as she was angry, dismayed at being deceived by the people she'd trusted. 'It wasn't the right thing. It wasn't right to lie to me.'

'No,' he said. 'I see that now.'

'Do *you* think . . . ' The breath caught in her throat and she had to start again. 'Do *you* think that she was murdered?'

Tommy lifted his hands and dropped them back down to his thighs. 'Why would anyone want to kill her?'

Helen gazed sadly back at him. Even now, she felt that he was being deliberately evasive. Pushing back her chair, she stood up and went over to the door.

'Where are you going?' Tommy asked.

'To my room. I'll see you later.' Helen ran up the stairs and into the bedroom, flinging herself on the lower bunk and curling up into a ball. She hoped Tommy wouldn't come after her. She needed time to think, time to absorb it all.

Wrapping her arms around her knees, she stared at the wall. *Murder.* It was a hard, cruel word. If she'd been told earlier, when it had happened, she might have been able to come to terms with it. Or was it something you could never come to terms with? She realised suddenly that Janet must have known, and her grandmother, too. No wonder Janet had been so eager to be rid of her. She was the kind of person who valued respectability above all else – and murder always came with a hint of scandal.

There were tear marks on the wall where posters had been ripped down, small ragged stripes of white showing through the purple paint. After Joe had moved out, Karen had decamped downstairs and Helen now had the room to herself. She hadn't bothered to replace the pictures. It would have felt too much like tempting providence, as if the very act of personalising the space would provoke the fates into snatching it away from her. Despite Tommy's declarations that she was a Quinn, that she would always be welcome at the Fox, she was secretly afraid of being moved on again.

There was still one poster remaining on the wall which Karen had either forgotten about or maybe just hadn't wanted. David Cassidy, in fur boots and jeans, smiled down at her from across the room. She had long outgrown her crush on him, but there was still something comforting about his presence. It reminded her of Saturday evenings at Gran's, when she'd curled up on the sofa to watch *The Partridge Family*.

Over the years, Helen had learnt to cope with a lot of things, but the prospect of change still disturbed her. Murder made everything different. How couldn't it? But who would want to kill her mother? No sooner had she asked herself the question than Joe Quinn's angry face sprang into her mind. But surely even he wasn't capable of that. She shivered, hugging her knees even tighter.

It was getting on for five o'clock when Karen opened the bedroom door without knocking and said, 'Tea's ready.'

'I'm not hungry.'

Karen stared at her. 'You sick or something?'

'Yeah, something like that.'

Karen looked at her some more, then gave a shrug and left.

Helen rolled over on to her back, put her hands behind her head and gazed up at the springs of the upper bunk. It wasn't a lie: she did feel sick, sick to her stomach. Every time she thought about the murder, it made her want to retch. To think there was someone out there who had killed her mother and got away with it. No one had been punished, no one brought to justice. It wasn't fair and it wasn't right. Why hadn't Tommy done something about it? Lynsey Quinn had still been his sister, even if they had gone their separate ways.

Ten minutes later, Yvonne yelled up the stairs, 'Mouse? Moira's here to see you. Shall I send her up?'

Helen leapt off the bed, flung open the door and leaned over the banisters. 'No!' she said. 'I don't want to see her!'

Yvonne peered up. 'Are you sure. She says—'

'I don't care what she says. I don't want to see her. Not ever! Tell her to go away.'

Yvonne gave a shrug. 'If that's what you want.'

'It is.'

'Okay, I'll tell her.'

Helen thought she saw a sly glint of satisfaction in Yvonne's eyes as she turned away and went back towards the living room.

# 30

Tommy sat down on the edge of the bed and bent over to untie his shoelaces. He was dog-tired and ready for some kip, although whether he would get any was another matter altogether. Mouse had stayed in her room all evening and he'd missed her presence in the pub. Not just because of the hard work she always did, but because he liked having her around.

'Do you think I should have tried to talk to her again?' he asked, glancing over his shoulder.

Yvonne, propped up by a couple of pillows, was flicking through the pages of a magazine. She looked up, her expression vague. 'Huh?'

'I was saying, do you think I should have tried to talk to Mouse again? I don't like to think of her shut up in that room all on her own. All this, it's been a right shock to her. It's knocked her for six.'

'She'll be fine.'

Tommy eased off his shoes and then removed his socks. He

stripped off the rest of his clothes, dropping them on the floor.

'For God's sake,' Yvonne said, 'there's a perfectly good chair two inches away from you. Why can't you put your clothes on that?'

Tommy leaned over, picked up the bundle of clothes and shoved them on to the chair. 'Happy now?'

'Thank you.'

As he crawled into bed, he took a moment to study his wife. Her hair was in curlers, her face covered with a greasy-looking cream. Not the prettiest sight in the world. He thought regretfully of Shelley Anne, sleeping alone in her little flat in Hoxton. Now there was a woman that could give a man some comfort when he really needed it.

'What?' Yvonne asked, sensing his eyes on her.

'How do you know she'll be fine?' Tommy asked. 'She might clear off like the last time she was upset. I mean, someone tells you that your mother might have been murdered, it's hardly the easiest bit of news to come to terms with.'

'She was only a kid back then.'

'She's not much more than a kid now.'

Yvonne sighed and put down the magazine. 'Well, I told you, didn't I? I said it was no good keeping it from her, that it was bound to come out eventually. But oh no, you and Moira knew best. Now look where it's got you.'

'Ta, that's really useful. *I told you so.* Just what I needed to hear.'

Yvonne's mouth took on a sulky pout. 'I'm only saying. No point having a go at me because it's all gone tits up.'

Tommy lay down and turned on his side so that he had his

260

back to her. The worst thing was that she was right. In fact, Moira had wanted to tell Mouse the truth, but he'd persuaded her not to. And now the poor woman was getting the cold shoulder. He remembered Moira's face as she'd left the pub this evening, her eyes full of tears. Shit, he'd really fucked up this time.

He closed his own eyes, not wanting to think about it any more. A couple of minutes later, Yvonne turned off the lamp and the room was in darkness. Tommy lay very still, willing his mind to stop whirring. Mouse would come round eventually. He was sure she would. He'd have another talk with her tomorrow and try and smooth things over.

Yvonne's breathing changed as she slowly drifted into sleep, but Tommy remained wide awake. Mouse wasn't his only problem. The rift between Connor and Joe hadn't improved in the last few days either. In fact, if anything, it had grown worse. Now the two of them weren't even on speaking terms. He wasn't sure what it was all about and he didn't want to become involved. Getting caught in the middle of that pair was always a big mistake.

'How long is he going to be here for?' Yvonne had asked this afternoon. 'Why can't he go back to his own place?'

'You know why not.'

'Well he can't sleep on our bloody sofa for ever. He was stark bollock naked when I got up this morning, not even a blanket over him. The girls don't need to see that when they come down for breakfast.'

'Okay, okay. I'll talk to him.'

He hadn't, though. And thinking of Connor reminded him that he'd never changed the locks. And what about the missing baseball bat? Where the hell had that gone? He tried to recreate the scene when his brother had smashed the bat down on the table, and the altercation that followed. Terry Street had taken the weapon off him, but what had happened to it then? Terry said that he'd left it by the side of the table. Well, it wasn't there now. Still, any of the customers could have picked it up and taken it home with them. He'd have to get another one.

Unable to sleep, Tommy blinked open his eyes again. At first the room seemed black, but gradually it took on shades of grey, until he could make out the outlines of the dressing table, the window and the door. Was Mouse awake too? He thought of the day they had gone to the cemetery and scattered the ashes in his mother's grave. Poor Lynsey. He had let her down badly, and now he had let her daughter down too. Fucking up, it seemed, was his speciality. Now all he had to do was figure out how to put things right.

# 31

Helen roamed through the empty rooms of the Fox, dragging the cloth across the tables in an absent-minded fashion. It was three months now since she had learned the truth about her mother's death, and she was still trying to come to terms with it. Winter had turned to spring, the snow replaced by blue skies and sunshine. The sun was currently slanting through the windows, skinny stripes of light that danced with motes and turned the floor a honey colour.

She hadn't seen Moira Sullivan since that fateful day when Shirley had tottered across the car park with a bottle of vodka in her hand. Moira had tried to heal the breach between them, calling round to the flat on half a dozen occasions and phoning maybe twenty times, but Helen's answer had always been the same. *I don't want to talk to her.* A few weeks back, she'd even received a letter, but she'd torn it up without reading it and thrown the pieces in the bin. Since then, she'd heard nothing more.

Helen wasn't sure why she was able to forgive Tommy but not Moira. Perhaps it was because Tommy was a bloke and they always got things wrong. She had viewed Moira as her closest friend, told her things in confidence and believed they had a special bond. But all the time this great dark secret had been lurking in the background.

Now, when she walked down the high street, Helen always avoided Connolly's and the undertakers'. In fact, she rarely went down the street at all, preferring instead to take a circuitous route along the winding back alleys and so not risk the chance of accidentally bumping into her. Of course Moira could have just turned up at the pub when she was working, but somehow Helen knew that she would never publicly force the issue like that.

Tommy, whenever he got the opportunity, still nagged her about it. 'At least hear her out, love. Moira's got a good heart. She never meant to ... She's really cut up about this.'

But Helen remained adamant. 'What's she going to say that I haven't heard already? It's a waste of time.' She knew that she was being stubborn about it, unfair even, but she still felt too badly hurt to even think about making up.

Although there was nothing left to clean or polish, she continued to prowl between the rooms like a cat marking her territory. So many things changed, and rarely for the better, but at least the Fox remained the same. Yet again her life had been turned upside down, but within the four walls of the pub she retained some sense of security.

As she came to the last and smallest of the three rooms, Helen dropped the cloth on the table and sank down into a chair by the fireplace. On the shelf to her side was an old paraffin lamp, and with peculiar fondness she remembered the blackouts of the previous year. Despite the lack of electricity, Tommy had refused to close the pub, choosing instead to light it with lamps and candles. There had been roaring log fires and even an old piano rolled down the street from Mrs Cohen's house to replace the silent jukebox. The locals, without the company of the TV or the warmth of their two-bar electric fires, had come in droves, making their way from their homes by torchlight.

Helen smiled as she recalled those evenings. There was something about adversity that brought out the best in people. It was that spirit of the Blitz thing. Instead of complaining, everyone had pulled together and the atmosphere had been warm and friendly. She leaned back and sighed, her smile slowly fading. It was not good, she thought, to be always looking over her shoulder, searching for happiness in times that had gone. She would end up like one of the old women who came in here, sipping on their glasses of gin, their rheumy eyes yearning for an age that had passed.

Briskly Helen rose to her feet and went through to the main room. She had to keep busy. That was the trick. For as long as she was occupied, there wasn't time to dwell on the past. And with tonight being a Friday, keeping busy shouldn't be a problem.

Tommy was behind the bar, whistling softly as he poured the float into the till. He looked up and gave her a tentative smile. 'Hi, Mouse. You okay?'

'I'm good, thanks. You?'

'Yeah, pretty good.'

She was aware that there remained a sense of awkwardness

between them, that they were not completely relaxed with each other. It would pass eventually, but in the meantime, they were still communicating in a rather strained and overly polite manner. Today, she had gone to school and stayed there, so she hadn't seen Tommy since last night.

'I was thinking I might go over the cemetery tomorrow,' he said. 'Put some flowers on the grave. You want to come with me?'

'Okay.'

'After closing, then?'

Helen nodded. 'Okay,' she said again.

Tommy looked pleased, as if her decision to accompany him was one more step on their journey towards reconciliation. He closed the till and started laying the ashtrays out across the bar.

Helen looked towards the corner where Joe and his gang would gather later in the evening. Friday was milk-round day. The protection money would be collected and brought back to the pub, the cash passed over discreetly in plain brown envelopes. Some of it would go straight out again in wages, backhanders to the local cops and to the wives or mothers of the men who were in jail. The rest would find its way into Joe Quinn's pocket. Whenever she saw Joe, a shiver ran through her. She could never quite shake that suspicion that he'd had something to do with her mother's death.

Connor, thankfully, hadn't stayed at the flat for long. A few weeks after the incident with the bat, he'd moved back in with Joe. Although there was no love lost between the two men, they still preferred to live together. That way, each could keep an eye on what the other was doing. That, at least, was

Helen's interpretation. She could think of no other reason for their cohabitation.

The rows, of course, hadn't stopped. Whenever they were in the pub, Connor watched his father with dark, suspicious eyes. And Joe always took pleasure in finding ways to wind him up. It was rare that the two of them managed to get through an evening without a quarrel about one thing or another. There was so much tension bubbling under the surface that eventually it would have to blow. With any luck Helen wouldn't be around when the big bang finally happened.

She glanced back towards the bar, wondering if Frank would show tonight. Lately, she had taken to avoiding him whilst trying not to make it obvious, a tricky balancing act that was none too easy to pull off. She couldn't help wondering if, like the others, he had known about the murder. It he had, then it shed a different light on his niceness to her, a niceness that was born of pity rather than any genuine liking. She couldn't bear the thought of being pitied by him.

A few weeks ago, she had spotted Frank in the cemetery. She had been to visit the lion – its great stone solidity still a comfort, even if her dreams of Narnia had long since disappeared – and had seen him striding along the main thoroughfare. Quickly, she had slipped back between the trees. There was something about that determined stride that spoke of a man on a mission. Where was he going? Torn between curiosity and her desire to avoid an awkward meeting, she'd waited until he'd swerved on to one of the narrower paths before making the decision to follow him.

Like a furtive private eye, she had moved cautiously forward, skulking behind bushes in case he glanced over his shoulder. But he hadn't looked back, not once. After a few yards he'd veered on to the grass and stopped abruptly in front of a white marble headstone. She could only see his back, but even with that limited view she was aware of the tension in his body. There was a rigidity about his pose, a sense of breath being held, of resolve being stiffened.

A few minutes passed before he crouched down and laid a small posy of flowers at the foot of the stone. He stayed in that position for a while, his head bowed, before slowly rising to his feet again. His hand lifted slightly and dropped back to his side, then he turned and walked away.

Helen had waited until he was out of sight before emerging from her hiding place. Tentatively she'd approached the grave, almost on tiptoe, as if the sound of her footsteps might carry across the cemetery. As she'd read the words on the stone, a soft gasp had escaped from her lips.

*ELEANOR ANNE MEYER*
*Beloved wife of Frank*
*Died 5th May 1963, aged 24*
*Rest in peace*

Helen had stood there for longer than he had, reading and rereading the inscription as this new and revealing piece of information had established itself in her mind. Frank had been married and his wife had died. Today was the anniversary of her death. Her sadness at the woman's young age, at his loss, was accompanied by a more uncomfortable emotion – a feeling of guilt. He hadn't chosen to share the tragedy with her; what she had learned had been acquired through snooping. It was another reason why she had been avoiding him lately. Every time she looked at him, she was reminded of what she knew.

'A penny for them?' Tommy said, suddenly breaking into her thoughts.

Helen shook her head and forced a smile. 'I'd be robbing you.'

He gazed at her curiously for a moment, then glanced down at his watch. 'Five o'clock. You ready?' he said.

'Go for it.'

Tommy walked across the bar, pulled back the bolts and swung open the door. And another night began at the Fox.

# 32

Terry Street put on his gloves, took the suitcase from the top of the wardrobe, laid it on the bed and flipped open the locks. Carefully he removed the bat, the handle still covered with the film of polythene he'd wrapped around it months ago. He held it in his hand for a moment, feeling the weight and imagining the sound it would make as it arced through the air towards its target.

He placed the bat in a navy blue sports bag on top of a clean pair of trousers and a shirt, then zipped the bag up. How did he feel? Excited, apprehensive, slightly nauseous, if he was being honest with himself. But he had no intention of backing out now. This was his one big chance to grab what he wanted. He glanced at his watch – almost time. One drink to steady his nerves and then he'd be off.

He poured himself a stiff Scotch, sat down on the couch and ran through the plan. Preparation: that was the most important thing. He'd already made the call from a phone box on the Caledonian Road.

'Joe, I need a word alone before you go to the Fox tonight.'

'Yeah, what's the deal?'

'It's good, but I'll tell you later. How about I pick you up around half eight? We can talk on the way.'

And Joe, who was always paranoid about who might be listening in on the line, hadn't pressed him any further. 'Half eight, then. And don't be bloody late.'

'I won't. Oh, and could you do us a favour? Don't tell Connor about this, will you? If he knows something's in the pipeline, he'll be on my back all night trying to find out what's going down. Let's just keep it between the two of us for now.'

'I don't tell him nothin',' Joe had grunted before replacing the receiver.

Terry put his glass on the coffee table and checked his pocket for the keys. One for the Jaguar and one for the cellar at the rear of the Fox. Both had come courtesy of Connor, who hadn't even noticed they'd been missing for the half-hour it had taken Terry to get the copies made and the originals returned to his jacket.

Although confident that it would work, Terry was smart enough to know that no plan was foolproof. He had made five practice runs and on only one occasion had something unexpected happened. A drunk, with his head between his knees, had been throwing up outside the cellar door. Had the run been for real, the plan would have been scuppered, but the chances of lightning striking twice were slight. Anyway, if there were any problems, he always had the choice of abandoning the project and leaving it until another day.

Thinking of it as a project enabled Terry to remove any personal feelings he might have for Joe. He respected the man for building up the firm from nothing, but that was about as far as it went. Brutal and charmless, Joe Quinn had few redeeming features. He was an ugly man with a black soul. All things considered, Terry would be doing the world a favour by getting rid of him.

He glanced at his watch again, knocked back the rest of his drink, then grabbed the bag and went out of the door. It was dark now, with a chill in the air. Ignoring his own car, he walked around the corner to where the white van was parked. He'd picked it up for a song – cash, no questions asked – and would dump it when the deed was done. Battered but familiar, it was the kind of vehicle that nobody looked at twice.

He climbed into the van, took the bat out of the bag and slid it under the seat. Later, he'd remove the film and leave the weapon for the cops to find. Was Lazenby ready? He'd better be. Terry neither liked nor trusted the man, but he knew that he needed him. A cop with influence in the West End could make a real difference to a firm. No surprise raids or midnight knocks on the door, no interference with the toms. Soho was the cash cow of London, and he intended to milk it.

Terry made his way over to the south side of Kellston, where Joe had set up home in a fancy block of flats called St George's Court. It was a three-storey building with balconies on every floor, a marble-tiled foyer and a wide front lawn. There was no sign of the Jaguar. That was good. It meant that Connor had already gone on ahead to the Fox. He was always there on Friday nights, hand outstretched as the dosh came in from the milk round.

Terry pulled in to a parking space in front of the block and killed the engine. He checked that the coast was clear – no one going in or coming out of the flats – then got out of the van, walked quickly to the front door and pressed the buzzer for Flat 6. There was a full minute's delay before Joe deigned to answer on the intercom.

'Yeah?'

'It's me. It's Terry. I'll wait for you down here.'

He went back to the van and lit a fag. His hands weren't shaking, but a thin trickle of sweat was running down the back of his neck. He knew that he would always remember this night, either as the final step on the ladder to success or the time he got himself banged up for life. Either way, nothing would ever be the same again.

It was another five minutes before Joe ambled out of the flats. He was a solid, fat man with an immense beer gut and several more chins than nature intended. Despite his weight, he could be fast on his feet when he needed to be. It didn't do to underestimate him. Tonight he was dressed in a beige lightweight summer suit with shirt and tie.

Terry flashed his lights and Joe walked over to the van and opened the passenger door. He leaned down with a scowl on his face. 'Why the fuck are you driving this heap of junk?'

'Because the Merc's in the garage,' Terry said. 'Some bastard reversed into me over Hackney way. Anyway, fuck the motor, are you getting in or not?'

As if it might be contaminated, Joe stared dubiously at the rust and the worn upholstery before eventually climbing in. 'Jesus,' he said, sniffing noisily, 'it stinks in here. Where d'you get this fuckin' death trap?'

Terry jumped a little at the words, as if Joe, perhaps subconsciously, knew what he was planning. He pulled hard on his fag and threw the butt out of the window. 'It ain't a death trap, boss. She might not look too pretty but she runs like a dream. Anyways, it's just a lend off a mate until I get the Merc back.'

Joe pulled a face as if it was beneath his dignity to be seen in anything so shabby. 'Some mate,' he snorted.

Terry pulled the van out on to the drive and started back towards the Fox. Now that the first part of his task had been completed, his heart had started to thump in his chest. He gripped the wheel, trying to steady his nerves. *Start talking*, he told himself. *Start talking before Joe picks up on the vibe.* 'I was up West last night and bumped into Liverpool Larry at the Bell. He was with a geezer called Mendez. You ever heard of him?'

Joe shook his head. 'There a point to all this?'

'Sure there's a point. Mendez is Liverpool's supplier, a sharp guy, Colombian. I reckon we could do business with him.'

'We already got a supplier.'

'Not a reliable one, though. How many times have we been let down in the past year or so? And every time there's some wannabe ready to slide in and fill the gap. Supply and demand, boss. There's a fuckin' big demand and we ain't got a regular supply.'

Joe didn't look convinced. He had reached the stage in life where he wanted things to be safe and easy and comfortable. 'You don't know this guy from Adam. Could be the fuckin' law playing silly buggers.'

'Nah, he ain't the filth. Liverpool can vouch for him.

They've been doing business for over a year now. Anyway, I said I'd talk to you, see how the land lies. I've got a number if you're interested.'

While Joe mulled it over, Terry's brain began to race. They were minutes away from the Fox. Had he covered every angle? Would he have the nerve to go through with it? He thought about the blood. Splatter was what he had to be wary of, blood and bone flying through the air. The spare clothes in the bag were just in case he had to get changed.

'Is Connor at the Fox?' Terry asked.

'Where else would he be?'

Yeah, predictable, that was the Quinns. They had never quite mastered the art of surprise. Terry left a short pause before asking, 'He didn't want to know what you were doing, then?'

'Sure he wanted to know, but it ain't none of his business.'

Terry gave a nod. Good. Something else ticked off the list. He'd been counting on the pleasure Joe always took in winding up his son. 'He'll be well pissed off. I'll keep shtum about the Colombian until you've had time to think it over.'

The traffic lights on the corner of Station Road were on red. Terry pulled up, praying to God that the coast would be clear when they got to the pub. There was still time for him to change his mind, but he knew where that would leave him: attached to a firm that was rotting at its roots. Joe wouldn't relinquish power until he was in his grave.

The lights turned to green and Terry moved off, indicating right. He swung on to Station Road and then took another right into the dimly lit car park of the Fox. The entrance to the pub was round the corner and invisible from here. His heart was still pumping, the adrenalin streaming through his body. *Keep your cool. Don't blow it.* The steering wheel was damp from where the fear was leaking from his palms.

Quickly his eyes raked the space, alert to any customers arriving or leaving by car, searching for stray drunks or crack-happy toms who might be doing business in the gloom. Everything was quiet. And yes – his luck was in – the silver Jag was parked in its usual place by the cellar door.

He pulled the van up next to it, creating a visual barrier between the car and the street. This way, no one passing by on Station Road would be able to bear witness to what was going to happen next. 'Christ, Joe, what's that?'

'Huh?'

'I think someone's smashed into the back of the Jag.'

Joe was out of the van faster than a greyhound from a trap. 'Stupid fuckin' bastard!' he muttered, presuming that Connor had been practising his usual careless driving.

Terry, after one final look around, bent down and grabbed the bat from under the seat. He jumped out of the van and strode around to where Joe was hunched over, peering at the rear end of the Jag.

'I can't see nothin',' Joe said.

And those were the last words he ever spoke.

In one swift, easy motion, Terry lifted the bat above his head and brought it down with all his force on the older man's skull. There was the cruel sound of wood on bone, a dull, dense fracturing, before Joe slumped forward, fell against the boot and slid slowly to the ground.

Terry crouched down and peered at his former boss. There was no doubt that he was dead. Even in the cloak of shadow, he could be sure of that. The wound was gaping and bloody, a pulp of flesh and bone and tissue. Joe's eyes stared glassily into the darkness.

Thinking that he was about to hurl, Terry leapt to his feet and pressed his knuckles hard against his mouth. Whatever he did, he mustn't throw up. It was done now. It was over. He waited for the feeling to pass before lowering his hand and gulping in the cool night air.

He gazed down at the body and then checked his watch. Only a minute had gone by, and yet it felt like longer. Time seemed to have slowed, as if the world was turning on a different axis. He listened for a distant siren, afraid that someone had already called the cops. But that was crazy. No one had seen him. Nobody knew. And if he kept his nerve, nobody ever would.

Quickly he scrabbled in his pocket for the keys. It took all his strength to heave the fat corpse off the ground and into the boot. He could smell the sharp, metallic stink of blood, and other odours too – sweat and fags and musky aftershave. He tried not to breathe too deeply.

To make the body fit, he had to push and shove and bend the legs. By the time it was done, his lungs were pumping.

Terry gave Joe Quinn one last look before slamming shut the boot. Well, it was the end of an era – but also the beginning of a new one. He did the rest of what he had to do, and then he went into the pub and ordered a pint.

# 33

Tommy lined up the eight pints of bitter on the bar and put his hand out for the money. 'That's a quid twenty.'

'Put it on the old man's tab,' Connor said.

'He ain't got a tab.'

Connor grinned as he picked up two of the pints. 'And bring the rest over, will you?'

Tommy shook his head. 'You think I got time for personal deliveries? I'm rushed off my feet here, in case you ain't noticed.'

'So get the kid to do it,' Connor said.

Tommy glanced towards Mouse, who was perched on a stool at the end of the bar, drinking a Coke through a lime-green straw. 'The kid's got a name, and she's on a break at the moment. Get one of the boys to come over, or use a tray.' He dumped a round metal tray on the counter and held out his hand again. 'Come on, a quid twenty. I'm not running a bleedin' charity here.'

'I already told you, these are down to the old man. We've

been waiting over an hour already. The least he can do is buy us a pint.'

Tommy, who was too busy for an argument, waved a hand and turned to serve the next in the queue. While he was sorting those drinks, Connor started to load the pints on to the tray.

'So where is the old man?' Tommy asked. 'It's not like him to be late on a Friday.' He glanced towards the corner, where Fat Pete, Terry Street and the rest of the crew were sitting.

'Said he had some calls to make. He'd be along later.'

Tommy could tell from his tone that Connor wasn't best pleased. 'You two had a ruck, then?'

Connor narrowed his eyes. 'What makes you say that?' he snapped. 'What you heard?'

'Nothin'. Just asking. No need to go off on one.' Tommy was used to his brother's moods, and his paranoia. You only had to look at him the wrong way and he'd start accusing you of plotting against him. 'You got the Jag, then?'

'Yeah.'

'Good.' Joe had lost his licence a couple of months ago for drunk driving, and now Connor had the job of ferrying him around. Tommy was glad that the old bastard couldn't get behind the wheel for a while; it made the streets a safer place. 'How's he gonna get here, then?'

'How should I know? Maybe he'll get off his fat arse and walk.'

Tommy raised his eyebrows. 'When hell freezes over.'

'Not my fuckin' problem,' said Connor, before picking up the tray and making his way back towards the boys.

It was another half-hour before Tommy was able to take a

break. He poured a couple of Johnnie Walkers and took them over to where Frank was sitting by the window, flicking through the evening paper. 'Sorry to keep you waiting, mate,' he said, setting the drinks down on the table. 'Bit short-staffed tonight. One of the girls called in sick.'

'No worries,' Frank said. 'You look knackered.'

'Yeah, the price of being busy. Still, I ain't complaining.'

Frank took a sip of whisky and gave a nod. 'I just called by to let you know that everything's smooth over at Dagenham. I went to see Alfie this afternoon.'

Alfie Blunt, who had managed the shop in Romford, was working with them again on the second long-firm fraud. Often managers were paid to be the scapegoat, to take the blame and do the time when a fraud was finally uncovered, but Alfie preferred his freedom. With a mate in the travel business, he was able to find out when a respectable man with a common-sounding name was emigrating. Once he was out of the way, Alfie would take on his identity and trade as a businessman with a clean record. At the moment he was calling himself Martin Leigh.

'Those new TVs are shifting,' Frank continued, 'and the stereos. We'll be putting in another order at the end of next week.'

'Good. I'll drink to that.' Tommy was glad to hear it. He was learning patience, but that didn't stop him wishing time away. The sooner the fraud came off, the sooner he could be freed from the shackles of Yvonne. He glanced over to where she was sitting with Carol Gatesby. The two of them had managed to waylay Terry Street on his way back from the gents' and were now flirting outrageously with him.

Frank lit a cigarette and sat back. Following Tommy's line of sight, he laughed and said, 'Terry had better watch it. That Carol'll eat him for breakfast.'

'Oh, I reckon he can take care of himself.' Tommy noticed how Terry's eyes flicked continuously towards the door and knew that he was waiting for Joe to walk in. Terry had come a long way in the past few years, helping to build up the firm and in the process making himself indispensable to the old man. Yeah, he was a smart one all right, but nice with it. You couldn't help liking him.

'So where's Joe tonight?'

'Good question.' Terry looked up at the clock on the wall. It was twenty to ten. Connor had already called the flat twice from the phone in the hall, but there had been no reply. The boys were getting restless, wanting their money for the weekend. No one, however, had been prepared to go round to St George's Court. If Joe was busy – and busy usually meant shagging some tart – then he wouldn't appreciate the interruption.

Mouse passed by with her hands full of dirty glasses and a distracted expression on her face.

'She okay?' asked Frank.

'Hard to tell,' Tommy sighed. 'You know what she's like. She don't say much at the best of times.'

'Poor kid.'

'You think I should have told her about Lynsey?' Tommy asked.

'Not my place to say. Hard to keep secrets in a place like this, though.'

Tommy reckoned she was coming round gradually. She

281

was certainly talking to him more, although the thawing in relations didn't extend as far as Moira. 'It ain't the easiest thing in the world to tell someone.' He finished his drink and rose to his feet. 'I'd best get on. Give us a shout when you want another.'

Frank gave a nod and went back to reading his paper.

By closing time, Joe still hadn't turned up and the boys began to drift away, grumbling about their boss's failure to show. Connor, who had taken control of the cash, leaned against the bar with a big fat grin on his face. He tapped the bag with the money in it. 'Maybe I'll go find myself a game of poker. What d'ya reckon, Tommy? I might get lucky like you did.'

'You won't feel lucky when the old man catches up with you. Just go home, huh?'

'It's Friday night,' Connor said. 'What the fuck do I wanna go home for?' He took a step back, stumbled against a table and laughed like a drain. 'I'm gonna go up West and win meself a fuckin' fortune!'

It was only then that Tommy realised how pissed Connor was. He couldn't let him take the Jag; he was likely to wrap it round the nearest lamp post. And even if he did manage to make it in one piece to the West End, he was drunk enough to blow all the money in a casino. Tommy held out his hand. 'Come on, give me the keys and I'll drive you back.'

'Nah,' said Connor. 'I can drive, man. Ain't nothin' wrong with me.'

'Give me the keys and you can have another drink.'

Connor thought about this for a moment. 'Scotch?' he asked.

'Anything you want.' Tommy reckoned that one more wouldn't make any difference. He gestured with his hand. 'C'mon, the keys.'

'Get me the drink first. And make it a double.'

While Tommy was sorting the Scotch, Yvonne came behind the bar and glared at him. In a stage whisper that just about anyone could have heard, she hissed, 'Don't even think about letting him stay here tonight. I'm not having him throwing up all over the sofa.'

'He's not staying here. Five minutes and I'm taking him home.'

'You'd better,' she said, before pursing her lips and strutting through to the hallway. Tommy listened to her clumping noisily up the stairs before turning back to Connor. He held the drink in one hand and stretched out the other. 'Keys,' he demanded, wiggling his fingers.

Connor took the keys out of his pocket and dangled them in front of him. 'Here you go, bruv. They're all yours.'

The exchange was made, and Connor retired to the nearest bench, where he sat back, lit a fag and put his feet up on one of the chairs.

As the staff herded the last of the customers out of the door, Frank came up to the bar. He looked over at Connor, and then back at Tommy. 'You want a hand getting him home?'

'Are you sure? I'll have to leave the Jag at the flats. It'll mean walking back.'

'That's all right. I could do with the exercise.'

'Thanks, mate. I wouldn't say no. It'll be a bugger getting him up those stairs.'

Frank perched on a bar stool while Tommy saw the staff

out and locked up behind them. Mouse, meanwhile, had started gathering up the dirty glasses.

'Why don't you leave those, hon,' Tommy said, 'and we'll sort them in the morning? You've done enough. Get yourself off to bed.'

'Okay,' she said. 'Night, then.'

'Night, love.'

Connor smirked at her. 'And no sneaking out after everyone's asleep. You don't want to get yourself in trouble.'

Mouse's cheeks blushed red, although Tommy wasn't sure if it was from embarrassment or rage. 'Cut it out!' he snapped at Connor.

'Shit, I was only giving some friendly advice. No need to bite me head off.'

'Well keep your advice to yourself.'

Frank gave her a nod. 'Night, Mouse. Sleep well.'

'Night,' she said, before hurrying through to the hall.

Tommy waited until she was out of earshot before addressing his brother again. 'Just leave the kid alone, can't you? She's got enough problems without you adding to them.'

Connor knocked back his Scotch and slammed the glass down on the table. 'You think, Tommy boy? I reckon she's on to a bloody good thing and she knows it. Got her feet well under the table here.'

Tommy raised his eyes to the ceiling. 'Let's go then, shall we?' He glanced at Frank. 'You ready?'

'As I'll ever be.'

Connor was swaying as he stood up, so Tommy and Frank took an elbow each, manoeuvred him behind the bar and half walked, half dragged him along the hall and out of the door.

The car park was empty now, apart from the silver Jaguar. They bundled him into the back of the motor, where he slumped sideways and promptly fell asleep.

Tommy got into the driver's seat and wound down the window, partly to keep himself awake but mainly to freshen the atmosphere. His brother stank of beer and fags and sweat. He glanced at Frank and grinned. 'Just try not to breathe too deeply.'

'Believe me, I'm trying.'

By now it was a quarter to twelve. The streets were quiet as the Jaguar purred sweetly towards the south side of Kellston. The traffic lights were on their side, and within a few minutes they had left behind the shops and the identical rows of two-up, two-down terraces and were driving instead past larger detached houses with garages and manicured front gardens. Tommy frowned. 'I still can't figure what Joe's up to. I mean, what's he playing at not turning up like this?'

'Your old man's a law unto himself.'

'True.'

Frank gave a yawn. 'Fancy the dogs during the week? Wednesday, maybe?'

'Yeah, sounds like a plan. I'll see if I can get some cover.' Tommy indicated left and turned into the drive of St George's Court. He was almost at the flats when he saw the blue flashing light in his rear-view mirror. 'Ah, for fuck's sake! What's their game?'

Frank looked over his shoulder. 'Hey, Connor, wake up. We've got company.'

Connor gave a grunt. His eyes briefly flickered open before instantly closing again.

Tommy slid the Jag into the pool of light spilling on to the forecourt from the foyer and switched off the engine. He watched as the panda car drew up behind them and two uniformed officers got out. He didn't recognise either of them; they weren't local filth, unless they were both new to the station. The older of the two, a thin-faced man with cropped grey hair and sergeant's stripes, came over to the driver's side and leaned down.

'Is this your car, sir?'

'My dad's,' Tommy said. 'He lives here.' He gestured with his head towards the slouched figure in the back. 'So does my brother. He's had a few, so I thought I'd drive him home.'

'Are you aware that your left rear light isn't working?'

'No,' Tommy said politely. 'Sorry, I didn't realise.'

'Could I see your driving licence, please?'

'Sure.' Tommy reached into the inside pocket of his jacket, took out his wallet and passed over the licence. 'Here.'

'Thomas Quinn,' the officer said, reading off the details.

'Yeah, Tommy Quinn. That's me.' While the thin-faced guy was checking over the licence, his partner was prowling around the Jag, peering at the tyres. 'I'll let Dad know about the light. I'm leaving the motor here. He can get it fixed in the morning.'

'Would you mind getting out of the car, sir?'

'What for?' Tommy said. Although they were going to have to get out anyway – Connor would need to be hauled up to the flat – he still resented being told to do so by the filth. And there was the money to worry about, too. The bag full of cash was sitting on the back seat.

Frank threw him a warning glance. 'Come on,' he said.

'The sooner we get this over with, the sooner we can go home.'

Tommy reluctantly did as he was asked. He looked towards his father's living-room window on the first floor, but there was no light showing. As Frank got out of the Jag and pulled himself up to his full height, Tommy saw the officers exchange a look. If things turned nasty, neither of them fancied taking him on.

'Would you mind opening the boot, sir?'

'Jesus,' muttered Tommy as he leaned back into the car and took the keys out of the ignition. 'Haven't you lot got anything better to do?' He walked to the back of the car. As he turned the key in the lock, there was a split second when he was aware of Connor shifting in the back seat and Frank bowing his head to light a cigarette. And then the boot swung slowly open.

## 34

It was after one o'clock and Helen was still awake, waiting for Tommy to come back. She shifted on to her side, peering into the darkness. What was taking him so long? Perhaps Connor had kicked up a stink, or there'd been a row with Joe, or maybe he'd just dropped by Frank's place for a nightcap on the way home. Whatever the reason for his absence, she couldn't sleep until he was safely in his bed.

She stared at the thin slice of light creeping under the door. An ominous feeling was tugging at her guts. An image of the smashed Jaguar jumped into her head, the metal crushed and crumpled, Tommy slumped over the wheel. And what about Frank? She gave a shudder and pulled the blankets tighter around her.

Suddenly there was a loud hammering on the back door to the pub. Helen sat bolt upright, her heart in her mouth. She heard the door to Yvonne's bedroom open and the sound of her footsteps as she padded along the landing. Grabbing her dressing gown, Helen leapt out of bed and rushed to the banisters. From here, she could see the hallway two floors down, and she watched as Yvonne hurried down the stairs.

'Who is it?' Yvonne called out as she approached the door.

'It's the police. Open up!'

Not an accident, then, thought Helen. The cops didn't shout like that when they'd come to break bad news. So what were they doing here? She thought of the Molotov cocktails that Fat Pete had put together in the kitchen – but that had been years ago. Surely they couldn't have found out about the bombing of the Lincoln.

As Yvonne unlocked the door and opened it, Helen sped down to the next landing. She leaned over again so she could see the policeman standing there. He was a tall guy in a grey suit, a man with mean eyes and a smug expression on his face.

'Mrs Quinn?'

'That's me. What do you want?'

He flashed his badge at her. 'DI Leach. Your husband's been arrested, Mrs Quinn.'

'What?'

'For the murder of Joe Quinn.'

Helen's eyes widened as she felt the shock run through her bones. Her knees began to shake and the hairs on the back of her neck stood on end. Joe was dead? Murdered? And Tommy . . . No, it couldn't be true. It was crazy, ridiculous, wrong.

Yvonne stumbled back, steadying herself on the table by the door. 'Joe's . . . Joe's dead? He can't be. I mean . . . ' She emitted a short, hysterical laugh. 'And you've arrested Tommy? You must be out of your mind.'

The copper flapped a piece of paper in her face. 'We've a warrant to search the place.'

'A warrant? What the fuck for? There's nothing here. You can't just—'

But the rest of Yvonne's objection was lost as the uniformed officers behind the detective rushed into the hallway like an invading army, some dashing into the bar, others swarming up the stairs to take possession of the first floor.

Helen stood frozen with panic, her hands gripping the banisters. One of the coppers stopped and spoke to her. 'You okay, love? Maybe you should wait in the living room.' But she didn't move. She couldn't. She was still standing there when Yvonne came upstairs, her face white as a sheet.

'It's not true,' Helen said. 'It can't be.'

By now Karen and Debs, woken by the noise, had joined them on the landing. They were probably less shocked by this invasion than Helen was. It wasn't the first time that their home had been invaded by the law, and they had learned long ago to take it in their stride. But what they hadn't heard yet was exactly what the coppers were doing here. It was the only occasion when Helen had ever felt sorry for Yvonne. Having to break the news to your kids that their dad had been arrested for the murder of their grandfather was a truly unenviable task.

'What's going on, Mum?' Karen asked. 'Where's Dad?'

Yvonne shook her head. 'Come on, we can't stay here.' She marched through to the living room, which was already in a state of disarray. The cushions had been thrown off the sofas, the contents of the dresser strewn across the floor. 'Look at the state of this bloody place!'

'Mum?' Karen asked again.

'In a minute,' Yvonne snapped back. Then she turned, put her arm around her daughter and gave her a hug. 'Sorry, hon. Just sit down, yeah, and I'll make us all a hot drink.'

'I'll do it,' Helen said. She needed to be doing something, anything, to keep herself occupied. And she didn't want to be there when Yvonne broke the news to the girls. She couldn't bear to hear those words again, couldn't bear to see their faces when they found out what was happening.

In the kitchen, three young officers were rooting through the kitchen cabinets and searching under the sink. Helen put the kettle on and then went to the fridge and took out a pint of milk. She felt like she was on automatic pilot, her hands working without her brain really thinking about it. Everything had assumed an odd, dream-like quality, and she felt – or at least hoped – that she would suddenly wake up and discover it had all been a nightmare. *Tommy arrested for murder.* It didn't make sense. Something must have happened at St George's Court. A row, a fight that had turned into ... but no, it just wasn't possible to accept. Not Tommy. He'd put up with Joe all these years. Why would he suddenly do such a thing?

The kettle boiled and she made a pot of tea. All the time she was aware of the presence of the police officers, their fingers delving into every nook and cranny of the kitchen, their eyes constantly flicking towards her, as if her purpose in the kitchen might involve something more sinister than the mere act of making a brew. What were they looking for?

Helen put the mugs on a tray, along with spoons and a bag of sugar – weren't you supposed to drink hot, sweet tea for shock? – and took it through to the living room. The cushions had been put back on the sofa, and Yvonne was sitting in the middle with her girls either side.

'There's been a mistake,' she was saying while she puffed hard on a cigarette. 'They've fucked up. They've got the wrong man. Your dad would never do a thing like that. You see, it'll all be sorted out by the morning.'

Karen and Debs were leaning heavily against their mother, looking more like children than teenagers. Their faces were pale and drawn. Helen couldn't grieve for Joe Quinn – she had always hated him – but she understood how it felt to lose someone you loved. And murder, with its cold brutality, was even harder to deal with.

As she put the tray down on the coffee table, Helen could hear footsteps overhead and realised with a start that the police were going into every room. A wave of anger and resentment rolled over her. She could imagine them rummaging through the drawers of the dressing table, their gloved hands pushing aside her pants and bras, their fingers quickly discovering the shell-covered box with the precious mementoes inside. Would they open it?

Of course they would. She hated them for that. It felt like a violation. No one touched that box but her. It was the one thing that she truly owned in a world where everything else seemed on loan.

DI Leach came to the door of the living room. 'Mrs Quinn?'

Yvonne turned to look at him, her eyes full of loathing. 'What?'

'Do you have the keys for the cellar?'

'No,' she snapped.

'Are you sure? Only if that's the case, we'll have no other choice but to break the door down.'

Helen watched as Yvonne tried to balance out her reluctance to do anything to help the law against the unnecessary damage they would cause if she didn't. Eventually, realising that it was pointless to withhold the keys, she jerked a thumb towards the kitchen. 'In there. There's a spare set in the cutlery drawer.'

'Ta,' DI Leach said sarcastically. 'That's very helpful of you.'

Yvonne gave a snort and stubbed out her cigarette with a series of hard jabbing motions. She glared at the man as he went through to the kitchen and retrieved the keys. In return, he made a show of jangling them in his hand as he crossed the living room again.

'Bastard!' Yvonne hissed as soon as he was out of earshot.

Helen passed round the mugs of tea and the four of them sat quietly for a while. The girls, she was certain, were still hanging on to the slim threads of hope that their mother had offered: there had been a mistake, the police had got it wrong, Tommy would be coming home in the morning. She noticed Karen's gaze sliding over and over towards the armchair that Joe had always occupied when he was living here. Well, there was no mistake about Joe Quinn. He was dead and gone and would never be coming back.

The police had abandoned the first and second floors now and had gathered in the bar. With no sign of the search uncovering anything incriminating, Helen's hopes were beginning to rise too. But then, just as there appeared to be one tiny light on the horizon, there was a sudden commotion downstairs, a series of shouts, a thump and scuffle of heavy boots against the wooden floor. Yvonne visibly jumped, her head jerking round to stare out at the empty landing.

Debs clutched hold of her mother's arm. 'What is it, Mum? What's happening?'

'I'm not sure, love.' Yvonne went to stand up, but then as quickly slumped back down again. There was nothing she could do, and she knew it.

It was another five minutes before DI Leach appeared at the door. 'Mrs Quinn? Would you mind coming downstairs with me?'

Helen saw Yvonne take a deep breath before she slowly rose to her feet. The girls clung on to her arms until she gently shook them free. 'I won't be long,' she said. 'You stay here, eh? I'll be right back.'

Karen and Debs, obeying their mother's request, remained on the sofa. But Helen had no intention of staying put. She hurried out on to the landing, waited until Yvonne and the inspector had reached the bottom of the stairs and then followed them down. A cool rush of air greeted her in the hallway. The back door was open and she could see into the car park, where the cops had set up a dazzling set of lights. Men in white overalls were crouched on the ground, carefully examining a stretch of concrete outside the cellar.

Helen absorbed all this in a matter of seconds before sidling up to the entrance to the bar. She was just in time to see DI Leach lift a large transparent plastic bag and dangle it in front of Yvonne. Helen's heart missed a beat. Inside the bag was a baseball bat, the wide end clearly bloodied, the handle decorated with red and blue twine.

'Have you seen this bat before, Mrs Quinn?'

Yvonne stared hard at it before shaking her head. 'No.'

'Are you sure?'

Yvonne didn't hesitate this time. 'Yeah, I'm sure.'

'We'll be checking it for prints, so if there is anything you'd like to tell us ...'

'I've said, haven't I?' Yvonne folded her arms defensively across her chest. 'Now can I get back upstairs? I've got two frightened kids who've just lost their grandad and had their father arrested and their home turned upside down.'

*Two kids*, Helen noted, rather than three. Even at this desperate time, she still felt the pain of rejection. It was as if she was invisible. She didn't matter, didn't even exist. Her gaze flicked quickly from the bat to the rows of tables littered with glasses and ashtrays and scrunched-up empty crisp packets. She wished now that she had stayed to tidy up. She might have heard something, seen something that would cast a light on the killing of Joe Quinn.

DI Leach, becoming aware of Helen's presence, lifted the bag a couple of inches higher and fixed her with his cold copper eyes. 'You ever seen this before, love?'

Yvonne looked over her shoulder and threw her a warning glance, but it wasn't needed. Helen knew enough to keep her mouth shut. She quickly shook her head before retreating and fleeing back upstairs. The image of Connor swinging the bat towards Joe flashed into her mind, and her stomach turned over. She knew with a terrifying certainty that Tommy would not be coming home tomorrow. Perhaps he would never be coming home.

# 35

Tommy sat in the hard plastic chair, leaning forward with his elbows on the table. He'd been interviewed briefly last night before being banged up here at Cowan Road. Had he got any sleep? He didn't think so. Every time he'd come close to dozing off, that nightmare picture would spring into his head again – his father curled up in the boot of the Jag, his dead glassy eyes gazing blindly up at him. The shock of it remained, as did the lingering taste of vomit in his mouth.

He picked up the cup of coffee and took a few fast gulps, hoping to raise his caffeine level to the point where his brain might finally kick into gear. His solicitor, David Montgomery, sat beside him, shuffling papers. The news he'd brought, over an hour ago now, wasn't good. The missing baseball bat had been found hidden in the cellar of the Fox, and Connor's prints were all over it.

Tommy still couldn't quite believe that Joe Quinn was dead. Despite his father's violent lifestyle, there had always been something invincible about him. He was the type of man who would stay alive just to spite the Devil. But he wasn't alive. Not any more. He was laid out on a cold slab with his skull caved in.

DI Leach watched him slyly from across the table. 'Come on, Tommy. Give it up. We all know that Connor did it. You really want to go down for murder too?'

Tommy didn't reply.

'This is how I see it,' Leach said. 'Connor has a fight with your old man on the way to the Fox. It gets out of hand. He kills him in the car park, panics, dumps the body in the boot of the Jag and then walks into the pub. When did he tell you, Tommy? When he arrived, or later, when he'd got a few bevvies inside him?'

'No comment,' said Tommy.

Leach gave a dry laugh before reaching down to pick up the plastic bag. He dumped it on the table, jabbing an index finger in the direction of the contents. 'You recognise this bat, Tommy?'

'No comment.'

'Sure you do. Isn't it the bat you used to keep under the bar?'

Tommy wondered how the copper had found out about that. Who had he been talking to? Or had Connor told him? No, Connor wouldn't be saying anything. He'd be keeping shtum, like he always did. Tommy's gaze settled on the bat, with its dark stain. His dad's blood. He felt a shifting in his guts.

'And it's not the first time that your brother's attacked him, is it? Wasn't there an incident in the Fox a few months back?'

'No comment.'

'We've got witnesses who say Connor threatened your father, that he came into the Fox with this very same bat and . . . Well, you were there, weren't you?'

Tommy gave a shrug. He thought about last night, trying to recreate the moment when Connor had arrived at the pub. Had there been anything different about him? But what the hell did *different* mean? His brother had never been what you could describe as normal. Still, surely there would have been some telltale sign that he'd just committed murder?

'So, what was the plan?' Leach continued. 'To drop Connor off at the flat – he was too pissed to be of any use by closing time – and then drive somewhere quiet to dump the body? Was that the idea?'

Tommy stared silently back at him. He didn't know the exact time his father had been killed. The post-mortem was probably being carried out even as they spoke, but it could be hours before he heard the result. He thought about Connor sitting in the corner with Fat Pete, Terry and the rest. He thought about Connor coming to the bar and getting the drinks. *Put it on the old man's tab.*

The other copper, DS Penn, smiled at him from across the table. He was younger than Leach, with a round moon face and overly pink lips. There was something almost childlike about his features. 'It's okay, Tommy,' he said gently. 'We get it. Connor's your brother. He put you in a difficult position, an *impossible* position. You didn't know what to do, yeah? We understand that.'

Tommy gave him a thin smile back. The whole good cop/bad cop routine didn't wash with him. He'd heard it all before.

'You must have been in shock,' Penn continued in his soft, wheedling voice. 'Who wouldn't be? Something like that – well, it's hard to take in. And if Connor didn't mean to kill him ... Maybe it was an accident, huh? He just meant to threaten him with the bat, but he lost control, hid the body and then came running to you for help.'

Tommy figured that Penn didn't know much about his brother if he thought he'd go running to anyone. But then the cop was just fishing, trying to get him to take the bait. Once he admitted that he knew about the killing, they'd have all the evidence they needed to charge both him and Connor.

'Or maybe you were in on it all along,' Leach said, coming back on the attack. 'Maybe you and Connor planned it together. He does the murder and you dispose of the body? Is that how it was, Tommy?'

Tommy took another slurp of coffee. Outwardly, he was doing a pretty good job of keeping his cool, but inside, a sharp, jagged feeling of panic was starting to take hold. He could see how it looked, how it would look to a jury. Who was going to believe his story? Even his own brief thought he was lying. He had seen it in Montgomery's eyes, in the way he'd pursed his lips. His only hope was if Connor came clean, admitted to murder and swore that Tommy had known nothing about the body in the boot. But what were the chances of that?

# 36

Terry Street strolled along Baker Street, took the Clarence Gate entrance to Regent's Park and made his way to the boating lake. It was a warm spring morning and already the paths were beginning to fill with people. He lit a fag as he walked, eyeing the girls in their flimsy dresses. He was looking forward to summer, when, God willing, even more flesh would be on show.

There were a couple of empty benches, and Terry sat down on one. He glanced at his watch. He was early – it was only a quarter to eleven – but then he'd been up since the crack of dawn. He'd had a restless night, a part of him constantly alert for that knock on the door. But it hadn't come. And now he knew it never would.

Already Terry had started to blank out the murder of Joe Quinn. He thought instead about what he'd done afterwards – the concealing of the baseball bat in the cellar, the smashing of the rear light on the Jag and then his casual appearance in the Fox. Yeah, he'd carried it off pretty well, he thought, chatting to Fat Pete and Vinnie, expressing the right amount of surprise at Joe's failure to show. At closing time, he'd left shortly before the others, driving away in the van and setting fire to it on a patch of waste ground over Clapton way. Although there had been little chance of anyone associating the van with Joe's murder, he couldn't afford to take the risk.

A breeze rippled the surface of the water, making the tethered boats rock back and forth. A couple of teenage boys were out on the lake, rowing haphazardly, their laughter floating through the air. It wasn't that long, Terry thought, since he'd been that age too – carefree and guilty of nothing more heinous than underage drinking and lusting after girls. But he had made his choice, and nothing would bring back his innocence now. The deed was done and he would learn to live with it.

Another ten minutes passed before DI Tony Lazenby sat down beside him. 'Terry.'

Terry gave a nod. The inspector, he noticed, was looking even more pleased with himself than usual. 'You got news, I take it?'

'Yeah, they charged Connor Quinn this morning. Murder. He's going down for a fucking long stretch.'

'Good,' said Terry. Although he had never had much doubt that this would be the outcome, he was still relieved to hear it. He gazed out across the lake, pausing before he asked the question. 'And the other two?'

'Not yet, but it's only a matter of time.'

'Shit,' muttered Terry. 'That wasn't supposed to happen.' He hadn't counted on Tommy refusing to let Connor drive the Jag home. It was the one fly in the ointment. He had no gripe with Tommy Quinn or Frank Meyer. 'Why couldn't the stupid bastards just have left well alone?'

'Well, that's the problem with going to war, mate. There are always casualties. Still, I wouldn't worry about it.' Lazenby gave a low, repulsive laugh. 'It's another Quinn off the streets. That has to be something to celebrate.'

Terry, however, didn't share this point of view. His conscience, so far as Joe and Connor were concerned, was clear – they had both deserved what they got – but Tommy had never caused him any grief. Still, there was always a chance that he'd get off when it came to trial.

'You heard from the others?' Lazenby asked.

By the others, Terry knew that he meant the members of the firm. 'Yeah, Fat Pete rang me early this morning.' He'd done a good job, he knew, of acting shocked. *Jesus, what? What? How? When, for fuck's sake?* 'We're meeting up later in the Hope and Anchor.'

'They reckon Connor did it? Any doubts?'

'Nah, they think he's guilty as sin. It's all sweet.'

'Best keep it that way, then.'

Terry frowned at the instruction – he didn't need some bent cop telling him what to do – but held his tongue.

'The Cowan Road boys will pull you in at some point,' Lazenby continued. 'Sooner rather than later. Make sure you've got your story straight. I take it you have got an alibi for the time Joe died?'

'No problem. I've got a bird who'll vouch for me. She'll say that we spent the evening together before—'

Lazenby waved a hand. 'Spare me the details,' he snapped.

'You think I give a flying fuck? You just stick to your side of the bargain and I'll stick to mine.'

Terry gazed out across the lake again. His alibi wasn't watertight, but then no one would know the exact time Joe had died. The bird in question, a hooker called Jeannie Kent, would swear that she had spent the evening at his flat before they'd walked down together to the Fox. There, at about a quarter to nine, they'd separated. She had watched him go inside the pub and then carried on round the corner to her sister's place. He didn't think Jeannie suspected him. It was normal practice in situations like this for any villain connected to the victim to make sure they had an alibi. No one wanted to spend unnecessary hours down the nick because they'd been unfortunate enough to be on their own when the incident took place.

'Now we just need to wait for the dust to settle,' Lazenby said. 'Take your time, huh? Don't go rushing in, trying to take over the firm. They'll need a bit of time to get used to the idea that Joe's dead and gone.'

Terry leaned back and lit another cigarette. 'You can skip the advice. I know what I'm doing.'

Lazenby gave him a scornful look. 'I've heard that from smarter men than you, mate, and most of them are six foot under now, or banged up for so long that they may as well be dead.'

But Terry knew that he wasn't most men. And with no one left to challenge his leadership, he'd be running the show in a matter of months. 'I'll bear it in mind.'

'Do that,' the inspector said, rising to his feet. 'I'll be in touch.'

'Have a nice day,' Terry said drily.

'Oh, I don't think it could get any better.'

Terry watched him stride off along the path. Lazenby was a snide, arrogant bastard and one day he'd get what was coming to him, but not just yet. For the time being he was useful, and for as long as he was useful, Terry would tolerate him. He glanced back towards the lake. What next? He had a few hours to spare before he met up with the lads. Maybe he'd go over to the Fox and offer Yvonne his sympathy.

# 37

It was a fortnight now since Tommy, Frank and Connor had been charged with the murder of Joe Quinn, but for Helen it still hadn't sunk in. Bewildered, she staggered through the days, trying to make sense of a situation that was senseless.

For a week after the murder the Fox had been closed, but now it was open again and busier than ever. The regulars had returned, along with a number of new customers, all in the thrall of a ghoulish curiosity about what had taken place in the car park. They whispered in corners, revelling in the scandal of an unnatural death. When she was working, Helen moved silently among them, trying to close her ears to all the gossip and conjecture. It was hard enough living with it; she didn't want to hear about it too.

She glanced across the pub to where Maureen Ball, the temporary manager, was cashing up after the lunchtime shift. Helen didn't like the woman – she was hard-faced and loud – but then she probably wouldn't have liked anyone who had taken the position. So far as she was concerned, the only person who belonged behind that bar was Tommy.

It was Terry Street who'd suggested bringing Maureen in. 'I know you don't want to think about it, love,' he'd said to Yvonne, 'but every day the Fox remains closed, you're losing money. You've got the kids to think about. And Tommy, too. It won't help him if he thinks the business is going down the pan while he's banged up.'

It hadn't taken Yvonne long to decide to reopen. And as it turned out, she got on like a house on fire with Maureen. The two of them would spend hours together, chatting in the bar or upstairs at the kitchen table. Maureen had been all kindness and sympathy, but Helen still didn't trust her. There was something false about the woman, something cold and calculating.

Helen ran a cloth over the last of the tables and said, 'I'm done here. You need a hand with anything else?'

'No, love, it's fine. You get off. I'll see you later.'

After Tommy's arrest, Helen hadn't been to school once. Since Karen and Debs had left Kellston Comprehensive, she no longer had the same protection and she couldn't bear the thought of all the pointing and sniggering. She would be the granddaughter of the murdered man, the niece of the murderer, a freak and a weirdo. As no one at home had objected to her bunking off, she'd simply carried on. Here, at least, she could feel that she was being useful, helping Tommy while he was away.

Helen went upstairs to her bedroom and stood by the window, biting her nails. She wasn't sure which was worse – being in the bar surrounded by gossips, or being up here alone. Her fears had a habit of creeping up on her when she wasn't occupied, and that was exactly what was happening now. Unable to control her thoughts, she started rolling through her interview with the policewoman, trying to recall exactly what she'd said.

The room at Cowan Road had been small and stuffy. She'd been interviewed by a female officer, a middle-aged woman called Lesley Jakes. 'Now there's nothing to worry about, Helen. All you need to do is tell the truth and everything will be fine.'

But it was the truth that Helen had been concerned about. Which part of the truth would be good for Tommy and which part would be bad? She understood how words could be taken and twisted, distorted until they meant something else entirely. She had looked anxiously towards the woman beside her – a social worker type who, because Helen was underage, had been drafted in to sit with her – but nothing useful had come out of her mouth.

'Don't worry, dear. You're not in any trouble. Just take your time and answer the questions honestly.'

Yvonne could have been the one offering support, but she had claimed to be too upset to sit in on the interview. In some ways, Helen had been glad of it. She would have been even more on edge with Yvonne's eyes boring into her.

Lesley had given her a kindly smile. 'You understand the difference between right and wrong, don't you, Helen?'

'Yes.'

'And you know it's wrong to lie?'

'Yes.'

Things had carried on in much the same vein for a couple

of minutes, until it was established that Helen Beck had a moral backbone and would never, under any circumstances, try to deceive the police. There were other questions, some of which she couldn't remember, and then Lesley had introduced the subject of the Quinn family.

'Did they argue a lot, Helen? Your grandfather and your uncle?'

'Which uncle?'

'Well, either of them.'

Helen had shrugged. 'Sometimes, but then everyone argues, don't they? Joe didn't live with us any more, so we didn't see that much of him.'

'But he still came into the pub.'

'Sometimes,' Helen had said again. An image of Joe's cold, cruel eyes had jumped into her head, and it had taken every inch of her willpower to stop herself from shuddering.

'And there was one occasion, wasn't there, a few months back, when your uncle Connor arrived at the Fox with a baseball bat?'

Helen hadn't been able to deny it. She had given a small nod of her head. 'Yes.'

'That must have been scary for you.'

'I didn't really see much. I was in the back room. I mean, I heard some shouting and that, but . . . I don't know. By the time I got there, it was all over.' She hadn't been trying to cover up for Connor – there would be lots of witnesses to the attack that night – but rather to distance herself from the actual event. Yvonne's only words of advice, uttered just before Helen had left the flat for Cowan Road, had been: *Don't tell those bloody bastards anything or they'll have you up in the dock giving evidence at the trial. And believe me, hon, it won't be for the fuckin' defence.*

It hadn't been much longer before Lesley Jakes had moved on to that fateful night. 'So, do you remember seeing your uncle Connor when he came into the Fox on Friday?'

'Yes.'

'And did you think there was anything unusual about him?'

'What do you mean?' Helen had asked.

'Was he acting oddly? Did he seem upset, angry, confused?'

Helen had frowned, pretending that she was thinking about it. 'There were a lot of people in that night. I was helping out, collecting glasses and that. I didn't . . . I wasn't really taking much notice of him.'

Lesley had tipped her head to one side, watching her carefully. 'You didn't speak to him, say hello?'

'I don't think so.'

'Do you not get on with your uncle, Helen?'

Helen had given another shrug. 'It's not that. It's just that I don't know him very well. He's not been out of prison that long. We haven't . . . you know . . . spent much time together.'

It was only when they had come to the final part of the evening that Helen's nerves had really begun to jitter. She had held the glass of Coke with two hands, aware of the shake in her hands and the dryness of her lips. Lesley had glanced down at her file and then looked up again.

'So, after the Fox closed, it was just the four of you left in the bar? Your two uncles, Frank Meyer and yourself.'

'Yeah. I mean, yes.'

'And how was your uncle Connor then?'

309

'He was a bit tipsy, I suppose.'

'Tipsy?'

'He'd had a few drinks.'

Lesley had leaned forward, putting her elbows on the table. 'Was he being . . . difficult?'

Helen had shaken her head. 'I don't understand.'

'I mean, was he arguing with your uncle Tommy?'

'I don't think so. I was clearing up. I wasn't . . . I wasn't really listening to them.'

Lesley had left a long pause, as if Helen, given time, might wish to add something. But Helen had kept her mouth shut. When it had become clear that nothing more was going to be said, Lesley had changed tack.

'And why was Frank Meyer still there? Did he often stay behind after closing time?'

'Sometimes,' Helen had been able to answer truthfully. 'He and Tommy are mates. He only lives down the road.'

'Is Frank friendly with Connor, too?'

Helen had hesitated, trying to work out what Lesley was getting at. She'd been so determined not to say anything incriminating that her head had started to ache. 'Not especially.'

'Were the three of them planning to go on somewhere?'

'No, I don't think so.' Yvonne's warning had leapt into her mind again. But if she said nothing, then mightn't she be withholding evidence that could help to clear Tommy and Frank? She had to make it clear that the two of them had known nothing about the body in the boot of the Jag. Taking a deep breath, she'd quickly carried on. 'I reckon Tommy was worried about Connor driving, that's all. He asked him for the car keys and said he'd take him home. Frank offered to give him a hand.'

'In what way?'

'You know, getting Connor into the car and that.'

'So your Uncle Tommy thought that Connor had had too much to drink, yes? That he wasn't fit to drive?'

'Yes.'

'And then what happened?'

'That's it,' Helen had said. 'I was tired and I went up to bed.'

'So you didn't hear anything else that was said? You didn't see them leave?'

'No.'

And that, as far as she could recall, had been pretty much the end of the interview. Had she said the right things? She still wasn't sure. Now she leaned against the side of the window, gazing down on the street and the people passing by. She frowned. It didn't seem right that life was carrying on as normal when Tommy and Frank were locked up, waiting to be tried for a crime they hadn't committed.

Placing the palm of her hand against the pane of glass, Helen wondered, just for a second, if it was possible that Tommy had been aware of what Connor had done. Usually they at least cleared up the dirty glasses on a Friday night, but not on this occasion. *Why don't you leave those, hon, and we'll sort them in the morning.* Had he wanted to get rid of her? But no sooner had the thought entered her head than she pushed it away. Tommy had been tired, irritated by Connor's behaviour, but he hadn't been afraid – and no one, surely, could fail to be afraid if their brother had confessed to murder and their

311

father's body, bundled into the back of a silver Jaguar, was lying less than twenty yards away.

Helen moved her hand from the window and rubbed at her face. She felt guilty for allowing the thought to even enter her mind. She felt drained, exhausted by the horror of it all. Glancing towards the bed, she recalled Frank's last words to her: 'Sleep well.' But she knew that she couldn't and wouldn't ever sleep well again until the two men she loved were free.

# 38

Helen turned up the collar of her coat, surprised by the coldness of the wind whistling down the main thoroughfare of the cemetery. Spring had passed, barely noticed, into summer, and then summer into autumn. Finally, winter had arrived, and so too had the trial of Tommy, Frank and Connor.

All week the pub had been unusually quiet at lunchtime, with most of the regulars finding more diverting entertainment at the court of the Old Bailey. The trial had been in progress for four days now. Helen had wanted to go too, was desperate to go, but Yvonne had asked her not to.

'I'd rather you didn't, love,' she'd said. 'Obviously I can't let the girls hear all the gory details of what happened to their grandad. Or their father's part in it all. It wouldn't be right, would it? And if they can't go ... well, perhaps it would be better if you didn't either.'

Helen hadn't quite got the logic of the argument, but the meaning of it was plain: if she even thought about stepping foot inside court, Yvonne would not be pleased. And so in order to keep the peace, she had stayed at home, relying on others to keep her up to date with what was happening. Some things she learned from the customers, blatantly eavesdropping on their conversations. Other snippets – and they were only snippets – she gleaned from Yvonne. But the bulk of her information came from Pym, the odd little man who had hung around Joe like a bad smell. Bribing him with beer and cigarettes, she sat him down in the small rear room of the Fox every evening and listened to his version of the day's events in court.

Pym took a certain pleasure, she thought, in relaying bad news. And to date, it had all been bad. Although the charge of murder had been dropped against Tommy and Frank, they were still accused of attempting to dispose of a body. The post-mortem had showed that Joe had died somewhere between the hours of seven and nine, hours when Tommy had been serving in the pub and in clear view of everyone. Frank too had got himself an alibi, spending the early part of the evening having dinner at Connolly's before walking down to the Fox with a couple of the regulars who'd been eating there too.

The defence were claiming that Tommy had acted in innocence, insisting on driving his brother home simply in order to make sure he got there safely. The prosecution, however, were pushing the idea that Connor would only have relinquished the keys to a car containing the corpse of his father if Tommy had agreed to help him to get rid of it. With Connor so drunk as to be a liability, Tommy and Frank must have decided to drop him off at the flats before proceeding with the ghastly business of disposing of the evidence.

'And the jury?' she'd asked. 'What do you reckon they believe?'

Pym had shaken his head before fixing his small beady eyes on her face. 'Ah, I don't like the look of that lot. Already made up their minds, I reckon.'

Helen shivered as she turned on to the smaller path and wound her way round to Irene Quinn's grave. It had been months now since she'd last seen Tommy. She had gone to Brixton prison once on a visit with Yvonne and the girls, but it had all felt strange and awkward, as if she was intruding on a family occasion. Tommy had put on a brave face for them all, but she could see that he was scared. Karen and Debs, still grieving for their grandfather, had shifted uneasily in their seats, wanting to believe in their dad's innocence, but not entirely certain of it.

The jail, with its walls and locks and peculiar smells, had been an intimidating place. Helen had been aware, throughout the visit, of being under the scrutiny of the prison officers – the screws, as Tommy called them – their eyes following her every move. The atmosphere, taut and unnatural, had wrapped itself around them all, inhibiting normal behaviour. Even Yvonne, never usually short of things to say, had been oddly quiet.

As Helen reached her destination in the cemetery, she took a bottle of water from her bag. Crouching by the grave, she pulled the dead flowers from the memorial vase, dropped them on the ground and replaced the stagnant water. 'Hello, Mum,' she whispered as she carefully arranged the six white lilies.

She rose slowly to her feet and sighed as she gazed down at

Irene Quinn's headstone. There had been some talk of inter-
ring Joe's ashes here, but thankfully Yvonne had decided to
wait until after the trial was over. It wasn't up to her to make
decisions like that, she'd grumbled, and for once Helen had
agreed with her. The idea of having the remains of Joe scattered in the same place as her mother made her stomach turn
over. She wasn't sure that Irene would be all that happy about
it either.

It was too cold to hang about. With a heavy heart, Helen
began walking back towards the Fox. She wondered what
news there would be this evening, trying desperately to hold
on to hope but at the same time aware of it gradually seeping
away. With Connor still loudly and aggressively proclaiming
his innocence, the prosecution were having a field day. The
evidence was stacking up: the constant rows, the attempted
assault with the baseball bat, the very public death threats.

Connor, of course, was not the type to plead guilty. If he'd
been caught with the bloodied bat in his hand and the body
at his feet, he'd still have sworn blind that he'd had nothing to
do with it. He was going to go down – there seemed little
doubt of it – and the tragedy was that he might take Tommy
and Frank down with him.

Helen strolled back to the high street and crossed Station
Road. As usual, she hurried through the car park, not wanting to linger near the place where Joe had died. For weeks
after his murder, a strip of police tape had remained by the
cellar door, fluttering in the breeze. Eventually, unable to bear
it any more, she had snatched it up and thrown it in the bin.

After unlocking the back door, she locked it behind her
again and started walking up the stairs. She was almost at the

316

top when she became aware of Yvonne's voice coming from the living room.

'Can you credit it, the little slut just turning up like that? Brazen as you like.'

'I'd have slapped her face,' Carol Gatesby said. 'I'm telling you, I would. The bloody cheek of it!'

'I wish I had. And that top she was wearing. Jesus, you should have seen it, Maureen. Tits hanging out, everything on show. The little tramp doesn't know the meaning of the word decency.'

Hearing Helen's footsteps on the landing, they all stopped talking and looked over their shoulders to where she was standing by the door.

'Oh, it's only the girl,' Maureen said dismissively.

Helen, who had wanted to ask about the day's proceedings – Yvonne was back earlier than usual – now felt too embarrassed to do so. She could see that they were all on the booze, their glasses brimming with vodka and ice. The bottle on the coffee table was already half empty. 'Is everything okay?'

'Sure it is,' Maureen replied. 'Nothing for *you* to worry about.'

Helen gave a nod, ignoring the slight. 'Good.' Maureen, taking her cue from Yvonne, always treated her with something akin to scorn. She had been intending to make a cup of tea before the pub opened in fifteen minutes, but that would mean walking through the living room in order to get to the kitchen. Imagining the resentful silence that would descend while she was brewing up, she decided to leave it. The women wanted to talk and they didn't want her listening.

After retracing her steps along the landing, Helen began climbing the next flight of stairs.

She was only halfway up when the trio resumed their conversation. Was it Shelley Anne they were slagging off? It had to be. Although usually disapproving of men who cheated on their wives, Helen wasn't so judgemental when it came to Tommy. Yvonne was the kind of woman who would try the patience of a saint; nothing was ever good enough for her. Not that that excused her uncle's infidelity, but it went some way towards explaining it.

In her bedroom, she got changed into a pair of black trousers and a black T-shirt. Most of her wardrobe, against the current fashion, was strictly monochrome. She preferred black or white to more garish colours, although whether this was down to a desire to be different or simply to blend into the background she hadn't quite figured out.

After brushing her hair, she tied it back in a ponytail and then took a look in the mirror. She frowned at her reflection. Her face seemed too pale, and there were dark circles under her eyes. Sleep didn't come easily to her these days; she tossed and turned, dozing and waking, her dreams mingling with the nightmare reality of the trial.

The trial. Her lips parted slightly in a sigh. Shelley Anne, wisely or not, had chosen to risk Yvonne's wrath by attending court. Shouldn't she have done the same? Maybe Tommy would think that she didn't care. And Frank, too. No, she shouldn't have given in to Yvonne's demands. Whatever the consequences, she should have followed her heart instead of her head.

Helen left the room, ran down the two flights of stairs and

went into the bar. While Maureen was still occupied, she poured a pint of Best and snatched a pack of John Players and a box of matches from the shelf. She took the beer and the fags through to the small room at the rear of the pub and left them on the table by the fireplace. Bending down, she put a light to the kindling under the logs and then went back to the main room and did the same.

It was only as she stood up that she realised that Maureen was now behind the bar.

'Hope you're intending to pay for that pint,' she said, giving Helen a surly look.

Jesus, the woman had eyes in the back of her head. 'Of course.' Helen scrabbled in her back pocket for some change and put the coins down on the counter. 'Here.'

Maureen scooped them up and dropped them in the till. 'I suppose it's for that little creep Pym. I don't know why you have to keep buying him drinks.'

Helen could have retorted that she wouldn't need to if Yvonne would actually keep her up to speed with what was happening in court, but seeing as she'd got away with nicking the fags, she decided not to go there. 'He's okay, and it's only the odd pint.'

Maureen gave a snort before walking round the counter, going over to the doors and pulling back the bolts. It was five o'clock exactly. Outside, a small group of customers had already gathered. Pym was the third one in, hurrying towards the rear of the pub as if afraid that someone might try to snatch his freebies. He was dressed in a shabby overcoat that looked too large for him. A green scarf was tied loosely around his neck.

Helen followed behind, aware that he hadn't even bothered to greet her – not so much as a nod – so eager was he to reach the table. She pulled out a chair and waited patiently while he ripped the cellophane off the pack of fags and lit one with a shaking hand. His fingernails, she noticed, were ingrained with dirt.

It was only after he'd taken a few fast draws and a large slurp of beer that he finally lifted his head to acknowledge her. 'Woman trouble today. Did you hear?'

'You mean Shelley Anne turning up? Was it Shelley Anne?'

'Yeah, it was her all right. Large as life and twice as . . .' Pym licked his lips in a lascivious fashion. 'Shame she don't work 'ere no more. Used to brighten the place up, that girl.' He lifted his eyes towards the ceiling. 'Course, her upstairs weren't too pleased. I mean, you wouldn't be, would you, havin' yer husband's bit on the side show her face. Thought she were gonna have a fit. Spent the whole morning staring daggers at her, and then come lunchtime it all kicked off.'

'But what happened in court?'

'That's what I'm saying, ain't it? The two of 'em had a real go, screaming at each other like—'

'Not with Shelley Anne,' Helen interrupted. 'With Tommy. With the trial.' She only had a limited amount of time before Maureen would be on her back about getting some work done. 'How's it looking for him?'

Pym, who'd clearly been relishing his account of the cat fight, seemed disappointed by her lack of interest. 'Well, we'll know tomorrow.'

'Tomorrow?' she echoed, startled.

'Yeah, ain't they told you? They did the summing-up today. The jury's out. There should be a verdict in the morning.'

'And what do you think?'

Pym gave a shrug. 'Makes no odds what I think.'

Helen stared at him, trying to contain her exasperation. 'But how did it go? Is there any chance for Tommy?'

Pym took another drink while he thought about it. 'In my opinion ... well, it ain't looking so good. I reckon the jury think he's guilty. Why else'd Connor hand over the car keys like that?'

'Because he was drunk,' Helen said, her voice rising as anger and frustration bubbled to the surface. 'Because he knew Tommy wouldn't leave it alone. Because he decided it was best to give in, let Tommy run him home and then get rid of the body later.'

Pym raised both his hands as if shielding off an attack. 'No need to shoot the bleedin' messenger, love. I'm just sayin' it how it is.'

'Sorry,' she said quickly. 'I didn't ... Sorry.'

'Anyways,' he said slyly, 'what would have happened if Tommy had taken the keys back to the Fox with him? What would Connor have done then?'

Helen didn't have an answer to that.

Pym tapped the side of his head. 'You've got to think like the jury, see. They reckon Tommy had to be in on it. Everyone knows there was bad feeling between him and Joe. It weren't no secret. And there's the bat, too. Found it down in the cellar, didn't they?'

'But Connor had keys. He must have hidden it there.'

'He could have. Or Tommy could have.'

The pub was starting to fill up, and Helen knew she didn't have much longer. Those glasses wouldn't collect themselves. 'And Frank Meyer?' she asked quickly. 'What about him?'

'If Tommy's guilty, Frank's guilty too. That's how they'll figure it.'

'Christ,' she murmured.

'Last day tomorrow,' Pym said, staring dolefully down at what remained of his pint.

Helen wasn't sure what he was more dismayed about – the trial coming to an end or the fact that his supply of free beer and fags was about to run dry. She couldn't suss him out. Did he have any feelings, good or bad, as regarded Joe? Was he sorry that he was dead, or did he not give a damn?

'What?' he said curtly, aware of her scrutiny.

She shook her head. 'Nothing.' Pushing back the chair, she quickly stood up. 'I'd better get on.'

Pym waited until she was almost at the entrance to the next room before speaking again.

'One other thing,' he said.

Helen looked over her shoulder at him.

His eyes flicked up towards the ceiling again. 'If I was you, love, I'd watch my back.'

'What?'

But Pym wasn't prepared to say anything more. He turned his head away and reached out for his cigarettes.

# 39

The next morning dawned cold and grey. A great blanket of cloud hung low in the sky, spilling out a torrent of rain. Helen lay in bed, listening to the rattle of the window pane. She heard Yvonne get up, followed by Karen and Debs. She heard the bathroom door open and close, the flush of the loo, the gurgle in the pipes as the water ran through them.

It had been just after four o'clock, the loneliest time of the night, when Helen had first woken up and realised what she had to do. She'd go mad if she was forced to stay here waiting for news on the outcome of the trial. It didn't matter what Yvonne said: today she was going to be there.

Helen wondered how the girls could bear to go to work when the verdict on their father was about to be announced. But then again, she knew that it was different for them. They had loved Joe Quinn and were still trying to come to terms with his murder. Although they wanted to believe that Tommy was innocent, they didn't share her con-

323

viction. The appearance of Shelley Anne at court hadn't done much to help matters either. Yvonne, angry and humiliated, had told them both about Tommy's infidelity. So now they had a dad who was not only charged with attempting to dispose of a body, but who'd also been cheating on their mother.

Helen waited until she was sure that Karen and Debs had left before getting out of bed and going to the bathroom. While she showered and brushed her teeth, she could feel the tension growing in her guts. In a few hours, everything would be different. Either Tommy and Frank would be cleared and life would begin again, or ... No, she couldn't bear to think of the alternative.

Looking through her limited wardrobe, Helen finally chose her black Mary Quant dress with the white collar. She put it on, along with her black woollen tights and a pair of black shoes, and looked in the mirror. It was really more the kind of thing you'd wear in the evening, but she didn't have anything else that was smart enough. Well, it would have to do. She brushed her hair and put on some make-up, a little eyeshadow and a light smear of lipstick.

Yvonne, who was sitting at the kitchen table with her hands wrapped around a mug of black coffee, glanced up as she came into the room. 'Jesus, what are you so dressed up for?'

Helen took a deep breath. 'I'm coming with you to the Old Bailey. I can't wait here. I just can't.'

Yvonne opened her mouth as if about to object, but then just gave a shrug.

Helen, expecting an argument, was surprised by the reaction.

Perhaps Yvonne was simply too hung-over to embark on an argument. She'd been on the vodka again last night, knocking it back like there was no tomorrow. Her face looked pinched and tight, her eyes still slightly glazed.

Helen made herself a cup of tea and sat down. There was cold toast on a plate, and although she wasn't hungry, she forced herself to eat a slice. In the silence of the room, every bite she took sounded unnaturally loud. She watched Yvonne, while pretending not to, wondering how she would cope if the worst came to pass.

Five minutes later there was a loud knock on the back door followed by the sound of the door opening and closing. 'Only me!' Carol Gatesby called up the stairs.

Yvonne lifted her head and looked through to the living room and the landing beyond. 'In here,' she said when her friend was close enough to hear.

Carol swept into the kitchen, shaking her wet umbrella. 'Jesus, it's pissing down out there.' Leaning down, she pecked Yvonne on the cheek. 'You okay, darlin'? Oh, daft question, course you're not. You want me to make you another coffee?'

'No, ta.'

Carol propped her wet umbrella against the wall, pulled up a chair and sat down beside Yvonne. Only then did she acknowledge Helen, with the faintest of smiles. 'Don't usually see you at this time of day,' she said, as if Helen made a habit of lounging around in bed for most of the morning.

Helen stared straight back. The only reason Carol Gatesby hadn't seen her for the past four mornings was that she'd deliberately stayed upstairs until they'd left. 'I'm coming to court with you.'

Carol's eyebrows shot up. 'Really?' She glanced over at Yvonne, as if expecting to hear an immediate denial, but Yvonne only sighed and reached for her cigarettes.

There was the sound of a car pulling up outside. Helen rose to her feet and went to the window. 'Terry's here,' she said, watching as he swung the sleek dark blue Mercedes in beside Tommy's Capri.

'He's early,' Carol said, looking at the clock.

Terry Street got out of the motor and ran his fingers lightly through his hair. He was wearing a smart grey suit, white shirt and charcoal-coloured tie. He had altered, Helen thought, since Joe's murder. He seemed older somehow, more serious. He was still charming, still good-looking, but he'd acquired a harder edge. She saw him glance quickly towards the cellar, as if he too was incapable of crossing the car park without being reminded of what had happened there.

There was a quick rap on the back door before it opened. 'Yvonne?' he called up. 'Are you ready? I thought we'd go a bit early, try and beat the traffic.'

'We'll be right down,' Carol called back. 'Just give us a minute.'

'I'll wait in the car.'

Helen stayed by the window, watching as he strolled back to the Mercedes. She had noticed how Terry's position within the firm had shifted over the last six months. He was, perhaps, a natural leader, and even the older members of Joe's entourage deferred to him. They all still met in the Fox every Friday, only now Terry was the one who was making decisions and distributing the cash.

'You ready, love?' Carol said to Yvonne.

326

Slowly, Yvonne stood up. 'I don't know why we're bloody bothering. We all know what the verdict's going to be.'

'Oh, don't be like that,' Carol said. 'You can never tell with them juries. He might get lucky. All it takes is for one of them to think he might be innocent and—'

'He *is* innocent,' Helen said, turning to look at the two women. 'He shouldn't even be on trial.'

Carol gave her a thin smile. 'Of course he is,' she replied, although her tone suggested otherwise. 'Course he is, love.'

Yvonne put on her coat, stubbed out her cigarette and took a long look around the kitchen, as if it was her, not Tommy, who might not be coming home again. Then without another word, she made for the stairs.

Once they were in the car and heading towards central London, Yvonne perked up a bit. She clearly liked being in the Mercedes; it was large and comfortable and smelled pleasantly of leather. Seated in the front passenger seat, she assumed an almost queenly stance, her back very straight, her shoulders pushed back. 'Thanks, Terry. It's good of you to do this.'

'It's no trouble. I'm going there anyway. And you don't want to be getting the bus in weather like this.'

Helen, who was sitting behind Terry, could see his dark eyes in the rear-view mirror. She could see them but she couldn't read them. What kind of verdict did *he* want today? As Joe's right-hand man, he must be looking for some sort of vengeance. She wondered if he thought Tommy was innocent or guilty. The latter, she suspected, although that in turn made her wonder why he was being so helpful.

Terry kept up a steady stream of chat as he was driving,

trying to distract Yvonne from the ordeal ahead. Carol joined in too, leaning forward so she wasn't excluded from the conversation. Only Helen was silent, her thoughts spinning in her head, her emotions bubbling so close to the surface that she was afraid of bursting into tears.

She found herself thinking about Moira, wishing that they hadn't fallen out. She'd not heard a word from her since Tommy had been arrested. That was over six months ago now. She should have swallowed her pride, put aside her anger and gone round to see her. It was at times like this that you needed your friends.

By the time Terry drew up outside the Old Bailey, Helen's heart was drumming in her chest. She clambered out of the car, her legs weak and shaky, her stomach starting to churn again. Gulping in the cold, wet air, she tried her best to steady her nerves.

'I'll park the motor,' he said. 'You go on in. I'll see you later.'

For a moment the three of them stood motionless on the pavement like lost children abandoned by a parent. Then Carol took control. Taking Yvonne by the elbow, she gently propelled her towards the entrance to the building. As Helen tagged along behind, she gazed up at the dome topped by a bronze statue of a woman, a sword in one hand, a set of scales in the other. What kind of justice was Tommy going to get today?

It felt like forever before they were eventually allowed into the public gallery. There had been a slow-moving queue as everyone was searched and their bags examined. Then, after they had got their seats, there was another long wait before the court officials and the lawyers drifted into the room beneath. Helen noticed Terry Street arriving, but he didn't come to sit with them. Instead, after giving a nod to Yvonne, he joined Fat Pete and Vinnie across the other side.

When the accused were brought into the dock, a ripple ran through the crowd. Helen looked first at Tommy. He was thinner, she thought, than the last time she'd seen him. The first thing he did was to gaze up into the gallery, his eyes searching for familiar faces. When he finally found them, he gave a small smile. But there was a glimpse of disappointment there, too. He'd been hoping, she realised, to see his two daughters sitting alongside Yvonne.

Connor was angry and impatient, his emotions out of control. As if unable to stand still, he shifted from foot to foot, glaring at the cops and the lawyers, unable even at this late stage to resist the impulse to try and intimidate. She could see his chest quickly rising and falling as if he was about to explode.

Of the three, Frank was the one who seemed the most composed. Or was he simply better at hiding his feelings? He stared out impassively across the courtroom. Helen willed him to glance up, to be aware that she was there, rooting for him, but he didn't once lift his gaze.

When the jury came in, Helen scrutinised their faces. Did they look towards the dock or did they avert their eyes? About half and half, she reckoned, so that didn't help much. Eight men and four women shuffled into their seats, adjusting jackets and smoothing skirts before eventually settling down.

Everyone stood up when the judge made his entrance. Not long to go now. They all sat down again. Helen lifted her hand and chewed on her knuckles. It was Connor first. After a few preliminaries, the foreman of the jury, a tall, thin man with a pair of half-moon glasses balanced on the end of his nose, rose to give the verdict. The judge asked the usual question, his tone neutral, almost bored, as if he had made the request too many times before. *Do you find the defendant guilty or not guilty of murder?*

There was only a second's delay. 'Guilty.'

Connor's face twisted with rage. 'No!' He slammed his fist down and then pointed at the jury. 'You fuckin' bastards! I didn't do it! I swear I didn't do it!' As the screws dragged him out of the dock, he was still screaming at them. 'I'll kill you! I'll kill the whole fuckin' lot of you!'

In the gallery, there was a murmur of voices from the firm. Joe Quinn's killer might have been brought to justice, but there was little to celebrate. He'd been murdered by his own flesh and blood. Helen glanced across at Terry. He had his head bent towards Vinnie, nodding as he listened to what the other man had to say. She only watched him for a second before looking back towards Tommy.

Tommy's face had visibly paled. She saw him take a deep breath and briefly close his eyes. It was, she thought, a kind of gathering-in before his own fate was decided. Beside her, Yvonne crossed and uncrossed her legs, unable to sit still. Helen twisted her hands in her lap, then leaned forward, saying a silent prayer. *Please God, let the jury find him innocent.*

The foreman waited for the question, fiddling with his tie while he kept his gaze fixed firmly on the judge rather than the dock. His response to the question was swift and brusque. 'Guilty.'

Helen heard the gasp escape from Yvonne's lips at the same time as she saw Tommy's shoulders slump. A look of horror, of disbelief, passed across his face before he bowed his head. Frank placed a hand on his arm and murmured a few words. Helen wrapped her arms around her chest as panic swept though her body. It couldn't be happening. It was wrong, evil, a travesty of justice. Not Tommy. They couldn't lock him up for something that he hadn't done.

The shock of it had barely begun to sink in before Frank Meyer received a guilty verdict too. Unlike Tommy, he showed no surprise. He gave only a small shake of his head, a gesture that seemed more resigned than anything else.

And then, before Helen knew it, both men had been led away. A howl of despair caught in her throat. She covered her face with her hands and wept.

# 40

It was over a week now since the sentencing, but Helen still hadn't even begun to accept it. How could she? She was walking around in a fog of disbelief. *Ten years.* It was brutal. It was impossible. Her eyes would fly open in the middle of the night, and for hours she would stare blindly into the darkness, wondering if Tommy and Frank were awake too.

Connor, of course, had got life, but she couldn't bring herself to feel any pity for him. If he'd pleaded guilty, even to manslaughter, the jury might have accepted that his brother had known nothing about the killing. But Connor's lies had been corrosive. In the end, the jury hadn't believed a word he'd said.

A bright winter sun was shining as she walked along the high street. Even the weather was wrong. It felt like a mockery for the sun to show its face when the two people she loved most were banged up in some stinking cell. She thought ahead to all the seasons that would need to pass before they were free again. A thin groan escaped from between her lips.

All around her people were going about their business, oblivious or maybe just indifferent to what had happened. Another bunch of thugs who had got what they deserved. Wasn't that what most of them thought? They bought their groceries, went in and out of the bank, stood and chatted on street corners. She felt an involuntary spurt of anger, wanting to lash out. Didn't they care that two innocent men had been sent down for a crime they hadn't committed?

Helen went into the Spar, picked up a basket and pulled the shopping list from her jeans pocket. She sauntered up and down the aisles, not in any hurry to return to the Fox. The flat was weirdly quiet. The four of them walked around on tiptoe, as if someone lay dying in one of the bedrooms.

Yvonne, who had spent most of the last week drinking vodka in her dressing gown, had finally got dressed this morning, done her hair, put on her slap and announced that they had to get on with things. Although she and Helen had never had the best of relationships, Helen was aware of the need for them to pull together. That was why she had offered to come out and do the shopping. The fridge was almost empty and the list was a long one.

It was almost one o'clock when Helen got back to the pub, a couple of carrier bags hanging from each arm. She went around the rear of the building, pushed open the door and climbed the stairs. The jukebox was playing in the bar, Bryan Ferry singing 'The "In" Crowd'. There was the usual buzz of conversation, the familiar chink of glasses. She didn't work the Saturday lunchtime shift, but she'd be back on duty in the evening.

She went to the kitchen and dumped the bags on the table. 'Yvonne?' There was no reply. She went back into the living room. 'Yvonne?' She turned, intending to go and unpack the groceries, but then stopped dead in her tracks. An old brown suitcase was leaning against the wall. Her old brown suitcase, the one that had lived on top of the wardrobe for the past four years. She frowned, confused as to what it was doing there.

Yvonne suddenly appeared at the door with a fag in her mouth. 'Sorry, love,' she said, with an expression that was about as far from apologetic as one could get. 'But it was never meant to be permanent, was it?'

Helen stared at her. 'What?'

'It's going to be hard enough staying afloat without another mouth to feed. I just can't do it. That bloody lawyer took every last penny we had.'

Helen glanced towards the suitcase again, the light slowly dawning. 'So you're kicking me out? Is that what you mean?'

'Well, it's not as though you don't have family of your own. You can go back to Farleigh Wood. You've still got relatives there. I'm sure your aunt won't mind.'

'And have you talked to Tommy about this?'

Yvonne gave a shrug, folding her arms across her chest. 'Tommy's not here, is he? And he's not going to be, not for a bloody long time.'

Helen stared at her in disbelief. She couldn't leave the Fox. It was her home, the only place she felt safe and secure. 'But what about the pub?' she asked, aware of a pleading edge to her voice. 'I can help out. I can do more. I can—'

'I'm selling it,' Yvonne said. 'Me and the girls, we can't stay here. Not after what's happened. We need a fresh start. I'm going to flog the place and then we're off to Spain.'

'Spain?' Helen repeated, dumbfounded. 'How can you go to Spain? What about visiting? How are you going to see Tommy if you're living hundreds of miles away?'

'He doesn't need us to visit him,' Yvonne snapped. 'He's got his fancy piece for that.' She took an angry drag on the cigarette, her eyes full of bitterness and venom. 'No, it's for the best. The sooner we get away from here, the better. Terry Street's already made me an offer and I'm going to accept. We'll be off as soon as the paperwork's gone through.'

'Tommy won't let you sell it. Does he know? Have you told him?'

Yvonne gazed scornfully back at her. 'He hasn't got a choice, love. The pub's in my name, not his. They wouldn't give him a licence, not with his criminal record.'

Helen, flustered as she was, could still see that there was no point in further argument. Everything had been decided. She understood now why Terry Street had gone out of his way to be so helpful. And she understood too why Pym had warned her to watch her back. 'So what are you saying – that you want me to leave right now? Right this minute?'

'It's for the best,' Yvonne said again. 'There's no point in dragging it out. I'll explain to the girls when they get back from work. I'm sure they'd have liked to say goodbye, but ... Well, they've been through enough. You understand that, don't you? It's nothing personal, love, we all just have to move on.'

Helen had a panicky feeling in her chest. She was about to

be thrown out on to the street and there was nothing she could do about it. Where was she going to go? Janet didn't want her – she'd made that perfectly clear four years ago. And since then the only communication between them had been an exchange of cards every birthday and at Christmas. She was on the verge of blurting this out, but pride held her back. No, she wouldn't give Yvonne the satisfaction.

'Okay,' she said. 'If that's what you want.'

Yvonne took a drag on her cigarette and gave a weary sigh. 'It's not what I want, Mouse. It's just the way it has to be.' She walked over to the table, laid the cigarette in the ashtray and took her purse from her bag. 'Here,' she said, holding out three five-pound notes to Helen. 'Take this. It should keep you going for a while.'

Helen stared at the money, wanting to refuse it but knowing she'd be a fool if she did. Reluctantly she reached out a hand and took the notes from Yvonne. She shoved them in her jeans pocket and turned away. So this was it. The end of her life at the Fox. She picked up her suitcase, took a deep breath and walked out of the door.

# 41

Outside, Helen screwed up her eyes against the bright winter sunlight. She could barely believe what had just happened. She felt shell-shocked, angry, confused, disoriented. Where was she going to go? What was she going to do? For a while she stood at the back door with her suitcase at her feet. She felt utterly and completely lost. Yvonne hadn't even had the grace to give her time to get organised, to make other arrangements. One minute she was living at the Fox; the next she was homeless.

She took another deep breath. What she mustn't do was fall apart. She wasn't a child any more. She was fifteen, almost sixteen, and more than capable of taking care of herself. Except it didn't feel like that at the moment. She was scared, that was the problem. It was a quarter past one on a November afternoon, and in a few hours it would be dark. Reaching down, she picked up the suitcase and began to walk.

As she crossed the car park, Helen glanced back over her shoulder. She remembered the first time she'd come here, sitting quietly with Tommy in the white Cortina, thinking that this was the last place on earth that she wanted to be. But then gradually, over the years, it had become the only place. She loved the Fox almost much as Tommy did. It would break his heart when he found out that Yvonne had sold it.

She blinked back the tears, not wanting to get sentimental. The pub was just bricks and mortar, nothing else. It was only the people who lived in it that mattered, and now that Tommy was gone, the building had lost its soul. She gave it one final, regretful look before heading for the high street.

As she trudged past the shops, she tried to work out what to do next. There were hostels for homeless people, she thought, but she didn't know where they were and she didn't have the courage to stop and ask anyone. Would she be allowed to stay in one anyway? Perhaps she was too young. They might take her and put her in a home. No, she wouldn't be able to bear that. She would rather sleep on the streets than be taken into care.

It was only as she was approaching Connolly's that she suddenly thought of Moira. But she couldn't ask her for help. How could she? She had pushed her away, refused even to speak to her. She felt ashamed now of how she'd behaved. It was hardly surprising that for all the time Tommy had been on remand, Moira had remained silent. Not a single phone call. Not one visit to the pub. She had decided, perhaps, that the Quinns were more trouble than they were worth.

And yet Helen couldn't quite believe this. Moira, above all

else, had a big heart. Surely she wouldn't turn her away in her hour of need? But still she hesitated, racked by guilt and remorse. It would be unfair to just turn up on her doorstep, saying she was sorry, expecting her to put a roof over her head. Or was that just her pride speaking? She wasn't good, she knew, at asking for favours.

Stopping outside the café, Helen peered through the window. She saw Paul Connolly behind the counter, and a waitress weaving between the tables, carrying a tray. She couldn't see Moira, though. And then she remembered that it was Saturday, and that Moira didn't usually start her shift until the evening.

She began walking again, wondering if Moira still went to the cinema in the afternoons.

She remembered the last film they'd seen together, *The Great Gatsby*. She thought of Jay Gatsby floating lifeless in the pool. She thought of Joe Quinn bundled in the boot of a car with his skull caved in. She gave a shudder, sickened by the horror of it all.

Despite the sun, there was a cold wind biting at her face and fingers. Where were her gloves? She had had them when she was out shopping. She must have taken them off and left them in the kitchen at the Fox. She wondered what else she might have left there. She glanced down at the suitcase, aware that Yvonne had done the packing. Was the photo of her parents there? And the shell-covered box? And the old sock with thirty pound notes folded neatly inside it? She was going to need that money now that she was out here on her own.

Helen crossed the road as the undertakers', Tobias Grand

& Sons, came into view. She stood back on the pavement and stared up beyond the gold-lettered sign to the window above. Moira's living room overlooked the street, with the bedroom and the kitchen at the rear of the building. There was no sign of life. She dropped her gaze to the undertakers' window, covered by wide net curtains. There was no sign of life here either. Death lay hidden behind the discreet shield, bodies waiting to be buried, silk-lined coffins waiting to be filled. She felt another shiver run through her.

Next to the entrance to the undertakers' was the door to Moira's flat. Helen put the suitcase down, raised her hand, paused only for a second and then rang the bell. Above the noise of the traffic she listened for the sound of footsteps coming down the stairs. Nothing. She rang again, wondering if she should walk round to the cinema and try to catch her there. And then, just as she was about to leave, the door suddenly opened and Helen found herself staring at someone she had never seen before. The girl was about nineteen, with long, straight wheat-coloured hair and pale blue eyes that still looked full of sleep despite the time of day.

'Yeah?'

Helen gazed blankly back at her for a moment. 'Er, is Moira in?'

'Who?'

'Moira, Moira Sullivan.'

The girl shook her head. 'Sorry. Never heard of her. Are you sure you've got the right address?'

Helen felt her heart sink. 'She used to live here.'

The girl gave a shrug. 'Sorry,' she said again.

'You don't know where she's gone, then?' Helen knew the

question was pointless even as she asked it. The girl didn't have a clue who she was talking about.

'No idea,' she said, and closed the door.

Helen picked up the case again and trudged back across the road. Maybe Paul Connolly would have Moira's new address. But why had she moved? She'd lived in that flat for years. What if she was dead? she thought suddenly, with a jolt. What if she'd got sick and gone to hospital and never got better? Although she knew it was unlikely, Helen was so used to losing the people she loved that this bleak possibility continued to dog her thoughts as she retraced her steps, pushed open the door and stepped inside the steamy café.

She went up to the counter, where a woman was paying for her food. She could feel her stomach twisting as she waited to be served. The woman, an elderly lady, was taking forever, counting pennies out one by one from her purse. But eventually it was done and Paul Connolly turned his attention to her.

'Yes, love. What can I get you?'

'Tea, please,' she said.

'One tea coming up.'

As he filled the mug from the big metal urn, Helen put her elbows on the counter and asked as casually as she could manage, 'Is Moira working tonight?'

'Moira?' he repeated, and then shook his head. 'No, love. Moira doesn't work here any more. Not for months.'

Although relieved that there wasn't worse news, Helen still struggled to hide her disappointment. 'Oh, do you know where she's gone?'

'Sorry, sweetheart,' he said. 'She moved away a while back.'

Helen gave a nod. 'Thanks.' She paid for the tea, picked up the suitcase and the mug and carried them both over to her favoured table. Pulling out a chair, she slumped down listlessly. So, she was too late. She should never have allowed herself to hope. Moira was gone and she would probably never see her again.

As she gazed out of the window, Helen suddenly remembered the letter she'd received, realising now what it must have been about. Moira had been writing to say that she was leaving. Maybe she had included her new address, or a phone number. But Helen would never know. She had ripped it up without even looking at the contents, and chucked it in the bin. How could she have been so stupid, so childishly unforgiving? Well, she was being punished for it now.

She took her time over the tea, glad at least to be out of the cold. The sun had gone in and the light, even though it was only two o'clock, was beginning to fade. She knew that she had no other choice but to throw herself on the mercy of her aunt. The thought of this filled her with such dismay that she wanted to put it off as long as possible. Should she ring first? There was a phone box outside the café. But if she called, Janet might find an excuse as to why she couldn't come. It was probably best to just turn up.

It was half an hour before Helen finally left Connolly's. She lugged her suitcase back across the street – it seemed to be getting heavier with every step she took – and went to stand by the bus stop. She would need to go to Chingford and from there get another bus on to Farleigh Wood. Ten minutes later, a Chingford bus arrived. Helen shuffled forward in the queue, but just as she was about to get on, she changed her mind and stood aside. She wasn't ready yet. She would wait and get the next one.

Three more buses came and went, but Helen still couldn't bring herself to do it. She could imagine the look on Janet's face when she turned up unannounced. Her aunt was not the type of person who would refuse her entrance, but it would be done grudgingly and it would be made clear that she wasn't welcome. At the thought of this, Helen moved away from the bus stop, leaned the suitcase against the stretch of wall beside Moira's old flat and gazed dolefully along the high street.

An hour later, she was still standing there when the door to the flat opened and the girl with the long straight hair came out. Helen watched as she crossed the road and went into the Spar. As if oblivious to the cold, she was dressed in a fringed brown suede miniskirt and a bright yellow blouse. A few minutes later she was back, clutching a bottle of milk in one hand and a pack of cigarettes in the other.

As the girl approached the door, she stopped and looked at Helen. 'Still here, then?'

Helen gave a light shrug, trying to smile but not quite succeeding.

The girl glanced down at the suitcase. 'So what's the deal? You running away?'

'No.'

'Your parents kick you out?'

Helen shrugged again. 'Something like that.'

'What's your name, then?'

It was on the tip of Helen's tongue to say Mouse – the name she had got so used to over the past four years – but at the last moment she stopped herself. That part of her life was over. It was time to start again. 'Helen. Helen Beck.'

'I'm Lily,' the girl said. She handed over the pint of milk. 'Here, hang on to this for a sec.' She dug into her back pocket, took out a key and unlocked the door. As she stepped inside, she glanced over her shoulder at Helen. 'Well, come on. Don't just stand there. Do you want to come in or not?'

# 42

The inside of Moira's old flat was familiar and strange at the same time. The same furniture was there, although the curtains were different and all the books and ornaments had gone. It was also a lot untidier. Magazines were strewn across the coffee table, along with dirty glasses, empty wine bottles and an overflowing ashtray. The gas fire was on, making a soft hissing noise. Helen put down the suitcase and handed back the pint of milk.

'Excuse the mess,' Lily said. 'I had a few mates round last night. You want coffee?'

'Thanks.' Although Helen would have preferred tea, she was grateful for anything hot. While she'd been hanging round the bus stop, the cold had crept into her bones.

Lily went into the kitchen and put the kettle on. Then she came back into the living room, crossed her arms over her chest and looked at Helen. 'How old are you, then?'

'Sixteen,' Helen lied.

Lily's eyebrows shifted up as if she didn't quite believe her. 'My mum kicked me out when I was fourteen. Well, not my mum so much as her fancy man. Not that she made any objection. To be honest, I was glad to get out of there. He was a real creep, couldn't keep his hands to himself, if you know what I mean.'

Before Helen had a chance to reply, Lily had returned to the kitchen. There was the sound of running water and the clatter of cutlery being thrown into a bowl. Helen stood in the middle of the room, not quite sure as to what to do next. The invitation had been so unexpected that it still felt faintly unreal.

'You going to sit down, then?' said Lily as she came back with a couple of mugs of coffee. She shifted the dirty glasses to one side and put the mugs on the table.

Helen perched on the edge of the sofa, carefully watching the girl while pretending not to. 'Thanks.'

Lily curled up in the armchair like a cat, ripped the cellophane off the pack of cigarettes and offered one to Helen. 'Smoke?'

Helen shook her head. 'No thanks.'

Lily lit one and leaned back. 'So this mate of yours – Maggie, was it?'

'Moira.'

'Yeah, Moira. That's it. She used to live here, did she?'

Helen gave a nod.

'It must have been a while ago. I've been here for . . . God, it's almost six months now.'

'We kind of lost touch,' Helen said.

'So what's the plan? What are you going to do now?'

Helen's plans, such as they were, wouldn't have filled the back of a postage stamp. 'I don't know. I've got an aunt in Farleigh Wood. I was thinking of going there, but . . .' She didn't need to finish the sentence for Lily to understand what she meant.

'But you don't get on with her.'

'Not really,' Helen said. She took a sip of the coffee. It was strong and sweet, with a bitter aftertaste.

'So what's the deal with the parents? Why'd they kick you out?' Lily took a drag on the cigarette and smiled. 'Hey, you don't have to tell me if you don't want to. It's none of my business, right?'

Helen hesitated, not sure as to how much to say. 'It's kind of complicated.'

'It always is, love.' Lily stared at her for a few seconds, then asked, 'You got any money?'

Helen looked warily back at her. Was this why she'd been invited in? Was the girl going to rob her, steal all her money and then throw her back out on to the street? She thought of the three five-pound notes in her jeans pocket and the saved cash that might or might not be in the suitcase. 'Not much,' she said. 'A couple of quid.'

Lily tilted her head to one side and laughed. 'There's no need to look like that. I'm not a bleedin' mugger.'

Helen blushed furiously. 'I know. I didn't—'

'I was just thinking we could get some cider, have a drink. I've got a stinking hangover. It's the only thing that gets rid of the headache. I just spent the last of my cash on fags, but I can pay you back tomorrow.'

'Tomorrow?' Helen repeated, thinking that she didn't even know where she'd be tonight, never mind the next day.

'Sure. I mean, you need somewhere to stay, don't you? You're welcome to kip on the sofa if you can stand the mess. I've got spare blankets and stuff.'

Helen stared at her, wondering if she'd heard right. 'Do you mean it? I can really stay here?'

'Course you can. You know, until you get yourself sorted.' Lily glanced towards the window. 'You don't want to be out there on your own, love. It's not safe. There's all sorts wandering the streets at night. So what do you say? You fancy that drink or not?'

Helen didn't have to think twice. With her only other alternatives being an embarrassing plea to Janet Simms, or sleeping under a bridge in a cardboard box, the choice was an easy one. She jumped up, her despair fading into something more akin to hope. 'Shall we go and get that cider, then?'

Two hours later, Helen was lying stretched out on the sofa. She wasn't used to alcohol, and it had gone straight to her head. It had cut through all her inhibitions, too. Now she was talking to Lily like she'd known her all her life. She'd already told her about her childhood in Farleigh Wood, and now she'd moved on to what had happened at the Fox.

Lily, who never seemed to watch or even read the news, was totally unaware of the drama that had taken place. 'So he was murdered by his own son?' she said, her eyes wide and incredulous.

'Yeah, and now Tommy's in jail too, even though he didn't have anything to do with it. Yvonne's going to sell the pub and go to Spain.'

348

'Nothing like sticking by your man. She sounds a real piece of work.'

'She's that all right. And when he comes out, he's going to have no pub, no home, no nothing. How could she do that to him?' The booze was drawing Helen's emotions to the surface. She wiped away the tears with the back of her hand. 'She's such a cow.'

'You okay, hon?' Lily asked.

'Yeah, I'm okay.'

'Well, you're best out of it, from the sound of things. What you need is a fresh start. Life's too short to be stressing about the past.' Lily took a large swig of cider. 'That bitch sounds just like my mum. She used to put me in care every time she got a new bloke. I was in and out of them homes like a bloody yo-yo.'

Helen turned her head to gaze at her. Lily seemed so smart and confident that it was hard to believe she'd had such a background. 'What about your dad?'

'What about him? He's a complete waste of space.'

'My dad was a copper,' Helen said.

'You're kidding?'

'No, for real. I don't remember him, though. I was only young when he died.'

'Oh well, at least he had a job. My old man never did a day's work in his life.'

'I've got bad blood,' Helen said. 'That's what Joe Quinn said.'

Lily gave a snort. 'There's no such thing,' she said. 'You've just been unlucky.'

'Unlucky,' Helen said. 'That's one way of putting it.'

The two girls looked at each other and burst out laughing. Suddenly, with a friend to share things with, life didn't seem so grim. Helen knew that she was drunk – they were both drunk – and she was glad of it. She didn't care about tomorrow, or how she might feel. The booze slid through her veins, giving everything a rosy glow.

'Have you thought about a job?' Lily said. 'What are you going to do?'

'I can find work in a bar or a caff. Maybe I can get some shifts in Connolly's.'

'That won't pay much, not at your age.'

Helen knew this was true. Although she had a bit of money in reserve, it wouldn't last long when she was having to fork out for rent and bills and food. 'I'll think of something.'

'I know how to make some decent cash,' Lily said. 'If you're interested.'

'Yeah? How's that, then?'

Lily gave her a sly smile. 'Well, what is it that all men want?'

Helen stared back at her in horror. 'No way, I'm not—'

'Oh, I don't mean *that*. Haven't you heard? There's more than one way to skin a cat.'

# 43

The next morning, Helen woke up with the headache from hell and a stomach that seemed intent on ejecting its meagre contents. She rushed to the bathroom, reaching it just in time to lift up the lid and throw up in the toilet. Leaning over the bowl, she retched a few more times before dropping her forehead on to the cool porcelain rim and swearing to God that she would never touch a drop of alcohol again.

Ten minutes later, when she felt just about able to stand, she stumbled back to the kitchen and put the kettle on. While she was waiting for the water to boil, she searched the cupboards until she found a bottle of aspirin. She took two, hoping it would be enough to dull the hammering in her head.

When the tea was made, she slumped down at the kitchen table, rubbing her eyes as she tried to remember the events of the previous night. She had said too much, she thought. The booze had loosened her tongue and removed all her natural reserve. But still she was grateful for the bed that Lily had provided her with. Glancing towards the window, she saw that it was grey outside and pouring down with rain. She wondered how long she would have waited before finally getting on a bus and going to Farleigh Wood.

After the tea was drunk, Helen went to have a shower. This proved to be a more arduous task than she had first envisaged, the water constantly changing from hot to cold and back to hot again. She found a bottle of shampoo in the bathroom cabinet and managed, eventually, to get the vomit washed out of her hair. Shivering, she dried herself quickly on the towel that was hanging on the rail.

Back in the living room, she opened the suitcase for the first time since leaving the Fox and dug out some clean clothes. Nervously she rummaged through the contents until she found the sock with the money in it. It was all there. The photograph of her parents had been packed too, as well as the shell-covered box and the old *A to Z* of London.

Sitting back on her haunches, Helen gave a sigh of relief. After burying the sock again – she thought she could trust Lily, but she couldn't be sure – she pulled out the road map and flicked through the pages. She was about to close it when she came across a neatly folded sheet of paper tucked in near the back. Her heart gave a tiny jolt as she opened it out. Written on the still crisp ivory-coloured notepaper that her gran had always used, in her grandfather's familiar slanting handwriting, was a set of directions to Kew Gardens. It was a trip that must have been made long ago, but still it stirred up her emotions. In the choppy waters of a world she had always struggled to understand, her grandad had been like an anchor, strong and steady and constantly reassuring.

For a while Helen held the piece of paper in her hand, before carefully placing it back in the *A to Z*. She knew it was no good hankering after the past; what was gone was gone, and she had to get on with her life. She would not grow attached to anyone else, she decided. It was too painful to lose the people you loved.

It was chilly in the flat, but as it wasn't her home, she didn't feel free to put on the gas fire. Instead, she took a sweater out of the case and pulled it on over her T-shirt. She ran a comb through her damp hair and glanced towards the bedroom. It was almost eleven, but there was still no sign of movement from Lily.

Helen made another mug of tea, took another aspirin – the first two didn't seem to be working – and then, with nothing else to do, set about cleaning up. She collected the empty bottles and threw them in the bin. She put the dirty glasses in the sink, along with all the used plates and mugs, and did the washing-up. She wiped down the surfaces in the kitchen and then moved on to the living room. By the time she was finished, the place was immaculate and her headache had receded a little.

It was midday before Lily finally put in an appearance. She came out of the bedroom wearing nothing but a long white T-shirt with a picture of Mickey Mouse on the front. 'Morning,' she mumbled. Then she gave a shiver. 'Christ, it's freezing in here. Why haven't you put the fire on?'

Helen, who was sitting on the sofa making a list of things to do, looked up and pulled a face. 'Sorry, I didn't ... you know, with it being your flat and everything.'

Lily bent down by the fire, put a match to the gas and crouched there for a while rubbing her hands together. 'That's no reason to freeze to death.'

'Do you want a brew?' Helen asked. 'The kettle's just boiled.'

'Oh, black coffee, please. That'd be great.' Lily stood up again and gazed around the room. 'God, you've been busy. I hardly recognise the place.'

'I only did a bit of tidying up.'

'More than that, love. It was a right tip. Ta, you've done a grand job.'

'Well, it was good of you to give me a bed for the night.'

'No skin off my nose,' Lily said. 'Now, how about that coffee? And then we'd better get to work if we're going to pay the rent this week.'

And so, that afternoon, Helen's education into Lily's world began. It started with hot tongs to curl her hair, and then a lesson on applying make-up so she could look a little older than she actually was.

'The punters won't complain, love – they like the young ones – but the cops might pick you up if you look under eighteen. You'll have to watch out for the filth; they're all over the place and they're not in uniform, so you just have to sniff 'em out.'

'I can do that,' Helen said. From time to time plain-clothes detectives had come into the Fox, sniffing around after Joe Quinn and the firm. Tommy had always pointed them out, and after a while she had learned to spot them for herself. 'I know you explained it all last night, but tell me again how it works, this corner game thing.'

'It's easy,' Lily said, as she patted loose powder on to Helen's face. 'We head up to Soho and hang around some clip joint until a likely punter comes along. It won't take long, trust me. You tell him that you're working for the club and that you can't get away straight off, but you'll meet him round the corner in fifteen minutes. Say you've got a flat there, somewhere you can go.'

'And then?'

Lily laughed. 'And then you take the cash and leg it, love – once they're out of sight, of course.'

'But what if they won't pay?'

'Then you walk away. But that doesn't happen very often. Most of them are so desperate for it, they've left their brains in their pants.'

Helen gazed into the mirror, absorbing all this information while her face was being gradually transformed. 'Don't they go to the cops? Don't they report it?'

'Well, what if they do? The law aren't going to waste their time trying to find you. Be like looking for a needle in a haystack. And anyway, most of the punters don't even bother. They're too scared of their wives and families finding out that they've been after a quickie on the quiet.'

Helen, who was nothing like as confident as Lily, bit down on her lower lip. 'It's still risky, though, isn't it?'

Lily's eyes met hers in the mirror. 'That's half the fun of it,' she said. 'You're not getting cold feet, are you?'

Helen knew that it was too late to change her mind now.

Anyway, how else was she going to survive? 'No, no way. I'm fine. I'll do it.'

After the make-up was completed, Lily raided her wardrobe for clothes. The two girls were more or less the same size and height, and after numerous garments had been tried on and discarded, Helen found herself dressed in a black leather miniskirt and a silky red scoop-necked top. The black platform shoes were a size too small, but she managed to squeeze her feet into them.

'Well, what do you think?' asked Lily.

Helen frowned at herself in the full-length mirror. She certainly appeared older. However, she thought she looked not so much like a tom as a rather ludicrous impersonation of one. 'Are you sure I look all right.'

Lily stood back and gave an appraising nod. 'You'll make a bomb.'

At five o'clock, they walked down to the station to catch a bus to Piccadilly. Helen, who wasn't used to platform shoes, tottered unsteadily on them, occasionally clinging to Lily's elbow for support. Lily found this hilarious and didn't stop laughing all the way down the road.

They were both wearing fur jackets over their skimpy tops, which Helen was thankful for. She was worried, however, that she might bump into someone she knew – Yvonne, perhaps, or Karen and Debs – and kept a watchful eye out while they waited for the bus. Knowing that the Fox was only a hundred yards away gave her a strange yearning feeling in her stomach. She tried not to think about it. She was moving on, leaving that part of her life behind her.

It was only when they were sitting upstairs on the bus that

Helen's nerves began to kick in again. 'What if I can't do this?' she asked, turning to Lily. 'What if I do something wrong or nobody's interested?'

Lily gave a laugh. 'Believe me, hon, you won't have any problems. The guys will be queuing up. You should see some of the girls working round there – they're out-and-out dogs.' She lit a cigarette and took a puff. 'And don't worry, I'll be with you. I won't leave you on your own.'

Helen stared out of the window, trying to remember every-thing she'd been told. What if she blew it? What if she was so nervy and awkward that the punters smelled a rat?

'You'll be fine,' Lily continued. 'I mean, what would you rather do – spend a few hours making a ton in Soho or sweat your guts out in a café for a weekly pittance and a few lousy tips?'

Put like that, Helen could see the logic of it. 'How much do I ask for?' she said, realising that she hadn't even covered this basic question.

'Oh, it depends what they're after. Anything from thirty for a quickie to . . . well, whatever you think you might get.'

'That much?' Helen said, shocked by the amount. She hadn't earned that in a week at the Fox.

'You kind of have to play it by ear, check out their clothes, their shoes, work out how much they might be willing to pay. Just stick by me and you'll soon get the hang of it.'

At Shaftesbury Avenue they got off the bus and walked up Dean Street into the centre of Soho. Helen had never been there before, apart from an afternoon shopping trip to Carnaby Street with her mother. And Soho at night was a very different place. It was the bustle she noticed first, the crowds of people on the streets. Slowly she took in the neon signs, the strip clubs and porn shops, the hustlers and the pimps, the toms waiting to do business. There was so much female flesh on offer, both in the pictures in the windows and in real life on the pavement, that she started to wonder how she'd ever compete. Girls in satin hot pants and Lurex halter tops stood in doorways with feather boas draped around their necks.

Lily, however, had none of Helen's doubts. She strutted along confidently, her head held high, her long hair swinging down her back. Men turned to look at her as she walked past, their eyes raking her body like foxes eyeing up a chicken. Helen tried to keep track of the street names, to remember her way back in case they got separated. She sensed the danger of the place they were in, felt the atmosphere humming with a barely suppressed excitement.

Lily finally stopped across the road from a club displaying a neon sign that said *Striptease*. It was squeezed into a row of similar establishments offering peepshows and films and exotic dancing. She gave a wave to the bouncer on the door and then blew him a kiss.

'That's Doug,' she said. 'He's sound. He'll get shot of any troublesome punters.'

Helen looked towards the giant on the door. He must have been six foot six or seven and had the broadest shoulders she'd ever seen. 'Troublesome?'

'You know, the ones who come back looking for you when you don't show up. Doug sends them on their way. They don't tend to argue with him.'

'No,' Helen said, still staring at him. 'I don't suppose they do.' Her nerves were starting to get the better of her again, giant butterflies flapping in her guts. She tugged self-consciously at the hem of the miniskirt. She felt exposed and embarrassed, as if she actually was about to sell her body.

Lily unzipped her jacket and took out a full half-bottle of vodka. She unscrewed the cap and passed the bottle over. 'Here, have a swig of this.'

Helen shook her head, wondering where the alcohol had come from. Hadn't Lily claimed that she had no money for booze last night? 'No thanks. I've still got a headache from that cider.'

'Go on,' Lily urged. 'It'll make you feel better, honestly it will.'

Helen hesitated, but then went ahead. She took a mouthful, swallowed it and grimaced. It was the first time she had ever drunk neat vodka. Although she didn't care much for the taste, she liked the warm glow that rose up from her throat. It took the edge off the fear, and she giggled as she passed the bottle back.

They had another mouthful each before Lily declared that it was time to get to work. She lit a fag and scanned the crowd with expert eyes. 'What you're looking for,' she said, 'are the nervy ones, the shy ones or the out-of-towners. All you have to do is catch their eye and smile. You can leave the rest up to them.'

Helen looked around. There were so many men, she didn't know where to start. They prowled the streets like hungry wolves, some shifty and furtive, others with a more predatory look in their eye. She shuffled from foot to foot, convinced that none of them would ever come near her.

It was Lily who was approached first. An overweight middle-aged man with a spare chin and a receding hairline sidled up to her.

'You looking for business, love?'

'Sorry, sweetheart, I'm busy,' Lily said. 'But my friend here might be able to help you out.'

Helen looked at her aghast. Lily grinned, gave her a little push towards him and stepped back into a doorway, leaving the two of them alone. Helen, aware of the man's eyes sweeping over her body, was immediately gripped by panic. What should she say? What should she do? She swallowed hard, feeling her pulse beginning to race.

'How much, then?' the man said. 'For the full . . . you know.'

Helen glanced quickly over her shoulder, but Lily was staring off down the street. 'Er . . . thirty?' she said tentatively, turning back to the punter. 'But . . . er . . . I can't . . . not right now. I mean, I can't get away right this moment. I'm supposed to be working for the club, you see? I'll have to talk to my boss and . . . er, it'll be about ten minutes or so.' The explanation came out in a rushed, hurried way, sounding – at least to her ears – about as truthful as the spiel from a second-hand car dealer.

'Ten minutes?' he muttered, pursing his lips.

'I'll have to talk to my boss,' Helen said again. All she wanted now was for him to leave her alone. She couldn't do this. She wasn't brazen enough. A sudden image of her grandmother jumped into her head, her face stern and disapproving. Oh God, this was all a big mistake. She shouldn't be here. She was completely out of her depth.

But then, just as she was on the point of taking to her heels, the man reached into his pocket, took out three crumpled ten-pound notes and pressed them into her hand. Startled, Helen gazed down at the cash for a second before shoving it into the pocket of her skirt. 'Round the corner,' she muttered. 'Brewer Street.' She plucked a number from the air. 'Number twenty-six. I'll meet you there. Wait by the door.'

As the man skulked away, Lily hissed at her from behind. 'Walk over to the club, make it look as though you're going in there.'

Helen did as she was told, forcing herself not to look towards the man. Was he watching her? Was he about to change his mind, to rush back and demand the return of his money? Her heart was beating hard in her chest as she sauntered over to the door as casually as she could manage.

Doug grinned at her. 'Don't worry, love. He's well gone.'

'Is he?' Helen said, her breath rushing from her lungs in a gasp of relief. She turned to stare into the crowd, but the man was nowhere to be seen.

Lily strode up and grabbed her by the elbow. 'Come on, let's get out of here.' She gave Doug another breezy wave. 'See you, hon.'

'You be careful,' he said to Helen. 'Watch yourself. There's some right nasty bastards out there.'

'Don't worry,' Lily said. 'She's got me to take care of her.'

Before Helen had a chance to say goodbye to the giant – he reminded her a little of Frank – Lily had propelled her away. 'Come on,' she said again. 'You can't afford to hang about.'

They hurried into a side street, and then another, Helen quickly losing track of the direction they were going in. She felt a mixture of emotions: elation at having succeeded in her task, and a creeping revulsion at how she had achieved it. 'You got any more of that vodka?'

'Sure.' Lily stopped by a sex shop and passed over the bottle. 'You did great. The first time's always the hardest. You'll soon get used to it.'

Helen took a swig from the bottle, slowly beginning to relax. 'God, I didn't think he was going to pay.'

'Oh, they always pay, babe – so long as you pick the right ones.'

'So what now?'

Lily tucked the bottle back inside her jacket and smiled. 'Now we go find ourselves another sucker.'

# 44

Christmas had come and gone, the New Year beckoning in 1975. And now it was February already. Tommy sat back on his bunk, trying to clear his head of everything but the music that was playing on the radio. But even as Cockney Rebel generously invited him to *Come up and see me, make me smile*, his eyes were inevitably drawn back towards the picture of his girls on the wall. He reached out a hand and touched their faces. It was too long since he had last seen them, and now they were miles away, living a new life in Spain.

Karen wrote to him occasionally, short, scrawled letters telling him about their house near the beach, her latest boyfriend or her job in a shop near the harbour selling T-shirts and flip-flops to tourists. She never mentioned the trial or what had happened. From Debs he had only received a card at Christmas. His older daughter, he knew, was still angry – angry about Shelley Anne, about his betrayal of her mother and the part he had played in attempting to dispose of the body of her grandfather.

Tommy had long ago given up protesting his innocence – at least to his family. It hurt that he wasn't believed by the two people he loved most in the world, but he knew that Yvonne would have been whispering poison in their ears. His soon-to-be ex-wife wasn't content with robbing him blind – Jesus, he should never have put the Fox in her name – but was determined to ruin his relationship with his daughters too.

After the trial, Tommy's first few months in jail had been a nightmare. While he'd been on remand, there had still been hope, but once that was swept away, the long term of imprisonment stretched ahead of him, the years filled only with emptiness. The first thing he had learned was to stop feeling sorry for himself – what was done was done; the second was to stop yearning for the day he'd be released.

What he couldn't stop, however, was going over the events of that fateful night. He played them over and over in his head, trying to spot the clues, trying to remember everything Connor had said and done. Had he been acting normally? But what was normal for Connor? He'd been crazy for most of his life. And his brother's anger in the courtroom hadn't helped matters either. The jury had taken against him, hearing only arrogance and lies in his evidence.

Tommy got out his cigarette papers and rolled a couple of skinny fags from his meagre supply of tobacco. With no extra cash coming in from outside, he had to make do with the weekly prison rations and the tiny salary he got from working in the print room. Yvonne, of course, hadn't sent him a penny since he'd been convicted.

He frowned as he lit one of the fags, pulling the smoke into his lungs. If only he hadn't taken the car keys off Connor. If only he'd just let him walk out of the Fox. If only Frank Meyer had cleared off after last orders and left him to deal with his brother alone. Tommy felt bad about Frank, really bad. He'd had no contact with him since the trial, didn't even know which jail he'd been sent to.

There was someone else Tommy felt guilty about too, and that was Mouse. Had she voluntarily gone back to her aunt's in Farleigh Wood or had Yvonne kicked her out? The latter, he suspected, although Karen claimed she had left of her own accord. Janet Simms, he was sure, wouldn't have welcomed the renewal of old responsibilities. Still, at least the kid was safe, with a roof over her head. Mouse was different to most girls of her age, less worldly, more fragile. Tommy sighed out a narrow stream of smoke. He had promised her a home for as long as she wanted it, but now – even though it was through no fault of his own – he had broken that promise.

Although it did no good to dwell on things you couldn't change, Tommy couldn't always help himself. He'd lost his girls, the Fox and most of his hopes for the future. The Dagenham fraud had probably gone for a burton too. As soon as the guilty verdicts had come in, Alfie Blunt would have ordered goods up to the credit limit, had a closing-down sale and scarpered with the cash. He was probably lying on a beach right now, soaking up the sun and sipping on a cocktail.

Tommy heard the flick of a page being turned on the bunk beneath him. He was sharing the cell with a taciturn Scot, which suited him just fine. There was nothing worse than being banged up with some hyped-up geezer who was desperate for a fix and wouldn't keep his mouth shut. Mal, who was serving a long sentence for a spate of robberies in Newcastle, spent most of his time reading true-life crime books, although whether this was pure escapism or an attempt to hone his skills, Tommy hadn't yet figured out.

There was the sound of heavy boots outside, and then the noisy clink of the key turning in the lock. A grey-haired screw came into the cell and looked up at Tommy.

'Quinn,' he said. 'You're wanted in the office.'

'What for?'

'Just shift your arse, will you. I haven't got all day.'

Tommy carefully put his fag out, saving the remainder for later, and climbed down from the bunk. 'You letting me out then, Mr Patterson? Finally realised that I'm an innocent man?'

'Yeah, right. You and all the others in here.'

The screw locked the door again and Tommy followed him along the landing. He glanced down through the tall metal rail at the wide safety nets strung from one side of the cell block to the other, a deterrent to any inmate who might get ideas about splattering their own, or someone else's, brains on the concrete below.

They went down three flights and then along a corridor. PO Patterson was about as chatty as Mal, but that didn't bother Tommy. The screw opened the office door, stood back to let him enter and then closed it again, remaining outside. In the office, seated behind a wide oak desk, was another, more senior screw called Colby. He had a serious look on his face.

'Take a seat, Tommy. Sit down, sit down. How are you?'

Colby's use of his Christian name set off alarm bells in Tommy's head. 'What's going on?' he asked suspiciously. 'What's this about?'

'Sit down, please,' Colby said again.

Tommy pulled out a chair, mentally preparing himself for bad news. He sat down and immediately leaned forward. All kinds of scenarios were running through his mind: a car crash, a drowning, a rampant fire sweeping though the house near the beach in Malaga. 'Shit, it's not my girls, is it? Tell me it's not my girls.'

Colby gave a quick shake of his head before clearing his throat. 'No, no, it's nothing to do with your daughters.'

Tommy sat back again, relief flooding his body. So long as his girls were safe, he could cope with anything else. 'What then?'

Colby picked up an opened envelope that was lying on his desk. 'You received a letter this morning. The censor thought . . . well, he thought I should have a word with you first.'

Tommy glanced at the handwriting on the front and recognised it instantly. Shelley Anne's. 'Ah,' he said.

Colby, who unlike some of the screws didn't relish the prospect of passing on bad news, pulled a face. 'I'm sorry, but—'

'It's a Dear John, yeah?' Tommy couldn't say he was surprised. He'd only seen Shelley Anne once since Christmas, and that had been an awkward visit. Despite her claims that she was going to stick by him, he could tell that she'd already started looking for a way out, that she wasn't prepared to wait around for the seven or so years of his ten-year sentence that he would need to serve.

'I'm afraid so.'

Tommy gave a wry smile and reached out for the envelope. 'Don't worry. I'm not about to top meself.'

Colby gave him a long look, as if trying to assess whether Tommy's response was genuine, or just the bluster of a man who didn't like to show his feelings in public. 'If you need to talk to anyone . . . '

'I won't,' Tommy said. 'It's okay. There's no problem. Me and Shelley Anne . . . well, it weren't anything serious.' And he wasn't broken-hearted, that much was true. Faintly disappointed, perhaps, but he'd soon get over that. Anyway, it was probably for the best. If Shelley Anne had stuck around, the first thing she'd have expected when he got out of jail was a ring on her finger.

'Would you like to read the letter here?'

'Nah,' said Tommy, standing up and preparing to leave. 'I'll save it for when I've got nothing better to do.'

# 45

As the weeks slipped into months, Helen gradually began to slough off Mouse's old, oversensitive skin and to grow a harder, more cynical shell. If she was going to survive, then she had to adapt. There was no room for shame or embarrassment. There was no place in Soho for shrinking violets. Within a year, she was proficient at her trade and went up West with Lily three or four times a week, earning money when she needed it, spending it as quickly. She drank too much, took up smoking and learned to fend for herself.

Her new life, although precarious, enabled her to survive. She had moved into the flat over the undertakers' on a permanent basis and was sharing the rent and bills, as well as the double bed. On the odd occasions that Lily brought a man home, Helen would be consigned to the sofa. There, she would put a cushion over her head and try not to listen to the noises coming from the bedroom.

The two of them, although they often travelled into Soho together, worked separately now. Tonight Helen was in Dean Street, smoking her way through her third cigarette while she scanned the meagre crowd for a likely punter. Since the beginning of February the weather had been icy, the rain freezing into slippery pools. She shivered, wondering if she was wasting her time. Anyone with any sense was sitting at home with the fire on full blast and a brew on the go.

From across the road, one of the local toms was giving her evils. They didn't like the corner game girls, who in their opinion wanted something for nothing and gave the rest of them a bad reputation. Helen could see where they were coming from, but she didn't give a toss. She glared right back, narrowing her eyes.

It was at times like this, when nothing much was happening, that Helen's mind would start to wander. She would think of Tommy and Frank and a small ache would blossom in her chest. Where were they now? She had no idea which jail they were in, or whether they were together or apart. She should have tried to find out, although she had no idea how. Perhaps someone at the Fox would have known, but she hadn't been back there since Yvonne had kicked her out.

Helen reached into her pocket, pulled out the bottle of vodka and took a few welcome swigs. The bottle, she noticed, was already half empty. Jesus, it was cold out here! The icy air stung her face, making her wince. She turned up the collar of her jacket but it made little difference. A man walked past and gave her a furtive sidelong glance. Helen smiled back at him. He carried on walking.

'Sod you,' she murmured.

She thought about calling it a night – she'd already been standing around for a couple of hours – but funds were low. If she was to leave now, she'd be going home empty-handed. Half an hour more, she decided, and then she'd quit before she froze to death. Looking around, she noticed Rixy walking by on the other side of the street and gave him a wave. He crossed over and came to speak to her.

'How's it going, hon?' she asked.

Rixy shook his head. 'Fuck all. How about you?'

'The same.'

Rixy was in his late twenties, a tall, skinny guy with dark Brylcreemed hair and a narrow moustache. He made his living from a blue film racket where he tempted punters with postcards showing scenes from a sex film, took their money to watch the film and then directed them up to the second floor of an empty building before hightailing it with the cash. 'Fancy a drink?'

Helen dropped the butt of her cigarette and ground it into the pavement with her heel while she thought about the offer. It would be good to get out of the cold, but she needed to make some money. 'Nah, I think I'll walk over to Greek Street, try my luck there.'

'I'll be at Leila's if you change your mind.'

'Okay.' Helen watched him go with some regret, a part of her wishing that she'd taken him up on the offer. At least she could have got her circulation back for a while. She rubbed her hands together, trying to generate some warmth. Leila's was a bar in Old Compton Street, a gathering place for the local toms, the pickpockets, the grifters and drifters and all the other lost souls who hovered on the edges of society. It was a good place to hunker down, exchange gossip and relax.

Helen knew that she hadn't refused Rixy's invitation just because she had to work. There was another reason, too. Although she'd got to know a lot of the faces around Soho – and was happy to have a drink or share a smoke with them – she remained reluctant to form any deeper friendships. Even with Lily she was careful not to get too close. After that first evening, she had never again spoken about the past. They had a laugh together and shared their grievances, but that was as far as it went.

Helen was about to set off for Greek Street when a man in his late thirties, wearing a smart navy blue suit, walked past her, stopped and then retraced his steps. There was nothing distinctive about him; he was an average-looking man, neither ugly nor attractive.

'Looking for business, sweetheart?' he asked with a smile.

His voice was softer than she'd expected, but the smile didn't quite extend to his eyes.

'Maybe,' she replied, doing her well-worn routine of glancing towards the club across the road. Even as she was doing this, she was in two minds as to whether she should give him the brush-off. There was something about the guy she didn't like. *Always follow your instincts.* That was what Lily had told her, and her gut feeling was saying no. At the same time, she was aware of her almost empty purse.

'Maybe?' he repeated. 'What does that mean?'

Helen looked at him again, her gaze taking in the expensive suit, the polished shoes and the gold wedding ring on the third finger of his left hand. There was nothing to worry about, she told herself: he was just a married man looking for a quickie before he went home to the boring routine of the missus and the kids.

She tilted her head towards the club. 'My boss is over there. I'm supposed to be working for the club, aren't I? I'm not allowed to ... well, I'll have to go over and sort out a break. I'll be ten, fifteen minutes at the most. I'll meet you in Bateman Street. Number sixteen. I've got a flat there.'

'How much?' he asked.

'Thirty. I'll need the cash up front.'

The man hesitated, but only for a second. After a quick look around, he took six fivers from his inside jacket pocket and handed them over to her.

'Ta,' she said, slipping the notes down the front of her blouse and into her bra. Then she strolled across the road, watching him from the corner of her eye. She was aware of him watching her too, but then he started walking towards Bateman Street. As soon as he'd turned the corner, Helen set off in the opposite direction. She would head for Oxford Street and catch a bus home from there.

She walked as quickly as she could on the slippery pavements. It had started to snow again, fast flurries of flakes tumbling from the sky. The tip of her nose felt numb. She was aware of having drunk too much on an empty stomach; her head was feeling fuzzy and her balance wasn't all it should be. A couple of times her heels slid on the ice and she almost fell over.

Concerned that she was making slow progress, that the man might realise what was happening and try to catch her up, Helen decided to stop walking in a straight line and instead veered right into Carlisle Street. She would go via Soho Square and that way reduce the chances of being found. Or would it? She was finding it difficult to think clearly.

As she walked, she kept getting a curious pricking sensation on the back of her neck. Again and again she turned to look over her shoulder, but there was no sign of him. It was just her imagination playing tricks. She heard the distant laughter of girls, the swish of a car going by. She glanced at her watch; it was almost nine o'clock. The streets were quieter than usual, the cold keeping people away. Maybe she should have stuck to the more direct route.

Helen was approaching the square when she sensed rather than heard the movement behind her. She whirled around, but already it was too late. As the man's strong hands clamped down on her shoulders, her heart almost leapt out of her chest.

'Haven't you forgotten something, love?'

Caught firmly in his grasp, Helen stared briefly into his hard, cold eyes before quickly looking around. Her gaze slid frantically to the left and the right.

'Don't even think about it,' he said softly, moving his hands closer to her throat. 'I could break your fuckin' neck in a second. Now where's my money?'

'I'm s-sorry,' Helen stammered. 'I've got no food or anywhere to stay. I didn't . . . ' She reached into her bra, retrieved the notes and held them up. 'Here, have it back. I'm really sorry. Honestly I am. I wouldn't have done it if I wasn't desperate.'

'Really?' he said, moving his face close to hers and breathing the word into her mouth.

Helen gulped hard as his fingers tightened around her throat. Should she take the risk and try and shout for help? There were a couple of young blokes passing on the other side of the road. All she had to do was yell and they'd come and help her ... or maybe they wouldn't. Maybe they'd just think it was a lovers' tiff. Maybe they wouldn't want to get involved. All these thoughts ran through her head in a matter of seconds. Her pleading eyes focused on the man again. 'Really. I swear to God. I've never done anything like this before.'

He removed his left hand from her neck, snatched the money from her hand and shoved it into his pocket.

For a moment, Helen thought it was over, that he'd been placated and now he'd let her go. But instead he put the hand back on her throat, leaned forward again and hissed into her face. 'You and me, sweetheart. We're going for a little walk.'

'No,' she said, making a futile attempt to struggle free of him.

'Don't make me angry, love,' he said, shaking her so hard that she gasped with pain and fright. 'You really wouldn't like it.'

Helen stopped struggling. Panic was coursing through her veins, her heart thrashing. She had to figure out a way to escape, but her head was spinning so fast that she couldn't think straight. He grabbed hold of her arm and started dragging her along the street. Someone will see, she thought. Someone will notice and call the cops. But then again, this was Soho. It was no rare sight to see a pimp mistreating one of his girls. And she looked like a tom. She was even dressed like a tom. As if reading her mind, he turned and glared at her.

'You think anyone gives a toss about what happens to a cheap little tart like you?'

'N-no,' she stuttered. 'But I'm sorry, really sorry. Please let me go.'

He gave a snort, his breath coming out like steamy cloud. 'You're not sorry. Your sort are never sorry.'

Before she had a chance to respond, he had yanked her off the street and into a dark alleyway that ran down the side of a row of sex shops. He slammed her up against the wall, the force of it sending a jolt down her spine. She closed her eyes, not wanting to see the expression on his face.

'Look at me!' he ordered.

Helen reluctantly opened her eyes and peered at him through the gloom. Her back was hurting and her legs had turned to jelly. 'Please,' she whimpered. 'I'm sorry. Please don't do this.'

'You don't even remember me, do you? And I don't mean tonight. I mean the first time you conned me out of thirty quid.'

Helen shook her head. Of course she didn't remember. After a while, all the faces became the same, hungry and eager and disgustingly pathetic.

He gave a nasty laugh. 'Well, why the fuck should you? I'm just one of hundreds, aren't I? Just another poor sucker who had the misfortune to cross your path.' He slapped her hard across the cheek, a stinging blow that sent her head flying back against the wall. 'Well, darlin', I'm going to make sure that you never forget me again.'

Helen, still reeling, instinctively raised her hands to try and cover her face, but he pushed them roughly aside. The next thing she knew, he was dragging her further into the alley, away from the faint orange glow of the street lamps, away from the curious eyes of any passers-by. She opened her mouth, intending to scream, but his hand instantly clamped over it.

'You make a sound, bitch, and it's the last one you'll ever make.'

He pushed her down on to the frozen ground and she fell hard, her legs twisting beneath her. One of her shoes came adrift and skittered across the ice. She tried to scramble to her feet, but in a second he was on top of her, his hand across her mouth again. She could feel the weight of him on her chest, squeezing the breath from her lungs. He slapped her again, and then again, each blow more ferocious than the last.

'Fuckin' bitch!' he spat. 'Bitch! Bitch!'

'Please,' she begged, through his thick, clammy fingers.

But nothing was going to stop him now. She could taste blood in her mouth. *Bad blood.* Joe Quinn's words rose into her mind, accusing her, mocking her. And soon, like Joe, she'd be cold and dead, feeling nothing, knowing nothing. This was where it was all going to end.

She could smell the man's sweat, and the faint, sickening scent of a musky aftershave. She felt him fumble for the zip on his trousers.

Helen lashed out, a primitive will to survive overriding her sense of fatalism. But this only infuriated him more. Grabbing her right wrist, he slammed her hand down hard against the ice. And then, before her brain had even properly registered the vile cracking sound, he was brutally pushing her legs apart. She heard his grunting breath, felt the ripping pain between her legs as he forced himself into her. She twisted her head to look at him. His eyes blazed down at her. Then he raised his fist and smashed it hard into her face, the force of the blow bringing with it an oblivion that she was grateful for.

# 46

Helen drifted in and out of consciousness, sounds clashing and colliding, dreams mingling and merging with a fuzzy, confusing reality. She was faintly aware of people coming and going, of footsteps on lino, of day turning into night and back to day again, but none of it made much sense to her. She was more vividly aware of pain, general pain, and then more specific agonies in her jaw and chest and stomach.

With a groan, she blinked open her eyes and saw the walls of a cool white room. She turned her head to find Moira sitting beside the bed. For a moment, fearing it was the remnant of yet another dream, she said nothing. Moira leaned forward and smiled at her.

'You're safe now, love. You're in hospital. You're going to be okay.'

Helen peered at her. She could not be real, could not be Moira, because Moira had left a long time ago. She had gone along with Helen's mother and her father and her grandparents. Tommy had gone, and Frank had gone too. There was no one left. Still, even if the woman was imaginary, she remained a comfort, a warm presence in an empty space.

Helen blinked, feeling a new throbbing pain in her eye sockets. She stirred a little, shifting as much as she dared. Each time she moved, a different part of her sent out a protest. Even her right hand felt heavy and strange. She gazed at the white plaster cast encasing her fingers. A memory was suddenly triggered in her brain – a man's mouth spitting out obscenities, the weight of his body on hers, the sharp cracking sound as he smashed her hand against the icy ground. No, she could not, would not remember these things. She would close her eyes and make them go away.

It was dark outside when she woke again. The curtains were pulled tight across the window. A thin, watery light illuminated the room, chasing the shadows into corners. She knew now that she was in hospital, that she was connected to a drip, that other tubes were invading her body. Soho, she thought, and immediately shuddered.

'Helen?'

The voice seemed to come from a long way away. She slowly turned her head. Moira leaned forward, laid a hand gently on her arm. Helen's mouth was so dry she could barely speak. 'How . . . how long have I been here?'

'A little while,' Moira said softly. 'Lie still. Don't try and talk. You're going to be fine.'

But although Helen heard the words, she could see something quite different etched on Moira's face. There was fear and worry and bewilderment. She switched her focus to a thin crack running up the wall. Bad things happen to bad people. That was what her grandmother used to say.

It was a few days more before Helen had recovered enough to understand how severe her injuries had been and how close she'd come to death. By then she was able to sit up and concentrate on what the doctors told her. She was able, finally, to have a lucid conversation with Moira too.

'It was a guy putting out the rubbish who found you,' Moira said. 'One of the local shopkeepers. Around midnight, that was. If it hadn't been for him going into the alley . . .'

Helen gave a shiver, knowing that this was what her attacker had thought of her – just another piece of trash to be pulped and then discarded.

'And the police have been here. They'll want to talk to you as soon as you're ready.'

Helen gave a quick shake of her head, a movement she instantly regretted. It sent a shock of pain down her cheek and along her shattered jawbone. 'No, I don't want to talk to them. I can't remember anything. It's all a blank.'

'Helen, we need to find out who did this. He could have killed you. Jesus, he came close enough.'

'I can't remember,' Helen said again. She was more than aware of the line the cops would be taking: that she was just another tom who'd picked the wrong punter. The place they'd found her, the clothes and make-up she'd been wearing would all point in that direction. But she also knew that she wouldn't be able to avoid the inevitable questions. The best she could hope for was to get it over and done with as quickly as possible. She knew in her heart, with a dull, despairing certainty, that the man who had raped her would never be caught.

Moira didn't ask what she'd been doing in Soho. Perhaps, like the police, she thought she already knew. They talked instead about what had happened before, about the murder of Joe Quinn, the trial and the terrible outcome.

'You should have called me,' Moira said, her eyes brimming with tears. 'After Yvonne threw you out. I'd have helped. You could have come to Portsmouth.'

'Portsmouth?' Helen said.

'That's where I went when I left Kellston. I put the address in the letter, and my new phone number. You did get the letter, didn't you? I've got a friend there who runs a wine bar. She offered me a job and ... well, I'd been in London all my life. I thought a fresh start might be a good thing.'

'I did get the letter,' Helen said. And then she had to explain why she hadn't opened it, why she'd thrown it away without so much as a second glance. 'I'm so sorry.'

Moira gave a gentle smile. 'You've nothing to be sorry for, love. We should have told you the truth when we had the chance. It was wrong to keep it from you. I can see that now.'

'None of that matters any more.'

'But I called,' Moira said. 'When the trial was going on. Three or four times. I heard what had happened and ... I gave my number to Yvonne. I take it she didn't pass it on to you.'

'No.'

'I thought you didn't want to talk to me, so ...'

A silence fell across the room. Out in the corridor a trolley rolled by, its wheels squeaking. Footsteps hurried past the door. Someone coughed. Helen felt a wave of fatigue roll over her. 'So what happens now?'

'As soon as you're better, you're coming home with me.'

'Home,' murmured Helen. Her eyelids, heavy as lead, were already closing again.

# PART FOUR
# 1981

# 47

Helen wiped the surface of the counter until it was gleaming, then poured out two mugs of tea, went through to the back and sat down at the table. She'd been on the go since five o'clock that morning, and now it was almost half three. The last customer had left, the door was locked and the rest of the day was hers to do with as she wished.

As she looked around, she gave a tiny sigh of contentment. Her feet might be hurting, but her soul was finally starting to heal. Although the past would never completely leave her, her dreams had ceased to be haunted by that terrifying night in Soho. Here, in the little sandwich bar in Camden Town, she was beginning to find some peace.

Moira had bought the place shortly after Helen had got out of hospital, using what remained of her father's inheritance and all her savings as a deposit. They worked from the crack of dawn until mid-afternoon making mountains of takeaway sandwiches and dispensing endless cups of tea and coffee. The bar, situated only twenty yards from the tube station, turned a decent profit, and Moira had already paid off half the mortgage.

Although London had recently been riven by conflict, with clashes in Southall, Brixton and Finsbury Park, Helen still felt safe in Camden. The sandwich bar was like a cocoon, a place of safety, of sanctuary. Moira had done as she had promised and provided her with a home. She had given her two, in fact – this place, where she spent most of her time, and the small flat above it, which had originally been rented out for extra income but which had become free six months ago. It had been a big step moving out of Moira's and into a place of her own, but Helen was glad now that she'd done it. She was twenty-one, a young woman, and living alone was one more step on the road to overcoming all her fears and insecurities.

Moira came in from the back yard, where she'd been putting out the rubbish, and went to wash her hands at the sink. 'Is it just me, or do I stink of fried bacon?'

'You and me both,' Helen said. 'Should we take it off the menu?'

'We'd have a riot if we did.'

'There's a brew for you here.'

Moira sat down and picked up the mug. 'Thanks, love. Just what I need.'

Helen watched as Moira raised the mug to her lips and blew softly across the surface of the tea. Usually she enjoyed this time of day, when the hard graft was over and they could sit comfortably together in the kitchen, but this afternoon she had something on her mind. She shifted in her chair, crossed and uncrossed her legs.

'What's the matter?'

'Nothing.'

Moira frowned at her. 'I know that face, Helen Beck. Don't tell me it's nothing.'

Helen smiled weakly back. 'Well, okay, I have been thinking about something.' She hesitated, took a breath and then said, 'It's about Mum. Do you ever wonder what really happened to her?'

'What do you mean?' asked Moira, her frown growing deeper. 'What *really* happened?'

Helen gave a shrug. 'Someone killed her and they got away with it. Don't you ever wonder who or why? It seems so wrong that there's someone walking around out there and . . . and they've not been made to pay for what they did.'

Moira glanced briefly down at the table before looking up again. Her eyes were full of sympathy and concern. 'I know it's hard, love, but sometimes you just have to let go.'

Helen knew that she wasn't just referring to Lynsey's murder but also to the vicious attack on Helen herself in Soho. Moira probably suspected that she was transferring her feelings about her own near-death experience to the actual murder of her mother. And maybe there was some truth in it. She couldn't do anything now about the brute who'd raped her, but maybe there was something she could do about her mother's killer. 'And what if I can't?'

Moira shook her head. 'You're just getting back on your feet. Going over all that again . . . well, it's going to stir up a lot of emotions. Do you really think you're ready, that you can cope with it?'

'No,' Helen said with a wry smile. 'But then I doubt I ever

will be. I just feel that it's something I've got to do.' She had the self-knowledge to understand that she was damaged, still fragile in many ways, but she was also aware that this was how she would remain if she couldn't lay the past properly to rest.

Moira gave another small shake of her head. 'I don't know where you'd even start. It was so long ago.'

'Maybe Tommy could help.' After she'd got out of hospital, it had surprised Helen to discover that Moira had stayed in touch with her uncle. The two of them exchanged letters, although Moira had never been to visit. Tommy was serving his time up in Durham and, having completed two thirds of his ten-year sentence, was due to be released at the end of the month.

'I don't know how, love. He didn't see her for years, not after she left Kellston.'

Helen thought about this for a moment, then said, 'Where's he going to go when he gets out?'

A light flush rose into Moira's cheeks. 'I've told him he can stay with me if he wants to. Just until he gets himself sorted. I've got the spare room now you've moved out, and ...well, it's not as if Yvonne left him with anything. You wouldn't mind, would you?'

'Of course not. Why should I? It'll be great to see him again.'

Helen, remembering Moira's revelation about her teenage crush, wondered if she still had feelings for Tommy. She might have teased her about it if her mind hadn't been pre-occupied by more serious matters. 'You know, there's something I've never understood. Tommy isn't the type to let things lie, especially when it comes to family. Why didn't he try and find out who killed her? They might have lost touch, but she was still his sister. I know he doesn't go looking for trouble, but it's not like him to walk away from something like that.'

Moira leaned forward, putting her elbows on the table. 'Maybe it was easier for him to believe it was an accident, to close his mind to the idea that she could have been murdered. He always felt guilty that he hadn't done more to help her out. He knew she was unhappy, that her life was a mess, but . . . ' The sentence tailed off into a shrug.

'I guess,' Helen said. 'But there must have been some sort of an investigation. I mean, once the police discovered that it was a suspicious death.'

'A pretty cursory one, I should imagine.'

'What makes you say that?'

The colour rose into Moira's cheeks again. 'They don't take much interest in girls who . . . They just presume . . . with the lifestyle she had and everything . . . '

'You mean because she was a tom.'

Moira stiffened at the words, her gaze momentarily flicking away from Helen. 'She had a lot of problems, love: the booze, the drugs and the rest. She never came straight out and said that was what she was doing, but . . . '

'It's okay,' Helen said. 'I understand. And I'm not going to judge her. How could I?' Her own experiences in Soho had taught her how tough life could be. She wasn't about to condemn her mother for making choices that were not so very far from her own.

'She did want you,' Moira continued. 'She *really* wanted you. Don't ever imagine that she didn't. But it was hard for her. That family, the Becks, they never gave her a chance, and Alan . . . your father . . . he was—'

'A pig,' Helen said drily. 'In every sense of the word.'

'Well, I suppose it wasn't easy for him, either.'

Helen smiled. It was typical of Moira that she wouldn't bad-mouth her father even though she'd loathed the man.

'Maybe I could drive up and see him. Tommy, I mean.'

Moira looked dubious. 'It might be better if you wait until he gets out. There's a lot of time to dwell on things in jail. You might . . . it might be tough for him to talk about her right now. It's less than a month. It's not so long.'

'I suppose,' Helen agreed, although she was inwardly disappointed. Now that she'd made the decision to start searching for answers, the thought of any delay filled her with frustration. 'So when was the last time you heard from her?'

'Oh God,' said Moira, rubbing at her temples. 'It must have been a few months before she died. She said everything was fine, the way she always did. She'd got a new flat and—'

'Was that the Samuel Street flat?' Helen interrupted. 'The one in Kilburn.'

'I think so.'

Helen nodded. 'Maybe that's the place to start.'

'But it was years ago, love. I doubt there'll be anyone living there who remembers her.'

'It's worth a try.' Helen finished her tea, took the mug to the sink and rinsed it out. 'I'll let you know if I find out anything.'

Moira looked startled. 'You're going over there now?'

'Sure. Why not? Well, I'm going to get changed first. I can get a bus from Camden station.'

'Do you want me to come with you?' Moira half rose from her chair. 'I don't mind.'

'No, I'll be fine,' Helen said, waving her back down. 'I'll give you a call later, yeah?' And then before Moira could raise any further objections, she made a hasty exit through the back door. The sun was still shining brightly as she walked around the side of the building to the main street and her own front door, a few yards from the entrance to the sandwich bar.

Upstairs, she stripped off all her clothes, chucked them in the washing machine and jumped under the shower. Fifteen minutes later, free of the smell of bacon fat, she pulled on her jeans and a white T-shirt, hurriedly dried her hair, grabbed her jacket and bag, and headed for the bus stop.

It was another half-hour and getting on for five before Helen reached her destination. She walked past the shops on Kilburn High Road, their windows full of royal memorabilia. The wedding of Prince Charles and Diana Spencer was due to take place at the end of the month. Although a part of her wanted to, she didn't really believe in fairy-tale romances – but then what did she know about romance? She hadn't had a date for over a year, and that had been a disaster. After a pleasant meal in a restaurant, Carl had walked her home, leaned in for a good-night kiss and she'd instantly gone into panic mode. She'd jumped back as swiftly as if he'd been wielding an axe in his hand. Needless to say, he hadn't called again.

Helen took a left and then a right, and finally found herself in Samuel Street, standing outside a shabby Victorian terrace. She glanced down at the scrap of paper in her hand – yes, this was definitely number twenty-eight – and then back up at the three-storey house. She presumed that 28B, the number she had written down, must be the middle flat. There were curtains at the window, but no other sign of life.

Helen stared up at it for a while. There was paint peeling from the sill and the glass had a grey, dusty look. It gave her an odd, shivery feeling standing outside the house where her mother had died. She looked down towards her feet. Lynsey must have walked on this bit of pavement too. It was eerie to think about it. Was there such a thing as ghosts? Did some part of her mother still linger in the atmosphere? Her eyes were drawn back up towards the window, but it remained as still, as blank as the first time she had gazed at it.

Helen wasn't quite sure, now that she was here, what exactly she was hoping to find out. That someone in one of the other flats might have known her mum? That they might have noticed who came and went? But as Moira had said, it had all happened so long ago. Even if one of the tenants had been around then, the chances of them remembering anything were slim.

Still, she hadn't made the journey to Kilburn to give up the minute she arrived. She walked up the short path and examined the bells on the door. There were three of them, A, B and C. No names. Her finger hovered on 28B, but she already knew that *that* particular tenant wouldn't have been around back then.

As she tried to decide between A and C, it suddenly occurred to her that she had no idea what she was going to say. She chewed on her lower lip, attempting to think of something that wouldn't make her sound deranged. *Hi, my*

*name's Helen. My mother died here in a fire. Did you know her?*
She pulled a face. No, that sort of thing wouldn't do at all.

Before she could talk herself out of it, she rang the bell for
Flat A, put her nose against the opaque glass in the door and
waited. There was no movement from inside. She tried to
peer into the hallway, but couldn't see anything clearly. She
pressed the bell again, but when there was still no response,
she tried C instead. Perhaps she had come too early. People
wouldn't be home from work yet.

Helen was considering going to get a coffee and coming
back later when she heard the clatter of footsteps coming
down the stairs. She quickly moved back from the door. It
was opened seconds later by a girl of her own age wearing
torn jeans, an off-the-shoulder pink T-shirt and a pair of Doc
Martens. The girl, who also had a punk haircut and a gold
ring in her lip, looked her up and down while lazily moving
a wad of chewing gum from one cheek to the other.

'Yeah?'

'Hi,' Helen said overbrightly. 'Sorry to disturb you. I
was ... er ... I was just wondering if you'd lived here for
long?'

'You what?'

Not a good start. And anyway, the girl was way too young
to have been around at the same time as Lynsey. She was now
looking simultaneously bored and suspicious, as if Helen was
about to try and sell her something. 'Sorry, I meant that I
knew someone who used to live here, but it was a long time
ago. I was hoping to talk to someone who ... Do you know
the other tenants? Do you know what time they'll be back?'

'Nah,' the girl said. 'No idea.'

'Oh, okay.' Helen hesitated, but couldn't think of anything else useful to ask. The only option was to come back later and try and talk to the others in the house. She was about to leave when the girl tilted her head to one side and gave Helen a long, cool stare.

'Who you looking for, then?'

'Her name was Lynsey, Lynsey Beck.'

The girl gave a shrug. It was obvious the name didn't mean anything to her. Why should it?

'Thanks anyway,' Helen said. 'It was a bit of a long shot. I just thought I'd ask.'

The girl took a step back, her hand reaching for the door, but then she stopped. Perhaps something in Helen's face, the expression of disappointment, prompted her to offer up a suggestion. 'Have you asked at the agents'?'

Helen shook her head. 'The agents'?'

'They're on the High Road. Matlin and Cope. They let out all the flats in this house.'

'Thanks,' Helen said, smiling at her. Perhaps her luck was on the turn. 'The High Road, then?'

'Next door to the Co-op.' The girl glanced at her watch. 'They'll be closed now, though. They shut at five.'

'Ah, okay. Never mind. I can always give them a call tomorrow.'

The girl gave a curt nod and closed the door without saying goodbye.

Helen was now in two minds: should she wait around for someone else to come back, or did she call it a day and head back to Camden? While she thought about it, she wandered down to the corner of the street. It would probably be a waste of time to stay here. It could be hours before anyone else showed up, and even when they did, they would probably have nothing more to tell her.

The trouble was that she felt too restless to go home. Now that she'd started, she wanted to get on with things. With the estate agent closed, there was nothing she could do there until they opened again tomorrow. It was a shame she couldn't talk to Tommy. He'd known her mother better than anyone, and surely he'd have contacts – people who knew people who knew people – in the circles that she'd moved in. That was the way it worked in Tommy's world. A few phone calls, a few favours called in, and the information was right there at your fingertips. But Moira was right: it wasn't fair to burden him with this when he was still in jail.

So who else could she turn to? One name leapt straight into her head: Frank Meyer. He'd been Tommy's best friend at the time her mother had been murdered. Surely Tommy must have talked to him, confided in him? Perhaps he could point her in the right direction. The only problem was that she didn't have a clue as to which jail he was in.

Frustrated, she raised her face to the blue sky and sighed. How did you find out these things? She didn't know where to begin looking. Unless . . . A seed of an idea was beginning to form. She rolled it around for a moment, weighing up the pros and cons. Perhaps she did know someone who could help her to find Frank. Too impatient to wait for a bus, she thrust out her hand as a black cab cruised past.

'Kellston, please,' she said to the driver as she climbed in the back. 'The Fox on Station Road.'

# 48

Helen felt her insides clenching as she stepped out of the cab and looked up at the pub that had been her home for years. More than once during the journey, she had leaned forward intending to tell the driver to take her to Camden instead. But then, thinking of what was at stake, she had changed her mind and settled back into the seat again.

The Fox hadn't changed much since she'd last been here, not on the outside at least. There were a couple of hanging baskets that hadn't been there when Tommy was running the place, but that was about the sum of it. She thought about the day Yvonne had kicked her out, her chest tightening at the memory of what had happened next. If she had never gone to Moira's flat, never met Lily, never embarked on that stupid, careless way of living, then ... But what-ifs never mended anything. She had made her own decisions and would have to live with the consequences.

Helen took a deep breath and pushed open the door to the

pub. Inside, the early evening customers were already settling into their pints, the tables about a quarter full, the air already redolent of cigarette smoke and ale. She walked through the rooms, glancing to either side, but didn't find who she was looking for. Never mind. If he was as predictable as she thought he was, he'd turn up eventually.

Helen went back to the bar and ordered a glass of white wine. There was a guy behind the counter she'd never seen before. He was in his mid-forties, with cautious eyes and a weak chin. 'Is this still Terry Street's place?' she asked him when he put the glass down in front of her.

'Yeah,' he said.

'You expecting him in tonight?'

The barman gave a shrug. 'Couldn't say.'

Helen glanced towards the corner where Joe Quinn's firm had always gathered on a Friday evening. Today was Friday. She looked back towards the barman. 'Can't or won't?'

'Who's asking?' he said, as if he'd learnt his script from an old gangster film.

She raised her eyebrows. 'I am. And a simple yes or no would suffice.'

'Would it?' he replied. 'Well, as I said—'

'Yeah, I get it. How about Maureen? Is she still here, or is that top secret too?'

'She's out back,' he replied after a short pause. 'Do you want to talk to her?'

Helen shook her head. 'No, ta. I was just wondering.'

He gave her a curious look, but then shifted along the bar to serve a waiting customer.

Helen took her drink and went to sit down at a table

where she could watch the door. So, Maureen Ball was still around. She felt a wave of resentment, even though she knew it was irrational. She still couldn't stand the thought of anyone other than Tommy running the pub. And soon he'd be out of jail but without any cash to buy back what was rightly his. Yvonne had well and truly taken him to the cleaners.

Leaning across to the next table, Helen swiped a copy of the evening paper that someone had left behind, and started to flick through the pages. More pictures of the lovely Diana, alongside news of riots in Moss Side, IRA hunger-strikers and ever-increasing unemployment figures. She knew that she was lucky to have a steady job with a decent income, not to mention a roof over her head. In fact, over recent years, everything had been going pretty well. She pondered for a moment on whether Moira was right about letting things go. That would be the safe option, maybe even the sensible one, but she just couldn't bring herself to do it. For as long as questions remained unanswered, she would have to go on searching.

Helen kept staring at the newspaper even though she was no longer reading it. Being back in the Fox brought with it an avalanche of memories, some good, some not so. But she had been happy here – at least so far as she knew what happiness was. Tommy had made her feel as if she belonged, and for that she would always be grateful.

It was close to seven when Vinnie Keane and a couple of other burly guys walked into the Fox. Helen was on her second glass of wine and her third cigarette. She'd more or less given up smoking, but the waiting had got on her nerves and she'd finally given in to the addiction and bought a pack of John Player's. While Vinnie went to the bar to order drinks, the other two settled down at the regular corner table.

Over the next ten minutes, more of the firm arrived, some of them familiar faces but most of them not. So, Terry Street had had a shake-up. It wasn't that surprising. After Joe's death, he'd have taken a good hard look at the army he'd inherited. A general liked to choose his own lieutenants and be surrounded by troops he could trust.

It was another quarter of an hour before Helen's patience was eventually rewarded. A small group of men, with Terry at the front, strutted in from the street. The barman, she noticed, had his pint on the counter before he'd even got there. She saw him lean forward and whisper something into Terry's ear. A second later, Terry turned to look at her. Helen stared right back, but she could tell he didn't recognise her. He had that look on his face, the wary look a man has when he thinks some bird he might have had a drunken shag with – and who he never thought to call – has just turned up to hassle him.

Terry gave her a thin smile, but she didn't smile back. He took his pint and walked over to the corner table. As soon as he was gone, she stood up and went to the bar. As it happened, it wasn't Terry she was here to see. It was the small scruffy man who had drifted in at the rear of the group and was now counting out his pennies for a half of bitter.

'I'll get that,' Helen said, reaching for her purse. 'And why don't you make it a pint?'

Pym, unlike Terry, recognised her instantly, but the sum total of his greeting was a small, abrupt nod. He gazed at her through pale rheumy eyes. He was just as skinny and just as scruffy as the last time she'd seen him. Despite the warmth of the evening, he was still wearing his tatty old overcoat.

'Do you have five minutes?' she asked. 'I'd like to talk to you about something.'

Pym glanced towards the group at the corner table, and then back at her, as if weighing up the pros and cons of their respective company. Then, clearly working on the bird in the hand principle, he nodded again and said, 'Got any fags?'

Helen bought a fresh pack of John Player's for him and ordered another glass of wine for herself. After she had paid, they went through to the table at the rear of the pub and sat down by the fireplace. Pym, who had not bothered to thank her for the drink, took a few hasty slurps, as though worried that she might be about to snatch it away.

Helen, aware that any small talk would be lost on him, skipped the preliminaries and launched straight into her request. 'I'm trying to track someone down,' she said. 'Frank Meyer. Do you remember him?'

'In jail, ain't he,' Pym said flatly.

'Yes, but I don't know which one. Do you think you could find out for me?'

'Maybe.'

'Good,' she said, taking his answer as a yes. 'And how long do you think that would take?'

'Depends,' Pym said slyly, his eyes darting down towards her bag.

'Naturally, I'd make it worth your while.' She took out her purse and slid a five-pound note across the table. 'But I need to know quickly. Can you do it by tomorrow?'

Pym palmed the fiver smartly, the note disappearing into the pocket of his overcoat. 'Tomorrow,' he repeated.

Helen rummaged in her bag until she found a scrap of paper and a pen. She wrote down two telephone numbers, the sandwich bar and the flat. 'Here,' she said, passing the piece of paper over to him. 'Call me any time. There's an answering machine, so you can leave a message if I'm not there.'

Thinking their business was completed, Pym picked up his pint and the cigarettes and rose to his feet. But Helen had other ideas. Seeing as she'd just spent a fiver, she decided that she might as well get her money's worth. 'There was one more thing,' she said.

Pym scowled and sat back down again. 'Yeah?'

'I want to get hold of the police reports on my mother's death. Do you know anyone who could help me do that?'

Pym stared at her for a while. 'Cops'll give 'em to you.'

'Eventually,' she said. 'How would I get them sooner?'

'Your old man was a cop,' Pym said, as if this answered her question.

Helen waited, but he didn't elaborate. 'And?'

'So find someone who knew him and get them to pull some strings.'

Helen could have reminded him that she'd only been a child when her father had died, but decided not to bother. Already a name had come to her. *Lazenby*. She had heard Joe and Terry talking about him years ago. 'Okay,' she said. 'Thanks.'

Pym got up again, and this time she did nothing to stop him. He shambled out of the room and back to the main part of the pub. He hadn't asked her a thing about her life since leaving the Fox; it was as if she hadn't been gone more than five minutes. He wasn't interested. And why should he be? He had a living to scrape and no time for catch-ups or reminiscences. It crossed her mind that she might not hear from him again, that she had just thrown a fiver away, but on balance she thought that she could trust him.

Helen sat and finished her wine. She rolled the name over her tongue again. *Lazenby.* There had been suspicions that he'd had a connection to the Gissings, that he'd had some involvement in the fire at the Fox. So, another bent cop, just like her dad. And one who had borne a grudge against Joe Quinn. Still, at least that gave them something in common. She would track him down and call him as soon as she got home.

# 49

DCI Tony Lazenby leaned back in his chair and gazed with interest at the woman sitting across the desk. The call had come through last night, a tentative voice on the other end of the line asking if he was the officer who had once worked with Alan Beck. When she'd explained what she was after, he had wondered at first if it was some kind of trap – the past come back to haunt him – but now he was sure that she was genuine.

'So,' he said. 'You're Alan's daughter.'

'Helen,' she said again, although she'd already introduced herself. 'Would you like to see some identification?'

He smiled at her. 'You've got all the ID you need on your face.'

'I'm sorry?'

'Your eyes,' he said. 'They're just like his.' It had given him a shock when he'd first noticed them, those distinctive blue-green eyes with their curving black lashes. She was an attractive girl, although he didn't think she knew it. His let his gaze slide quickly over her body. She was slim, with an oval face and a wide, generous mouth. Her hair, dark and silky, was chopped just below shoulder length.

'Are they?'

'Yes, they are.' With a slight jolt, he realised that she reminded him of someone else too – his ex-wife, Dana. He wasn't sure if this made him more inclined to like or dislike her. In truth, he had never thought much about Helen Beck except as the unfortunate mistake that had ruined Alan's life. And that, of course, wasn't her fault. It was all down to her slapper of a mother.

Helen Beck put her hands on the desk, linking her fingers firmly together as if to prevent any possible shake. 'I was hoping you could help me. Like I said last night, I know I could go through the usual channels, but I don't want to wait. So anything you could tell me – off the record, naturally – I'd really appreciate.'

Tony gave a nod. She had a pleasant voice, low and gentle, but he suspected it disguised something harder. She was nervous, certainly, but there was an edge of steeliness there too. Her gaze met his and didn't waver. He hadn't decided yet how much he was going to divulge. He needed to find out first how much of a threat, if any, she might be to him. What he had done, he had done for Alan's sake, but she was unlikely to see it that way.

Reaching out to his side, he tapped the brown folder that was lying on the desk. 'I was able to make a few calls, call in a favour or two, but you have to understand that—'

'That it's confidential, yes?' she said, interrupting him quickly. Her eyes dropped to stare hungrily at the folder. 'I won't mention it to anyone. I promise.'

'To be honest,' he said, 'I'm not even sure there's much in here that'll help.' He took a certain amount of pleasure in withholding the information, in making her wait. 'It's all fairly basic stuff, the police inquiry, the coroner's report ... Nothing, I'm sure, that you don't already know.'

'I don't know much,' she said. 'That's why I'm here.'

Tony gave a shrug. 'Okay,' he said. 'How about some coffee? It's only from the machine, but it's just about drinkable.' He stood up, deliberately glancing towards the file in order to make it clear that it was there for her to read as soon as he'd left. 'It'll be about ten minutes, yeah?'

She gave a nod. 'Ten minutes. Thank you.'

Tony checked his watch, then walked out of the office, closing the door behind him. He strolled down to the first floor, through the foyer and into Savile Row. While he waited for the time to pass, he checked out the suits in the window of a nearby tailor's. Helen Beck, he was sure, was going to be disappointed by what she read: no suspects, no leads, just the sordid murder of a cheap little tart in Kilburn. What she really needed to know was in his head, but he still hadn't decided whether he was going to share it with her.

Things had gone well for him over the past few years, with a promotion to DCI and a gradual tightening of control over business in the West End. Terry Street's rise to power had been swift and effective, and together they had carved out a decent portion of the trade – the drugs, the toms, the sex shops – that went on there. On the one hand, he didn't want to take any unnecessary risks, but on the other, he could see certain advantages in telling her some of what he knew.

Tony had made a few discreet enquiries and uncovered the rape that had happened in Soho. He hadn't heard about it at the time, or if he had, he hadn't made the connection with Alan Beck's daughter. It wasn't unusual for toms to run into trouble, but that had been a particularly nasty attack. Bad enough, from the looks of it, to get her out of the game for good.

He strolled back towards the station. Helen Beck might be fragile, but she was driven, too. He could see that. She wanted answers and she'd push to get them. If he played this right, he could make sure that the only grief she caused was for somebody else.

When he stepped into the office again, she was leaning back in the chair and the file was exactly where he'd left it. He put the plastic cup of coffee down in front of her and walked around the desk. 'You see what I mean?' he said.

Helen gave a nod. Her eyes were full of the expected disappointment. 'Not much to go on.'

'No,' he agreed, sitting down. 'Unfortunately, the trail – if there is one – tends to go cold pretty quickly.'

Helen pushed a strand of hair behind her ear and gave a sigh. 'So I'm wasting my time. Is that what you're saying?'

Tony didn't reply straight away. A silence filled the room until he finally spoke again. 'Can I ask you something?'

'Sure.'

'Why now? It's been a while.'

'I was young when it happened, only a kid. I didn't even know she'd been murdered until I was fifteen. An accident, that's what I was told.' She gave a wry smile, lifting her hand a little and letting it drop back lightly on to the desk. 'Oh, it wasn't their fault. They were only trying to protect me, but . . .'

'But you'd have preferred to know the truth.'

'Yes.'

Tony tipped back his chair and put his hands behind his head while he thought some more. She was a fascinating sort of girl – for a tart. Perhaps he would take the chance and go with his instincts. 'I might be able to . . . No, I'm not sure . . . I mean, they were only rumours.'

She leaned forward, her eyes lighting up. 'You know something?'

'They were only rumours,' he said again.

'Please,' she begged. 'I have to find out what happened, why she was killed.'

'And if you don't like what you find?'

'I'll deal with it,' she said firmly. 'So please, if you do know anything . . .'

'All right,' he said, with a feigned show of reluctance. 'I'll tell you what I've heard. But it didn't come from me, right?'

Helen Beck gave the barest of nods. Her wide lips parted a fraction as she waited for him to continue.

'You ever heard of a woman called Anna Farrell?'

Helen shook her head. 'Should I have?'

'She was friends with your mother, pretty good friends by all accounts. Sometimes she used the flat in Kilburn to entertain her . . . other friends. Anyway, this Anna Farrell used to go out with a man called Chapelle.'

'Who?'

'Eddie Chapelle. He's Maltese, a big name in the West End. Well, in the more unsavoury parts. Girls and gambling mainly. He got into escort agencies in the sixties. You know, high-class hookers for discerning businessmen, judges, politicians, that kind of thing.' He paused. 'It's a bit before your time, 1963, but you've heard of the Profumo scandal, right?'

'Yes, I've heard of it.'

'Well, the story goes that that was just the tip of the iceberg, and that Stephen Ward wasn't the only one procuring girls for men in high places. Chapelle was allegedly up to his neck in it too.'

Helen Beck frowned at him. 'Okay, but what does that have to do with my mother's murder?'

'Well, Chapelle was able to slip under the radar in '63, but he was arrested in 1970 on various charges relating to pimping, illegal gambling, tax evasion – you name it, he was charged with it. At the time, Anna Farrell was still his girlfriend. He was looking at a hefty sentence, and the law was looking for witnesses prepared to give evidence against him.'

'And was she – prepared to give evidence, I mean?'

'Who knows?' he said. 'But Chapelle may not have been prepared to take the chance. It could be that Anna knew too much, that her testimony – if she chose to give it – would send him down for a very long time.'

Helen's eyes widened. He saw her breath quicken, her chest rising and falling. 'And so what happened to her? What happened to Anna?'

'Good question. Nobody knows. She disappeared right after your mother was murdered. No one's seen her since.'

'You think she's dead?'

'Or still running scared. She might have figured she'd be next.' Tony leaned over, opened a drawer and took out a photograph. He slid it across the desk to Helen. 'This is her. This is Anna Farrell.'

Helen picked up the picture and stared at it. 'She looks a bit like Mum.' She glanced up. 'Don't you think?'

Tony gave a shrug. 'Perhaps.'

'Did my mother work for Chapelle too?'

'Probably.'

'You think he killed her, don't you?'

In mock protest, Tony quickly raised his hands. 'Hey, I didn't say that. Don't put words in my mouth.'

'Sorry. I . . . I didn't mean . . . '

'And anyway, he was banged up at the time, so he certainly didn't do it himself.'

'It wouldn't have stopped him getting someone else to do it, though.'

Tony gave a grudging nod. This was all going well, exactly as he'd planned. All he had to do was lay down the trail and the girl was bright enough to pick up the pieces and put them together. 'Like you said, the two women looked kind of similar.'

'So she could have been killed by mistake,' Helen continued. 'Is that what you mean? Whoever did it . . . they could have got it wrong, couldn't they?' She stared down at the photo again. 'Or maybe Chapelle was worried about her giving evidence too. Maybe he intended to have them both killed.'

'Look,' he said, 'we could come up with all kinds of

411

conspiracy theories, but it doesn't mean that any of them are true.'

'No, of course not,' she said, although she didn't look convinced. She picked up the picture. 'Can I take this?'

'Sure.'

As she placed it in her bag, he leaned towards her, his face full of concern. 'You can't go around accusing people of murder, Helen. You do understand that, don't you? And Chapelle . . . Well, he's not the type of man to stand back and ignore it. He's capable of pretty much anything.'

'He's out of jail, then, I take it?'

'Yeah, he only did a couple of years.'

'And now he's back in the West End.'

Tony paused. 'Yes.'

Helen rose to her feet and put out her hand. 'Okay. Thanks for seeing me. I appreciate it.'

Tony took her hand and shook it. Her palm was warm, and slightly damp. 'Promise me you won't do anything stupid?'

'Define stupid,' she said.

'You know what I mean.'

She smiled at him, turned and walked out of the office.

Tony stared at the door for a minute or two. Had he done the right thing? Eddie Chapelle wouldn't be happy when she came sniffing around asking awkward questions. It would make him mad, and when he was mad, he had a tendency to hurt people.

Slowly, he lowered his gaze to Helen's untouched cup of coffee. In truth, he didn't actually care whether she got hurt or not. What did it matter to him? There was a big fat plus side to all of this: if Chapelle saw her as a serious threat, he might decide to take her out of the picture. What was one more murder to a man like that? And if he did decide to dispose of her, then that would be the end of Eddie Chapelle.

He picked up a pen and tapped it lightly against the top of the desk. Yeah, he could see how this might pan out. If Chapelle went down for Helen Beck's murder, then all his West End business interests would be up for grabs. Tony's mouth slid into a smug, self-satisfied smile. It never did any harm to aim for a bigger slice of the pie. In fact, maybe he could move things along a bit. A word here and there, a few rumours that were bound to reach Chapelle's ears, and he could easily set the wheels in motion.

# 50

Helen climbed the stairs to her flat, unlocked the door and walked through to the living room. She dropped her jacket on the sofa, then went into the kitchen and put the kettle on. While she waited for it to boil, she ran through her conversation with Lazenby again. Could she trust him? Neither of them had mentioned Joe Quinn or the small matter of the firebombing of the Fox. She still had no idea if he'd been involved or not.

Helen had to admit that she'd taken an instant dislike to the man. There was something highly unpleasant, even odious about him. Absently, she rubbed at her bare arms, as if his predatory gaze might have left a slimy trail. But for all her distaste, she still reckoned that the information he'd given her was sound.

She delved into her bag and took out the photograph of Anna Farrell. It was a head-and-shoulders shot, a picture that had probably been taken in a photographer's studio. Where had Lazenby got it from? She hadn't thought to ask. There were a lot of things she hadn't asked, but it was too late now.

Anna definitely had a look of Lynsey Beck about her – long straight fair hair and brown eyes – and it was easy to see how a mistake could have been made. But if that was the case, then where was Anna now? Still on the run, or had Chapelle caught up with her? If the latter was the case, then there wasn't much hope of her being alive.

Helen made herself a brew, then settled down on the sofa and wrote down everything Tony Lazenby had told her, as well as what she remembered from the police reports. When she'd finished, she read it through a couple of times, making sure there was nothing she'd missed. She chewed on the end of the pen and gazed out of the window at the pale blue summer sky. It was almost six thirty on a Saturday night, and most girls her age were probably getting ready to go out on the town. Did she envy them their carefree pleasures? Perhaps a small part of her did, but the greater part was consumed by a need to find her mother's killer.

This afternoon, when they'd closed up the sandwich shop, she had told Moira that she was going over to Kellston to see Lily. She didn't tell her about the intended visit to West End Central police station, or her phone conversation with DCI Tony Lazenby the evening before. Moira had been so obviously relieved to hear that nothing particularly useful had been gleaned from the tenant in the house at Kilburn that Helen hadn't had the heart to tell her the rest of her plans. Moira's relief, she knew, was only down to concern; she was worried for her well-being, for her safety, and perhaps, bearing in mind today's revelations, she was right to be.

The lie about Lily, however, sat uneasily on Helen's conscience. The truth was that she hardly ever saw her former friend these days. They had drifted apart, their lives taking different directions. Helen hadn't been back to Soho since she'd been raped, but Lily still roamed the same old streets, still playing the game and risking the odds. The last occasion they'd met up, over a year ago now, had not gone well. There had been an awkwardness between the two of them, a tense and edgy atmosphere.

The phone interrupted Helen's thoughts and she jumped up off the sofa. 'Hello?' she said into the receiver.

There was a beeping sound as someone dropped coins into the slot of a phone box, and then a male voice came on the line. 'I've got it for you.'

'I'm sorry?' It took a moment for Helen to realise it was Pym. Her heart skipped a beat. 'Oh, you have? That's great.' She was still holding the pad in which she'd been writing up her notes on Lazenby. She put it down on the table and flicked over to a fresh page. 'Okay, fire away.'

'He's on the Mansfield,' said Pym.

Helen started. 'What?'

'The Mansfield,' he repeated. 'Carlton House.'

'But . . . but he can't be. He's in jail. He can't be out yet. He got the same sentence as Tommy, and he isn't due to be released until the end of the month.'

'Yeah, well,' Pym grunted. 'Maybe Tommy got himself in bother, got time added on. Look, I ain't got all day. Do you want this address or not?'

Helen's fingers tightened around the pen. Her pulse had begun to race. 'Yes, of course.'

'Number seventy-four,' he said. 'You got that?'

She quickly scribbled it down. 'Seventy-four Carlton House.'

'That's it.'

'Thanks,' Helen said. 'Thanks very much.' But she'd barely got the first word out before the line was disconnected. For a moment she listened to the dialling tone, before carefully replacing the phone in its cradle. She stared down at the address, barely able to believe it. Frank Meyer was out of prison and he was living back in Kellston.

# 51

Helen stood gazing down at the piece of paper, trying to decide what to do next. Her initial instinct was to grab her jacket and dash straight round there, but maybe she needed to think things through first. Frank Meyer might not welcome uninvited guests turning up on his doorstep. He couldn't have been free for long and was probably still adjusting to life on the outside. Was it fair to hurtle round to Kellston and burden him with all her problems?

She decided, on balance, that it would be better to wait until tomorrow, when things might be clearer in her own head. The sandwich bar was closed on Sundays and so she had a free day. After a while, she sat back down on the sofa, still trying to absorb the fact that Frank was out of prison.

Helen rummaged in her bag and found the pack of John Player's that she'd bought in the Fox. With a slightly shaking hand she lit one and inhaled deeply. What would Frank be like after serving seven years inside for a crime he hadn't committed? There had never been any doubt in her mind of his innocence. The prosecution, she was certain, had twisted and manipulated the evidence to make him look guilty. Just like they had with Tommy.

She tapped the cigarette against the side of the ashtray, trying to put herself in Frank's shoes. How would she feel if it had been her? Bitter, she thought, and angry. All those years snatched away, with nothing to show for them. How old would he be now? She had never known his exact age but presumed that, like Tommy, he must be in his early forties.

She smoked the cigarette, then stubbed it out and gazed around the living room. She'd painted the walls a pale mossy green and decorated them with three quirky Paul Klee prints. Not to everyone's taste, she imagined, but she liked them. The sofa was a darker shade of green and pulled out into a double bed for when she had visitors. Except she never did have visitors, not the type who stayed over, anyway.

Helen tapped her heel restlessly on the ground. The evening loomed ahead of her, long and empty. What was she going to do with herself? Watch some TV, perhaps, or go over the Lazenby notes. She wondered what Frank was doing and what had brought him back to Kellston. She got up and walked over to the window. She watched the people passing by beneath her, people with places to go, friends to meet.

Suddenly she knew that she couldn't put it off. Now that she had Frank's address, she had to see him. The thought of waiting until tomorrow was too much to bear. She went to the bedroom, changed into her jeans and a clean white shirt, pulled a comb through her hair and put on some lipstick. Then, before she could change her mind, she hurried through to the living room, shrugged on her denim jacket, grabbed her bag and rushed out of the flat.

Once outside, she tried to decide between catching a bus and travelling by rail. From Camden station she could get an overground train to Dalston and from there another one to Kellston. The latter would be quicker than the bus, but it wouldn't be quick enough. She was too impatient to wait around for public transport.

For the second time in two days, Helen stretched out her hand and hailed a black cab. It was an expensive way to travel, but it saved hanging about. She gave the cabbie the address and settled back in the seat as he did a perilous U-turn and headed for Kellston. They were barely fifty yards down the road when she started questioning the wisdom of what she was doing, spending the rest of the journey in a state of heightened anxiety. What would she say to Frank? How would he react to her turning up out of the blue? What if he didn't want to see her? What if he wasn't there? What if was there but he had company, a girl perhaps? Oh God, there were just *so* many reasons why she shouldn't be arriving unannounced.

By the time the cab drew up outside Carlton House, Helen had almost talked herself out of it. It took every effort of will for her to resist the temptation to ask the driver to take her back home. Butterflies were dancing in her stomach as she paid the fare and then watched the cabbie drive away. Well, she thought, looking around, there was nothing else for it. The time had come to gather her courage and put aside her reservations.

As she walked tentatively along the path, she recalled the

times she'd spent on the estate as a kid, roaming the dank, gloomy passageways. Back then, she'd been both afraid and intrigued, but now she was only nervous. There was a threatening atmosphere to the place, a definite air of menace. Gangs of youths idled at corners, smoking joints or drinking beer as they stood and waited for something to happen.

The three tall towers of the Mansfield Estate had been built less than twenty years ago, but already they were starting to fall apart. Staring hard at Carlton House, she took in the crumbling mortar and the rusting balconies. She counted up seven floors and scanned the row of windows. Was one of them Frank's?

The evening was pleasantly warm, but she still gave a slight shiver as she started climbing the stairs. She could have taken one of the lifts, but the wafting smell of urine had been less than inviting. Anyway, it would take her longer if she walked. It would give her more time to prepare herself.

By the time she mounted the last flight, she was beginning to regret her decision not to take the lift. She reached the seventh floor, checked the numbers on the sign and turned left towards number seventy-four. When she was almost there, she stopped to catch her breath, gazing out over the balcony at the view of Kellston. From here, she could see the neat rows of terraces, the high street, the station and even the roof of the Fox.

When she had delayed for as long as she could, and her pulse was almost back to normal, she took the final few steps and came to a halt in front of Frank's door. It was shabby and battered-looking, the brown paint chipped and flaking. She couldn't see a bell and so she knocked lightly with her knuckles, then waited, her heart in her mouth. There was no response. Disappointed, she rapped on the door again, a series of harder, more impatient knocks. This time there was a clearly audible movement from within. She heard the sound of a bolt being pulled back and then the door swung open. Suddenly she was face to face with Frank Meyer.

'Yeah?' he said roughly.

Helen smiled up at him. She had almost forgotten how tall he was. He didn't look that different from the last time they'd met, although his hair was shorter and there was a slight hollowness beneath the cheekbones that hadn't been there before. He was sleepy-eyed and unshaven, possibly a little drunk. There was a definite whiff of whisky in the air.

'Hello, Frank,' she said.

A flicker of confusion passed across his face before her features finally registered with him. 'Christ,' he said. 'Mouse. Where the hell did you spring from?'

'Not so far away,' she said, trying to keep her tone light as old emotions rose to the surface. It was the first time anyone had called her Mouse in years. 'Aren't you going to invite me in?'

'Sure,' he said, standing back and waving her inside. 'Come on in. Welcome to the palace.'

As Helen stepped inside the hall, the first thing she noticed was the overwhelming smell of damp. She wrinkled her nose, trying not to breathe too deeply. Frank closed the door and ushered her through to the living room. The smell was just as bad in there, and her gaze quickly took in the torn black-speckled wallpaper, the grubby carpet and flimsy curtains.

There was hardly any furniture; only an old cream sofa with worn-out arms, and a small table. A bottle of Scotch stood on the table, along with a half-full ashtray.

Frank, seeing her expression, pulled a face. 'Beggars can't be choosers,' he said. 'It's somewhere to live until I get myself sorted.'

'Oh, I wasn't ... Yes, I'm sure it'll be fine. A lick of paint and—'

'And it'll still be a dump. Don't worry, I'm not planning on staying here any longer than I have to.' He put his hands on his hips and stared at her. 'Well, you've grown up since I last saw you.'

'It's been a while.'

'A lot of water under the bridge, huh?' He gestured towards the sofa. 'Grab a seat. Let me get you a drink. What would you like? I can do Scotch or Scotch. Or black coffee if you don't fancy that. There's no milk, I'm afraid.'

'Scotch, then,' she said. 'Thank you.'

While Frank went into the kitchen to fetch another glass, Helen perched on the edge of the sofa. She wasn't sorry that she'd come, but she wondered if it was wrong to try and involve him in her troubles. 'How have you been?' she asked as he came back into the room.

'Not bad. Yourself?'

Helen nodded. 'Surviving.'

Frank sat down beside her, poured her a drink and passed her the glass. 'Cheers,' he said. 'It's nice to see you again.'

'Thanks. And you.' She took a sip of the whisky. 'So how long have you been out?'

'About a week. Just under.'

'And was it . . . I mean . . . God, I don't suppose you want to talk about it, do you? Sorry.' She frowned and buried her nose in the glass again.

Frank gave a shrug of his heavy shoulders. 'It's over. That's all that matters. Finished, done with.'

Helen looked at him closely, trying to read his face. She wasn't sure what she saw there: relief, bitterness, despair, anger? Maybe all of them. Or none. It was hard to tell with Frank Meyer. She glanced around the room again, remembering his old flat overlooking the Green.

'You can't stay here,' she suddenly blurted out. 'You can't.'

Frank gave a low laugh. 'I've seen worse. And believe me, I'd rather be here than where I was last week.'

'No,' she said, shaking her head. 'It's not right. It's not fair. Nothing that happened was your fault, but you lost everything because of it.'

Frank's eyes met hers for a second before he looked away. 'It's in the past, Mouse. There's no point dwelling on it.'

She left a short pause before saying, 'These days most people call me Helen.' She didn't want him to think of her as the kid he'd known in the Fox. Those times were gone. She was a woman now, although she doubted if he saw her as one.

'Do they? I'll have to try and remember that.'

And then, on impulse, Helen said, 'You can come and stay with me in Camden. You know, just until you get sorted. It's not much, just a sofa bed, but it's comfortable enough.'

Frank smiled. 'Thanks for the offer, but I couldn't do that.'

'Why not?'

'Because you don't owe me anything, love. I'm not your responsibility.'

Helen frowned at him, realising that he thought she was there out of duty, or pity. 'That's not why I'm offering, not at all.'

'So why, then?'

Helen felt the old familiar blush creep on to her cheeks. Suddenly, she felt as awkward and self-conscious as that teenage girl who had furtively watched the door of the Fox waiting for him to come into the pub. She took a large gulp of whisky and put the glass down on the table. 'To be honest, you'd be doing me a favour.'

'And how do you figure that one out?'

'It's a long story, but let's just say that I'd feel a damn sight safer at the moment if there was someone else around.'

'A long story,' he said. 'Well, you'd better get started, then.'

# 52

It only took Frank a few minutes to gather his belongings together, and half an hour later they were back in Camden. Helen made some food – a quick bowl of pasta, to mop up the Scotch – and while they ate in the kitchen, she told him about everything that had happened since the trial. The only part she glossed over was her time with Lily. Although she trusted Frank, she didn't want him to pity her or to think of her as damaged.

'So,' he said. 'Terry Street owns the Fox now.'

'Yeah, Yvonne couldn't wait to get rid of it. She was on that plane before the ink was dry on the contract. Do you think Tommy might be able to buy it back?'

'If he can get the cash together . . . and if Terry's prepared to sell.'

'Big ifs.' She paused. 'What about Dagenham? Couldn't he raise some money from there?'

Frank, surprised, narrowed his grey eyes. 'How do you know about Dagenham?'

Helen had been aware of both of the long-firm frauds. 'Because you and Tommy used to talk about it when I was around. I guess you thought I was too young to understand.'

Frank laughed. 'We thought wrong then, huh?'

'I never said anything to anyone. I wouldn't.'

'The keeper of secrets,' he said.

Helen could feel his eyes on her, and blushed again. 'I wouldn't say that exactly.' She reached out for her glass of whisky, even though she knew she'd drunk too much already. 'If the job was never finished off, couldn't you—'

'It's too late,' Frank said, shaking his head. 'The minute we got sent down, Alfie would have cleared the stock, grabbed the money and got the hell out.'

'But you haven't been there, you haven't tried to contact him?'

'Waste of time,' he said.

'You don't know that. We could go over there tomorrow. I'm sure Moira would lend us the car.' But she could see that Frank thought it was pointless. 'Or you could start another one, begin again. Couldn't you do that?'

'If I had the money,' Frank said. 'These things cost to set up.'

'I have some. Maybe I could help out.'

Frank put down his fork and pushed his bowl aside. 'I don't think so.'

Helen, hoping that she hadn't offended his pride, stood up and put the dishes in the sink. 'Well, the offer's there.' She sloshed some water into the bowl and glanced over her shoulder. 'Do you want to go through to the living room?'

Frank took the bottle of Scotch with him and sat down on the sofa. Helen followed him through and curled up in the armchair. There were so many things she wanted to ask, but she wasn't sure where to start. After a short silence she said, 'So what made you come back to Kellston?'

'Isn't that what criminals do?' he replied drily. 'Return to the scene of the crime?'

'Except it wasn't your crime.'

Frank gave a shrug. 'Hell, we're all guilty of something.'

Helen couldn't understand how he could be so blasé about it. If she'd been sent down for something she hadn't done, she'd be awash with rage and bitterness. However, if it hadn't been for the whisky loosening her tongue, she would never have asked the next question. 'So what are you so guilty of?'

Frank's face immediately darkened. He fumbled for his cigarettes and lit one quickly. 'You don't want to know.'

'You mean that you don't want to tell me.'

He glanced across at her, breathing out a long, thin stream of smoke. 'Yeah, that too.'

'Okay,' she said. 'I didn't mean to pry.' She took another sip of her drink before changing the subject. 'Did Tommy ever talk to you about my mum?'

'Not really. I didn't even know he had a sister until . . .' He shifted on the sofa, leaning forward to tap the cigarette against the edge of the ashtray. 'So what's the plan, Mouse? Sorry, *Helen*. I'll get used to it eventually. What are you planning to do about Eddie Chapelle?'

'Talk to him, I suppose, try and find out what he knows.'

'And if he was involved, do you really think he's going to tell you?'

'I guess not.'

'And what are you going to do then?'

Helen gave a shrug.

'Not much of a plan,' he said, grinning.

She smiled weakly back. 'You got a better one?'

'Not yet,' he said. 'But if Mr Chapelle's got something to hide, I suggest we tread carefully.'

Helen felt a flutter in her chest as he said *we*. It was like an acknowledgement that she was no longer alone and that they were in this together. 'Are you sure you want to get involved? I'll understand if you don't. You've only just got out of jail.'

'Which means I've got nothing else to do.'

'Thanks,' she said. 'I appreciate it. I suppose you think I'm crazy doing this.'

'Does it matter what I think?'

'Yes,' she said.

'Then no, I don't think so. Sometimes, when you have loose ends, you have to find a way of tying them up. It's not doing that that drives you crazy.'

Helen gave a nod. 'And what about *your* loose ends? Connor let you go down for a crime you didn't commit. How do you come to terms with that?'

Frank hesitated for a moment, turning the glass around in his hand. 'I'm not sure that he did.'

'What?'

'I'm not sure that Connor killed Joe Quinn.'

Helen's brow creased into a frown. 'But he must have done.'

'Just like I must have known that the body was in the boot of the Jag.'

'It's not the same.'

Frank looked up at her. 'It might be.'

Helen didn't think so. She remembered Shirley tottering across the car park with the bottle of vodka in her hand. She remembered Connor coming up behind her, grabbing her arm and whirling her around, punching her hard in the face. He was capable, more than capable, of murdering Joe. 'They were always fighting. Connor threatened to kill him.'

'Threatened, yeah, but that's not the same as actually doing it.'

'But if he didn't, then who did?'

'Oh, I don't know. Someone who wanted Joe Quinn out of the way. Someone who needed a scapegoat. Connor was the obvious choice.'

'And what about you and Tommy?'

'Collateral damage,' said Frank. 'No one could have anticipated that Tommy would take the keys off him, refuse to let him drive. And I was just in the wrong place at the wrong time. That's the way it is sometimes.'

'So have you got any ideas?'

Frank smiled. 'Lots of ideas, but not a shred of evidence. There are plenty of firms who'd have liked to see the back of Joe Quinn, the Gissing brothers being right at the top of the list.'

The mention of the Gissings prompted another memory for Helen. 'Wasn't there a rumour that Lazenby was connected to them?' She wondered now if she'd made a mistake in going to see the chief inspector. But if she hadn't, then she'd never have found out about Eddie Chapelle.

Frank knocked back his whisky. 'Plenty of rumours about pretty much everything. Doesn't mean that they're true – or that they're not.'

There was another silence. Helen wondered if she should put some music on, but then worried that it might seem too . . . Too what? Too much like a date, perhaps. Instead she said, 'So what happened to all your things, the stuff you had in Barley Road?'

'It's in Tommy's lock-up.'

Helen, who'd thought she knew pretty much everything about Tommy, hadn't known about this. 'A lock-up?'

'In Dalston,' Frank said. 'I got a mate to clear out the flat and store everything there. I should go over sometime and pick up my clothes. I've been wearing the same shirt for the last three days.' He bent his face towards his shoulder and sniffed loudly. 'Can you tell?'

'Would you like the polite answer to that?'

'Sorry,' he said.

'It doesn't matter. Look, we could go to the lock-up tomorrow. And then go up to Dagenham, see if Alfie Blunt's still around.'

Frank laughed. 'You're not giving up on that one, are you? But yeah, it sounds like a plan.'

They carried on talking until midnight, when Helen helped him to pull out the sofa bed and then fetched some blankets and a pillow from the cupboard in the hall. 'There's plenty of hot water if you want a shower. And there's clean towels in the bathroom.' Her hand flew up to her mouth. 'Oh, I wasn't hinting. I just meant . . .'

'It's okay, I know what you meant. And thanks.'

'Good night then.'

'Sleep well,' Frank said.

Helen froze in the doorway, recalling with a tremble that those were the last words he'd said to her before he'd been arrested.

# 53

When Helen walked into the kitchen the following morning, it was to find Frank Meyer showered and shaved and wearing jeans with a clean, if slightly crumpled, grey T-shirt. He looked better than he had the night before, and none the worse for having consumed half a bottle of whisky. She, on the other hand, was suffering from a nagging headache and the feeling that she might have said too much.

'I made coffee,' he said, nodding towards the percolator.

'Good.' She smiled tentatively as she poured some into a mug. 'Have you had any breakfast?'

'I helped myself to toast. I hope that's okay?'

'Of course it is. Make yourself at home. Well, it is your home for as long as . . . Just ask if you need anything.'

'You've got a nice place here,' he said, as if he'd only just arrived and was noticing his surroundings for the first time.

'I like it. You sleep all right?'

'Like a baby.'

'Good,' she said again. She put a slice of bread into the toaster. 'There's cereal in the cupboard and eggs in the fridge. Are you sure you wouldn't like some more toast?' She knew that she was fussing, but she couldn't help herself. It would take a while to get used to having him around.

'I'm fine, thanks.'

While she was waiting for the toast to pop up, Helen went over to the window and looked down on the street. 'Ah, Moira's dropped the car off. I've got the spare keys. We can go over to Dalston and pick up your things.'

'Are you sure she doesn't mind?'

Helen turned around and went back to the counter. 'No, of course not. I often borrow it.'

'It's good of her.' He drank some coffee. 'So are she and Tommy . . . Are they an item now?'

Helen took the piece of toast and her mug, then went over to the table and sat down opposite him. 'An item? No, I don't think so. They're just friends.' She spread a thin layer of butter over the toast while she considered it some more. 'I think they're just friends.'

'You don't sound too sure.'

'She doesn't visit or anything. She offered, but I don't think Tommy wanted her to.'

'Sometimes it's easier that way.'

Helen took a bite of toast, chewed it and looked at him. 'Is it?'

'You have to try and forget about the outside world. Your world is that prison, that cell, the day-to-day routine. You start yearning for more and it'll drive you crazy. Acceptance, that's the thing.'

'And that's how you got through it?'

'More or less.'

Whenever Helen talked to him, she got the feeling that there were lines she should be reading between, things unspoken that she couldn't quite grasp. She didn't know Frank well enough, perhaps, to fully understand him. Quickly, she ate the toast and finished off her coffee. 'You ready, then?'

The Sunday morning traffic was light, and twenty minutes later they were in Dalston. Frank guided her around the back streets until they reached a car repair shop with a row of lock-ups running along beside it. Helen stopped the Ford Fiesta and switched off the ignition. The garage was closed and there was no one else around.

'How come I never knew about this?' she asked as they got out of the car.

Frank grinned. 'Well, I guess Tommy had his secrets like everyone else. And he probably didn't want Yvonne to find out. We used to keep stock here if we ran out of room at the shop.' He took a bunch of keys from his pocket and walked towards the lock-ups. 'I know the guy who runs the place, Billy Kent. He was the one who cleared my flat out for me.'

'What happened to the MG?'

Frank nodded towards the garage. 'Billy flogged it. Not much point in having it sitting around for seven years. Plus, it helps to have a bit of extra cash when you're inside.'

There were two large padlocks on the door. Frank unlocked them both and rolled up the metal shutter. The inside of the lock-up was about the same size as a regular residential garage, with boxes stacked along the left-hand side. To the right were four large wooden crates, a rusty lawnmower and various bits of junk. The place had a damp, musty kind of smell.

While Frank started rooting through the crates, pulling out the articles he wanted to take with him, Helen wandered over to the boxes. Most of them were sealed, but a couple at the end only had the flaps tucked under. Out of curiosity, she flipped open the first one and found a heap of Christmas decorations: long strands of tinsel, coloured baubles, even an angel with a single lacy wing.

'Hey, look at these,' Frank said.

She turned to see him posing in a pair of sunglasses. 'Very smart.'

'Ray-Bans,' he said. 'Are Ray-Bans still cool, or have I missed the boat?'

'They're still cool.'

'Good.' He pushed them up on to his forehead and then crouched down and carried on sorting through his stuff.

She watched as he put a pile of LPs to one side. 'Aren't you bringing those?'

'Do you think I should? I don't want to clutter up your place.'

'I don't mind, so long as there's no heavy metal. My head can't cope with heavy metal.'

He selected a few from the pile and read the names off the covers. 'Dylan, Van Morrison, Ry Cooder. Anything too objectionable there?'

'No.'

'Okay, I'll bring them along.'

Helen closed the decorations box and opened the next, smaller one. There was a crumpled red coat folded over on top. Some of Yvonne's old things, she thought at first, before recalling that Yvonne didn't even know about the lock-up. She picked up the coat and shook it out. It had black trim at the collar with black buttons down the front and at the wrists. At first it seemed only faintly familiar, but then it hit her like a lightning strike. *The coat had belonged to her mother.* She remembered her wearing it when she came to Camberley Road. Helen's hands began to tremble. She drew in her breath, her lungs constricting.

The gasp alerted Frank, who stopped what he was doing and looked over at her. 'What is it?'

'This was my mum's,' she whispered. She raised it to her face and buried her nose in the fabric. If she'd been hoping for some lingering scent, she was quickly disappointed. The coat had a strange, acrid smell. 'What's it doing here?'

Frank stood up and came over to her. 'Tommy must have ... he must have collected her things from the flat after ... '

'You didn't know they were here?'

He shook his head. 'I guess he didn't know what to do with them. He couldn't bring himself to throw them away and so he just stored them here. Maybe he thought that ... I don't know. Maybe he thought that you might like to have them one day.'

Helen put the coat to one side while she rummaged around in the box. There were a few other items of clothing, none of which she recognised, as well as a couple of brightly coloured fruit bowls, a plastic carrier bag containing numerous strings of beads and an old watch that had stopped working long ago. Right at the bottom she came across a metal tin and pulled it out to look at it. It was about ten inches wide, silver-coloured, with scorch marks across the surface. In the top right-hand corner were the initials LQ painted on in a child-like hand.

'It looks like an old petty cash tin,' Frank said.

Helen tried to open it but it was locked. She shook it and could hear something shifting around inside. 'LQ,' she said, touching the initials with her fingertips. 'She must have had this when she was living at the Fox.'

'You want me to try and get it open?' Frank glanced around the garage. 'I'm sure there's something in here we could use.'

But Helen quickly shook her head. Whatever was inside had been important enough for her mum to want to keep private. She didn't want to look at it in some musty lock-up in Dalston. She wasn't ready yet and she didn't want to get emotional in front of Frank. 'It's okay. I'll take it back with me, open it at home.'

'Would you like me to put the box in the car? I'm pretty much done here.'

Helen placed the tin back in the box and then laid the red coat carefully on top. 'It's all right. I can carry it. It's not heavy.'

They loaded up the boot with Frank's clothes, records and a few chosen books. He would pick up the rest of his stuff when he had a more permanent place to live. 'Are you okay?' he asked as she placed the box in an empty corner.

'Why shouldn't I be?'

'Because they're your mum's things and you didn't know they were here. You're not mad, are you? Only Tommy's always tried to do right by you – even if he did sometimes screw it up.'

Helen gave him a wry smile. 'Hey, I was mad at him for not letting me know she'd been murdered. This doesn't really compare.' She thought of Tommy going to the wrecked flat in Kilburn and picking through what remained of his sister's belongings. 'I wonder if he went to Samuel Street on his own.'

'Probably. He didn't say anything about it to me.'

'It can't have been easy for him, knowing what happened there. To be honest, I'm surprised anything survived the fire.'

Frank closed the boot. 'He probably meant to give them to you when you were older.'

'Maybe.'

Helen leaned her elbows on the roof of the car while Frank went and secured the lock-up. The sun was shining and she could feel the heat on the crown of her head and her shoulders. She wondered if finding her mum's things was some kind of sign. Did she believe in messages from the other side? Here she was, just beginning an investigation into the murder, and suddenly the box turned up. A mere coincidence, or something more? She was inclined towards the latter and found it vaguely comforting.

'Home, then?' asked Frank.

'It's early yet. Let's go to Dagenham and check out the shop.'

Frank slid the sunglasses back over his eyes. 'There won't be a shop. We'll be wasting our time.'

'Well I've nothing better to do. How about you?'

'It'll be a wasted journey.'

'You can't be sure of that.'

'I can't be sure that the sun's going to rise tomorrow morning, but it's a pretty good bet.'

Helen held up the car keys and jangled them in front of him. 'I'll let you drive. So long as you're careful. You still remember how to drive, don't you?'

Frank leaned across the roof and held out his hand. 'Now you're talking. Maybe that trip to Dagenham isn't such a bad idea after all.'

# 54

Frank drove with a casual disregard for the Highway Code, his left hand sitting lightly on the wheel, his right elbow jutting out of the open window, speeding along the quiet Sunday streets as if Dagenham might disappear if he didn't get there within the next half-hour.

'What's the hurry?' Helen said.

'No hurry.'

But he didn't take the hint and slow down. And Helen, not wanting to be a back-seat driver, had to be content with gritting her teeth and hoping for the best. She watched him out of the corner of her eye, studying the left-hand side of his face, the curve of his jaw and the sharply defined cheekbone. His eyes, although she knew they were grey, were shielded by the aviator shades. She wanted to know what made him tick, who the real Frank Meyer was, but he was a man who didn't willingly give much away.

It was about ten past eleven when they got to Dagenham. Despite the sunshine, it seemed a grey sort of place, neglected and run down. Helen was reminded of Kellston; it had a similar air of despondency about it. 'So where was it, the shop?'

'Broad Street. We're almost there.'

'And what's it called?'

'Leigh's,' he said. 'At least it used to be.'

A few minutes later, Frank pulled up beside a neat row of shops. There was a chemist, a butcher's, a toy store and a newsagent. He stared out of the window with a resigned expression on his face. 'You see,' he said, slapping his palms lightly against the wheel. 'He's well gone.'

'Which one was it?'

'That one. The toy store. Except it was electricals back then.'

Helen looked over at the bright red sign: *Gibson's Toys*. The window was full of teddy bears, Barbies, train sets and Corgi cars. 'Maybe he's branched out.'

'Yeah, I bet he has. All the way to the Caribbean.'

Helen was starting to regret ever having suggested the idea. Perhaps she should have let things lie. Frank had already convinced himself that he'd lost everything – and accepted it – before she'd butted in and insisted on coming here. Still, it would be stupid to leave without even trying to find out where Alfie had gone. She opened the car door and got out.

'What are you doing?' he asked.

She bent down to answer him. 'I'm going to take a look.'

'What for? It's closed. It's Sunday.'

'Well, what do people do on Sundays?'

Frank gazed back at her. 'I don't know. Stay in bed, go to church, make pointless journeys to Dagenham?'

'Ha ha,' she said. 'How about stocktaking? There could be someone in the back.' She walked over to the door and peered through at the Aladdin's cave within. For a second, with her nose pressed hard against the glass, she felt like a little kid again. She rapped on the door, but nobody answered. She tried again, harder this time, but there was still no response. Frank came up behind, leaned over her shoulder and looked inside. She was aware of the closeness of him, of his body almost touching hers. Had it been any other man, she would have shied away, but with him she didn't feel the need. 'Just don't say I told you so,' she murmured.

'Ah, it was worth a punt.'

She turned to look up at him. 'How can you be so calm about it?'

Frank gave a shrug. 'What's the point of getting stressed? It won't change anything.' He started heading back towards the Fiesta. 'Come on, let's go find someplace to have a coffee.'

Helen was about to follow when she had another idea. Instead, she started walking towards the newsagent's. 'Hang on. Just a minute.' Inside the shop, a middle-aged man with a slight paunch – too much temptation from the chocolate selection perhaps – was standing idle behind the counter. She said hello, smiled nicely and bought a pack of cigarettes, even though she didn't want them. As she was paying, Frank came in and stood beside her.

'I thought you were giving up,' he said.

'I am . . . soon.' She put the cigarettes in her pocket. Just as she was about to leave, she stopped and said casually to the

443

newsagent, 'Oh, I don't suppose you know Mr Leigh, do you? The guy who used to run the electrical shop?'

It was a shot in the dark, but one that paid off. 'You mean Marty?' he asked.

'Yeah,' Frank interrupted. 'Marty. You any idea where he's gone?'

The man looked up at Frank, alerted perhaps by something hard and edgy in his tone. Frank's sheer size often intimidated people, and Helen could see suspicion passing over the newsagent's face. If they weren't careful, he would clam up and tell them nothing. Quickly she tried to rectify the situation.

'Frank's an old mate of Marty's. They used to go to school together.' She gave him a subtle nudge with her elbow. 'Didn't you, love?'

There was a pause before Frank said, 'Yeah, that's right. Me and Marty go way back.'

'Only we've been away,' she continued chattily. 'In Scotland for a few years. It's awful how you lose touch with people, isn't it? We were just passing by and noticed that the shop had changed hands. We were hoping to track him down, have a catch-up, you know, but ... I don't suppose you've any idea where we could find him?'

The man seemed to soften a little, although he threw another wary glance towards Frank. 'Moved, didn't he,' he said, stating the obvious.

Helen waited patiently, not pressing him, careful not to appear too keen. She was suddenly reminded of those nights in Soho, of the tentative punters who would pause for a few seconds after listening to her spiel, wanting to believe her but not quite sure if they should. Instinctively, she did what she had always done then – provided her most seductive smile and waited for the pay-off.

'Well,' the man said, 'don't suppose it's a secret or nothing. Sold the old place, didn't he? Personally, I reckon that was down to *her*. She never liked it much round here.'

'No,' Helen agreed, taking another chance. 'You could be right. She was always saying that to me. I never got it myself, but there's no pleasing some people.'

'You're not wrong there. I mean, it might not be everyone's cup of tea, but I've been trading here for going on thirty years now.'

'Thirty years?' Helen repeated. 'That's amazing. Still, I'm not surprised.' She glanced around the shop with an expression that she hoped relayed a suitable sense of respect and admiration.

He nodded, clearly gratified by the response. 'So, you want to know where old Marty's gone?'

'We would,' she said. 'It'd be great to see him again. We're only in town for a few weeks, and so . . .'

'Now let me see,' he said, stroking his chin. 'It was over Angel way if I remember rightly.' He paused and frowned. 'Or was it?'

Helen felt Frank shift impatiently beside her, but he had the sense to keep his mouth shut and wait.

'Now hang on, it's been a few years. Let me see. Yes, I think it was the Holloway Road. Yes, I'm pretty sure it was that way. *She* was keen on Holloway, I remember that.' He paused. 'Yes, somewhere in that direction.'

'Thank you,' Helen said. 'We'll try there, see if we can find him. Thanks for your help.'

'That's all right. Pass on my best if you see him. Tell him Barry said hello.'

'Barry,' Helen repeated dutifully. 'We will. Thanks again.'

The two of them walked out of the shop, saying nothing until they were back inside the Fiesta.

'Christ, Mouse,' Frank said, grinning. 'How did you get to be so devious?'

'I have *no* idea what you mean. I'm not devious. I just did what any normal person would do if they were looking for an old friend.'

Frank raised his eyebrows. 'Well, I always said you were smart.'

'I can't be that smart,' she said. 'If I was, I wouldn't be letting you drive this car.'

Frank laughed and turned on the ignition. 'Fancy a trip to Holloway?'

# 55

They had been searching for half an hour and had made two circuits of the area, including Holloway Road, Canonbury Road, Liverpool Road and Essex Road, before they finally hit the jackpot on Upper Street, not far from Angel tube. The wide double-fronted shop stood between a record store and a greengrocer's and had the name *Leigh's* emblazoned in gold across the top.

'There!' Helen said, pointing. 'Over there, to the left.'

Frank turned his head to look, almost running into the car in front as the traffic lights switched to red. He managed to brake just in time, but the driver of the Vauxhall was less than impressed. He honked his horn, wound down his window and gave Frank the finger.

'What's wrong with the geezer? I stopped, didn't I?'

'Ignore him,' Helen said. 'He's just jealous of your cool shades.'

'You could be right. I do look particularly handsome in them.'

Helen gave a snort and looked over at the shop again. The window display contained just about anything electrical the modern home could want, including cookers, fridges, washing machines, vacuum cleaners, kettles, irons, televisions, record players, radios and hairdryers. 'That has to be it, doesn't it?'

'Yeah, though it doesn't mean that Alfie's still running it. He could have sold it on to someone else.'

'Wouldn't they have changed the name?'

Frank gave a shrug, perhaps not wanting to get his hopes up again. 'I just don't get it,' he said. 'Why wouldn't he have finished what we started? It's been years. All he had to do was organise a closing-down sale and then scarper with the cash.'

'Maybe he scarpered over here.'

'No,' Frank said. 'If this is his shop, then he's still trading under the same name. He couldn't be doing that if he'd pulled the rug out from under the creditors.'

'*Cherchez la femme*,' Helen said.

'Huh?'

'Didn't you hear what Barry said: *She never liked it much round here*. Maybe Alfie had another reason for staying put.'

Frank pulled a face, as if the idea of Alfie Blunt choosing a woman over a fast buck was about as likely as a rank outsider romping home at Kempton Park. 'You reckon?'

They drove around for a while until they found somewhere to park, and then walked back to the shop. It was closed, of course, but they peered in through the window just like they'd done at the toy store. Helen rapped on the glass, but nobody responded.

Frank put his hands in his pockets. 'Not to worry. I'll come back tomorrow.'

Helen reversed a few steps and peered up at the windows on the first floor. 'There's a flat upstairs. Maybe it belongs to the shop. The tenant might have a phone number for him.'

'Worth a go, I guess.'

They went to the door at the side of the shop and Helen rang the bell. There was too much traffic for them to hear the sound of footsteps from inside, but thirty seconds later the door was pulled open and they were face to face with a short, wiry man with a freckled complexion and a shock of red hair. As he looked at his visitors, his expression turned from mild curiosity to one of astonishment. 'Frank!'

Frank took off his sunglasses and put them in his pocket. 'Hello, Alfie. Long time no see.'

Alfie Blunt still had his mouth hanging open, gazing up at Frank as if he'd just seen a ghost.

Frank gave him a hard-edged kind of smile. 'So, Alfie. I think you and me need a little chat.'

'It's Martin,' he hissed, glancing anxiously back over his shoulder. 'What are you ... I didn't realise ... I didn't ...'

'Marty?' called a woman's voice from the top of the stairs. 'Who is it? Who's there?'

'It's nothing, love. It's just a rep.' He quickly pulled the open door ajar so she couldn't see his visitors.

'What? On a Sunday?'

'I won't be a minute,' Alfie yelled back, before returning his attention to Frank and Helen. 'You've got to go,' he urged, flapping his hands as if he was driving away a pair of unruly beggars. 'I'll meet you in the Black Lion. It's round the corner from the tube. Ten minutes, yeah?'

'I don't think so,' Frank said. 'I'm not moving one fucking inch from here until you give me what I'm owed.'

'You'll have your money, I swear. But you have to go now.'

'And let you do a bunk?' Frank said. 'I don't think so. You could be out of here and—'

'I won't, okay? I've got a wife and kid. Where am I going to go? I'll be there. I swear I will.'

Frank looked dubious, but Helen nudged his elbow. 'Come on, it'll be fine.'

Alfie gave her a nod and then dashed back inside, closing the door smartly behind him.

Frank glared hard at the door before turning to Helen. 'The minute we walk away, he could clear off. All he needs to do is pack a bag and—'

'And what? He's got a business here, and a pretty good one by the looks of it. He's hardly going to abandon that. Or his wife and kid. He'll turn up. You can be sure of it. He won't want you bashing on his door again in half an hour.'

Frank raked his fingers through his hair and glanced up at the windows to the flat. 'Let's hope you're right.'

'A fiver says I am.'

'Fighting talk. Okay, you're on.'

'Right, let's find that pub.'

The Black Lion was exactly where Alfie Blunt had said it would be, round the corner from Angel tube station. Frank ordered a pint and Helen had an orange juice. Although her headache had receded, she couldn't quite face the prospect of more alcohol.

They took their drinks to a quiet corner of the pub and settled in to wait. Frank lit a cigarette, then sat back and laughed. 'Jesus, did you see the look on him when he spotted me? I thought he was going to have a heart attack.'

'Well, maybe it's a shock, you turning up like this.'

'Maybe? What do you mean by *maybe*?'

'I don't know. He hasn't made much effort to prevent you finding him, has he? He's even kept the name of the shop.'

'There is such a thing as sheer stupidity.'

Helen took a sip of her orange juice. 'So what are you saying exactly? That you choose to do business with stupid people?'

Frank, who was in the process of lifting his pint to his lips, promptly put it down again. He gazed at Helen and grinned. 'There's no good answer to that one, is there?'

Fifteen minutes passed and there was still no sign of Alfie Blunt. Helen was starting to wonder if she'd just thrown a fiver down the drain when he suddenly came hurrying into the pub, out of breath, red-faced and apologetic.

'Sorry, sorry ... the missus ... Margaret ... I had to ... ' He plumped himself down on a chair and took a few seconds to catch his breath. 'Well, it's good to see you again, Frank. How have you been doing?'

'Just fine,' Frank said. 'But much better now that I've found you.'

'I weren't hiding anywhere, mate. I didn't want to get in touch, send a letter or nothing. I know those screws read everything. I reckoned you'd find me soon enough once you got out.'

'You reckoned right.'

'Look, would you two like some privacy?' Helen asked. 'I can go and sit somewhere else for a while if you want to talk.'

'No, stay where you are,' Frank said. 'You know all about it anyway. I'm sure Alfie here doesn't mind.'

'Martin,' Alfie insisted again, keeping his voice low. 'Call me Martin or Marty. Alfie's dead and gone. He don't exist no more.'

'Okay, *Marty*, why don't you get me up to speed with what's been going on?'

Alfie had a quick glance round, making sure that none of the other customers were earwigging, before shifting his chair even closer to the table and leaning forward. 'It's like this, right. We was all geared for the sale – you know, like we planned and all – and then you and Tommy ... well, I weren't sure what to do after that, and so I just kept trading, thinking you might get a message to me or something. But I didn't hear nothin' and the shop began to do well, and so ...'

'So you just carried on?'

'Seemed like the smartest thing to do. I wouldn't screw you over, Frank, not you and Tommy. We're a team, ain't we? I reckoned I'd just wait until you got out, and then ...'

'You saying it never crossed your mind?' Frank asked. 'You could have gone ahead and scarpered with the cash.'

Alfie grinned at him. 'I ain't saying it didn't cross me mind. I wouldn't be human, would I? Course I thought about it for a moment. But that's all it were, just a passing thought. There's three shops now, Frank. It's a good little business. Plenty of profit.'

'Good,' Frank said. 'You won't have any problems raising credit, then. We can get things back on track, go ahead with the closing-down sales and—'

Alfie gave a few rapid shakes of his head. 'I can't do that, Frank. How would I explain it to the missus? She ain't gonna want to leave here. She's got family down the road. And she don't know about ... she don't know nothin' about Alfie Blunt. So far as she's concerned, I'm straight as a die.'

Frank made a light growling noise in the back of his throat. 'Your family situation doesn't interest me, mate. All I want is my money.'

'Look, just hear me out, okay?' Alfie wriggled in his chair, as if he couldn't get comfortable. 'There's options, right? We could sell one of the shops, maybe even two of them, raise some cash that way. Or you and Tommy, you could just take a share of the monthly profits, use them to start something new. I've put some readies aside, Frank. I can get them for you soon.' He reached into his inside pocket and took out an envelope. After another quick glance around the pub, he slid it across the table. 'There's a ton here. It's all I can get for now, but I'll go to the bank first thing tomorrow.'

Frank slid the envelope into his own pocket and stared at Alfie. 'How much are we talking about?'

'A few grand, but like I said, we can think about flogging off the other shops. You can look through the books, decide what you want to do. But these shops, they're good little earners. Everyone wants electricals. Long-term, we could make a mint.'

Helen looked across at Frank, trying to figure out what he was thinking.

Frank sat back and folded his arms across his chest. 'And what if I don't like any of your options?'

'Aw, Frank, give us a break. I could have screwed you over but I didn't. I've spent the last seven years working like a dog. There's a decent business here, all above board and no hassle from the law.' Alfie looked at his watch. 'Why don't you go away and have a think about it, come over and see me tomorrow?'

Frank gave a nod. 'I'll do that.'

Alfie scraped back his chair. He looked at Helen and said, 'Nice to meet you, love.' Then he put out his hand to Frank. 'Tomorrow, then.'

They shook hands and Alfie hurried away.

Frank and Helen finished their drinks and left the pub. 'So what do you think?' she asked as they got back into the car.

Frank switched on the ignition and pulled away from the kerb before he answered. 'I'm not sure what to think right now. I'll take a look at the books tomorrow, but I guess I'll have to wait for Tommy to get out before making any final decisions.'

'It's funny really, isn't it?'

'Funny?'

Helen smiled at him. 'You've just done seven years inside and you've come out a legitimate businessman with a share in three profitable shops.'

The corners of his mouth curled up. 'Legitimate, huh? Well, that's certainly a first.'

'Oh, and you owe me a fiver.'

'And here was me hoping that might have slipped your mind.'

'I see,' she said. 'So you expect Alfie Blunt to pay his dues but you're not so keen when it comes to your own debts?'

Frank laughed, took the envelope out of his pocket and threw it on to her lap. 'Here, take it out of there.'

'It's okay,' she said, handing it back. 'You can buy a take-away tonight instead. I fancy a Chinese.'

'Chinese it is.'

They were approaching Camden when Helen noticed that Frank kept glancing in the rear-view mirror. 'What is it?' she asked, turning to look over her shoulder at the traffic behind.

'I'm not sure, but I think we may have a tail. There's a red Audi that's been with us since Islington. Could just be travelling in the same direction, but I reckon I saw it earlier, too.'

'Where is it?'

'About four cars back, behind the black cab.'

She kept on looking, but couldn't get a clear view. 'No, I can't see it properly.'

Frank flipped on his indicator. 'Right, let's take the scenic route and see if he stays with us.'

They cut up into Kentish Town, went as far as the tube station and then swung a right and started to wind around the back streets, away from the main stream of traffic. The red car followed them, keeping its distance.

'Not much doubt about that, then,' Frank said. 'I'm going to pull in by that bus stop down there. Try and get a look at his face as he goes past.'

As he flipped on the indicator, Helen leaned forward. The red Audi slowed a little as the driver realised what was happening and then accelerated again, speeding past them so quickly that she only caught a glimpse.

'Mid-thirties,' she said. 'Short brown hair, wearing sunglasses. Sorry, that's about it.'

Frank left the engine idling while he lit a cigarette. 'Now who the hell would want to be following us around?'

'It's creepy,' Helen said, shivering a little. 'Do you think it's to do with my visit to see Lazenby?'

'Hard to say. Have you talked to anyone else about Eddie Chapelle?'

Helen shook her head. 'Only you. You think this is down to him?'

'Could be.'

'But Tony Lazenby's the only person who knows about Chapelle's connection to my mum. At least, he's the only person who knows that I'm trying to find out about her murder.'

'Yeah,' Frank said, pulling hard on the cigarette. 'If there's one thing I've learnt in life, it's never to trust a copper.'

'But why would he . . . ? I don't get it. I don't understand.'

Frank gave her a sideways glance. 'Just be careful, okay? Don't get anywhere on your own for a while.'

'What? You think that—'

'I think someone's had their cage rattled and they're not too happy about it. We'll stick together, yeah? Wait and see what happens next.'

Helen pulled a face. 'Is that what you call a plan?'

'Best I can come up with at the moment. You got a better one?'

'No.'

'Right, let's go home.'

As Frank turned the car around, Helen kept her eyes peeled

for their shadow. A ripple of fear ran down her spine. She was afraid, she couldn't deny it, but a part of her felt strangely exhilarated too. Maybe, finally, the truth about her mother's murder was starting to unravel. It hadn't taken much – a single visit to Tony Lazenby – but already someone was worried enough to put a tail on them. She sent up one of her silent prayers to the heavens. *Please God, keep us safe.*

# 56

It took Frank less than thirty seconds to break the lock with a screwdriver and prise open the old tin. 'Here.' He pushed it across the kitchen table without flipping open the lid or looking inside. Then he stood up and went through to the living room.

Helen was grateful for his tact. She sat for a while staring at the initials in the right-hand corner. She wondered how old her mother had been when she'd painted them on. Her hand hovered over the tin while she braced herself for whatever might lie inside. Memories, she thought – and they weren't always easy to deal with. She took a deep breath and opened it.

The first thing she came across were photographs, pictures of herself as a baby, as a toddler, in school uniform, in a blue velvet dress for a kids' party. She took them out and laid them to one side. Next there was a picture of her mum and Tommy when they were children, standing outside the Fox with their mother. She had never seen a photograph of Irene before. Her maternal grandmother, a slim blonde woman, had a nice face and a pleasant smile but also an undisguised weariness about her eyes.

Helen stared at the picture for a while before placing it on top of the others. Next there was a birth certificate confirming that she was the child of Lynsey and Alan Beck. And also her parents' marriage certificate. She found a crayon drawing that she couldn't remember doing, a hotchpotch of coloured circles that might have been balloons. Her name was unevenly scrawled across the bottom of the page.

She continued to work her way through the box, uncovering receipts, buttons, a broken silver link bracelet, used cinema tickets, an unopened sachet of sugar, a couple of tiny pebbles and a pale pink feather. She had no idea what these mementoes had meant to her mother, but she knew that they'd meant something: tiny remembrances, perhaps, of happier times.

At the bottom of the box was a small heap of envelopes, six in all, addressed to Mrs L. Beck at the Samuel Street address in Kilburn. Helen's first thought was that they might be love letters. She smiled, wondering if there had been someone special in her mother's life after the disappointment of her marriage. As she took the letter out of the first envelope and unfolded the sheet of paper, her smile instantly froze. Instead of the sweet nothings she'd been expecting, there was a brutal threat written in bold black capitals. YOU ARE A BITCH AND YOU ARE GOING TO DIE.

Quickly, Helen snatched up the next one. KEEP LOOKING OVER YOUR SHOULDER, BITCH.

And then the next. YOU DESERVE EVERYTHING YOU GET.

The other three were in a similar vein, short and to the point, nasty and threatening. She could feel her heart thumping in her chest as she gazed down at them. Her hands were shaking, damp, and she had a sick feeling in her stomach. Grabbing the first envelope, she stared at the postmark. It had been sent from Holborn in 1970, a few weeks before her mum had been murdered.

'Frank,' she called.

He came into the kitchen with a bottle of beer in his hand. 'You okay?'

Helen gestured towards the notes lying on the table. 'I . . . I found these. They were in the bottom of the tin.'

He sat down beside her and picked up the notes, one after the other. 'Christ,' he murmured.

'You think Chapelle sent them? Or got someone else to send them? You know, to warn her off about giving evidence.'

'Could be,' he said. He examined the envelopes, peering at the postmarks. 'All sent from different parts of London.' He sipped on his beer and pondered for a few seconds. 'Not sure if it's really his style, though. If he wanted to give her a warning, he'd be more likely to send one of the boys round. Why bother with this kind of thing?'

'Perhaps he just wanted to scare her.'

'Easier ways of doing it.'

'But there has to be a connection.' Helen raised a hand to her mouth and chewed on her knuckles. 'God, why didn't she go to the cops? Why didn't she tell them?'

'I don't suppose they'd have done much. The best she could

have hoped for – and that's presuming she was prepared to give evidence – would be witness protection. And that would have meant changing her identity, moving away and probably never seeing you again.'

Helen played with the notes, picking them up and putting them down again. 'At least she'd have been alive.'

'But did she even know enough to be a threat to Chapelle?'

She shrugged. 'She was friends with Anna Farrell. Anna was Chapelle's girlfriend. Well, according to Lazenby. And girls talk to each other, don't they? Anna could have told her all kinds of stuff.'

'She could have,' Frank agreed. 'But it would only have been hearsay. Surely Anna was the one he'd be more concerned about.'

'So he killed them both. Just to be sure. She's probably dead too, don't you think?'

Frank sat back, frowning. 'I don't know.' He played with the beer bottle, revolving the neck between his finger and thumb. He was quiet for thirty seconds, and then he said, 'You sure you want to carry on with this?'

Helen gave a nod. 'Of course I do. I *have* to.' She swallowed hard. Suddenly, after the tail that had been put on them and the threatening notes to her mother, the danger had become more real. 'I'm not scared of him,' she lied, although the tremor in her voice betrayed her.

'Sometimes it's good to be scared,' Frank said. 'Especially of men like Eddie Chapelle.'

# 57

For the next few weeks, Helen divided her time between working in the sandwich bar and finding out everything she could about Eddie Chapelle and Anna Farrell. While she was buttering bread and doling out teas, Frank was either in Islington, sorting out business with Alfie Blunt, or up West making discreet enquiries about Chapelle.

On Wednesdays, which she had off, she and Frank took the Northern Line up to Hendon and went to the Colindale newspaper library, where they trawled through the mass of microfilm, searching for anything that could be relevant to her mother's murder. The library had been Moira's suggestion, and through its archives they had found out a little more about Anna Farrell: she had been a model and socialite in the early sixties, a rising star mixing with the glitterati, but by 1970 – when she was thirty-two – she had more or less slipped out of view. There had been a couple of convictions for soliciting in 1967 and 1968, but since then nothing else.

On Chapelle, however, they'd compiled a much larger dossier, none of which made for comfortable reading. Eddie Chapelle had been arrested on numerous occasions, usually in connection with pimping, pornography or gang warfare in the West End. In 1969, there had been a particularly nasty killing: a man called Raymond Deed had been brutally murdered, slashed and stabbed, his head almost severed from his neck. Chapelle had been in the frame, had even been charged, but the case had never gone to trial.

Lynsey Beck's death, on the other hand, had barely registered with the media. They had found only one mention, and that was in the local Kilburn paper, a narrow six-inch column reporting the fire in Samuel Street and the death of the tenant. There was no suggestion of foul play.

Helen squinted through the windscreen as they approached Camden, the early evening sun in her eyes. They had the windows open and a warm breeze caught her hair and sent it flying back over her shoulders. Since getting his money from Alfie, Frank had bought himself a second-hand motor, another MG, although this one was white. Now that he had some cash, he was free to move out and find his own flat, but as yet he hadn't suggested it.

He was only staying, she knew, because he didn't want to leave her alone while she was digging up the past and possibly stirring up trouble. She wondered if she was a burden, if she'd involved him in something he'd rather not be doing. The thought made her uneasy. She wanted him to stay, but she didn't want him to feel under any obligation.

It was strange how quickly she'd got used to having him around, to waking up each day and finding him in the kitchen, the smell of toast and coffee wafting on the air. Every morning the bed was reconstructed as a sofa and the blankets piled neatly in the corner of the room. He was easy to get along with and she looked forward to the time when work was finished and she could race upstairs to the flat to see him again.

This afternoon, they had spent several hours tracking down old friends and acquaintances of Anna Farrell, but had little to show for the effort. Of the few they had managed to find, nobody was prepared to say much, although whether this was down to fear or ignorance was impossible to fathom. On the whole, they had been met with only shrugs and frowns. No one knew where she was. No one had heard from her for years. No one seemed to care.

'Are we wasting our time?' sighed Helen as Frank cruised into the parking space outside the sandwich shop.

He turned off the ignition and glanced at her. 'Not giving up already, are you?'

'Did I say anything about giving up? I just meant . . . I don't know . . . Maybe we're not looking in the right places.'

Frank's mouth curled a little at the corners. 'Ah, the *right* places. You should have said.'

'Now you're laughing at me.'

'As if.' He made an effort to straighten his face. 'But seriously, you have to be patient with these things. If we keep going, something useful will turn up eventually.'

Eventually felt like a long way off for Helen. 'I hope so.'

They got out of the car and went on up to the flat. They had barely been inside a minute when the doorbell rang.

'You expecting anyone?' asked Frank. He went over to the window to take a look outside.

'Oh, it's probably Moira. She said she might drop by this evening.'

'Maybe you should—'

But Helen didn't catch the end of what he was suggesting. She was already on her way downstairs. As soon as she opened the door, she regretted it. Standing on the pavement were three men, two of them as tall as Frank, the other – the one in the middle – with a face that she instantly recognised from the photographs she'd seen in the papers. Her heart leapt into her mouth as she found herself staring into the cold, steely eyes of Eddie Chapelle.

'Hello, Helen,' he said.

She went to try and slam the door, but was way too slow. One of the goons stepped forward, inserting his heavy boot into the gap and shoving the door back, forcing her to retreat. The other two followed in his wake until all four of them were huddled together in the cramped hallway.

Eddie Chapelle gave a weary shake of his head. 'That's not much of a welcome, Helen. I'm disappointed. I thought you'd be pleased to see me.'

She could feel her heart thrashing, her mouth turning dry with fear. She knew what this man was capable of; she'd read and heard enough to comprehend the kind of danger she was in. 'W-what do you want?' she eventually managed to stammer out.

He fixed her with that intimidating stare again. 'Isn't that the question I should be asking?'

Frank suddenly appeared at the top of the staircase. 'What the—'

'Don't even think about it,' Chapelle said, looking up at him. 'We're just here for a chat. There's no need for any nastiness.'

The very next second, Helen felt the cold pressure of steel against the nape of her neck. One of the goons had a gun to her head. She drew in her breath, her gasp clearly audible.

Frank gave a nod and raised his hands. 'Okay, okay. I get it.'

'Stay where you are,' the other thug said. 'Don't move a fuckin' muscle.' He also had a gun, a black revolver that he kept aimed at Frank as he jogged up the stairs. Quickly, he ushered Frank around the corner and out of sight.

'And now you,' the first goon said to Helen. 'Up the stairs and take it slow, huh? No sudden movements.'

Helen did as she was told, her legs shaky. It was only a few minutes since she'd been bemoaning their lack of progress – but this wasn't the kind of progress she'd been hoping for. When they got to the living room, Frank was already in the armchair, with the thug standing guard behind him.

'There's no need for all this,' Frank said. 'What's with the shooters?'

Chapelle threw him a sneering glance but otherwise ignored him, turning his attention back to Helen. 'Sit down, sit down,' he said, waving towards the sofa.

Helen lowered herself into the corner, keeping her eyes on him. Eddie Chapelle was a dapper man in his mid-fifties with grey hair and a thin, sharp face. Although he was of medium height and build, the size of his two companions made him seem almost petite in comparison. 'What do you want?' she asked again, trying to keep the panic she was feeling out of her voice. 'What are you doing here?'

Chapelle remained on his feet, watching her carefully. 'A little bird tells me you've been asking questions behind my back. I don't like that, Helen. I prefer to conduct my business face to face. More honest that way, don't you think?'

Helen looked up at him. Despite her fear, anger was blossoming inside her. Was this the man who had killed her mother? It was more than likely. And if he was going to kill her too, she felt determined to find out the truth before he did. 'You don't think I have a right to know what happened to my mum?'

'Every right,' he said slyly. 'But what makes you think I can help?'

'Because you knew her. Lynsey Beck. She used to work for you.'

Chapelle frowned and pursed his lips. 'A lot of girls work for me. Many girls. Why should I remember her?'

'Nineteen seventy,' said Helen. 'She was friends with Anna Farrell.'

'Ah, Anna,' he said. 'Now I do remember Anna. A very attractive woman. We were also ... *friends* for a while. But your mother, no, I don't think I recall her.'

Helen took a deep breath. 'When you were in jail, she received threats, notes telling her to keep her mouth shut. Are you saying you didn't send them?'

'Threats?' he repeated, his eyebrows lifting. 'And you think ... ? But how would that be possible if, like you say, I was in jail?'

Helen couldn't tell if he was being genuine or not. He was the kind of man, she imagined, who lied with such regularity that it was virtually second nature to him. She answered his question with one of her own. 'If you've got nothing to hide, why are you so bothered about what I might be doing?'

Chapelle pulled a face. 'A man has his ... reputation to consider. Mud sticks, my dear. You start accusing people of—'

'I'm not accusing you of anything. Somebody killed her,' Helen said. She could feel Frank's eyes on her – he was probably willing her to shut up – but she refused to meet his gaze. 'I'm just trying to find out who that was.'

'And looking in the wrong direction, I'm afraid.' Chapelle tilted his head and gave a sigh. 'I don't wish to be dragged into this business. Do you understand?' He leaned down suddenly, grabbed hold of her chin, yanked it towards him and pushed hard into her cheeks with his thumb and forefinger. 'Do you?'

'Keep your hands off her!' Frank said. He lurched forward, but the goon wasn't having any of it. In one swift, brutal motion, he smashed the butt of the gun against the side of Frank's head, sending him sprawling to the ground.

Helen let out a cry. She instinctively tried to move, to help, but Chapelle tightened his hold. He grasped her shoulder with his left hand, his fingers like an iron grip. 'Don't worry about your boyfriend,' he hissed. 'He's not dead ... yet.'

Frank, as if to verify the statement, gave a low groan from where he was laid out on the carpet.

Chapelle stared hard into her eyes. 'Look at me, not him. And listen to me good, because I don't like to repeat myself. You stay away from me and my business. I hear you're still poking around, and next time ... well, next time it won't be such a friendly visit. You got it?'

Helen gave a nod.

'You got it?' he asked again.

'Yes,' she croaked.

'Good.' He let go of her, turned to his goons and gave a fast flicking gesture with his hand. The two thugs, like well-trained Rottweilers, immediately walked over to the door. Chapelle gave Helen a long final stare. 'Let's hope we don't meet again.'

As soon as he had gone, she jumped off the sofa and crouched down beside Frank. 'Are you okay? Are you all right?'

Slowly, he pulled himself up into a sitting position and leant his forehead briefly against his knees. Then he touched the side of his head and winced. There was blood in his hair. 'Jesus, what did he hit me with? A bleeding brick?'

'Don't move. Let me get something.' Helen rushed into the kitchen and ran a clean cloth under the cold tap, then wrung it out and took it back into the living room. She kneeled down again and dabbed tentatively at the wound, trying to stem the flow of blood. 'Sorry,' she said. 'I'm so sorry. This is all my fault.'

Frank looked at her. 'Why? Did you hit me?'

'No,' she said. 'But—'

'Then it's not your fault.'

'You know what I mean. If I hadn't started . . . if I hadn't . . . I never meant for you to get hurt.'

'Here, let me do that,' he said, reaching up to take the cloth from her.

Helen felt the breath catch in the back of her throat as his hand collided with hers and their fingers became briefly intertwined. Their eyes met, and for a moment their faces were so close that their lips could have touched with only the barest of movements. Flustered at the thought of it, she quickly turned her head to one side and pulled her hand away. 'We should go to the hospital. You may need stitches.'

Frank frowned, as if trying to fathom out what had just happened. Or maybe it was the pain he was frowning at. 'What I really need,' he said, as he pressed the cloth firmly against the cut, 'is a stiff Scotch.'

Helen, glad of an excuse to leave the room, jumped to her feet and went back into the kitchen.

'You may as well bring the bottle,' he called out. 'I get the feeling I'm going to need it.'

She returned with the bottle of whisky and two glasses and sat down on the floor near but not too close to him. She poured out a large measure and passed it over. 'How are you? That's a nasty cut. It's still bleeding. Are you sure you don't want to go to hospital?'

Frank knocked the drink back in one, winced and then sighed. 'Ah, that's better. No, honestly. I'm going to have a headache, but there's no lasting damage.'

Helen poured him another whisky and then picked up her own glass. She took two large gulps, feeling the burn as it slid down her throat. 'Do you know, when he was here . . . I really thought . . .'

'I know,' he said. 'The idea crossed my mind too. It's not every day you get a visit from Mr Chapelle and live to tell the tale.' He looked at her over the top of his glass. 'And it's not everyone who'd have the guts to do what you did. I was impressed, Mouse.'

Helen flushed at the compliment, even though she felt she didn't deserve it. 'What's there to be impressed by? I was terrified.'

'But you still went ahead and asked the questions. It was a brave thing to do.'

She bowed her head before raising her face to look at him again. The shock of it all was only just beginning to sink in. 'Brave or stupid?' Briefly she pushed her fist against her mouth, thinking of how much danger she had put him in. 'You were the one who got hurt.'

'I'll live.'

'No thanks to me.'

Frank shifted back and leaned against the armchair. He laid the bloodied cloth on the coffee table and lit a cigarette. 'I knew what I was getting into. I don't blame you, so don't start blaming yourself.'

Helen understood what he was saying, but it was hard for her to see it that way. She felt responsible for what had happened. She was responsible. Quietly she said, 'He did kill her, though, didn't he? He did kill my mum.'

Frank hesitated before replying. 'Well, I'd swear that he had Anna Farrell killed. That's what he's worried about. But I'm not so sure about your mother. I don't think he was faking when he claimed that he didn't remember her. I mean, why would he bother to pretend?' He pulled on the cigarette while he pondered some more. 'My gut instinct says he came here only because of his connection to Anna's death. I could be wrong, but that's the way I see it.'

It wasn't the answer that Helen had wanted. She thought back over the encounter with Chapelle. It was true that he

471

hadn't shown even a flicker of recognition at the name of Lynsey Beck, but that could have been a deliberate ploy to put her off the scent. It didn't mean anything. Not really. Men like him wore deceit like suits of armour. 'He's hardly going to admit it, though, is he?'

'I suppose not.'

'But you think I'm wrong?'

Frank's shoulders lifted a fraction before dropping again. 'All I'm saying is that his main interest, his main worry, seemed to be Anna Farrell.'

Helen, who needed things clear-cut – she wanted justice for her mother – was reluctant to give up her main suspect. Chapelle had the motive and the means. He could easily have paid one of his goons to commit murder and then torch the flat afterwards. 'But why would Lazenby have put his name forward if he didn't have anything to do with it?'

Frank gave a snort. 'Why do bent coppers do anything? Because there's some advantage in it. Because he wants to cause Chapelle grief. Perhaps he's got a grudge. I don't know. All I do know is that you can't trust Lazenby any more than you can trust Chapelle.'

'But if Chapelle didn't kill her, who did?'

Frank swirled the whisky around in his glass. 'Whoever sent the notes? Perhaps we're confusing two completely separate issues. Maybe there was someone else who wanted her dead.'

'God,' said Helen, rubbing at her eyes with the heels of her hands. 'If that's the case, then we're back to square one. How do we even begin to find out who it was?'

Frank didn't seem to have an answer to that one.

'So what next?' she asked.

'That's up to you.'

Helen's gaze dropped from the wound on his temple to the bloodied cloth lying on the coffee table. She'd caused enough damage for now. It was time to pull back for a while. 'I think we should leave it until Tommy gets home. It's only a few days. Let's wait and see what he says.'

# 58

Terry Street, although inwardly raging, kept his expression composed as he gazed back at Lazenby. The man was a liability, a dangerous, interfering fool. You didn't fuck with the likes of Chapelle unless you wanted to end up in a wooden box. But Lazenby, of course, thought that he was bloody invincible, thought that he could get away with anything.

'Don't you see?' the copper said, almost knocking over the bottle as he refilled his glass. It was one o'clock in the morning and he was drunk on triumph and whisky. 'He'll have to try and get rid of her. She's digging too deep and she isn't going to stop. There's only one sure way to shut her up, and when he makes that choice—'

'You'll be there to put the cuffs on.'

'You've got it. He's already paid her a visit, thinking he can scare her off. All I have to do now is tip him the wink that it hasn't worked out, that she's still shooting her mouth off about how he murdered her mother, and he'll have to come up with a more permanent solution.'

Terry gave a nod, giving nothing away. He'd spent the last five years building a good working relationship with Eddie Chapelle – they owned three gambling establishments together, a few clubs and a string of strip joints – and now Lazenby was about to blow it all out of the water. For years, the rival firms in the West End had been at war with each other, fighting over territory, over ownership of pubs and clubs, until it had reached the point where they were inflicting more harm on each other than anything the filth could come up with. Barely a week went by without a firebombing or a stabbing. Someone had to find a way to keep the peace, and he was the one who'd come up with the perfect compromise.

He lit a fag, still pleased with his idea and with the way it had panned out. The plan had been a simple one. Instead of single ownership, all of the clubs were to be split between the major firms, so they had half, third or quarter shares in each establishment. With everyone getting a fair share of the profits, there was no reason to attack each other. Of course there were still disagreements, petty squabbles and personal vendettas, but on the whole, life was a lot calmer. Everyone had benefited from the deal, and for the moment, a truce was holding.

That truce, however, could easily be shattered. Eddie Chapelle was one of the major players, an influential one, and if he was taken out of the picture, the whole balance would shift. There'd be a renewed tussle for power and everything would fall apart. Before long they'd be back to their old ways, tearing each other to pieces instead of concentrating on the cash that could be made.

'So what do you think?' Lazenby said smugly. 'Once he's history, we can clean up.'

Terry took a long drag on his cigarette. He was all for cleaning up, but he knew that this wasn't the right time or the right method. Lazenby was incapable of seeing the bigger picture. If he succeeded in banging up Chapelle, they would lose more than they'd gain. It would be a bloody disaster. This wasn't a thought, however, that he chose to share. Instead, he nodded his head, feigning an enthusiasm that he didn't feel. 'Sounds good to me.'

'Lucky you've got me around, huh?' Lazenby said. 'As soon as he tries to top Helen Beck, as soon as he's arrested, we can move in and grab his share.'

'Easy,' Terry said. 'A piece of cake.' He remembered the girl who'd collected the glasses in the Fox. Tommy Quinn's niece. But she'd been called something else then. Mouse, that was it. She'd been a quiet, serious little thing, not like Tommy's two flirty daughters. It was strange to think of her stirring up trouble for someone like Chapelle. 'What if you don't get there in time? What if he does top her?'

Lazenby gave a careless, drunken shrug, as if it didn't really matter. 'Then we get him for murder rather than attempted murder. Either way, we get the result we want.'

Terry, who had long ago learnt that there was no room for a conscience in the world he had chosen to inhabit, still felt a spurt of revulsion at the copper's callous response. However, his decision as to what to do next would be driven only by practical considerations. He glanced at his watch and rose to his feet. 'Sorry, but I have to be somewhere. Are we done?'

Lazenby looked up at him and smirked. 'What's the hurry? You got a bird keeping the bed warm for you?'

'Yeah, and she's the impatient type.'

'Best not keep her waiting, then.'

'Call me,' Terry said, before turning away and walking out of the club. Outside, he breathed in the cool night air as he cut down Lancaster Place on to the Embankment. To his right, the dark expanse of the Thames glittered with reflected light and he stopped for a while to watch the river flow by.

Terry didn't often think about the past – what was done was done – but Lazenby's talk of Helen Beck had revived old memories. He found himself thinking of Joe Quinn, about a conversation they'd once had in Connolly's. He could still see the older man's fingers deftly rolling up a fag, could still hear the warning tone in his voice. It wasn't so long ago, and yet it felt like a lifetime. Then there had been the firebombing of the Fox, the attack on Stott's pub, the elimination of the Gissings. And then . . .

Terry shook his head, not wanting to remember *that* particular night. But now he'd started, he couldn't find a way to stop. Joe was sitting beside him, frowning, scowling, whingeing, because he was travelling in a rusty old van. The stink of him. Yes, he'd never forget that smell: whisky and tobacco overlaid with a pungent unpleasant aftershave. *Where d'you get this fuckin' death trap?*

The Thames ran strong and steady. Terry gazed at the water, but all he saw was Joe getting out of the van and hurrying over to the silver Jag. That moment when time had stood still. He could have changed his mind, but he hadn't. Instead he had reached down under the seat and grabbed hold of the baseball bat. He instinctively flexed his fingers, feeling again the warm, sticky polythene wrapped around the handle. Out of the van, a few steps and . . .

It was the sound that haunted him most, the crunch of wood against bone. He screwed up his eyes, listening to the water lapping beneath him, but all he heard was that sound again. It resounded in his head, a constant reminder of what he'd done. Yet he knew that if it hadn't been him, it would have been someone else. Joe Quinn's days had been numbered, no matter how you looked at it.

Everything Terry had now – the power, the influence, the money – was down to that one defining action. And he wasn't going to let a fucker like Lazenby screw it all up. No, it was time to let go of this particular association, to sever the ties in a permanent fashion. The copper had served his purpose; he was no longer needed.

Terry carried on walking until he came to a phone box. He looked around, making sure he had no unwanted company, before opening the door and slipping inside. He dug into his pocket for some loose change, picked up the receiver, dialled the number and waited. The call was answered after a couple of rings.

'Yeah?'

'It's Terry Street. Put Eddie on the blower. I need to talk to him.'

# 59

It had been late afternoon by the time Moira got back from Durham with Tommy. Helen and Frank had gone round to the house for what proved to be an emotional reunion. There had been hugs and kisses and a few tears. The men had gone through that ritual back-slapping routine before sliding easily back into the old banter as if it had only been seven weeks rather than seven years since they'd last seen each other.

The champagne had flowed along with the beer and the whisky, and by the time they sat down to eat they were all a little drunk. Helen watched her uncle from across the table. If prison had left a mark, it wasn't immediately obvious. To her, he seemed like the same old Tommy, solid and reassuring, with that familiar wide smile on his face.

There was plenty of conversation and lots of laughter as they tucked into roast beef and all the trimmings. There was wine too, bottles of red and white. The atmosphere was upbeat and cheerful until the subject of Yvonne came up. Then Tommy's face clouded over, his eyes flashing with anger. He looked across at Helen.

'I'm sorry, Mouse. That woman's a bitch. She had no right to throw you out like that.'

Helen shook her head. 'It doesn't matter. It's all in the past now.' Earlier, she had glossed over her time with Lily, making light of it, pretending that nothing important had occurred until Moira had come back on the scene. So far as she knew, he was not aware of the attack, the rape, that had taken place in Soho, and that was how she wanted to keep it. Moira had promised to keep quiet, and it seemed that she had kept her word.

'You've hardly told me anything about that time. How did you cope, love? Jesus, you were only fifteen.'

'I was okay. I got jobs. I managed.'

'Yeah, but what sort of jobs?'

Helen, finding herself put on the spot, shifted uncomfortably in her seat. She didn't like lying to Tommy, but it was preferable to telling him the truth. 'Oh, this and that. In pubs and cafés mainly. I didn't stay anywhere for long. I got by. I was fine.'

Tommy studied her closely. He had an inkling, perhaps, that something was being kept from him. He leaned forward as if about to interrogate her more closely, but then Frank came to the rescue with a quick change of subject.

'So have you thought about trying to buy back the Fox?'

Tommy leaned back again. 'Fat chance of that! Yvonne wiped me out. There's the cash from Alfie, but I'll still be well short.'

'I dunno. Once the shops are sold, you'll have a fair few quid. And you could always get a partner.'

Tommy gave a shrug. 'Even if I could find someone, Terry wouldn't sell.'

'He might. From what I've heard, he spends most of his time up West these days. And anyway, he owes you. I bet he got that pub for a song when Yvonne flogged it to him. No harm in asking, is there?'

Helen, who was sitting beside Frank, turned her head to look at him. 'Why don't you invest? The two of you could buy back the Fox together.'

'Who, me?' Frank laughed. 'I don't know anything about running a pub.'

'You don't need to.' The thought of Tommy getting back what was rightfully his and Frank having a reason to stick around suddenly seemed like an ideal outcome. Despite all the bad things that had happened at the Fox, she was still attached to the place, still felt as if a part of her belonged there. 'Tommy will do all the hard work while you sit back and rake in the profits.'

'Oh yeah?' said Tommy, grinning. 'Not sure I like the sound of that.'

Frank laughed again, but didn't commit himself one way or the other. Helen decided not to press him. Perhaps he had other plans. Perhaps in a week or two he'd pack up his belongings and leave her flat for ever. What reason did he have to hang around? The prospect of him going away put a dampener on her earlier elation. Even if Tommy did get the Fox back, it wouldn't be the same without Frank.

The conversation shifted again. Tommy nodded towards

the injury on the side of Frank's head. 'So are you going to tell me what happened?'

'It was just a scrap. You know how it is.'

'Don't give me that,' Tommy said. 'You don't get into scraps. Or hardly ever. And when you do, you sure as hell don't come out looking like that.'

Frank lifted a hand to briefly touch the wound. The cut was starting to heal, but the bruising had spread down the side of his face in wide arcs of yellow and purple. 'It's nothing.'

'So what's the big deal?' Tommy asked. 'Why are you holding out on me? Come on, I want to know.'

'It was my fault,' Helen piped up. She hadn't wanted to tell him what they'd been doing – not tonight, at least – but she didn't want Frank to have to lie for her either.

Tommy grinned again. 'You, huh? What you been doing, Mouse – practising your left hook?'

There was a short, awkward silence. Helen didn't know where to begin. Tommy glanced around the table, sensing the sudden change of atmosphere. 'Anyone gonna tell me what's going on?'

Helen cleared her throat. She wasn't prepared for this, and had a jumble of thoughts running round in her mind. Quickly, she tried to put them into some kind of order. 'I've been ... we've been trying to find out what happened to Mum.'

Tommy's smile began to fade. 'You know what happened.'

'No, I mean what *really* happened. I want to know who killed her.'

Tommy stared at her, and then at Frank. His face had grown pale. 'Who the fuck did that to you?'

'One of Eddie Chapelle's goons.'

Tommy shook his head. 'Jesus Christ! What were you thinking? You've been messing with Eddie Chapelle?'

'More the other way round,' Frank said drily, touching the bruises on his face again.

'Are you mad? Are you both mad?' Frank turned to Moira. 'Why didn't you tell me about this?'

'She didn't know,' Helen said. 'Not all of it, anyway. She only ... she only knew that I'd been round to where Mum used to live in Kilburn. It's not her fault. I asked her not to say anything until you got home.'

Tommy pushed aside his plate, knocked back the wine he'd been drinking and reached for the bottle to pour another glass. He took a few fast swallows and then lit a cigarette. 'Tell me,' he said. 'Tell me everything.'

Helen took a deep breath before embarking on a stumbling account of the last few weeks.

She told him about Kilburn, about going to the Fox, and about how she eventually found Frank. She told him about her meeting with DCI Tony Lazenby, the records he had let her see and the rumours about Anna Farrell that he'd shared with her.

'Lazenby?' Tommy growled. 'You really thought that lying scumbag was going to help you? He couldn't stand Lynsey's guts. The bastard would have stabbed her in the back soon as look as her.'

'I didn't have a choice,' Helen said. 'I know what he is ... who he is ... but there was a chance he might give me something useful. And he did. He gave me Chapelle.'

Here, Tommy interrupted her again, putting his elbows on

the table and glaring at Frank. 'And you thought this was a good idea? Fucking with the likes of Eddie Chapelle?'

Frank scowled back at him. 'A good idea? No, not in the slightest. But all she was trying to do was to find out who killed her mother, *your* sister. Would you rather I'd left her to do it on her own?'

Tommy pulled hard on the cigarette, releasing the smoke in a long, angry stream. 'It's got nothing to do with you.'

'Christ, Tommy, don't you want to know the truth?'

'It was an accident,' Tommy said. 'She fell, she banged her head, a candle got knocked over and it set fire to the flat. *That's* the goddamn truth.'

There was a hush around the table. Moira laid her hand gently on Tommy's wrist. 'You can't be sure.'

Tommy snatched his arm away. 'Why can't you all just accept that she's dead and gone and that's the end of it?'

'It's not the end of it,' Helen said. 'She was threatened before she died.'

'What?'

'There were notes,' Helen explained. 'We went to the lock-up and found the box; you know, the cardboard box with some of her things in it. You must have got them from the flat. Her red coat was there. Do you remember?' She paused, but Tommy said nothing. 'There was a metal tin and inside it were threats, notes that had been sent to her. Someone wanted to kill her.'

Tommy got up from the table and began to pace around the living room. He took two more drags on the cigarette before stubbing it out in the ashtray. 'This has got to stop,' he said. 'Promise me you'll stop.'

Helen gave a small shake of her head. 'I can't.'

He walked over to the window and then turned back, his hands clenching and unclenching. 'You have to. For God's sake, Mouse, there's only one way this is going to end. Is that what you want? I won't let you carry on. I won't. It's bloody madness.'

What had started as a celebration had suddenly turned sour. Moira tried to intervene, to bring some peace to the proceedings. 'Perhaps it would be better if we all calmed down and talked about this in the morning.'

'I am calm,' Helen said, rising to her feet. Now that it was out in the open, she wanted to finish what she'd started. 'I understand how you feel, Tommy, but this is something that I have to do. I can't just let it rest. If Chapelle did murder her, then—'

'You don't know what you're messing with!' Tommy yelled at her. His face had changed colour again, a great red stain covering his cheeks. 'You're crazy! You know that? You're completely fuckin' crazy.'

Shocked, Helen's mouth fell open. He'd never shouted at her before, never looked so angry. This wasn't the Tommy Quinn she knew. Afraid of what she'd unleashed, she shrank back. For the first time she recognised his father in him, was reminded of Joe Quinn's quick temper and brutal ways.

'Don't you care who else you're putting in danger?' he ranted. 'It's not just about you. It's not just about fuckin' you!'

'Hey, cool it,' Frank said warningly, quickly scraping back his chair and moving between the two of them. 'What the hell's the matter with you?'

'What the hell's the matter with *you*?' Tommy yelled back.

485

'Keep out of it! I've told you – this is none of your fuckin' business!'

For a second, as the two of them locked eyes, Helen thought they were going to come to blows, but then Tommy whirled around and went back to the window. 'It's got to stop. All of this. Right now.'

Helen shook her head again. 'It's not as simple as that. It's my choice,' she said. 'I'm sorry, but—'

'Your choice? Your bloody choice?' Tommy slammed the palm of his hand against the window pane, making the glass shudder. 'For fuck's sake, do you *want* to get her killed?'

There was a sudden eerie silence in the room, like the aftermath of a bomb going off. Tommy's fist rose quickly to his mouth, but it was too late to retract the words. He twisted around, his gaze jumping frantically from Moira to Frank to Helen.

'What?' Helen murmured.

'I meant . . . I meant *yourself*. Do you want to get yourself killed?'

'No you didn't,' Frank said. 'What the hell's going on?'

Helen wrapped her arms around her chest, her heart beating hard. She felt her legs start to shake, to give way, and slumped back down into the chair. All the time she kept her eyes fixed firmly on Tommy. She could see that he was sweating, could see the veins on his neck standing out. She opened her mouth to speak, but nothing came out.

Frank stared at him too, his expression one of disbelief. 'Jesus Christ, she's still alive, isn't she?'

'No,' snapped Tommy. He raked his fingers through his hair and looked away. 'How could she be?'

'Don't give me that shit,' Frank said. 'Just tell us the bloody truth.'

Moira stood up and walked around the table. Her eyes were wide, her voice a mixture of sharpness and bewilderment. 'Tommy? What's going on? Is it true? Is Lynsey . . . ?'

For a second, Tommy looked as though he was going to deny it again, but then a wave of weariness seemed to flood over his body. A thin groan slipped from between his lips. He went over to the sofa, sat down and buried his face in his hands.

For a while, no one else moved or said anything. They were like players on stage, waiting for the next line. All eyes on Tommy. But he wasn't ready yet. Helen could almost see his inner struggle, the desire to speak battling with a long-held silence. She could barely describe what she was feeling herself. There was pain and anger all wrapped up in a kind of numb, desperate hope.

Moira sat down beside Tommy and put her hand on his arm again. This time he didn't pull away. 'Just tell us the truth, Tommy. For Helen's sake.'

Tommy looked up at her. His voice was quiet, strained. 'I'm so sorry, Mouse. I didn't . . . I couldn't . . . '

Helen felt a suffocating sensation in the depths of her chest. She couldn't breathe properly. She snatched at the glass of wine beside her and took two large gulps. 'Is she . . . is she still alive?' Her voice rose an octave, becoming almost shrill. 'Tell me, Tommy. I have to know. Tell me!'

Tommy held her gaze for only the briefest of moments before bowing his head again. 'I think so. Yes.'

Helen's whole body jerked, her fingers tightening so hard

around the glass that it instantly shattered. Blood and wine flowed down her hand, but she wasn't aware of it. She was aware of nothing but that one stark word. Yes. Her stomach turned over, bile rising in her throat. She couldn't think straight. A kind of ecstasy shot through her heart, piercing it with a desperate yearning. 'You *think* so?' she whispered. 'What the hell does that mean?'

'I can't be sure.'

Helen felt hot and cold at the same time. A weird tingling sensation travelled down her spine. A few minutes ago, her mother had been dead, mourned over, her ashes scattered, but now, like Lazarus, she had risen from the grave. She shook her head, trying to make sense of it all. She would have jumped up from the chair if her legs hadn't felt so weak. Instead she leaned forward, her whole body trembling. 'Tell me, Tommy. Tell me everything.'

# 60

Tommy had always wondered if and when this day would come. He'd tried to push the truth to the back of his mind, to deny its existence, although it had still come back to haunt him in the dark, silent hours of the middle of the night. He had lived with the secret for too long. Like a cancer, it had grown inside, becoming harder to bear as the years passed by. In jail, the burden of it had pressed down on his conscience: everything he'd done and said, all the lies, the deceit, the pain and the anguish.

He could see Mouse waiting, breathing in short, shallow gasps. She would never forgive him. How could she? He watched as Frank poured her a glass of brandy and placed it on the table. Moira fetched cotton wool and antiseptic for the cut on her hand. He frowned, remembering the blood on a different carpet, the horror of what he had done.

He stood up again and returned to the window, keeping his back to Mouse. He couldn't bear to look at her, to see the expression in her eyes. There was still a grey light outside, although the day was almost done. He stood and stared down at the traffic, but all he saw was a young woman in a red coat. Now that the time had come, he felt fear and awe and an odd sense of relief.

'Lynsey called me on the night it happened. It was late, after the pub had closed, and she was crying. I couldn't make sense of it at first, what she was saying, what she was telling me. I hadn't heard from her in years, and . . . Well, she was in trouble, big trouble. I told her to stay where she was and I'd come over. I gave Yvonne some bullshit story, took the takings from the till, got in the motor and drove to Kilburn.'

As Tommy spoke, he was transported back to that night all those years ago. He was driving again through the dark, a light spring rain spattering against the windscreen. He was trying not to speed in case he got stopped by the law. All the traffic lights seemed to be on red. While he waited, he drummed his fingers impatiently against the steering wheel, feeling the dread spreading through his guts.

When he finally arrived at the flat, Lynsey opened the door straight away. She was still crying, her face red and swollen, mascara smeared under her wide, frightened eyes. It had been over a decade since he'd last seen her. She dragged him quickly into the hallway and up the stairs. *You have to help me, Tommy. Please. I don't know what to do.*

There was a lamp on in the living room, and the curtains were closed. He had a few fleeting impressions – cream walls, a plush red sofa, a glass-topped coffee table – before his gaze came to rest on the body of the woman. She was lying face down on the floor, her long fair hair matted with blood. He bent down, touching the still warm skin of her neck, making sure there was no pulse. He turned to look up at his sister. 'Who is she? What happened?'

Lynsey had her hand over her mouth, the tears flooding down her cheeks. 'I don't know what happened. I swear I don't. I came home and she was there. It wasn't me. I didn't do it.'

Tommy believed her. In her present state, he didn't think she was capable of lying to him. He felt some relief that she wasn't responsible, rapidly followed by a wave of confusion. 'Why ain't you called the cops? If it's nothing to do with you, then—'

'I can't,' she wailed. 'Oh God, he's going to kill me. He's going to kill me too.'

'Keep it down,' he said, quickly standing up again. 'You want to wake up the whole bloody house?'

Lynsey buried her head in his shoulder, clinging on to him. 'What am I going to do? I can't call the cops, I can't. He'll find out, and then . . . ' She dissolved into sobs, the rest of her fears muffled and incoherent.

Tommy could feel the sharp tips of her fingernails digging into the soft flesh of his back. Gently he pushed her away from him. 'Do you have anything to drink? Brandy? Do you have brandy?'

For a second, she seemed unable to comprehend what he was saying, but then abruptly she nodded, pointing towards a cabinet in the corner.

Tommy walked across the room, opened the cabinet and grabbed a bottle of Courvoisier from inside. Then he took hold of Lynsey's wrist and pulled her into the kitchen, closing the door behind them. 'Sit down,' he said. He found a couple of glasses and poured two stiff shots. 'Drink it,' he ordered. He knocked his back in one and poured another. Only then, with the brandy coursing through his veins, did he feel able to properly listen to what she had to say.

The story, as she told it, was garbled and disjointed. Tommy had to keep stopping her to get things straight. Gradually the facts began to slot together and the picture became clearer. The dead woman's name was Anna Farrell. She was a mate of Lynsey's who sometimes used the flat to entertain her friends. Tommy knew what she meant by 'friends' – clients, punters, men who preferred their sexual encounters to be in comfortable surroundings rather than on street corners. Lynsey hadn't been expecting Anna that night – she usually phoned if she was coming round – but she'd been out herself and might have missed the call. Anna had a key and would have let herself in.

Lynsey lit a cigarette. She smoked rapidly, with a shaking hand, her eyes continuously darting towards the door and the horrors that lay beyond. She told him about Eddie Chapelle, Anna's boyfriend, and how Anna had introduced them and she'd started working for him too. 'Weekend parties. You know the sort of thing: rich guys, country houses out in Kent and Surrey.'

'And now he's in jail.'

'It's me he wants dead,' she whispered. 'Not Anna.'

Tommy frowned at her. 'And how do you figure that one out? If she's his girlfriend, she's the one who's got all the dirt.'

'No, he trusts her. He knows she'd never grass on him.' Lynsey shuddered. 'I'm telling you, he sent someone . . . sent someone to kill me, and they got it wrong. They found Anna here, thought she was me and—'

'You can't be sure of that,' Tommy said.

'I am. Just before he was arrested, it all kicked off. The last party I went to, Eddie only gave me half of what he'd promised, and I was shooting my mouth off to him – you know what I'm like – saying I'd make him pay, let everyone know what he was up to. I didn't mean it. But then after he was arrested, I started getting threats, notes sent through the post. And then last week there was a car. It was following me down the street. I swear, Tommy, it followed me all the way from Kilburn station.' She jumped up. 'I've got to get away. I've got to get away from here.'

'And go where?' Tommy asked.

'Anywhere, for fuck's sake! As soon as he finds out it wasn't me . . .'

'He'll come after you – or get someone else to. Are you going to keep running for the rest of your life? And what about your kid? Are you just going to abandon her?'

Lynsey's hands flew up to her face again, her features twisting with fear. 'Oh God, what if he goes after Helen? I can't let him . . . Christ, Tommy, what am I going to do?' She slumped back down into the chair, defeated and helpless.

Tommy's mind was racing, searching for a way out. If she reported all this to the cops, it would mean witness protection, relocation, a new identity. And that was only if they believed her story. What if they didn't? They might even charge her with murder. Plus, it wouldn't stop Chapelle from trying to get his revenge. From what he'd heard of the bastard, he was perfectly capable of going after the kid. He drank

493

some more brandy, knowing that the decisions he made in the next few minutes could mean the difference between life and death. 'Have you got a passport?'

Lynsey shook her head.

'Ireland, then. You could go to Dublin.'

She stared at him, the tears rolling down her cheeks. 'But he'll still be looking for me. And it won't stop him from hurting Helen. Maybe even worse. He's violent, vicious. You've no idea what he's capable of.'

'So take her with you.'

'And how am I supposed to do that? I can't just turn up at the house in the middle of the night. You really think that old cow would let me take her?'

'Tomorrow,' he suggested. 'We could go to Chingford, book into a B and B and pick her up from Farleigh Wood in the morning. You could pretend you were just taking her out for the day. The two of you could be on the ferry and on your way to Ireland before anyone even knows about . . .' His gaze slid towards the living room before returning to his sister again. 'It's the only way, love. Unless . . .'

'Unless?'

Tommy didn't want to say it, but there was another option. 'If Eddie thinks you're dead, then he won't be coming after you. Or Helen.'

Lynsey's eyes widened. 'What . . . how could . . . ?'

'Who's to say that isn't you, next door? If we arrange things right, we could make it look like you did die here tonight. Eddie won't be surprised if Anna goes missing. He'll just think she got spooked and did a runner.' Even as he was explaining, Tommy was aware of the awful repercussions of what he was suggesting. A part of him wanted to stop, to say it was a stupid, mad idea, but he couldn't see a better option.

'Me?' she said faintly.

'You know what that would mean?'

Lynsey stared back at him, her brown eyes full of fear and sorrow. 'I'll never see Helen again.'

Tommy felt an ache in his heart. To separate a mother and her daughter was a dreadful thing, but the alternative was terrible too. 'It needn't be for ever,' he said. 'Maybe later, in a year or two, we could ...' Unable to find the words, he glanced away. 'It's up to you. I'll go along with whatever you decide.'

'She'd think I was dead.'

'Yes.'

Lynsey's face crumpled. 'I couldn't do that to her.'

'So take her with you.' Tommy looked at his watch. It was twenty to one. 'But make your mind up, sis, and quick. If we're going to do this, we need to get a move on.'

She stubbed out her cigarette and sat for a while, her hands clasping and unclasping. 'If I take her, Joan will go to the cops and report it. And then Eddie will find out about it too. He'll know I'm still alive. He'll come after us both. He won't let it rest. I know he won't.' Her voice rose and broke. 'We'll always be waiting for ... Christ, I can't do that to her. If I leave her, then at least she'll be safe.'

'Yeah,' said Tommy. 'Eddie Chapelle will think you're dead.'

Lynsey gave a quick, frightened nod. 'I have to, don't I?'

'Go and pack a bag,' he said. 'Not too much, just the essentials. And make sure you leave some bathroom stuff,

your toothbrush, that kind of thing. It's got to look like . . . '
He cleared his throat before he continued. 'Did Anna have a
handbag with her?'

Lynsey nodded again.

'Take it with you. I'll get rid of it later.' He took the car
keys out of his pocket and pushed them across the table.
'After you've packed, go and wait in the motor. It's the white
Cortina parked down the street.' He paused and added, 'Oh,
and give me your wedding ring.'

'What?'

'Just do it, Lynsey. Don't fuckin' argue with me.' He
watched as she pulled off the gold band, held it for a moment
and then passed it over. He wondered why she still wore it –
it hadn't been a happy marriage – but now wasn't the time to
start asking those kinds of questions.

He walked back into the living room with her. She hurried
past the body, keeping her eyes averted. While she went to the
bedroom, he crouched down and looked around. There was
no sign of the weapon that had been used to kill Anna Farrell.
He stared at the bloodied hole in her skull, thinking that it
could have been Lynsey lying there.

He already knew what he was going to do – set fire to the
place and destroy as much evidence as he could. Gritting his
teeth, he took hold of Anna's shoulders and carefully turned
her over. His stomach lurched as he saw her face: empty and
dead. Her eyes, thankfully, were closed. A smear of bright red
lipstick had run from her mouth to her chin, giving her an
odd, clownish quality. He had a moment of doubt – what the
fuck was he doing? – but there was no going back now.

He tipped over the coffee table, making it look like she

496

could have fallen and caught her head against the sharp edge of the glass. If the cops thought it was an accident, they'd be less inclined to delve too deeply. But even if they suspected murder, they probably wouldn't put that much effort into an investigation. Lynsey Beck's arrest sheet would tell them all they needed to know about the kind of life she'd lived.

He heard a movement behind him and turned to see Lynsey standing by the door. She had an overnight bag hanging loosely by her side. 'Get out of here,' he said. 'Go and wait in the motor.'

She hesitated, her eyes glued to the body of Anna Farrell. 'What are you going to do?'

'The motor,' he repeated. 'Five minutes, yeah, and I'll be with you. Just go, okay?' He was struggling to keep it together, thinking that at any moment the bell might ring and the cops would be waiting downstairs. Logic told him that they couldn't know about the killing yet, but that didn't stop the dread. He could feel his heart hammering in his chest, the blood pumping manically.

Her voice was small and hoarse and scared. 'Thanks, Tommy.'

He gave a nod, waited until she'd started the descent of the stairs and then picked up Anna Farrell's left hand. He took off the two rings she was wearing and slipped them into his pocket. Her hand was still loose, still warm – she couldn't have been dead for that long – and he was able to slide on the wedding band. It was a bit loose, but that didn't matter. It would be a way of identifying the body later.

He jumped up and went back to the kitchen, where he quickly washed and dried the glasses and made sure they were free of prints. He placed one of them in the cupboard and held on to the other. He found a carrier bag and dropped the bottle of brandy into it. No point in wasting good booze, and Lynsey, he was sure, would need a drink later. Returning to the living room, he left the bag by the door to the hall.

With a tea towel wrapped around his hand, he took a bottle of vodka from the cabinet, and splashed half the contents over Anna and the surrounding area of carpet. He screwed the lid back on and left the bottle and the glass lying beside her. There were three candles on the window ledge, and he laid them on their sides by the body, making it look as though they had fallen from the coffee table. He scattered a few cushions, magazines and newspapers, then he took out his lighter, lit two of the candles and held the flame close to the open pages of the *Evening News*. For a second he hesitated – was there a different way, a better way than this? – but he knew there was no going back now. He waited until the pages had caught alight, until a small fire had started to burn, before muttering a brief prayer and heading for the stairs.

It was only as he was leaving the house that Tommy thought about the other tenants. Shit, what if the fire became raging and they didn't get out in time? All the windows, apart from the one in Lynsey's flat, were in darkness. The people on the ground and top floors were probably asleep. He dithered on the doorstep. It was one thing setting a corpse alight; quite another being responsible for the inadvertent cremation of the rest of the residents.

In the end, he drove to the first phone box he could find and made a 999 call, claiming that he'd just been walking past a building that appeared to be on fire. He gave the address clearly, but provided only a garbled name before hanging up smartly. It was the best he could do, and he hoped it would be enough.

The journey up to Liverpool was long and fraught. But the ferry, he decided, was a better bet than the airport. There was less chance of anyone being able to track Lynsey down. They didn't speak much. They were both in shock, and anyway, there wasn't a lot left to say. They both knew that they would probably never see each other again.

When they stopped at a garage for petrol, Tommy emptied out the meagre contents of Anna Farrell's small handbag – two lipsticks, a compact, a bottle of aspirin, keys and a purse. There was twenty quid in the purse, and he took the notes and offered them to Lynsey. 'Here.'

She shrank back, shaking her head. 'I can't.'

Tommy put the notes in his own wallet and dumped the rest of the stuff in the bin. He understood her reluctance to take the money, but callous as it sounded, Anna didn't need it any more. He'd add it to the rest of the cash he had and give it to her later.

It was hours before they finally reached Liverpool. They parked up and waited near the ferry terminal, neither of them sleeping, until the sun rose and a new day dawned. They found a café, drank strong black coffee laced with brandy and smoked too many cigarettes. He told her not to call him, not to contact him, until she was sure that it was safe. He gave her the cash he had taken from the till of the Fox. He promised to keep an eye on Helen, to make sure she was okay.

Lynsey faced her future with dull resignation. As she

hugged him goodbye, her eyes were full of emptiness. After the ferry set sail for Dublin, Tommy dumped Anna Farrell's rings in the water. Then he stood and watched the boat until it became nothing more than a tiny dot on the horizon.

# 61

After Tommy had stopped speaking, Helen was overly aware of the stillness of the room. Of all her emotions – and there were many of them – anger was the first to rise to the surface. 'All this time, you've known that she was still alive. How could you?' she hissed. 'How could you do that to me?'

Tommy turned from the window and finally met her gaze. His mouth twisted down at the corners. 'I'm sorry, love. I'm so sorry. It was . . . I didn't know what else to do.'

As she leaned forward, Frank placed a hand on her shoulder. She wasn't sure if it was protective or restraining, but she quickly shrugged it off. 'You let me think she was dead. You came to her funeral. We scattered her ashes on *your* mother's grave. You let me go through all that, and it was nothing more than a filthy, dirty lie.'

'I couldn't tell anyone, not if Chapelle was going to come sniffing around. It was the only way to keep her safe. If he found out . . . I couldn't take that chance.'

Helen stood up, a sourness in the pit of her stomach. She gave a choked, despairing laugh. 'So where is she, then? Where's she hiding out?'

Tommy shook his head. 'I dunno. I swear I don't. She might still be in Ireland. She might not. She could be anywhere. We haven't spoken since that day, and that's the God honest truth.'

'The truth,' she repeated mockingly. 'And what the hell would you know about the truth?'

'Don't be too hard on him,' Frank said. 'It was a tough call.'

Helen gave him a glare. She had expected, hoped that he would be on her side, and didn't appreciate his response. 'You think he did the right thing?'

Frank raised his eyebrows. 'I didn't say that. All I meant was that it must have been a hard choice. People were going to get hurt no matter what he did.'

'Not *people*,' she retorted sharply. 'Me.'

Moira was sitting on the sofa, a stunned expression on her face. Her gaze, full of bewilderment, jumped to each of them in turn before finally settling on Helen. 'What are you going to do?'

It was a question Helen couldn't answer, not right at that minute anyway. She felt as if she couldn't breathe, as if the walls of the room were slowly squeezing in on her. All she knew was that she had to get away. As she grabbed her bag and made for the door, she heard Moira calling out after her, but she didn't stop. She needed air and she needed it fast.

Outside, Helen ran as quickly as she could in her black high heels. The evening air was cool but her face was burning hot. She was still frantically trying to absorb what Tommy had revealed: her mother was alive, her mother had made a choice, her mother had chosen to abandon her. She felt sick and confused. Her heart was pounding in her chest. Her head was spinning, anger battling with grief and despair. Somewhere, someplace else, Lynsey Beck was getting up every morning and going to bed every night. Did she ever think about the daughter she had left behind?

Helen only slowed to a walk when she was certain that she hadn't been followed. She was at Chalk Farm tube station, not that far from home, but she didn't want to go back to the flat.

That would be the first place they'd look, and she needed time on her own. She glanced around for a cab but couldn't see one. Instead, she ducked into the station, bought a southbound ticket and went down on to the platform.

Almost immediately there was a faint rumbling and a stirring of the air. Seconds later, the train came rushing out of the tunnel. As the doors opened, she got on quickly, glancing over her shoulder to check that she was still alone. There were plenty of seats and she chose one as far away as possible from the other passengers.

As the doors closed and the train moved off again, she caught her own reflection in the glass of the window. A girl with red lips and lost eyes. A girl dressed in a sleeveless black cocktail dress. Her fingers fluttered up to her throat, touching the string of pearls. They had been a present from Moira for her twenty-first birthday.

Helen passed the journey in a daze, barely noticing the stations or the passengers getting on and off. In her mind, she stumbled blindly through the past, searching for answers that could not be found. Her anger had subsided, shifting into something dull and hollow. She almost missed her stop, only alerted at the last moment by an announcement over the intercom. *Leicester Square.* She leapt out of her seat, out of the train and on to the platform.

When she was up at street level again, she realised that she should have grabbed her jacket on her way out of Moira's flat. It wasn't freezing, but the evening was chilly enough to make her shiver. She strode up Charing Cross Road to Cambridge Circus, and then headed west. Without really thinking about it, she already knew where she was going.

In Soho, the streets were buzzing, the place alive with noise and light. The smells of food and dope and traffic fumes drifted on the air. She had been drunk earlier, tipsy at least, but Tommy's revelations had shocked her back into sobriety. The cut on the palm of her hand was starting to hurt, a throbbing ache that made her wince. She found an off-licence and bought a half-bottle of vodka and a pack of cigarettes.

For the next half-hour, she wandered aimlessly around, revisiting the old haunts she had once known so well. She walked among the dealers, the punters and the pimps. She studied the toms with their hungry mouths and blank, empty eyes. What was she doing? She had no idea. She drank and smoked and tried to blot out the horror of what she had learned.

Terrible things had happened to her here on these streets, but terrible things had happened in other places too. Maybe this was where she belonged. She had bad blood – that was what Joe Quinn had said, and it was true. She had *his* bad blood, and her father's and her mother's. It ran in her veins, an inherited evil she could never be rid of.

Helen was in Brewer Street, leaning against a wall, when the man approached her. He was a tall, shifty-looking bloke in his mid-forties. He kept his hands in his pockets, his gaze darting left and right as he sidled up to her. 'How much?' he muttered.

She felt a shudder of revulsion as she looked him up and down. 'More than you can afford,' she said.

His face tightened, a cruel expression entering his eyes. 'Try me.'

And she knew in that moment that this man wanted to hurt her, that his lust was full of loathing too. Although all her natural instincts railed against it, she didn't immediately dismiss his proposition. A small voice was whispering in her ear. Bad girls did bad things, and perhaps this was nothing more than she deserved. 'Make me an offer.'

He leaned in towards her, scowling. His sour-smelling breath made her flinch. 'What's the game, darlin'? What you playing at?'

Helen stared back. 'No game,' she said.

'So I ain't got all night. Name your fuckin' price.'

Helen hesitated, aware that the decision she made would be irrevocable. She felt like she was standing on the edge of an abyss – one simple step and she would fall off the edge and descend into a nothingness from which she could never return. And suddenly, through all the rage and rejection and self-pity, she had a moment of clarity: she could be a victim for the rest of her life, or she could start fighting back.

Quickly, she shook her head. 'I'm not interested. You've made a mistake.'

He glared at her and then reached out to grab her wrist. 'Don't fuckin' mess with me, you bitch!'

But Helen wasn't afraid. He might be a nasty piece of work, but she'd known worse. 'Get your filthy hands off me.' Snatching away her arm, she stared back at him, her eyes full of contempt. 'Just push off, okay? Push off or I'll call the cops.'

Aware that the altercation was starting to attract attention, the punter decided to back off. His eyes were two cold slits, his mouth tight and angry. He gave her a final black look before turning his head and spitting on the ground.

Helen watched as he strode away, and then started walking in the opposite direction. She'd only gone a few yards when there was a familiar voice behind her.

'You're not an easy person to find.'

She spun round to find Frank Meyer standing there. A few hours ago, there was no other face she would rather have seen, but a lot had changed since then. 'What do you want?' she snapped. 'What are you doing here?'

'To talk.'

'No thanks. Just leave me alone, huh?'

'Ten minutes,' Frank said. 'That's all I'm asking. You can spare me that, can't you?'

Helen carried on walking, and he tagged along beside her. She wondered how much he had heard of her exchange with the punter. Enough, she was sure, to get the gist of the conversation. 'How did you find me?'

'I checked the flat and you weren't there, so Moira suggested . . .'

Helen gave him a sideways glance. Her past life, her life with Lily, could never have stayed a secret for ever, but she hadn't wanted him to find out this way. 'She told you, didn't she?'

'She didn't tell me anything. She just suggested looking here.'

'So now you think I'm a whore.'

'So now you're telling me what I think.'

Helen kept on walking. She was quiet for a while, and he didn't say anything either. As they turned on to Wardour Street, she looked at him again. 'I thought you wanted to talk.'

'Not here. Let's go back to Camden.'

'I don't want to go to Camden.'

'Just you and me,' he said. 'There won't be anyone else there.'

'No.'

'Come on,' he wheedled. 'I'll make a deal with you. Come back to the flat for an hour, and then if you want to come back here, I'll drive you myself.'

'You can't drive. You've had too much to drink.'

'We'll get a cab, then.'

Helen chewed on her lower lip, recalling another deal Frank had made, many years ago. The two of them sitting in Kellston cemetery after Joe Quinn's attack on her in the cellar. Frank trying to persuade her to go back to the Fox. The memory, bittersweet, brought a lump to her throat. 'You said ten minutes. You said you only wanted to talk for ten minutes.'

'So we'll split the difference. Call it . . . half an hour.'

'That's not—'

But before she could make any further protests, he had hailed a passing black cab, opened the door and quickly ushered her inside.

Helen sank back into the seat, a terrible exhaustion washing over her. She wasn't sure if she was too drunk or not drunk enough. She had downed a fair bit of vodka, but the sharp pain in her heart remained. 'I don't know why you're doing this. There's nothing left to talk about.'

Frank settled down next to her, not too far away, not too close. 'We'll see.'

# 62

Walking into the flat, Helen felt like she was entering a
stranger's home. It was all familiar to her – the furniture, the
curtains, the lamps, even the two empty glasses sitting on the
coffee table – and yet none of it seemed to belong to her. It
was another Helen Beck who had lived here, a different girl,
with dreams and aspirations. Her life had been nothing but a
house of cards, and now, with just a breath of truth, it had all
come tumbling down.

Frank went through to the kitchen and put the kettle on.
She followed him, standing by the door and watching as he
got out the coffee and sorted mugs and spoons and sugar and
milk. They had barely spoken in the cab, the driver's presence
too much of a deterrent for any real intimacy. She had huddled into the corner and stared out at the flashing lights, at
the crowds of people. She had wanted to get lost in those
crowds. She had wanted to disappear for ever.

'You going to sit down?' he asked.

Helen slipped off her shoes and left them by the door. She padded into the kitchen, the lino cool beneath her feet. The metal box was still on the table, and she pushed it aside, hating everything it represented. She saw Frank looking at her, and frowned. 'You see? She didn't even bother to take this with her. That's how much her precious memories meant.'

'I'm sure she loved you,' he said.

'So why didn't she take me with her?' The tears sprang into her eyes, and she brushed them away roughly. She still had the same aversion to crying in company that she'd had as a kid. 'Why did she leave me at my grandmother's?'

He spooned the coffee into the mugs and glanced over his shoulder. 'Maybe she figured that Chapelle would check to see if you were still around. She had to make him believe she was dead, and she couldn't do that if she took you with her.'

'Because no decent mother would ever leave her child behind, huh?'

'You don't think it may have been *you* she was protecting?'

Helen felt the anger rise inside her again. 'Why are you defending her? She was only interested in saving her own skin. She didn't give a damn about anyone else.'

'I'm not defending her. I'm just trying to see it from her point of view. If she had taken you, she'd have been looking over her shoulder for the rest of her life, wondering when Chapelle was going to catch up with you both. What kind of a life is that for a kid, for anyone?'

Helen gave a snort. 'So you're saying she did it for me?'

'Maybe, partly. Is that so difficult to believe?' He put the mug down in front of her and pulled out a chair on the other side of the table. 'And I wasn't taking sides earlier when I said it was a tough call. All I meant was that I didn't know what I'd have done if I'd been in Tommy's shoes.'

'Told the truth?' she suggested. 'Told me that my mother wasn't *actually* dead.'

Frank gave a curt nod. 'Yeah, perhaps you deserved the truth. But you were, what – eleven years old? He barely even knew you then. And the longer you keep a secret like that, the harder it is to let it go.'

She pulled a face. 'So he was just going to pretend for ever?'

'Perhaps he thought it was better that way. How would you have felt if you'd found out that she was still alive but that nobody knew where she was?'

'Like I feel now,' she shot back. 'Angry, betrayed, rejected, bitter, twisted. Do you want me to go on?'

He gave her a wry smile. 'Best not. I might start feeling sorry for you.'

'It's not funny.'

Frank placed his elbows on the table and balanced his chin on the roof of his hands. 'No, it's not. But you can deal with this, Mouse. You're stronger than you think. Don't let it destroy everything.'

'What, just come to terms with it and move on? That simple, is it?'

'No, sorry, I didn't mean to sound flippant. All I'm trying to say is ... Shit, I dunno.' He studied her carefully and sighed. 'Look at you. Despite everything, all the rubbish you've been landed with, you've still managed to make a decent life for yourself. You're young, smart, beautiful. You can do anything you want.'

Helen felt the colour rise into her cheeks. He might have called her smart before, but he'd never called her beautiful. To hide her blushes, she bent her head to the mug and took a sip of the coffee. It was hot and strong and sweet. She frowned. 'You've put sugar in this. I don't take sugar.'

'For the shock,' he said.

'That's only for tea.' She paused, then said, 'And you don't know anything about me, not really. I've done all sorts of stuff. Bad stuff. I'm not the girl you think I am.'

Frank shrugged it off. 'We've all been there. So you're not perfect, so what? I've made mistakes.' He hesitated, as if in two minds as to whether he should continue. He chewed on his lower lip for a few seconds, and then said, 'I was married once, you know.'

'Eleanor,' she said softly.

Frank looked at her, surprised. 'How did you know that?'

'I saw you once in the cemetery. You were visiting a grave and I was . . . I was curious. So I waited until you'd gone and then went to take a look.'

'You never said anything.'

'I felt bad about finding out that way. It felt like I'd been snooping. And I figured that if you wanted me to know, you'd tell me.'

He placed his hands on the table and linked his fingers together. There was a tightness to his jaw, a muscle twitching at the corner of his mouth. 'Ellie. She was called Ellie. And I wasn't a good husband. Not in any way. We used to live in Kellston. It was years ago. She got ill and . . . Well, you're supposed to be there when the person you love gets sick, but I couldn't cope with it. I felt bitter and angry and trapped. Do

512

you know where I was on the day she died?' He gave a small, hollow laugh. 'I was out in a pub, getting drunk.'

'I'm sorry.' Helen instinctively reached out to touch his hand, but then stopped herself. Instead, she pretended she'd been reaching for the metal tin. She pulled it towards her and lifted the lid. She stared at the contents for a second and then raised her eyes to him again. 'Why are you telling me all this?'

'Because people make mistakes, big ones. They mess up. And sometimes the mess is so immense it can't ever be put right. All you can do is try and find a way to live with it.'

Suddenly Helen understood how he had managed to accept the unfairness of his jail sentence with such apparent equanimity. He had viewed it as a punishment for a different crime. He might not have been guilty of attempting to dispose of Joe Quinn's body, but that hadn't mattered. A more corrosive kind of guilt had been eating away at his conscience. 'And have you?' she asked. 'Found a way to live with it?'

Frank forced a smile. 'Let's just call it a work in progress.'

Helen, aware that they hadn't talked like this since he had moved into the flat, felt a mixture of emotions. She had longed for him to confide in her, to trust her, to share the secrets of his life, but now that he had, she felt that it was all too late. She remembered the imaginary friend she'd created back when she was eleven – Ella – and thought how odd it was that that name and the name of his wife were so similar. To cover her confusion, she took the envelopes out of the tin and put them on the table. She pulled the notes out and laid them side by side, staring hard at the threats that had been sent to her mother.

'She must have been scared,' Frank said, looking down at them.

As Helen studied the thick, crisp notepaper with its bold printed warnings, something niggled in the back of her mind. She frowned, but whatever was there was too elusive, too vague for her to grab hold of.

'What is it?'

She shook her head. 'Nothing. I don't know. I just ... It doesn't matter.' She glanced up. 'Anyway, I've made a decision. I'm going to go away, leave London, start again somewhere new.'

'Go away, or run away?' There was a sharp edge to his voice that hadn't been there before.

'Either. Both. Why not? It worked for my mother.'

'How do you know? You've got no idea what her life's been like.'

'And whose fault is that?' She found herself wondering if her mum had married again, if there were other children. Somewhere out there she could have half-brothers and sisters she had never met.

'You've got family here. Don't turn your back on them, Mouse. Moira loves you. You're like a daughter to her. And Tommy—'

'Tommy's never stopped lying to me from the first day we met.'

Frank leaned back and folded his arms across his chest. 'So what would you have done if you'd been in his shoes?'

'Told me,' she said. 'Told me that it was all a lie, that she wasn't really dead.'

'Even if that might have put her in danger?'

'I wouldn't have told anyone else.'

Frank considered her answer for a moment. 'Maybe he thought that the truth would cause you even more pain, that it was better to have a clean break. Or maybe he just didn't think at all. Perhaps he did what he had to do and then simply tried to muddle through the consequences.' He drank some coffee and put the mug back down on the table. 'Don't turn your back on him, Mouse. He's not in the best of places himself. He's been banged up for the past seven years, his daughters are hundreds of miles away and he's lost everything he ever worked for.'

While Frank talked, Helen played with the notes, idly running her fingers across the smooth white paper. And it was then, suddenly, that it came to her. The breath caught in the back of her throat, and she felt a jolt run through her body as she finally made the connection. Surely it couldn't be ... it wasn't possible. Well, there was only one way to find out. She jumped up and ran out of the kitchen.

Her sudden departure took Frank by surprise. 'Mouse?' he called after her. 'Are you okay?'

Thirty seconds later, she came back with the old *A to Z* in her hand, sat down again and flipped it open.

Frank watched her, bemused. 'What is it? What are you doing?'

Helen flicked through the pages until she found the list of directions that her grandfather had written. She gazed at it for a while, and then slid it out and passed it over to Frank. 'Look at this.'

He read through the route, raised his eyes and gave a shrug. 'I don't get it. Kew Gardens? What am I—'

'Not the writing,' she said hurriedly. 'The paper. Look at the paper.' She pushed across one of the threatening notes. 'Does it look the same to you? Does it feel the same?'

Frank rubbed the paper between his fingers. 'Well, yeah, it could be. But isn't this stuff kind of common? It's just standard writing paper, isn't it?'

Helen shook her head. 'No, it's not your Basildon Bond or anything like that.' She took back the sheet that had come from the *A to Z*. 'See, it's thicker. Gran used to buy it from a shop in Chingford. She liked nice notepaper. She had a thing about it.' Her thoughts were racing now, spinning around and tumbling down on each other. 'I mean, it's not so rare that someone else couldn't have used it, but . . .' She shook her head again. 'What are the chances?'

'You think your grandmother sent these threats?'

Helen raised a hand to her face and bit down on the knuckle. Had her middle-class, God-fearing, moralising grandmother really been capable of such a thing? 'I'm not sure.' She bent and studied the sheets of paper. The threats had been boldly printed, and she couldn't swear that it either was or wasn't her gran's handwriting.

'Why would she do that?'

Helen, unable to sit still, quickly stood up again. She went over to the sink and then back to the table. 'She wouldn't. I mean, not ordinarily. But when she got ill . . . I don't know. She changed. She wasn't herself. Maybe something snapped inside her. She couldn't forgive Mum for getting pregnant, for trapping her son. They were always rowing about it. I suppose this could have been a way of getting back at her.'

'Well, she certainly did that.'

Helen held on to the back of the chair as the full force of this new possibility washed over her. 'It was because of the threats that Mum presumed she was the intended victim, not Anna. She reckoned Eddie Chapelle was out to get her. But if he didn't send them, then . . .'

Frank finished the line of thought for her. 'Then one of his thugs simply followed Anna Farrell to the flat – or even posed as a punter – and got rid of the one person who could have been a real risk to Chapelle when his trial came round.'

'But according to Tommy, Mum reckoned that Anna was sound, that she'd never grass up Chapelle.'

Frank gave a weary sigh. 'Yeah, but men like Eddie Chapelle don't leave things to chance. They like to make sure the odds are stacked in their favour.'

'And what about the car that followed her?'

'If there was one. The driver might have slowed down for any number of reasons, but she was so jumpy she presumed it was to do with the threats.'

Helen sank back down into the chair and rubbed hard at her eyes. She had a sinking feeling in the pit of her stomach. If this was true, then . . . Pain squeezed at her heart as she thought of everything that had happened as a consequence. There was a short silence, broken only by the thin, trembling hum of the fridge. After a while, she lowered her hands and looked over at Frank. 'It was all for nothing. She wasn't in any real danger. She could have called the cops, answered their questions, carried on with her life. She could still have been here now.'

'You don't know that for sure.'

The past flickered through Helen's mind like a reel of old

film. She imagined her mother sitting in Connolly's, lifting her eyes to see Alan Beck for the first time – that fateful moment that had changed everything. She saw the cherry blossom trees in Camberley Road, her grandmother's scowl as the copper waited by the garden gate, the coffin in the church, the fair-haired man who said he was her uncle. Then there was fire, the flames that had devoured Anna Farrell and almost destroyed the Fox. A scattering of ashes. A stone lion in Kellston cemetery. Frank Meyer sitting on the grass, talking to her, persuading her to go back home. There was Tommy's smile, Joe Quinn with his angry, lashing tongue, Moira's kindness. She saw herself leaving the cinema one night, her head full of love and betrayal, lies and deceit. Jay Gatsby lying dead in a swimming pool.

'Mouse?'

Helen barely heard him. The reel had moved on to a cold night in Soho, to a man with a wedding ring who she knew she couldn't trust. She felt the frozen ice against her back, the pain as he beat her, the force of his hate. She had almost died that night, but somehow, miraculously, she had been given a second chance.

'Mouse?'

Helen started, and blinked. 'Huh?'

'Will you tell him? Will you tell Tommy about the notes?'

She frowned, thinking of what it would mean to break such news to him. 'Should I?'

'Why wouldn't you?'

Helen smiled faintly, understanding where he was going. To keep a secret in the hope of protecting someone else was a risky business. If she told him, he would have to live with the knowledge that he had made a terrible mistake. If she didn't . . . well, that made her as guilty as him when it came to withholding the truth.

'It's your choice,' he said. 'I'll stick by whatever you decide.'

She glanced down at the floor before slowly raising her gaze again. 'Do you think she's still out there somewhere?'

'You could always look for her.'

'And what if she doesn't want to be found?'

Frank paused for a second. 'I'd want you to look for me if I ever went missing.'

Helen felt her heart skip a beat. It was the nearest he had ever got to expressing any real feelings for her. 'Would you?'

Frank held her gaze for a few seconds, and then said, 'Okay, I'll make you a deal. Stay here tonight, sleep on it, and if you still want to leave tomorrow, I won't say another word. In fact, if you want me to drive you to the station . . .'

Helen lifted her eyebrows. She tried to keep her voice light, but she could still hear the tremor in it. 'What is it with you and your deals?'

'What can I say? I'm a creature of habit.'

'Nothing's going to have changed by tomorrow.'

'Not tomorrow or the day after. Maybe not next month or next year, but eventually . . .'

'It'll all get better?'

'It might,' he said. 'Stick around and see what happens. Running away never solved anything. Take it from someone who knows.'

Helen waited. She wanted him to say that he didn't want her to go, to ask her to stay, but perhaps that was hoping for too much. Frank Meyer wasn't the type of man who put his cards on the table. Their eyes locked for a second and something passed between them. She wasn't sure exactly what it was, but she felt a surge of strength, of hope. She could take a chance, or she could walk away. The decision was hers. But deep down inside, she knew that she'd already made the choice. She sat back, a smile tugging at the corners of her mouth. Even bad girls did the right thing sometimes.

# Don't miss the next Kellston novel

# STREETWISE

Ava Gold's employment options are rapidly shrinking
and, not wanting to go back to driving minicabs, she lands
herself a trial run at being nightclub owner Chris Street's
personal driver. Chris is one of the men about town
in Kellston, East London, and is initially suspicious
of having a female driver, but Ava soon
proves her worth, and beyond.

Still, working for one of the notorious Streets – who
have a past history of violence reaching back to the
boom time of the sixties – is never going to be easy.
Chris' ex-wife is newly involved with his worst enemy
and his younger brother Danny and his crazy girlfriend
are up to something that will pull Ava into a world
of blackmail, murder, sex and greed . . .

\*

'Well into Martina Cole territory'
*Independent*

# Out February 2014